Siam
Nights

J. F. Gump

Preface

Siam. The very word conjures up images of an exotic, far away, land. Now known as Thailand, old Siam is a romantic country filled with rice paddies, pineapple fields, ancient Buddhist temples, lumbering elephants, and deadly cobras. From the mountains in the north to the beaches in the south, Thailand offers every visitor a wondrous treasure of excitement and adventure.

The Thais are a polite and gracious people who find a reasons to smile, even under the worst of circumstances. It has earned Thailand the nickname, "The Land of Smiles". The name is well deserved.

Siam Nights is love story; a tale of human drama set in Pattaya, a resort city located on the eastern shore of the Gulf of Siam. Visitors from around the world come to enjoy its tropical beaches, its incredible golf courses, and its fabulous shopping bargains. But the characters in this novel find more than they ever expected in Old Siam.

For readers unfamiliar with Thailand, Baht is the local currency and is worth about 3 cents U.S. A wai is a polite greeting with hands held in a prayer-like fashion, a kilometer is about .62 miles, Thais measure bus trips by hours instead of by distance, buses are the most affordable means of travel, and U.S. Eastern Standard Time follows Thailand time by exactly 12 hours. I'm sure there are other things I should tell you, but these are the ones that come first to mind. I have included a basic map of Thailand for your convenience.

Acknowledgements

Thanks to everyone who has supported my work. A special thank you to my fans who bought my trilogy from Bangkok Book House, and to my family who allowed me uninterrupted time to write.

~~ J. F. Gump

Chapter 1

Tippawan Bongkot urged her rickety motorbike through the early morning streets of Phitsanulok. Determination lined her soft-tanned face. She turned right onto a dusty side street and coasted to a stop at the front of her mother's house. The windows were dark. The Nan River rippled in the background. She tilted her watch toward the solitary street lamp—it was five o'clock.

Tippawan bit nervously at her lip. Her mother was always in a bad mood, especially when she was awakened before she was ready to get up. Common sense told her to leave but her heart insisted she stay. She hesitated for a minute as she struggled with her indecision. Finally she got off the motorcycle, squared her shoulders, and walked to the front door. She knocked until the lights flickered on and irritated mumbling reached her ears.

A second later the door squeaked open and her mother appeared at the narrow gap. Her hair was disheveled, her eyelids puffy. Endless wrinkles lined her weathered face.

"I'm sorry if I woke you, Mama." Tippawan kept her tone calm.

"What are you doing here in the middle of the night?" the old woman grunted and motioned her daughter inside.

"It's almost morning."

"It looks like nighttime to me." Nui's eyes focused on the suitcase tied to the back of the motorcycle. "And where do you think you're going?"

"I'm going to Pattaya, to visit my brother." Her prepared answer sounded weak now that she had said it aloud.

The old woman tilted her head back and stared down her

1

classic Thai nose. "That place is evil. You don't belong there. None of my daughters belong in Pattaya."

Tippawan choked back her first response. Her mother was referring to her older sister Itta, but she was nothing like Itta. She had come only to tell her mother she was leaving, not to argue with the sharpest tongue in Phitsanulok. She kept her calm. "I can't stay here Mama, you know that. I don't have a job or anything."

Nui sighed loud enough to be heard halfway to China. Her expression softened but only a little. "You should go to your sister's house in Chiang Mai. It's better there, safer."

"There are no jobs in Chiang Mai, or Bangkok either; I've checked already. Everyone says I can find work in Pattaya or Phuket. Anan lives in Pattaya and I can stay with him until I get settled. I'll be safe with Anan. "

"What about your trouble with Sawat—and the police?"

This time Tippawan sighed. Just hearing Sawat's name irritated her. "I talked with the police yesterday. One nice lieutenant said maybe I won't have to see them so often if I'm working in Pattaya."

"Did he promise it or just say it?"

Tippawan tried to smile but couldn't. She looked away from her mother's pointed stare. "He only said it. He told me to call before my next meeting and he would let me know for sure."

Nui reached out and grasped Tippawan's hand. "There are bad people in Pattaya; you must be careful." She gripped tighter. "Don't be like your sister Itta. You have enough trouble already."

"Don't worry, Mama," Tippawan whispered. "I'm going to Pattaya to find a job, a real job. Maybe I'll work with Anan." She glanced at her watch. "I have to go; my bus leaves at six. Tell Yai he can use my motorcycle while I'm gone. So can you."

Without another word she stepped outside, untied her suitcase from the motorbike, and hurried away. At the main road she hired a tuk-tuk taxi to the bus station.

Her mother was right, Pattaya was evil. But at the moment anyplace would be better than Phitsanulok. A thrill rushed through her as her bus entered the highway south toward Bangkok.

Chapter 2

"Earth to Mike. Beam me aboard, Mike. There's no intelligent life out here."

Mike Johnson glanced at his watch and then at the half-finished report sitting on his desk. He picked up his radio and thumbed the talk button. "I've got bad news Randy, there's no intelligent life in here either. What's up?"

"Me and the other guys are leaving early. We're gonna have a few beers and grope some female flesh. The van leaves in ten minutes. Are you ready?"

Mike smiled to himself. It was Saturday and it had been a hard week. There was nothing he wanted more than to get away from the job-site and suck down a few beers. He glanced at the stack of contracts and invoices waiting to be entered into the cost report. "I can't. Have our driver come back and get me after he has dropped you guys in Pattaya. I should be finished by then."

"Whatever you say. I'm going to Soi 8 later. Maybe you can meet me there."

"I doubt it, Randy," Mike responded. "You're a bad influence. Besides, I have other plans."

"Lek again?"

"Screw you, Randy." Mike keyed his radio on and off several times. "I think my battery is going dead. Maybe I'll see you guys later."

"Roger that. I'll send Kriengchai back for you. Don't keep him late."

"I'll be ready when he gets back." Again Mike eyed the stack of papers. "At least I think I will."

He sat his radio back into the charger and concentrated on his typing. For the hundredth time this week he wished he had a competent assistant.

Mike had been working in Thailand for over two years. Sometimes it felt like forever, but at other times as if only a few weeks had passed. He clearly remembered his apprehension when he'd first arrived at the Bangkok airport. Looking back his fears seemed ridiculous, but at the time they had been unsettling. It had taken months to adjust to being a minority, and he'd never gotten used to the tropical climate.

The weather Southeast Asia came in three basic seasons: hot, extremely hot, and hot with rain. The Thais claimed there was a cool season but he hadn't noticed. He supposed his body had been habituated by too many years of frigid winters and air conditioned summers to ever become accustomed to the unrelenting mugginess.

A few of his co-workers had experienced serious homesickness during the first months after arriving in Thailand, but Mike never did. Actually he'd been relieved to be away from the craziness of his family in the US. He glanced at his watch; his driver would be back within the hour. He stopped his mental meandering and focused on the monthly report.

Chapter 3

Tippawan stared through the window at the lush Thailand countryside. Since the bus wasn't moving she could take everything in with a slow, casual glance. To her left was a large tapioca field. To her right sprawled an equally large pineapple field. Dividing the two fields and scattered helter-skelter across them were coconut trees.

To Tippawan's inexperienced eye everything looked ready to harvest, ripe for the picking. But she wasn't a farmer so she didn't really know. The only thing she knew for sure was that it was damned hot inside the bus. The occasional breeze that found its way through the open windows did nothing to ease the assault of the late morning sun.

The bus had broken down halfway between Phitsanulok and nowhere. For several kilometers the coach had limped along, its engine alternately sputtering, backfiring, and then roaring back to life. Finally it had died altogether. An hour had passed since the driver called for a backup but it hadn't yet arrived.

Trickles of sweat snaked through her hair, across her cheeks, and down the back of her neck. Her clothes clung to her damp skin as if fastened by some perverted form of post-it note glue. Tippawan didn't like to sweat; it wasn't lady-like. Besides, it would make her smell like the farangs, the foreigners who came to Thailand on holiday.

Outside, the coconut fronds and tapioca stalks stood nearly motionless in the stagnant air. She was tempted to join the other passengers who had abandoned the bus in favor of the cooler outdoors but the blazing sun gave her second thoughts. Better to smell like a farang, she decided, than have the sun darken her skin.

Tippawan, like most Thai women, preferred her skin to be as white as possible. Dark skin marked the caste of common laborers while light skin elevated one to the status of the educated and affluent—or at least something other than a peon. She chose to sweat it out inside the bus. She prayed to Buddha that the backup would come soon.

Tippawan was her given name but everyone knew her as Math. In Thailand, nicknames are more common than not. Usually the nickname has little or nothing to do with the person's given name. For instance, Math's oldest sister's name was Chalamsee but everyone knew her as Nuang. Her brother's given name was Peebanlat, yet everyone knew him as Anan. Math didn't know where her nickname came from. In English *Math* is a shortened word for *mathematics*, the study of numbers and calculations. In Thai the word *Math* means nothing, it's a nonsense word. Her nickname was a mystery she had never asked about; she just accepted it in Thai lady fashion.

Math had been born and raised in the city of Phitsanulok in north-central Thailand. Except for the short time she had worked in Bangkok, she had lived her entire life in Phitsanulok. Now she was headed to Pattaya on the eastern seaboard of the Gulf of Siam to visit her older brother Anan. He wasn't really that much older, but at her tender age of twenty-three two years seemed like a lot.

Anan had always been ambitious and he had done well. Two years earlier he had quit his full-time job as a graphic artist to start his own advertising business in Pattaya. A silent partner had provided the seed money and Anan had provided the sweat equity. The first months were mostly an exercise in survival. Some weeks he made no money

During those lean times Anan had borrowed money from Math to help pay his bills and put food in his stomach. At the time she'd had little cash to spare but she gave him what she could afford. Anan had never repaid her, but she had never pressed him about it either. That wouldn't be a polite—especially since he was her brother.

Anan's business catered to Pattaya's bustling tourist trade. Now was the so-called *high season* and Math was sure his business must be booming. She knew Anan was making money because he had recently bought himself a house and two motorcycles. To have so much at such a young age made him the richest person in their family.

Math hadn't been so lucky. Her own short-lived career had ended just a few weeks ago. After less than six months at her first real job with a finance company in Bangkok, her position had been terminated. It had happened so quickly, yet looking back she realized she should have seen it coming.

The finance company had been in the business of making loans on cars, trucks, and motorcycles. Math had been hired to work in collections and repossessions. When the Thai economy went into meltdown, loan defaults soared. The banks that had been supporting the finance company suddenly stopped. Worse, they demanded full payment on past-due advances. In an incredibly short time, the whole thing fell apart. The finance company folded and the employees were let go.

Oddly enough Math felt responsible for the company's failure —not because she had done anything wrong, but because she believed she was a bad luck charm. Luck had never been her friend since the day she was conceived. She had little doubt that if the finance company hadn't hired her, it would still be in business. She was sure her very presence had been enough to destroy everything. She knew her bad luck had somehow overflowed the bounds of the finance company and brought the entire Thai economy to ruin. Bad Luck Lady! She called herself that sometimes. Bad luck to everything. Even to this stinking bus.

There was a sudden bustle of activity outside as the stranded passengers scurried from the scanty pieces of shade they had found. Math pushed up from her seat and looked back. There sat another bus. She grabbed her purse and headed for the exit. Before she was even halfway to the door the driver announced that the coach behind them wasn't their backup. It was just another bus with a few empty seats. The other driver had stopped to help however he could. An elderly couple and a woman with two babies were the lucky ones ushered aboard.

Math trudged back to her seat. Suddenly it felt hotter than ever. She didn't know how much longer she could take the heat. If the backup didn't arrive soon, she would have to risk getting her skin darkened.

~~~

Tippawan "Math" Bongkot was conceived twenty-three years ago on a rainy night in early July. As confusing as it may sound, her biological father was not her mother's husband. Her mother, Nui, hadn't meant for anything to happen that night. Certainly the out-of-wedlock pregnancy hadn't been planned. It was a mistake that would haunt her forever.

At that time, Math's father, an uneducated man named Supit, had been struggling to keep food on the table. In their house empty stomachs and late rent payments had been the rule rather than the exception. Supit liked to drink and many of their family's missed meals had gone to pay for his Mekong whiskey. Whenever Supit drank, he was not a loving man. To the contrary he was a verbally and physically abusive drunk.

On the night Math was conceived, Supit had come home crazy drunk. His assault started with Nuang, their oldest daughter who was barely thirteen-years of age. When Nuang rejected her father's drunken fondling, he cornered her and began slapping at her with his open hand. When Nui demanded he stop, Supit turned on her with his fists. His assault that night was brutal.

Between blows Nui screamed for Nuang to take the younger children and run. When she was sure her children were away from the house, she fled into the night. She went to a friend's house for solace and protection.

Nui's friend took her in without question. He tended her wounds and crooned softly until her panic ebbed to calmness. Before that night had ended, the comforting touch of an old friend's hand stoked a fiery passion that neither of them could stop. In a minute it was over for the man, but for Nui it was only the beginning.

Within a month Nui began experiencing physical symptoms she knew all too well from three previous pregnancies. At first she ignored the symptoms, hoping against hope it wasn't true. After missing her third menstrual cycle, she knew she was pregnant. She also knew who the father was and he was not her husband. It wasn't the sort of thing that happened to a married and proper Thai lady; it was the sort of thing that happened to the whores in Bangkok and Pattaya. If anyone ever learned the truth, it would bring shame to herself and to her family.

Nui had been desperate but she couldn't afford a doctor— especially for something like the abortion of a bastard child. Supit's work had become even more sporadic, and they barely survived from day to day. He had even given up his Mekong whiskey. Nui toyed with the idea of going to the unborn baby's natural father for help, but she was too ashamed, too embarrassed.

In her fourth month of pregnancy Nui attempted a self-induced abortion with a potion given by a friend. Nui didn't know what the concoction was, nor did she care. She only wanted to stop the baby from being born. But the drug hadn't worked and Math emerged into the world on March 25th of the following year.

Math's true father had learned the truth when Nui was eight months pregnant. Her confession turned the man inside out. He had loved Nui for as long as he could remember. When they were both much younger, he had even planned to marry her, but his father made sure that never happened. Yet he had continued to fantasize of her having his child, even long after she had married Supit.

The day Nui told him she was pregnant with his baby had been the happiest and saddest of his life. Everything he had ever dreamed of was happening, yet he couldn't take pride in any of it. As right as it was, it was wrong. His shame was overwhelming. Out of embarrassment and self-imposed humiliation, Math's birth father entered monkhood on the day she was born.

Math had learned about her mother's attempted abortion in an overheard conversation when she was twelve years old. She was much older before she discovered that Supit, the father of her family, was not her biological parent.

~~~

Thirty minutes after the Good Samaritan bus had left, Math reached her moment of decision—dark skin or death by sweat. Dark skin really wasn't all that bad, she finally convinced herself. She stood and headed down the aisle.

As she neared the exit, there was another flurry of activity outside. Again she looked back. There sat another bus. It was empty. Thank Buddha!

Math picked up her pace and hurried toward the door. Her senses swooned at the temperature change when she stepped outside. After her dizziness eased, she transferred her luggage to the backup bus and then got in line with the other passengers.

The air conditioning of the coach felt like an icebox. Math took her seat, pulled her arms against her chest, and shivered at the coldness. After everyone had boarded and found seats, the bus pulled into traffic and sped south.

Chapter 4

Math had made the trip from Phitsanulok to Bangkok more times than she could remember. While working in Bangkok she had returned home almost every weekend. She had been up and down this road many times, but only a few when it was light. Funny how different everything looks in the daytime, she mused.

Away from the main roads, Thailand is mostly an agricultural country. The climate is perfect for crops like rice, pineapples, oranges, bananas, tomatoes, cashews, and an incredible variety of tropical fruits.

The road from Phitsanulok to Bangkok is an endless spattering of gas stations, produce stands, and impromptu roadside restaurants. Every few kilometers areas of denser population appear. There seems neither rhyme nor reason as to where these places are located.

These mini-villages all look much the same. On either side of the road sit short rows of two-story buildings constructed of concrete, bricks, and blocks. The ground-floor spaces are used for shops while second-floor spaces are for storage or apartments. Some people call them "shop-houses."

Math noticed that fewer than half of the shop-houses were in business. There were never many people around, either. The few locals she saw almost always stopped what they were doing to stare. Invariably, the children would wave as the bus passed by.

Being from the city of Phitsanulok, Math couldn't understand how these people lived in such seclusion. She couldn't imagine living in a place where you knew everyone in town, and when you met strangers it was through bus windows as they flew past at 100 kilometers per hour. How did these people survive? What work did they do to make money? Without a vehicle, their isolation would be complete. Math couldn't think of many worse ways to live.

The rest of the trip to Bangkok was uneventful. Math spent most of her time wondering if she smelled bad or not. From time to time, and as inconspicuously as possible, she sniffed at her clothes and her armpits. If there were any unpleasant odors, she couldn't smell them. She wondered if the farangs—the foreigners who visited Thailand—ever smell bad to themselves? She had no way to answer that question.

By the time the bus arrived at the Bangkok terminal, her sweaty clothes had dried and she had consumed the better part of three bottles of water. She went directly to the ladies room and washed herself as thoroughly as she could with the small cloth she carried in her handbag. A shower would have been better, but that would have to wait. At least for the moment she felt cleaner and less smelly.

Because the bus had arrived late in Bangkok, Math had missed her connecting bus to Pattaya. So had several others. A bus company representative pulled the stranded passengers aside and updated them on plans to get them to Pattaya.

The good news was that there were seats for everyone on a later bus. The bad news was that there would be a wait. What the representative didn't mention was that the later bus would be leaving at the height of Bangkok's notorious rush-hour traffic.

Math stood next to a young lady who was about her own age but who, in her opinion, was much more beautiful. Actually the lady wasn't more beautiful; it was just that Math had never considered herself as anything other than plain. The girl's skin was darker, but her well-formed body and near-perfect face easily overcame the dark skin stigma. She wore a heavy gold chain around her neck and an equally heavy gold bracelet on her left wrist.

"Hello. My name is Math," she whispered. "Are you going to

Pattaya on holiday?"

The girl eyed Math for a moment before answering, "No, I'm going to work with my sister."

"Oh, same as me, except I'm going to work for my brother," Math smiled. "Does your sister have a business in Pattaya?"

The girl laughed. "No, my sister works as a dancer in a nightclub. Her boss said he would hire me as a waitress or cashier or dancer or something. By the way, my name is Tana. What bar will you be working at?"

Math blushed as visions of her sister Itta flooded her thoughts. "I don't understand. My brother has his own business. Why do you think I would work in a bar?"

Tana put her hand on Math's arm. "Because all of the prettier and sexier girls eventually end up working in the bars. I did that last year during the high season. I had a few short times every week and made a lot of money. Really, I had a lot of fun, too." She smiled, waiting for a reply.

Math returned the girl's smile even though she didn't feel like smiling. She wondered what a *short time* was but was embarrassed to ask. From the way the girl said the word she had an idea of what it meant. If it was what she thought, she was sure she didn't want to talk about it. Tana's hand on her arm made her uncomfortable and excited at the same time. Long buried emotions rose.

Two years earlier, while attending the local technical college in Phitsanulok, Math had become very close friends with one of her classmates, a young woman named Kallaya. In time she had fallen in love with Kallaya—or so she'd felt—but she had never said anything. She wasn't sure if it was because she was embarrassed, or because she couldn't stand the rejection that might come. She had been crushed when Kallaya had gotten pregnant and then married. After that, Math had been very careful in her relationships with women. She never understood why she felt attracted to certain ladies. She often thought she must be a lesbian, but on the other hand she liked men, too. She was very confused about her emotions.

Math raised her arm to adjust the purse strap biting into her shoulder. The movement broke the contact with the girl's hand and she took a step away. "I don't think I'll ever work in a beer bar or any other kind of bar. If I can't work with my brother, I will find some other job or go back to my home."

Tana smiled. "That's what I said last year. We shall see what you do when you get to Pattaya."

Math didn't respond.

After an uncomfortable silence, Tana suddenly perked up. "I see a friend—a girl I know from Pattaya. I must say hello. Do you want to come with me?"

Math shook her head and the girl hurried away. She was relieved to see her go.

The bus company representative finished answering questions and returned to his other duties. The stranded passengers drifted off in various directions. Math found a seat away from the commotion of the bus terminal.

Exhausted from the heat of the broken down bus and the long ride from Phitsanulok, she propped her feet atop her suitcase and settled back. Within minutes she was asleep.

Chapter 5

Mike Johnson reviewed his weekly report one last time before saving it to the hard-drive. A minute later it was attached to an outbound email and headed halfway around the world to Pittsburgh. He had worked with computers most of his life but was still in awe of how the internet had changed the way people communicated.

He glanced at his watch—it was almost five. Through the window of the construction trailer he could see the sprawling structure of the new refinery. It would be operational before too many months, and then he would be going home. The thought left him with mixed emotions.

Mike had been in Thailand for more than two years and had long since gotten over any homesickness he'd ever experienced. His condo in Pattaya had become his home and his Thai friends and co-workers had become his family. He knew he should feel guilty for not missing his wife and his son, but he didn't. In fact, he dreaded the thought of going home. Mostly he felt guilty because he didn't feel guilty.

He spotted his driver relaxing in the front seat of the mini-van parked outside. Thai music blared loud enough to penetrate the thin walls of the construction trailer. Mike shut down his laptop, packed it into his computer bag, and left his office.

The job site was deserted. It was Saturday and everyone else had gone home more than two hours earlier. Mike would have done the same thing except for the report. He felt sorry that their driver had to come back for him, but it couldn't be helped.

"Khun Kriengchai!" he shouted as he neared the van.

J. F. Gump

At once the music stopped and Kriengchai was up and moving. "You go home now, Khun Mike?"

Mike stepped inside the van and took a seat. "Yes, it's time to go home."

The road from the refinery to Pattaya snakes through the exotic Thai countryside checkered with pineapple fields, chicken farms, and lumbering water buffaloes. The local residents had become so inured to construction traffic that the passing mini-van with its farang passenger went all but unnoticed.

Kriengchai stopped at a roadside market where Mike bought sodas for both of them. Kriengchai didn't open his, but then he never did. Mike knew he saved it for his children. Mike had met Kriengchai's family once. It was clear they were poor, but equally clear they were happy.

As they drove north on Sukhumvit Road, a ridge of black clouds edged its way northeast from the Gulf of Old Siam toward Chonburi and Bangkok. Mike figured someplace would get a downpour before long, but it wouldn't be Pattaya; the storm was too far north.

The forty-minute ride to his condo was filled with the usual heart-stopping adventures of the Thai traffic. Mike had never seen an accident in progress, but he had seen plenty of the end results. Most of them were gruesome. As often as not, motorcycles were involved. He had long ago stopped using motorcycles for transportation unless he had no other choice.

When they reached his condo, the driver scurried from his seat to slide open the side door of the mini-van.

"I'm sorry I kept you late," Mike said, stepping outside, his computer bag in hand. "Your family must be angry with both of us." He slid a five-hundred baht note from his wallet. "Please, take them to dinner on me," he smiled. "Maybe they will forgive us."

Kriengchai nodded and slipped the money into his pocket. "My family is never angry with you, Khun Mike, but I will take them to dinner for you anyway. Do you need a ride someplace tomorrow?"

16

SIAM NIGHTS

Mike knew Kriengchai's question was a gesture of politeness more than a symbol of servitude. He also knew that Kriengchai would use the five-hundred baht wisely, but wouldn't take his family to dinner. "No, Kriengchai. Tomorrow is Sunday. In America, Sunday is a day of rest."

Kriengchai smiled. "Same for me. When you rest, I rest. See you Monday morning. Have a nice weekend."

"Thank you, Kriengchai, I will." He turned and walked toward the condo lobby.

Mike had lived at the condominium complex longer than anyone else, including the managers. Jahl, the evening receptionist, was on duty.

"Sawasdee krup," he said when she looked up.

"Hello, Khun Mike," the girl smiled bright. "Will you be joining us for dinner tonight?"

Jahl had asked the same thing every Saturday since the new management had started their so-called *Weekend Feasts*. Mike had never once attended.

"I have other plans for tonight." It was his standard reply, even when he had no other plans. "Maybe next weekend."

"Okay, next weekend." Jahl's smile faded to a pout. "What you do tonight?"

It was a typical Thai question. Prying wasn't intended and truth wasn't expected. It was the Thai version of idle chit-chat. "I go with my friends," he gave the typical Thai answer.

Jahl rolled her eyes, handed him his key, and returned to her magazine.

Inside his condo he took a quick shower and dressed in clean clothes. He was taking his friend Lek to the grand opening of a new restaurant in Pattaya. With a little luck, this evening would turn out as he had been planning for the last few days. Buddha willing, he might even get laid. His wife in Pittsburgh was the last thing on his mind. He left the condo and walked toward the beer bar complex at Soi 2.

The sun had set but the concrete and asphalt continued to

radiate the day's heat into the humid air. If there was a breeze, it wasn't noticeable. He kept his pace slow—his Thailand shuffle he called it. It helped keep sweating to a minimum.

Toy's Bar was less than three blocks away, a casual five-minute walk. He slid onto a stool beneath an overhead fan at the backside of the bar. Lek was busy preening for their dinner date. She waved to say she would join him in a minute. "I have something to tell you," she mouthed at him.

No surprise there. She always had something to say. He double-checked his wallet to make sure he had his invitation. It was still there. He and three guests were invited to join the staff of the Amari Hotel for the grand opening of their new restaurant. He had asked Lek to go with him out of desire; he had invited Lek's sister Toy and her love of the week out of politeness. But he didn't mind; it made Lek happy, and Toy was fun to be around. It would be a good evening.

Chapter 6

Math was awakened by a firm but gentle hand shaking her shoulder. She looked up to see Tana's smiling face. "Come on," the girl was saying, her hand held out in assistance. "The bus is leaving. If we don't hurry, we'll miss this one, too."

Math took Tana's hand by reflex and allowed herself to be pulled from her seat. Together they walked to the boarding area. Math was relieved that Tana's seat was four rows away. She was tired and not in a mood for idle conversation.

The Bangkok sky had grown pale and an east-moving bank of dark clouds promised rain before nightfall. Rush hour was in full swing and the city streets were clogged with cars, buses, and motorcycles. After twenty minutes of little progress, the storm arrived and assaulted Bangkok with heavy sheets of rain and jagged bolts of lightning. The stop-and-go traffic became mostly stop.

She glanced at her watch—it was after six. Unless traffic cleared soon, it would be ten o'clock or later before they reached Pattaya. A prick of uneasiness jabbed at her. She had phoned her brother several times during the last two days but he had never answered. He had no idea of her plans and wouldn't be waiting for her when she arrived at the bus station.

When Math had left home earlier that morning, she had planned to arrive in Pattaya no later than five or six o'clock and then catch a motorcycle taxi to Anan's house. She liked to surprise people and thought Anan might enjoy her unannounced visit. Now she wasn't sure if she could find his house in the dark. She had been there only once and that had been more than a year ago. On impulse she dialed Anan's number from her cell phone, her *handy* as she called it. Again, there was no answer.

Time flew while the bus was going nowhere fast. Going nowhere fast, Math thought, pretty much described her life. It was going nowhere fast, slow, and at all speeds in between. Nothing was going right. She had no job, no money, and no man to love and take care of her. Now she was headed toward Pattaya on the slim hope that her life would somehow change for the better. More likely, with her luck, her brother would be out of business within a month.

If things didn't work out with her brother, she would do something else. Maybe she could find a job at a restaurant or a hotel. Tana's suggestion that she could work as a bar-girl entered her thoughts. She found the idea both gross and exciting.

She pulled at her bra strap, adjusting it away from the scar on her chest. It was an ugly scar that started at her cleavage and then streaked close beneath her left breast and across her side before stopping at the middle of her back. The scar was a constant reminder of her heart defect—a lifelong gift from her mother's failed abortion. It was a gift her doctors predicted would end her life before she turned forty.

Long before her tenth birthday, Math knew something was wrong. She couldn't keep up with the other kids when they played. She was always tired and out of breath. Sometimes her heart felt as though it would leap from her body. By the time she turned eleven, she had started fainting on a regular basis. When it became clear that something was terribly wrong, her mother took her to a doctor.

Nui and the doctor had spent a long time talking in private that afternoon. Nui was crying when she emerged from his office. The doctor took Math aside and explained everything about her heart. There were two options: surgery or death. Until the financial details could be arranged, Math was restricted to limited activity and she rarely left her house.

At the time her father had a job that provided their family with medical insurance, but the operation was very expensive and the insurance company refused to pay. Every day her mother called the insurance company and begged them to change their minds. Every day she hung up crying.

As the weeks multiplied into months, Math resigned herself to the fact that the doctor had been wrong. She had just one option, and it was not surgery.

One day several months after the doctor's diagnosis, Math slipped away from her house and went to the temple to pray. She had been to the temple many times in the past, but always with her mother or older sisters. She knew some of the monks who lived there and they had always been very kind to her.

That afternoon as eleven-year-old Math knelt praying, one of the monks entered the room. She had talked with him many times. His name was Jum. He watched her for a long time before coming to sit next to her.

"You look very sad," he said.

"I am sad," she replied. "I'm going to die."

The monk sat in silence for a long minute. "Why do you think you'll die?" he finally asked.

Math explained everything about her heart and the operation and the insurance company.

When she finished talking, the monk said, "I wish your mother had told me."

"I don't understand. Why would she tell *you* such a thing?"

"Never mind," he replied. "Come, we must pray for your health."

Math and the monk prayed together that day. She felt good knowing he had asked God and Buddha to help her. She left the temple happier than she had been in months.

Three days later the insurance company relented to Nui's daily begging and crying; they would pay for the operation. It was like a miracle. Math was positive that God had heard their prayers.

Two days before her twelfth birthday, Math underwent surgery to remove the excessive and dangerous blood vessel growth inside her chest. Her body had been doing its own version of a heart bypass and doing it all wrong. Blood vessels had sprouted in places they didn't belong and were growing haphazardly between veins and arteries. Her heart was being starved to death by her own body. At the time of her operation, the doctor's only promise had been that he would probably have to operate again.

It had been while she was recovering from that first operation that she learned about her mother's attempted abortion. She was lying in her bed at home, trying hard not to cry from the pain in her chest. Her mother was in the next room talking to Nuang, her oldest sister.

As the evening wore on, her mother's mood had shifted from worry and sadness to guilt and self-condemnation. While Math listened, small bits of truth bled out into the night, cutting deeper and colder than any surgeon's knife. Her own mother had tried to kill her before she was even born.

"Stop!" she had screamed, when she couldn't bear to hear more.

Nui had rushed to her side. "Is it your heart? Are you in pain?"

"Yes," Math had answered truthfully. Indeed, her heart was in terrible pain, but not from the surgery.

That night something died inside of Math and something also died between Math and her mother.

~~~

As the bus crept slowly out of Bangkok, the windows fogged over making it difficult to see outside. There wasn't much to see anyway except other buses, trucks, and cars inching forward, maneuvering for position. She closed her eyes, hoping she would fall asleep.

Memories from her recent past floated through her mind— memories of her ex-fiancé and the nightmare of their engagement, memories she wished she could forget. She tried to focus on something else but couldn't. The memories past took over.

Sawat Janchai was her ex-fiancé's name. Sawat was tall, thin, and handsome. Also, as she had recently learned, he was gay—not 100% gay but bisexual, which to Math was gay enough.

She and Sawat had become engaged and moved in together four months before she started her job in Bangkok. The job and the engagement were both finished now, and their relationship had turned into a nightmare that wouldn't stop. She wasn't sure it would ever end.

Sawat, like most Thai people, hadn't gone past the sixth grade because his family couldn't afford the tuition. But Sawat was street smart, a survivor. At the age of fifteen, he had disappeared from Phitsanulok and didn't return until he was twenty-one.

Math had been surprised the day they ran into each other. They had been friends and playmates when they were both younger, but she hadn't seen him for years. Sawat had changed so much she barely recognized him. They'd spent that afternoon talking about when they were kids and laughing at the silly things they had done. Later they brought each other up to date on their lives since they had last seen each other.

Sawat told her about his adventures with a Thai carnival group that traveled from city to city entertaining people at festivals and cultural events. His job had been to set up stages and to help load and unload the props and costumes. Sometimes he would perform in the shows. Sawat had been a roadie, a common laborer. After six years he had tired of his gypsy life and returned to Phitsanulok. He'd taken a job doing maintenance at the Big-C Shopping Center.

When Sawat finished the story of his life, Math updated him on her own. She had graduated from high school, endured a second operation on her heart, and was nearly finished with college. She told Sawat she was determined to get an education, even though her family was too poor to afford it. She had been selling clothes, make-up, perfume, and anything else people would buy so she could pay her tuition. Languages came easy to her, and she was at the top of her class in English. In less than a year she would graduate with a technical degree in computers and accounting. She was sure she would get a decent-paying job somewhere.

Math and Sawat dated on and off after that day at the Big-C. Usually they would go shopping or to a movie or out for dinner. Then last fall, at the Loy Krathong festival, Sawat had asked her to be his future wife. She had been so happy that someone loved her that she had said yes without hesitation. One week after his proposal they'd moved in together. Her mother and father had been against it because it wasn't proper and it wasn't polite. But Math didn't care; she only wanted someone to love.

Sawat was her first lover and she tried very hard to please him. The first two times they made love she reached an orgasm. After that she couldn't, no matter how hard she tried. Still she had taken pleasure in satisfying Sawat. She believed it was her duty to take care of her man and to make him happy.

By the following February, Math had graduated from college and had been hired by a finance company in Bangkok. The salary was okay and the company provided an apartment and insurance as part of her pay. She and Sawat decided to keep their small rented house in Phitsanulok. They agreed she would come home every weekend until he could find work in Bangkok, or until she found a decent paying job in Phitsanulok.

For this past Valentine's Day Sawat had bought her a cell phone. They couldn't really afford it, but she couldn't refuse it. The following week she had started her new job in Bangkok.

The bus hostess offering a complimentary meal interrupted her reminiscing of Sawat. Math welcomed the distraction though she merely picked at her food. Outside, the day had faded to near darkness beneath the thick clouds. As if on cue, the streetlights lining the freeway sparked to life. The bus was moving faster now but they were still inside the city limits of the sprawling megalopolis of Bangkok. With a population of more than ten million people Bangkok stretched for kilometers in every direction. Math glanced at her watch—it was seven o'clock. She had a sudden hope she would arrive in Pattaya by nine.

For a while she watched through the bus window as they passed a continuous stream of shops, malls, and factories. She was on the verge of sleep when uninvited memories of Sawat crept back into her head.

From the very day Math had started her new job in Bangkok, Sawat had been accusing her of having affairs with other men. It wasn't true, but he wouldn't listen to anything she said. His jealous rants upset her so much she sometimes became physically ill. There had been times when she wanted to end her relationship with Sawat, but her Thai sense of loyalty wouldn't let her and she continued to come home every weekend.

As the weeks passed, Sawat became ever more abusive—not physically, but verbally and emotionally. Not a weekend passed without an argument. He always found some reason to explode and storm out of the house. Recently he had become unresponsive to her presence. His blatant indifference had been the most painful of all.

Just before their engagement ended, Math had a one-night affair with a police captain in Bangkok. She hadn't planned it, but she hadn't rejected the policeman's advances either. She needed someone to love and Sawat already thought she was having an affair. She did it out of need and spite. Afterwards she felt dirty and cheap.

The guilt of her affair ate at her for two days before she decided she had to get away from Bangkok and what she had done. She asked her manager for some time off and it was granted. She went home on Thursday, a day earlier than usual. On her way to Phitsanulok she prayed silently for Sawat to be surprised and happy to see her.

When Math walked into their house that night, she found

J. F. Gump

Sawat in the midst of a sexual encounter—not with another woman, which she might have understood and been able to forgive, but with a man. And not just any man, but a lady-man, a katoey, a transvestite.

In an instant her shock gave way to outrage. The torrent of screaming and shouting that erupted from her was like a mindless beast. Emotions she never knew existed tore through her. Her fiancé, the man she was to marry, was having sex with a lady-boy. It was more than she could accept and reason deserted her.

With tears streaming she ran to the bedroom and found the small pistol Sawat kept in the dresser. She had the barrel snuggled tight beneath her left jaw when Sawat came into the room and shouted for her to stop. His presence refueled her rage. She lowered the pistol from herself and pointed it at him. Quickly she pulled the trigger. Bang! Bang! Bang!

Math jerked upright in her seat, heart pounding, sure she had heard gunshots. If she had, she was the only one. After a minute her pulse slowed to a gallop. She returned her thoughts to that night.

It had been the first time she'd ever fired a gun, but her aim had been very good. Two of her three shots found their mark. The impact of the .22 caliber bullets had barely made Sawat stagger, but the shock had made Sawat's knees buckle and he fell to the floor. Calmly she had laid the pistol down and called the police on her new cell phone.

Sawat's wounds hadn't been life-threatening or even very serious. The police had considered the whole affair a domestic matter and waited for Sawat to decide Math's fate. Typical of Thai law in such cases, the injured party could decide whether or not to press charges. Sawat had six months to decide, and he was in no hurry about it. Until he decided, Math was required to go to the police station every two weeks to report her whereabouts and her activities.

She had continued to work in Bangkok and returned to

Phitsanulok only to visit her family and to report to the police. Then, just two months ago, her job with the finance company had ended.

Math had contacted Sawat only once since the shooting. She had called to beg for his mercy and to ask him to drop the charges. In that conversation Sawat had made his feelings clear—if he couldn't have her, no one else would either.

Since then she had waited for the worst but it never came. Sawat just kept telling the police he hadn't decided. He still had eight weeks before the case would be dropped from the records. Meanwhile, the threat hung over her like a cobra poised to strike— like the deadly sword of the mythical monkey-man from Thai legends.

~~~

The bus bounced over a pothole, jolting Math awake. She looked out through the window. The rain had stopped and every trace of daylight had vanished. Outside there was little to see except passing cars and lights from the occasional roadside shops and restaurants.

She wasn't sure how long she had slept and she didn't see anything to help her know how far they had traveled. The only thing she knew for certain was that she was no longer in Bangkok. She flicked on her reading light and glanced at her watch. It was almost eight. She turned the light off and continued staring into the night, looking for a road sign that would tell her where she was. In a while she saw one that read *Pattaya—60 km.* Traffic was moving smoothly and the bus was far south of Bangkok's traffic and construction. With luck they would be in Pattaya by eight-thirty.

Math noticed a slight but unpleasant odor emanating from her armpits. Dear Buddha, how she needed a bath. She spent the rest of the trip realizing that she too could smell like a farang.

J. F. Gump

Chapter 7

The bus arrived at the Pattaya terminal at 8:40 p.m. Math collected her small cardboard suitcase from baggage claim and called her brother again. Still there was no answer. *Bad luck lady*, she thought to herself.

After competing with the other passengers for a motorcycle-taxi driver, she was on her way to Anan's house. At least she hoped she was. Her memory of where he lived had dimmed and the driver didn't know the street. She gave directions as best as she could remember. She wondered what she would do if she couldn't find her brother's house.

As they rode, she began to worry. She had heard the stories about motorcycle-taxi drivers taking young female fares onto lonely highways, and then raping them or worse. She remembered the short stretch of deserted road on the way to Anan's house and said a quick prayer for her safety. The driver swerved in and out of the traffic with brash recklessness. Maybe, she thought, rape was the least of her worries. Her prayers must have worked because fifteen minutes later she arrived unharmed at what she hoped was her brother's house.

She paid the driver and carried her suitcase to the small front porch. The door opened on her second knock. The man who answered wasn't Anan. A chill crept down her arms. "Who are you?" her voice quavered despite her effort to remain calm. Maybe she had the wrong house.

The man stared at her, his eyes glassy, his gaze penetrating and not polite. "Who are you?" he asked in return.

She didn't like the look on his face. She thought maybe he was drunk or on drugs. Then again, maybe she was just being paranoid. "I am Math," she said. "Anan is my brother. I have come to visit him. Is he here?"

"No," the man answered. "Was he expecting you?"

She felt a mild sense of relief, knowing she had the right house. "Where is my brother and who are you?"

"My name is Ziriwat. I'm Anan's business partner. I've heard him mention your name. Your brother has gone to Chiang Mai to visit your sister and to see about some business there. He didn't say how long he would be away. Maybe just a day or two."

"Why are you here? Anan never told me anyone lived with him."

"I don't live here all the time. Anan said I could stay here while he's gone. It's a nice house so I accepted his generous offer." Ziriwat paused and stared at Math for a long moment. "But I'm being rude. I haven't invited you inside your own brother's house." He turned away from the door and motioned at her with his hand, "Please, come in."

Math's female intuition sounded an alarm. She wasn't sure what to do but decided she had little choice for the moment. She forced herself calm, picked up her suitcase, and followed him inside. She was careful not to shut the door behind her. "Are you staying here tonight?"

"Well, yes," Ziriwat smiled. "You can stay, too, if you want. After all, it is your brother's house. You'll be safe here." His eyes scanned the length of her body.

Math's skin crawled at his blatant inspection. She wanted to turn and run, but she wasn't sure where she would go if she did. She wasn't sure the man could be trusted but for now she needed a shower and some time to think. Meanwhile she would try to find out exactly what sort of person he really was. It was possible her first impression could be wrong.

"Sure, I'll stay here. It *is* my brother's house and I feel safe enough," she said, trying to convince herself as much as Ziriwat. "Which bedroom can I use?"

He pointed to one of the doors. "I'll sleep there."

"Then I will sleep in there," she pointed to the other door. "Are there any clean towels? I need to shower. I've been on the bus since early morning and I'm very dirty."

Ziriwat found a towel and gave it to Math. She put her suitcase in the bedroom, and then went to the shower. She ignored his stares as she passed through the living room.

The water was barely lukewarm, but it felt good. Within five minutes she was finished and happy to be clean again. She wrapped the towel around herself and pulled back the shower curtain. There stood Ziriwat, ogling.

"You left the door unlocked," he smiled.

"It's cold in here," Math said, unnerved by his boldness. "I must get dry and into clean clothes." She grabbed the dirty clothes she had laid on the basin and hurried to her bedroom. She shut and locked the door. At that instant she decided her first impression of Ziriwat had been correct. She also decided not to spend the night. He might be harmless but she didn't trust him. The way he had looked at her was frightening. Buddha only knew what he might do if she stayed. Math slipped into clean clothes, combed her hair, and put on new make-up all in record time. She phoned her sister's number in Chiang Mai but the call wouldn't connect. She took a deep breath to calm herself, scrutinized her make-up in the mirror one last time, and then opened the bedroom door.

Ziriwat was sitting on the sofa. He stood when she stepped into the living room. "You look very nice," he said, giving her a brief inspection. "Are you going out?"

"I'm going to Soi 2," Math answered walking toward the front door.

"Going to work?" His tone was polite but his words were insinuating. His eyes drifted down, stopping where her tight black slacks hugged hips and thighs.

"No," she replied disdainfully. She remembered her earlier conversation with Tana about the work in Pattaya. "I don't even know what you are talking about. I'm going to see an old friend. I'll be back later. I should only be gone for a couple of hours." She forced herself to smile. "But I still plan to stay here. That's okay, isn't it?"

"Yes," Ziriwat answered immediately, his excitement rising at her unexpected promise. "I'll be waiting when you come home. You won't have to worry about coming back to an empty house. Do you need a ride? I have a motorcycle."

"Your offer is very kind, but I wouldn't want to impose."

"Mai pen rai, never mind," he said. "I was going to Pattaya anyway."

She struggled with her caution for a moment before deciding it would probably be okay if he drove her to Pattaya. He might try to slip into her bed if she spent the night, but she figured he would behave himself in public. "Thank you, I do need a ride. Would you mind if we don't leave for a few minutes? I'm hungry and would like to get something to eat. There's a restaurant on the corner down the street. I saw it on my way here. Could you pick me up there in fifteen minutes?"

Ziriwat didn't let his eyes leave her body. "Yes, fifteen minutes."

Math walked out the front door, happy to be away from her brother's partner. The guy gave her the creeps. She wasn't really hungry but she did want to meet the lady who ran the restaurant. Anan had told her that he and the owner were friends. Since she had no plans to come back to Anan's house until he came home, maybe the owner would know when Anan was returning.

Typical of many small Thai restaurants, this one was open-air with fans whirling overhead to help cool the customers and to blow away the flies. The cooking food smelled wonderful, but eating was the last thing on her mind. The restaurant owner was a slender woman whom Math guessed to be in her late thirties or early forties.

"Sawasdee ka, good evening," Math said politely as she sat at a table.

"Sawasdee ka," the lady replied. "My name is Mon. Can I get

you something to eat or drink? I make terrific spicy pork and delicious papaya salad."

"No, thank you," Math answered. "I'm not very hungry and I must leave in a few minutes. My name is Math; I'm the sister of Anan."

"I've heard Anan say your name. He has mentioned you and your sisters to me before. And a young brother too, if I remember correctly. I'm pleased to meet you, and surprised. Anan didn't say you were coming to visit."

"Khop khun ka, thank you," Math said. "Anan didn't know I was arriving today. When I called to tell him I was coming to Pattaya, he never answered his phone. I decided to come anyway. I never thought he would be away. I think I should have planned better but it's too late for that. Anan has told me you and he are friends, so I wanted to meet you. I was hoping you might know when he is coming home."

"I'm sorry, I don't know. He only said he would be gone for a couple of days, maybe longer. He went to see your sister in Chiang Mai. He's been talking about expanding his business there."

"Yes, I know that already. Anan's partner told me."

"Humph! Ziriwat!" Mon said the name harshly. "I don't like him much. He's been staying at your brother's house the last few days. I don't know what he's doing, but he's had some strange people stopping by since Anan left. If I were you, I wouldn't trust him. His family has a bit of money and he uses people. I don't know why your brother wants him as a business partner. I suggest you be careful around him."

"Don't worry," Math said, noting Mon's reaction, "I've seen enough of Ziriwat to know I don't want to be near him more than necessary. I've already decided I won't stay at my brother's house until he comes home. I have some money so I'll stay in a hotel."

It was a lie. Math had money, but not much. If she was lucky, she might be able to afford a cheap room for one night. She didn't know where she would stay. She had made a plan while she dressed, but it wasn't a very good plan.

J. F. Gump

"Some of the Pattaya hotels can be expensive," Mon warned. "And some of the things that go on there are not polite. You're welcome to stay at my house if you want."

"No, but thank you for your generosity. I'll be okay. If you could tell Anan to call me on my cell phone when he gets home, I would be most grateful."

"Of course I'll do that."

Math wrote her number on a piece of paper and handed it to Mon.

"Here, I'll give you my phone number too." Mon scribbled it down. "You can call if you don't hear from me or Anan, or if you need anything."

"Khop khun ka. You are as nice as Anan said."

"Mai pen rai, never mind," Mon said, blushing.

Ziriwat roared up on a motorcycle. "Ready to go?"

Math nodded and stepped away from the restaurant.

Mon gave Math a worried look as she climbed aboard the motorcycle. Ziriwat revved the engine and raced down the street.

Math wished Ziriwat would slow down but didn't say anything. She suspected he was trying to impress her with the motorcycle's power and his driving skills. She wasn't going to satisfy his ego by commenting on either. She held on tight and hoped for the best.

Within minutes they entered the northern part of Pattaya. Ziriwat turned right off Sukhumvit and onto North Pattaya Road. They passed the bus station where Math had arrived just an hour or so before. Gliding down North Pattaya they passed City Hall and the Thai Garden Restaurant. A minute later they turned left onto Second Road, heading south. Ziriwat stopped the motorcycle in front of the Big C Shopping Center. Across the street sat the outdoor beer bars of Soi 2.

"Do you need me to pick you up later? I can if you want."

"No, you don't have to do that," Math replied. "I'll pay a motorcycle-taxi to take me home." She had no intentions of going back to Anan's house until he came home from Chiang Mai. But Ziriwat didn't need to know that and she wasn't about to tell him.

"That could be dangerous for a beautiful young woman," he warned, true concern edged his voice.

"I can take care of myself," she said. "Thank you for the ride." With that she walked across Second Road toward the lights and music of the Soi 2 beer bars.

Standing at the top of the street and looking at the scene below, she realized it hadn't changed much since she had seen it last. She hoped she would find someone she knew. Her plan depended on it.

Math remembered the last time she had been in this part of Pattaya. It had been seven years ago when she was little more than a flat-chested, naïve, sixteen-year-old. She had traveled to Pattaya alone, looking for her second oldest sister Itta. She hadn't come on a whim or on holiday; she had run away from her home in Phitsanulok to escape from her father.

Three months after Math turned sixteen, her father Supit had come home drunk and in a foul mood. Within minutes a scuffle had erupted between him and her brother Anan. By the time Math realized what was happening, Supit had knocked Anan to the floor and was kicking him. Math intervened by pushing Supit away. Her distraction was brief but effective; Anan escaped through a window. Her father went into a rage at her interference. He hit her hard in the face. The blow knocked her down. She curled herself into a tight ball and pulled her arms over her head and her face. Supit went to the floor after her, flailing her back with his bony fists.

She wasn't sure how many times or how long he hit her. She passed out after the first few punches. When she finally awoke, he was gone. Her back ached terribly, inside and out. Lying there in agony, she knew she had to get away from the house and her father.

When the pain eased to a tolerable level, Math got up from the floor. She looked around the house, certain that at any moment her father would appear and resume his attack.

He was gone, but her mother was there and brutally beaten. Math washed her mother's face and helped her to bed. Then she stuffed a few clothes into a plastic bag and left the house. She had no idea where she would go, but with only ten baht in her pocket she knew it wouldn't be far. On impulse she decided to go to the temple. She knew they sometimes took abused women into the temple and gave them shelter. The motorcycle-taxi driver wanted her entire ten baht for the ride.

At the temple, the monk Jum took care of her. She had known Jum since she was a little girl. He was the monk who had helped her pray for a miracle when she needed her heart operation. While growing up, Math would talk to Jum whenever she was upset or in trouble. He always listened without criticizing or being judgmental. Sometimes he would offer advice and guidance. Over the years she had come to think of him as more than a monk – he was her good friend. But as close as she had always felt toward Jum, he was still a monk.

That night when she told what her father had done, she saw fury in Jum's eyes. He told her she must stay away from her father and suggested she stay at the temple for a few days. Since she had no money, she had no other options.

The next morning there was blood in her urine. There was nothing she could do about it except hope it was nothing serious. In Thailand, if you have no money, you have no doctor. She would either live or die.

After two days at the temple she felt better and was ready to leave. She had already decided she wouldn't go back to her home. She would go to Pattaya and stay with her sister, Itta. Math had no money for food or bus fare, but she had made up her mind and would go to Pattaya, even if she had to walk. At the age of sixteen she thought she could do anything.

When she told Jum of her plan, he worried she was too young to be traveling so far alone, especially without money. Jum coaxed her to stay, but she refused to change her mind. Eventually he gave up and said he would pray for her safe return.

As she walked away from the temple, Jum stopped her and pressed 500 baht into her hand. For bus fare and food, he told her. She accepted his money and promised to repay it when she could. Jum refused her promise. The only thing he wanted in return was for her to come and visit him when she had time.

"Hello, sexy lady," a man's voice shouted up at her from the bar below. "Come sit with me."

The man's words jolted Math from her thoughts. She blushed realizing how she must look standing there alone and staring at the cluster of bars and men.

She moved to the other side of Soi 2 where it wouldn't seem like she was eyeing the foreigners. She continued her scan of the bars from there.

~~~

Seven years earlier, when Math made her spur-of-the-moment trek from the temple to Pattaya, her second oldest sister had been working as a scuba diving instructor. She had no choice except to take Math into her home. No matter that it turned her life upside-down, she couldn't turn away her sixteen-year-old sister.

At that time Itta was living with a man from Scotland, but she had been careful to keep it hidden from her family. Math's unplanned visit changed all of that. Itta's secret was exposed.

While Math lived in Pattaya, Itta had taken her everywhere she went–even when she and her Scottish boyfriend went out drinking. They liked the bars on Soi 2 and went there almost every night. Her sister seemed to have a lot of friends who worked in the bars. A couple of Itta's friends, Som Jai and Nao, had befriended Math and treated her like a younger sister.

To sixteen-year-old Math, the glitter and excitement of Pattaya's nightlife had been overwhelming. The music, the lights, and the crowds of farang men drinking and laughing – she had never seen anything like it. She didn't even know places like this existed. She was totally enthralled.

Once, when Math told Itta that she would like to work in the bars when she got older, Itta had gone into a rage and spoke very harshly and very loudly to her. At the time she thought Itta might hit her. Itta hadn't hit her, but her outburst made Math realize she should never mention being a bar-girl again. Still, at age of sixteen the idea had excited her. It had excited her enough that she decided to study hard to learn English, just in case she ever did become a bar-girl.

Itta allowed Math to live with her for three months before insisting she return home and finish her schooling. During that time her father and mother had separated. When Math went home, she went to live with her mother.

Tonight Math saw no one she recognized. She took a deep breath, and then walked back across Soi 2 and into the nightlife of Pattaya.

Chapter 8

Math wandered through the maze of beer bars crowded with farang tourists drinking beer and laughing with friends. Music blared from every bar, each trying to be louder than the next. Smiling Thai ladies vied for the attention of the men.

She searched the faces of every bar-girl hoping to see Nao, or Som Jai, or anyone she knew. After twenty minutes and a lot of bars she gave up and went back to the top of Soi 2. As she considered what to do next, a lady on a motorcycle drove up and parked directly in front of her. When the woman removed her helmet, Math recognized her. It was Som Jai. She was older of course, but her face was unmistakable. "Sawasdee ka, Khun Som Jai," she said, unable to contain her excitement. "Do you remember me?"

Som Jai stared at her for a long moment before saying, "No, I do not."

"Maybe you remember my sister. Her name is Itta. She used to work here in Pattaya as a scuba diving instructor. Her boyfriend was a man from Scotland. I'm her sister. My name is Math. I met you a few years ago when I was much younger. Please say you remember me." Her heart raced in anticipation.

Som Jai smiled. She remembered Itta, but she didn't remember this girl. "Of course I remember Itta," Som Jai said truthfully before telling a lie. "And now that I think about it, I remember you too. My, haven't you grown up. The young lady I remember was a skinny teenager with barely lumps for breasts. How is your sister?

The last I heard she married that farang and moved away."

Math breathed a sign of relief. "Pee sao sabai dee, khop khun ka. My sister is well, thank you. She's living in Scotland with her husband. I'm embarrassed to ask you this, but I need help. May I ask a favor?"

Som Jai tensed but her smile stayed in place. Maybe this girl was Itta's sister, but maybe she wasn't. Som Jai measured her words before answering. "I will help the sister of my friend, if I can. What do you need? I hope it's not money, because I barely live week to week myself."

"Oh no, not money," Math answered. She told Som Jai the story about her brother and the man at his house. "I don't want to go back there tonight and I have no place to stay. I have a little money, but I think not enough for a hotel room. My brother should be home by tomorrow. I need a place to stay only for tonight. Would it be possible for me to sleep at your house?"

The tension faded from Som Jai's smile. If the girl was truly Itta's sister, the least she could do was give her a place to stay for one night. If she wasn't, well, she was bigger than the girl – certainly big enough to take her on if there was any trouble. "Of course you can sleep at my house, but you'll have to wait until I finish work. It will be late; you can ride home with me on my motorcycle. Meanwhile, let's stop standing in the street. I have to work, but you can sit at the bar and talk to some of the farangs. Just be careful. Most of the men are okay, but some aren't so good. They would love to get you to go with them for a short-time." Som Jai turned and strolled toward Toy's Fun Bar.

There were those words again, *short-time*. Now Math was certain she knew what it meant, but decided to ask Som Jai just to be sure. When they reached the bar, she said, "Som Jai, what is a short-time? I've heard it twice today already."

Som Jai laughed. "It's when a man and a lady go to have sex for an hour or so. Surely you know what sex is."

Math blushed and lowered her eyes from Som Jai's face. "Yes, I know what sex is. It's just that I've never heard those words before."

Now she had no doubt about the meaning. *Short-time* meant going to have sex for an hour or so. That was one thing she wasn't concerned with. After her recent break-up with Sawat, she had no intentions of getting involved with another man any time soon, maybe never again.

Som Jai gave her a soda to drink but didn't charge her for it. A few of the bar-girls stopped by to talk. Most wanted to know if she was going to work at the bar. She spent her idle time watching the farangs. None sat close which was okay with her. This was a good chance to practice her English, but she wasn't in the mood to talk with drunken strangers. She glanced at her watch. It was only ten thirty. It was going to be a long night.

At eleven o'clock, Som Jai came over and pointed down the street, "The big bosses are coming."

Math looked in the direction Som Jai had pointed. She saw two well-dressed Thai women, accompanied by two farangs. When they reached the bar, the women went inside the bar area while the two men sat on the outside with the rest of the customers. She wasn't sure if the *big bosses* were the ladies or the farangs.

"The older one is Toy and the younger one is her sister Lek," Som Jai whispered. "They own the bar. The two farangs are Lek and Toy's current boyfriends. Toy is really nice but not much of a business lady. Lek is okay but she's all business. I like Toy better. I'd better look busy." Som Jai started another tour of the bar.

Math watched the owners as they went about their business of greeting customers. She was impressed by the women's confidence in themselves. Especially the one named Lek. The woman left no doubt about who was in charge.

The two farangs had fallen into a deep conversation and barely paid any attention to the goings-on at the bar. After a few minutes, one of them waved Toy over. The younger, dark-haired, man said something that clearly upset her. Toy went to Lek and talked angrily while pointing at the two men. Lek only smiled. Finally,

J. F. Gump

Toy grabbed her purse and went to sit next to them.

At that moment Som Jai returned and Math lost interest in the farangs and the boss ladies. A few minutes later a man hugged Som Jai from behind. Math looked up to see the older of the two foreigners who had arrived with the boss ladies.

"Hello, Som Jai," the farang said. "How are you today?"

"Hello Mike," Som Jai smiled. I'm very well, thank you. Are you leaving?"

The man ignored Som Jai's questions. "Who's your friend?" He nodded toward Math. "Is she going to work here?"

"No, I don't think so," Som Jai answered. "She's the sister of my friend. She arrived in Pattaya just today. She's spending the night at my house. Where are you going?"

"I'm taking Toy's boyfriend Eduardo downtown. He has come to Pattaya twice now, but he's never been to South Pattaya. Toy insists on going with us. I guess she thinks we can't be trusted alone. We're leaving as soon as she comes back from the toilet. What's your friend's name? Does she speak English?"

Math answered the question herself. "I am Math and I speak English. Your name is Mike?"

Mike was surprised at how well she spoke English. He turned his full attention to her. "Your English is very good. Which bar do you work in?" Like most farangs, Mike assumed if a girl spoke good English, she must have learned it in a bar.

"I'm not a bar-girl," Math responded, her voice clipped. "I have never worked in a bar. I learned English in school. I studied very hard."

There was a pause while his insinuation, and her rebuttal, took effect. Then, for no reason other than impulse, she added, "You said you were going to South Pattaya. I've never been to South Pattaya. Would it be okay if I go with you and your friends? I'm tired of sitting here and I want to see everything in Pattaya. I promise I won't be any trouble."

Mike hesitated. "Are you sure? I'm taking Eduardo to a few places that aren't very nice. You might see things that would

42

embarrass you."

"I want to see everything in Pattaya," she repeated.

"Up to you," Mike said after a short silence. "I need to tell a friend at the Classroom Bar that I'll catch up with him later. I'll be back in a minute. We'll leave when Toy is ready."

Math watched the farang as he walked across the street toward the Classroom go-go bar. He was an older man; about 45 she guessed. She thought he was a little overweight, but to her most farangs looked overweight. If he smelled like a farang, she hadn't noticed. He had a kind face, but his moustache made him look serious.

As she waited for the farang to return, a growing sense of unease crept through her. She wasn't sure what she might be getting herself into by going to South Pattaya with total strangers. She searched the bar for Som Jai. She seemed to know the foreigner quite well. Maybe she could tell her something about him. If he was a bad man, she could always change her mind. She caught Som Jai's attention and motioned her over. "How well do you know the farang named Mike?"

"I've known Mike for a long time. He's very nice. He works in Thailand. Why do you ask?"

"I invited myself to go to South Pattaya with him and his friends. I just wanted to make sure I would be safe."

Som Jai laughed. "Mike will be a gentleman with you. If he's not, you tell me and I'll hit him. But don't worry, I guarantee you'll be safe with Mike. Just be careful how you act while you're here. Lek might not like it if you get too friendly. She treats Mike like he's her personal property."

Mike returned and their conversation was cut short.

"There's Toy," Mike said, pointing. "Let's go." He grabbed Math by the hand and led her over to Toy and Eduardo. "This girl, uh... I forget her name, wants to go with us," he said. "I hope no one minds."

"I am Math," she said, looking at Mike.

No one else spoke. There were no objections.

"Let's go then. I vote we grab a baht-bus," Mike suggested.

"No, we will take my truck," Toy announced, leaving no room for argument.

As they followed, Mike whispered into Math's ear. "We really should take a baht-bus. It's much easier and faster. There's no easy place to park downtown."

Almost before he had stopped speaking, Math shouted softly, but loud enough to be heard, "Toy, I think we should take a baht-bus, too."

Mike cringed.

"I'm not riding in a disgusting baht-bus," Toy shouted back pointedly.

Math looked at Mike. He shrugged and continued walking toward Toy's truck.

Pattaya has its own unique form of public transportation. Most people call them baht-buses, but a few people call them baht-mobiles. Picture a small pick-up truck with bench seats on either side of the bed and an open-sided, metal cap overhead. These trucks serve as the local bus transportation and baht is the local currency. Baht-bus! The baht-buses follow a set route around town. You get on, ride until you're close to your destination, and then you get off. It's cheap and convenient transportation.

Toy was the master of bad driving. She cut off more cars, motorcycles, and baht-buses in less than three kilometers than Math thought possible. Somehow she managed to miss every one. The rear seat of Toy's truck was very small. With two people in the back, it was overcrowded. The ride to South Pattaya was as scary as it was uncomfortable.

As Mike had predicted, there was no place to park in downtown Pattaya. Toy spent more time finding a place to park than it had taken for them to drive there. Then she had to pay 200 baht for the privilege.

Mike smiled at Math but said nothing. Instead he spoke to Eduardo, "Happy-A-Go-Go is this way." He led the way down a narrow street lined with shops, bars and restaurants.

The closer they came to Pattaya's famous 'Walking Street', the more crowded the sidewalks and streets became. Mike grabbed Math's hand and pulled her towards him. "In South Pattaya," he said, "it's better if the men and the bar-girls think you're with someone already. But if you're not comfortable, I will let go of your hand."

Instinctively she knew he was right. She squeezed her hand tighter onto his and allowed herself be pulled closer. Her eyes shined as she watched the endless procession of neon lights, sexy ladies, and drunken farangs. Loud music spilled out from the bars and filled the streets with a confusing mix of songs, one indistinguishable from the other. Street vendors hawked their wares, while the bar-girls and the katoeys (the transvestites), touted their own special wares. Her sister Itta had never brought her here, and neither had her family when they came to Pattaya last year to visit Anan. "Isn't this exciting?" she said to no one in particular.

Mike gave her a questioning glance. "Uh, yeah," he shrugged. "I suppose it is."

Toy and Eduardo either didn't hear or just didn't answer.

Within a minute they were entering Happy-A-Go-Go. The place was crowded with brown-skinned Thai ladies and drunken farangs. There were a few vacant seats scattered around the room, but none where four people could sit. The hostess asked them to wait for a moment while she found them a table.

In the center of the bar was a raised platform with brass poles, pulsating lights, and dancers in various stages of undress. Math saw the dancers, but pretended she didn't. Instead she looked around the room at the customers and the girls who weren't dancing.

In less than a minute the hostess returned to show them to their seats. Math and Toy sat with their backs to the dance stage. That was fine with her because she wouldn't have to look at the naked girls dancing. The music was loud and their conversation minimal. It wasn't a good place to talk. Besides, the men seemed more interested in the dancers than either Math or Toy. After about ten minutes, the stage lights dimmed and music changed. Two ladies replaced the dancers who had been on stage.

"Watch this," Mike said to Eduardo. "Tell me what you think. Is it real or is it an act?"

Math had no idea what Mike was talking about. She really didn't want to look at naked women but her curiosity got the best of her. She swiveled her seat toward the stage. Two ladies were dancing sensuously with each other, touching lightly, caressing softly. Math was entranced. Her imagination ran wild. She had never done that before, but she had fantasized about it often enough. She couldn't take her eyes away.

As the songs continued to play, the ladies on stage proceeded to make lesbian love to each other. It wasn't polite but it was exciting. When the show ended, the women left the stage and the other dancers returned.

Mike took her hand. "Sorry you had to see that," he said. "I told you there might be things you didn't want to see."

Her face was flushed from excitement and embarrassment. She hoped it was too dark for anyone to notice. "Never mind," she said. "I told you I wanted to see everything in Pattaya."

A few minutes later they had finished their drinks. Mike paid for everyone and they left. Outside, the streets were more crowded than before. It seemed that every person in Pattaya was in this part of town.

"Let's go to the Bamboo Bar," Mike suggested to no one in particular. Everyone followed his lead. After a moment he dropped back, pulling Eduardo with him so they could talk about the show at Happy-A-Go-Go. Math walked ahead, beside of Toy.

"So, why are you in Pattaya?" Toy asked. "Are you here on holiday?"

"No. I'm here to work with my brother. If he has something for me to do, that is. I lost my job in Bangkok and need money for food, rent, and everything. I don't know how much my brother can pay me. Maybe nothing. If he has no work for me, I'll find something else to do."

"Darling," Toy said, "You're a very good looking young lady and your English is excellent. If you ever need a job, you can work at my bar. The pay isn't good, but you can make extra money by going with my customers. With your looks and your English, you would make a lot of money from the farangs. You just have to be careful and use a condom to protect yourself."

"Hey," Mike shouted. "What are you telling her? She's a nice girl. She doesn't want to work in your bar or any other bar." He hadn't really heard much of their conversation but he had heard Toy say *condom* and guessed at the rest. The look on their faces said his guess was correct.

Math was surprised that Mike understood their Thai conversation. She was also surprised that he would care where she worked.

Mike hurried to catch up with the women. He took Math by the hand. "You can walk with me. Toy is my good friend, but working in a bar is not for you. You're too smart for that."

Math stopped walking. She barely knew this farang and now he was telling her what she should do. "You are not my boyfriend or my husband or my father," she said, lifting her face and jutting out her chin. "Where I work is up to me." She wasn't smiling.

Mike stared at her for a long moment before replying, his face was as serious as hers. "Yes, it's up to you if you want to be a whore. I think it would be best if you just shut up and come with me." He let his lips form an apologetic smile. He squeezed Math's hand firmly but gently and started up the street again.

She let herself be led rather than make a scene. Her pursed lips made it clear she was annoyed with his bossiness.

Two blocks later they stopped at a large, open-air bar with a live band and a dance floor. A mixture of Thais and farangs filled about half of the tables. The band played loud. A few people danced. A young lady showed them to their table.

The waitress took their orders, and Mike paid when the drinks arrived. The band started a new song, a slow song. "Do you want to dance?" he asked.

Either Math didn't hear him, didn't understand him, or was just plain ignoring him.

"I said do you want to dance?" he repeated louder, almost shouting.

Still she didn't answer, or even acknowledge he had spoken. Instead she turned and talked to Toy.

The music was loud and the women were talking low. Mike couldn't hear anything they were saying. He figured they were talking about him, and laughing at him too. "Little bitch," he muttered under his breath. He turned so he could watch the band and the couples who *were* dancing.

Three songs later he had finished his beer and Math had ignored him the whole time. He was bored and ready to leave. Also, he was anxious to get back to Lek. He felt guilty for coming to South Pattaya in the first place. Lek would probably be pissed at him if he were gone too long. He didn't want that, not tonight. He had special plans for later.

"Well," Mike said to no one in particular, "I'm going back to Toy's bar." He stood and walked to the street. The others left their half-finished drinks behind and followed.

I'm taking a baht-bus back," Mike announced when they reached the sidewalk. "I don't feel like walking to Toy's truck. Sorry Toy, I hope you're not angry with me too." He frowned in Math's direction.

"Never mind," Toy noticed his gesture. "I'll see you at my bar later."

As Mike crossed the street, he heard Math shouting, "Please, wait. Can I go with you? I don't want to walk back to the truck either." Actually, she didn't want to ride with Toy again, but out of politeness she didn't say that.

He grimaced but waited for the girl to catch up, then flagged down an empty baht-bus. The ride up Second Road to Soi 2 would take about ten minutes unless they ran into traffic, or unless the driver was trolling for new passengers.

Mike was surprised when she sat beside him. Considering the way she had been acting for the last half hour or so, he was surprised she was even sitting in the same vehicle with him. It was his turn to ignore her and he did it completely.

At Central Pattaya Road they just missed making it through the green light. Within seconds the baht-bus was surrounded by cars, buses, and motorcycles spewing out enough exhaust fumes to kill all but the hardiest.

Second Road is blocked from the sea breezes by a continuous row of hotels, bars, and shops. Tonight the exhaust fumes at the intersection of Central and Second hung squalid in the damp air. Mike breathed only when necessary. In a moment Math spoke. "Why do you care where I work?"

"I don't care where you work," he answered. "You can do what you want. I'm not your father or your husband or your boyfriend or anything else. Remember? What you do is up to you. I just don't like the idea of a nice and smart girl getting into that business. That's all I care about."

"Oh," she said, and then smiled for the first time since the subject had come up earlier. "I was just wondering. Are we almost to Soi 2?"

"Yeah, almost."

The light changed and the baht-bus continued up Second Road. Five minutes later they had arrived. Mike rang the buzzer to let the driver know they wanted to stop. They exited the bed of the truck and Mike handed the man a fifty baht note. It was more than the normal fare, but the driver hadn't stopped for any other passengers and that made the ride worth the extra money. When they entered Toy's Bar together, Lek gave them a cold, suspicious glare.

"I will talk to Som Jai," Math said, remembering Som Jai's warning about Lek.

"Up to you," Mike answered. He was glad to be rid of her. At the same time he felt like he was being dumped. "I'll talk to Lek," he added in a smart-ass tone. "At least she will talk to me."

"Up to you, too," she responded, just as tartly.

They went their separate ways. Math went to where Som Jai was sitting. Mike went to *his* seat.

Chapter 9

Mike's seat was a stool at the far end of the bar behind where the two-man band played. To the rear of his seat, and not more than fifteen feet away, was another beer bar with another two-man band. When both bands played, he couldn't hear what either was playing. He called it the music mix zone. Inside the music mix zone, it was actually quieter than most of the other seats at the bar. There a person could have a conversation without having to shout over the noise of the bands. Mike liked the music mix zone.

Lek sauntered around the bar, casting an occasional biting glance at Mike. After about ten minutes she walked to where he sat. "Who is the lady?"

"What lady?" Mike responded.

"Don't be a stupid man," Lek glanced in the direction of where Math sat talking to Som Jai. "You know what lady I mean."

"A friend of Som Jai's, I think," he answered. "At least that is what she told me. Why?"

"I think you went for a short time with her. Som Jai told me the girl is no good. A stupid bar-girl who used to work in Pattaya. Why would you go with a bar-girl?"

"Come on, Lek. I went with your sister and her boyfriend. That girl invited herself to go with us. We just went to a couple of places downtown. Why are you so concerned anyway? Lately, it seems like you don't want me anymore, so why should you care if I do go with another girl?"

Lek gave him a long stare. He was wrong. She still wanted

Mike, but he was the one who had been pulling away from their relationship. He still came to see her every day, but he never stayed long anymore. He had even stopped taking her home with him on Saturday nights. Tonight was the first time in weeks they'd done anything together away from the bar. He was the one who had been pulling away and his withdrawal hurt and angered her. Just when she had finally let her defenses down and decided to love him, he had distanced himself from her.

"I think you're mixed up. It seems you don't know what I want." She paused to gauge his reaction and then continued. "If you went with my sister, then where is she? I think you didn't go with my sister. I think you went only with that lady."

Mike sighed. "I took the baht-bus back because I wanted to get away from that lady, but she decided to come with me. What could I do? Your sister will be back in a minute. You'll see I'm telling the truth." He fell silent, frowning.

Lek recognized his expression. She had pissed him off. "Paw," she shouted to one of the girls behind the bar, "Bring Mike a beer. I will pay." She gave him a cool glance and walked away to visit other customers.

Always business, Mike thought, more irritated than angry. With Lek, business always came first. Well, fuck her. He tried to laugh it off, but couldn't. Numbing depression rubbed against his senses. He recognized the symptoms, but he couldn't stop them. The rest of the night was going to be shit.

He knew he should just go home, but he couldn't allow himself to leave just yet. Earlier he had taken Lek to dinner. It was part of a plan he had cooked up three days before. He'd decided that tonight he would wait for Lek to finish work and then see if she would go home with him. He hadn't done that in a while. He hoped things between them might be better if she went home with him tonight. Now, after the trip downtown with that girl, he was sure Lek wasn't going anywhere with him. He proceeded to drink one beer after another at a fairly steady pace.

By the time Toy and Eduardo returned from downtown he had

finished three beers and was working on his fourth. But today was Saturday and he didn't have to work the next day, and the chances of Lek going with him were slim, so what difference did it make if he got drunk? With luck, he mused wryly, he would be shit-faced within the hour.

He watched the ladies of the night talking and flirting with the farangs at the bar. Most of the men looked as drunk as he felt. They probably were. Som Jai sat with a customer who seemed more than a little interested in her. Mike figured she had a man for the night. Toy talked steady with that new girl Math. He knew she was trying to recruit the girl to work at her bar and it annoyed him.

None of the bar-girls came to talk with him like they usually did. They'd probably seen the conversation between him and Lek. He didn't care. He wasn't in the mood for a broken English conversation anyway. He was doing just fine watching the bar activities, listening to the undecipherable music, and drinking his beer.

Mike had long ago formed his opinion of the bar-girls and he felt sorry for most of them. The girls who work the beer bars in Pattaya are nothing like most people think. He had taken the time to know some of them as people and found that he liked them as friends. Most of the bar-girls are uneducated, but smart nonetheless. In Thai society, it often falls to the daughters to help aging parents and younger siblings survive. Sometimes the pressures of their responsibility are overwhelming. The menial jobs they find in their hometowns are mostly as farmhands and common laborers. The pay is barely enough to survive. Working in Pattaya is an option for the prettier ones, and it beats slaving in the hot sun twelve hours a day or longer. The girls aren't proud of what they do in Pattaya, but they're not ashamed of it either. For them it's a matter of survival. Mike didn't look down on them for their professions.

Then there was Lek. He remembered the day he had met her. It had been eight months ago and he had been enchanted with her from first sight. She was older than the rest of the girls in the bar, but the way she moved, talked, and directed everyone made it clear that she wasn't just another lady of Pattaya – she was the boss. He had pursued her shamelessly, and she had succumbed to his persistence. On the nights when Mike went to Toy's bar, he always sat on the same stool in the music mix zone. Before long, everyone but the weekend tourists recognized it as "his" seat.

The music mix zone. That was where Mike sat tonight. Lek was ignoring him, Toy and that girl kept pointing at him, and he was getting drunk. What a wonderful fucking evening this was turning out to be.

He was finishing what he had decided would be his last beer when Toy came and sat beside him. "Mike," she said, "Do you have two beds in your condo?"

"Why? Are you looking for a place to live?" His words came out thick, slurred, and cynical. The last few beers had done their job well.

"No," Toy answered, ignoring his tone. "That girl, Math, was going to spend the night at Som Jai's house, but Som Jai is going with a man tonight. She doesn't want Math to stay at her house when she's not there. I told her she could stay with you, if you don't mind."

He stared stupidly at her for a full minute. Finally, he said, "I have to talk to Lek for a minute." He stood and stumbled to where Lek was talking to a customer.

"Lek," he said louder than necessary to overcome the music. "Are you going to go home with me tonight or not?" It wasn't a polite thing to do or say so loud, but Mike was too drunk to know, or even care, what he was doing. A couple of the bar-girls looked in his direction.

Lek stood closer to her customer. She glanced briefly at Math before glaring at Mike. "No!" Her voice was even louder than Mike's had been.

Everyone in the bar stared in their direction. The band stopped playing. Mike could feel eyes drilling holes in his body. "Then I'll take some other woman home," he grunted.

"I don't care," Lek lashed back. "Fuck some bar-girl if that's what you want."

He stared at Lek trying to understand what had just happened. For the first time ever, he had directly asked Lek to go with him and she had rejected him. He turned and stumbled back to his seat, his face burned with embarrassment.

"The girl can come with me if she wants," he said, his voice tight. "Whatever she wants to do is up to her."

Toy smiled in satisfaction and walked to where Math was sitting. They talked for a minute, then Math came hesitantly to sit beside Mike.

"Are you okay?" she asked him, her tone meek. "You look maow. Err, I mean, I think you've had too many beers."

"I'll let you know when I've had too many beers." He shouted at one of the girls to bring him yet another.

Math said nothing.

Mike sipped at the beer for about ten minutes. The angry frown never left his face. Lek didn't say anything else, but her eyes shot pointed daggers at him and Math. Math didn't look in Lek's direction. She knew she was caught in the middle of something she didn't understand.

Finally Mike said, "I'm leaving now. If you want to sleep at my place, you can. I won't bother you if you don't bother me. Up to you." With that he stood and left the bar.

"Where are you going?" Lek shouted. When Mike didn't answer, she turned her glare toward Math.

Math had been having doubts about going with the farang, but now she was 100% sure she didn't want to stay at Toy's bar. For a moment she considered going back to her brother's house, but then decided that was a bad idea. She grabbed her purse and followed Mike. When she caught up to him, she took his hand. "I don't want to lose you," she said, but actually she didn't want him to fall and get hurt while she was with him. Together they started the three-block walk to his condo.

Halfway home, Mike stopped at a gas station. "I want to buy

water," he said as he wobbled his way toward the entrance. Math followed, still holding his hand.

Inside, the attendant spoke to Mike. Clearly, the man knew him. He gave Math a puzzled stare. In a moment he said, "Are you taking him home?"

"Yes," she answered. "Seems he had too much beer tonight."

The man only smiled. Mike stopped here almost every night on his way home. He would buy water, cigarettes, and beer. He was a regular customer. Tonight was the first time the attendant had ever seen him with a lady.

Mike stared at the cooler doors as if trying to decide which brand of water to buy. Since there were only two choices, Math wondered what was taking so long. After a minute, he selected two bottles of water, a wine cooler, and two bottles of beer. Math rolled her eyes. The attendant smiled.

"I need Marlboro Lights, too," Mike slurred. His words were unnecessary. The attendant had already laid them on the counter.

"Hey you," Mike said, looking at Math, "You want anything?"

She did. She went to the cooler and got two cans of iced coffee. Without even pausing, she proceeded to get a large bag of potato chips, some sweet snacks, a bag of nuts, a loaf of bread, and a can of Pepsi. She put them on the counter next to the things Mike had bought.

He stared at her incredulously. Nervy bitch, he thought. The attendant rang up the items, Mike paid, and they left. As they exited, the attendant said something in Thai. Math said something in return. Mike didn't understand what either one of them had said. At that moment, he didn't really care.

A few minutes later they passed between the mostly empty beer bars that lined either side of the narrow street leading to his condo. The girls at the bars had great fun shouting at Mike and making comments about his lady friend. Math blushed. Mike ignored them.

In the lobby of the condo, the night clerk seemed surprised to see Mike with a girl, but she only smiled and said hello. After a short elevator ride to the third floor and a twenty-foot walk, they were inside his room.

Mike raced to the air conditioner and turned it on. Next he put everything he had bought into the refrigerator, except for the cigarettes and one beer. He struggled briefly with the bottle opener before the cap flipped off and skittered across the floor. He sat in the swivel chair by the desk, lit a cigarette, and then looked at Math. "You can sleep on the couch. I'm going to read for a while and then I'm going to bed – alone. I think you understand what I mean. The bathroom is there if you want a shower." He pointed at a door, then picked up a book and proceeded to read.

Math had showered only a few hours earlier, but decided another one wouldn't hurt. Besides, it was obvious Mike wasn't going to start any meaningful conversation. She went into the bathroom, locked the door, and took a very long shower.

While toweling herself dry, she heard a thud outside the bathroom door. She didn't know what the noise was, but she was sure it wasn't good. In *quickly time* she put on her clothes, eased the door open, and peeked out expecting to see Mike passed out on the floor. He was passed out alright, but not on the floor. He was sitting upright in the chair. The book he had been reading lay on the floor.

She stared at him deciding what she should do. She noticed the swivel chair had wheels. Slowly she rolled him and the chair toward the bed but he didn't stir. She took him by the arm and shook him gently. He awoke enough to make unintelligible noises. After a minute of hesitation she pulled on his arm and he stood swaying. She put his arm across her shoulders and guided him to the bed. They fell together in a confused tangle of arms and legs.

After untangling herself, she stood beside the bed wondering what to do next. She thought about taking off his clothes but decided that was a bad idea. Instead she removed his shoes and pulled the blanket over him. Next she looked through the closets looking for extra blankets. Nothing. She looked in the bathroom and found a dry towel. It would have to do.

While listening to Mike's drunken snoring, Math helped herself to a can of iced coffee, a few chips, and a whole bag of nuts. She knew she shouldn't be eating this late at night but she was hungry and with his loud snoring sleep was out of the question. In a while she went to the bed and rolled Mike onto his stomach. His snoring stopped at once. She turned off the light, lay on the couch, and covered herself with the towel.

The air conditioner's fan ran full speed. The thin towel did little to stop the cold air blowing down on her. After a few minutes she was shivering and she was sure she would freeze to death by morning. She got up, turned on the light so she could see, and turned the air conditioner off. She switched the light off again and lay back down on the couch.

She was still cold. The towel was so short she could cover her feet or she could cover her shoulders but she couldn't cover both. She glanced at the bed. The blanket called warmly to her. After a few minutes she gave in. She abandoned the couch, walked quietly to the bed, and slipped under the covers.

The sheets were frigid. Math moved her feet around, hoping to find one spot that would be warmer than another. In a moment she found a spot much warmer. She pushed her feet in that direction until they encountered Mike's leg. He stirred when she touched him. For a minute she didn't move, afraid he would wake up, but he didn't.

Dear Buddha, his leg felt so warm. Inch by inch, she eased her body closer to Mike until her back was touching his. She lay there for a long time, absorbing his body heat. She wondered what her friends in Phitsanulok would say when she told them she had slept with a farang? Probably not believe her, she decided.

In a while she felt warmer and the sheets on her side of the bed felt less cold. Inch-by-inch, she moved away from Mike, pulled the blanket over her head, and fell asleep.

Chapter 10

Mike awoke the next morning when a ray of sunlight sliced through a crack in the curtains and shined on his closed eyes. He moved his head enough to put his face back into the shadows. He glanced at the clock. It was ten thirty. He was soaked with sweat, his mouth tasted like shit, and his bladder felt like it might explode at any moment. He didn't hear the air conditioner running which probably accounted for the room feeling like a sauna.

He got up from the bed, switched on the air, and staggered to the bathroom. He sat lady style rather than standing because he didn't trust his aim. He tried to recall last night but it was less than a blur. He didn't remember coming home. In fact, he didn't remember much of anything after Lek had given him the third degree about going downtown with Toy and Eduardo and that girl, whatever her name was. The liquid, brown-bottle, memory eraser had worked well.

With his bladder empty and very much relieved, Mike brushed his teeth and splashed cold water on his face. He groped for a towel but found none; he dried his face with the tail of his shirt. He caught a glimpse of his image in the mirror. He looked like shit but he wasn't surprised – he felt like shit, too.

Mike left the bathroom, took a bottle of water from the fridge, and then sat at his desk. He noticed a half-full bottle of beer. Must have been really drunk last night, he thought. He wasn't a person to stop halfway through a beer.

His eyes scanned the desk and the kitchen table. No

newspaper. He had forgotten to buy a newspaper. He would have to satisfy himself with doing crossword puzzles out of a book until he was awake enough to shower without drowning.

He lit a cigarette, took a drink of water, and attacked the puzzle on the first page he opened. By the time he'd finished the cigarette, the room had cooled a bit and his sweating had slowed to a clammy discomfort. The puzzle was only half finished, so he wasn't quite ready for the shower.

As he studied the crossword, a movement in the bed caught the corner of his eye. There was a lump under the covers and it was moving. He hadn't noticed it before, but then he had been so groggy when he got up that he wouldn't have noticed an elephant in his bed. A shot of adrenaline pumped through him.

He walked to the side of the bed. Definitely not a pillow. Carefully he pulled back the edge of the blanket. It was that girl. What the hell was her name? It was something weird but he couldn't remember what. He lowered the blanket and went back to his chair. As hard as he tried, he couldn't remember the girl coming home with him. What had they done last night? Did they have sex or something? He still had his clothes on, but she was in his bed. He wasn't sure what to do, so he just sat and stared.

After a few minutes of watching the mostly motionless lump, Mike's gaze wandered around the condo. It was a corner unit on the third floor. He had paid extra for an east-side view, away from the afternoon sun and the noise of Second Road. Drape-covered sliding glass doors accounted for both exterior walls of his corner unit. The inner walls were white plaster trimmed with dark wood. The condo came furnished with a bed, a sofa, two chairs, a coffee table, desk, kitchen table with chairs, a minimum of dishes, and a 19" color TV. It also came with cable, which meant he could watch a lot of Thai channels, a couple of bad English channels, or the Asian version of MTV. There were no pictures or other decorations to make it feel like a home. It was spartan, but it fit his lifestyle. Not much to take care of and a comfortable place to sleep.

The floors were cheap marble, which was good. Minor spills on marble wouldn't stain like carpeting and he didn't need a vacuum cleaner. He paid for maid room service, so the bed linens and towels were changed daily. They also mopped the marble floor every day. That thought made him hesitate. Slowly, he lifted his foot so he could see the bottom of his socks. Damn, still dirty.

Mike had an ongoing battle with the room maids. When they mopped, they would do it with dirty water. He had taken time to teach them to use fresh water when they mopped his floor, but he had to remind them every few days so they wouldn't forget. He had stopped getting angry about it. He had learned long ago that Thais don't react well to angry farangs. Also, he had learned that Thais have their own ideas about things. If their ideas matched with farang ideas, fine. If not, they would make a short-term effort to please and then go back to their old habits. For a newcomer to Thailand, Thai habits could be quite annoying if not downright frustrating. Mai pen rai, never mind, he muttered to himself, lowering his foot to the floor.

His eyes came to rest on the photo album sitting on the shelf unit opposite of the desk. He had brought it with him from his last trip home. Some of the Thais he worked with at the oil refinery had asked about his life in America, so he had taken the time to assemble pictures from his childhood, his school years, his time in Vietnam, and so on until the present time. They had been delighted to see Mike at the various ages of his life. For the last few months he had been adding a few pictures of Thailand every week or so.

That reminded him; he had some pictures he'd picked up on Friday night. Since the lump looked like it wasn't going to wake up anytime soon, and since the crossword puzzle wasn't getting done, he decided to kill some time sorting and selecting pictures.

Mike pulled the album from the shelf, laid it on the desk, and opened the front cover. Inside was a picture of himself as a baby not yet two years old. White hair, blue eyes. His hair had changed colors twice since then. First to brown and then to a mix of gray and brown. The next color would be total gray unless all of his hair fell out before then. He had a powerful urge to look at the top of his head with a mirror to see how much his bald spot was showing. Every year his bald spot got a little bigger, and it was becoming progressively harder to pretend he had any hair at all. In a few years he would save a bundle on haircuts. He found the thought wryly amusing.

A soft moan caught his attention. He glanced toward the bed. The lump was moving. One corner of the blanket raised and a brown, oriental face peeked out.

"So, you have decided to wake up, huh? I thought maybe you were going to sleep all day or maybe you were dead. How can you sleep with your head covered like that?"

The girl didn't respond. After a minute she slid the blanket back and sat on the edge of the bed. He was relieved to see she still had her clothes on. "What are you doing here anyway?"

"Khun Mike," she said, staring at the floor, "Don't you remember? You told Toy I could sleep at your house. I'm sorry I slept in your bed, but last night I was very cold. I thought maybe I would freeze to death. I wanted to wake up first and go back on the sofa but I didn't. I hope you're not angry with me."

He stared for a moment, wondering if she was telling the truth. "Yes, I remember," he lied, "I just don't understand how you could be cold. When I woke up this morning, it must have been a hundred degrees in the room. Don't you have any blood in your body or are you sick?"

"I have blood and I'm not sick," she retorted. "Last night I was cold, so I closed the air conditioner before I got into bed. I'm sorry. I didn't know it would get so hot. I think your room needs a fan."

"What my room needs is for little girls to keep their fingers off things that don't belong to them."

She hung her head. "I'm not a little girl, and I said I was sorry."

"Never mind," he sighed. "It's too late to worry about that now. Look, whatever your name is, if you sweated under that blanket half as much as I did, you probably need a shower. There's soap, shampoo, and toothpaste in the bathroom. If you need a toothbrush, I guess you can use mine."

"Khop khun mak ka. Thank you very much," she answered with a small smile on her lips. She picked up the towel she had carried to the bed with her and walked to the bathroom. Just before she closed the door, she looked at Mike and said, "I am Math."

While the girl was in the bathroom, Mike took the opportunity to clean up some of his bachelor's mess that the daily maid service didn't touch. Things like the magazines, books, and newspaper scattered here and there; the miscellaneous odds and ends of things he left laying on the desk and kitchen counter tops; the old food growing green and white fuzz in the refrigerator; and the curdled milk with an expiration date two weeks old.

While cleaning he found a discarded ice coffee can, an empty nut bag, and an open chip bag. It looked like she had pigged out while he slept. By the time the shower stopped he had finished straightening the place. He sat back at his desk and pretended to work on a crossword puzzle as he waited for her to emerge from the bathroom. He wait was short.

Math had been fully clothed when she went into the bathroom. Mike assumed she would be fully clothed when she came out. He was wrong. When she exited the bathroom she wasn't dressed, but wrapped in the bath towel instead.

"Khun Mike," she said, her voice shivered. "I'm cold." She ran on tiptoes to the bed and again became a lump under the blanket.

As she moved from the bath to the bed, he noticed that her arms, shoulders, and legs were still wet. She hadn't dried, but only wrapped the towel around herself. "If you wiped the water off, you wouldn't feel so cold."

She ignored his comment and said in a pleading tone, "Khun Mike, can you stop the air conditioner, please?"

Dear God, he sighed to himself, how do I get myself into these situations? He had barely stopped sweating and was just starting to feel comfortable. Now this girl, this intruder, wanted him to warm the room up again. Maybe she really didn't have any blood. Either that or she was crazy. He would be glad when she was gone. "Okay, just this one time, and only for a few minutes," he said and turned the air conditioner off.

As he walked back to the desk, he saw her clothes neatly folded on the bathroom countertop. On impulse, he stepped into the bath and collected them. This could be interesting, he thought, looking first at the clothes in his arms and then at the girl under covers in the bed. This could be interesting indeed. He put the clothes on the kitchen table, returned to his seat and waited.

After a few minutes the girl uncovered her head. "Can I have my clothes?"

"Sure," he said. "They're on the table." He pointed in that direction.

"I mean, can you bring them to me?"

"Who was your slave this time last year?"

"Please, Khun Mike. I'm not a bar-girl and I'm very shy. I would be embarrassed."

He didn't respond.

"Please," she pleaded again.

"Okay," he relented. He laid her clothes on the bed, thinking it could still be interesting.

She put on her clothes while remaining under the covers. He was impressed. He had tried that before and it wasn't easy.

Once her clothes were in place, Math sat up on the edge of the bed. "Last night, you maow."

Mike knew the words. She had said he was drunk last night. "Mai maow," he replied in Thai. "Maow mak mak." Not drunk, but super drunk, was his answer.

She laughed at his honesty.

"Did you have fun last night?" he asked. He couldn't remember everything that had happened. He hoped the girl could help fill in the missing time.

"You mean before or after you tried to kiss me? Khun Mike, why did you do that?" It wasn't true but it wasn't important. She wondered how much he actually remembered.

"I didn't try to kiss you," he said, sounding less confident than he hoped. "And quit calling me a coon. I'm tired of everyone calling me a coon."

"Well, before *that*," she said, "I had fun. I got to see some things in Pattaya, I got to talk to my friend Som Jai, I got to see you fight with your girlfriend, and I got to help you home after you drink many beers. Yes, Khun...uh...Mike. Yes, I had a lot of fun."

"What do you mean I had a fight with my girlfriend? I don't have a girlfriend."

"Oh, maybe I didn't understand about the lady named Lek. The way you and she talked, I thought you were girlfriend and boyfriend."

"Lek is only my friend," he said louder than he intended. He remembered how their relationship had withered over the last few weeks. "She is not my girlfriend!"

Math didn't say anything. She just lowered her head and stared at the floor.

"What's wrong with you now?" He spoke softer this time, but still too loud.

She looked up at him. "I have never heard a man ask a woman, who is just a friend, to go home with him and have sex."

He felt his face reddening. He didn't remember doing that, but he knew he might have if he had been drunk enough. Not so long ago he and Lek had been lovers of a sort. Everyone at Toy's thought of them as girlfriend and boyfriend. Lek used to go home with him but they had never had sex. She would always "take care my bar" until all her customers were gone. By then, Mike was usually very tired and always very drunk. On the nights when Lek had gone home with him he had been lucky just to get home, much less get anything else. Snuggling was the closest they'd ever come to physical intercourse. Recently he had started going home before Lek was finished with her work. Lek had never asked why he didn't wait for her anymore.

"Are you hungry?" he changed the subject. He knew she

would be. Thais were always hungry. Eating seemed to be their national pastime.

"No," she said, surprising him, "My stomach doesn't feel good."

"Probably from of all the junk food you ate last night," he pointed at the chip bag. "When was the last time you ate real food?"

Math blushed. "I don't remember; I think yesterday morning."

"Well, let's buy some real food and see what happens. If you can eat, fine. If you can't, that's okay too."

After Mike had showered, shaved, and put on clean clothes, they left the condo. They ignored the stares and sly smiles of the day-help as they walked through the lobby. Once outside of the condo, Mike considered where they should eat. He had a limited taste for Thai food, but figured he could suffer through one meal if necessary. He remembered that the restaurant down the street served a combination menu of Thai, American, and German food. They went there.

Math ordered a rice and pork breakfast soup and a cup of coffee. Mike ordered ham, eggs, toast, and orange juice. She was quiet while they waited for the food to be served. Her gaze wandered around the room.

Mike watched as Math gave the restaurant a close inspection. She was small-framed, almost frail. From walking next to her, he knew she was about 160 centimeters tall but probably weighed less than 45 kilos soaking wet. Her face was slightly longer than common for a Thai, but she was beautiful nonetheless. She had pulled her long black hair into a ponytail bound with a rubber band. Her eyes were almond-brown and almond-shaped. Her skin was lighter than most of the women he saw in Pattaya. No doubt she was proud of that. He noticed her eyes making short, furtive glances at the other customers. She seemed nervous. After a moment he asked, "Are you okay?"

"Yes," she answered. "It's just that I've never been to a restaurant with a farang before. I think everyone is looking at me like I'm a bar-girl."

"Well, screw them, if that is what they're thinking." he said. "As long as you and I know the truth, who cares what they think. By the way, you're wearing the same clothes today that you wore last night. Do you have a change of clothes?"

She wondered if he could possibly smell her, then decided he couldn't. He was just being observant. "Yes, they're the same. I have clothes, but I left them at my brother's house. I will call him after we finish eating. If he's home, I'll go back to his house to stay. I came to Pattaya to work with my brother. I didn't come to sleep in your condo."

Her comment caught him off guard. "Oh, yes, of course," was all he could think of to say.

When Math finished eating, she called Mon at the restaurant. Mike could understand a few of her words, but he couldn't keep up with the conversation. After a minute, she turned her cell phone off.

"My brother hasn't come home. I'll call him again later. If he still isn't home, I will go to his house and get some of my clothes." She hesitated for a moment before asking, "If he doesn't come home, could I spend another night at your condo again?"

Her unexpected comment unnerved him. He had to work tomorrow, and if she spent the night, he would have to leave her alone in his condo when he went to work. He had images of coming home and finding everything missing. The thought made him uneasy. He struggled with the question for a moment before answering. "Yeah, sure. Why not?"

"Thank you," she smiled.

"Ghep tung krup, my bill please," Mike called to the waiter. After he had paid, he turned to her and said, "Come on, I'll buy you some clothes to wear for today. You shouldn't be walking around all day in those tight slacks and dress shoes. I think a nice pair of shorts and some good sandals would be better. Besides, by the end of the day you will be smelling like some of the tourists if you don't change your clothes. If you're ready, we can go to the

Big C Shopping Center now."

They spent the next two hours shopping. First came the new clothes - shorts, shirt, and Dr. Scholl's sandals from the ladies department. Next they bought pineapple, cantaloupe, watermelon, milk, sodas, and more bread and water from the grocery section. Mike paid and they left the Big C. Outside, the temperature had reached its midday inferno. Their ten-minute walk home was heat-suffocating misery.

By the time they reached the condo, Mike's shirt was soaked and even Math had broken into a sweat. The room maids had come and gone, leaving the air conditioner off in their departure. Mike bee-lined to the control, turned the air conditioner on high, then stood in front of the vent and let the cold air cool his body and dry the sweat from his skin and clothes. Before he had even begun to feel comfortable, Math was complaining.

"Oh Mike, it's so cold in here," she said in an annoying whine.

"Then get under the blanket," he answered, "I'm not turning the air off yet."

"But I'm dirty from being outside. I would need a shower first."

"Then take a shower for crying out loud."

"I'm not crying out loud," she said indignantly.

Mike sighed. "It's just an expression. I mean take a shower and put on your new clothes. You will feel better."

"Okay," she replied and headed to the bathroom.

He noticed she didn't shut the door. He was tempted to walk over and look inside, but didn't. Instead he continued to stand under the cold air. When he felt better, he turned the air conditioner to a more normal setting, changed his shirt, and turned on the TV. The shower was still running. He walked to the desk and sat down. From his chair, he had a full view of the bathroom. After a few minutes the shower stopped. He watched as her hand reached out and pulled a towel from the rack. A moment later she stepped from the shower, the towel wrapped neatly around her body. When she saw him staring at her, she smiled.

"Please don't look," she said. "I am shy."

"Okay," he said and put his hand across his eyes. He kept two fingers cracked apart just enough that he could peek through. He watched as she walked from the bathroom to the bedside and removed the tags from her new clothes. He watched as she finished laying out the clothes, and then loosened the towel and let it unwrap from her body. He watched as she finished drying her hair and wiping the water from her shoulders and arms.

Her breasts were small but well formed. Her buttocks and her legs were a work of art. Her stomach was flat and smooth. There wasn't an ounce of fat anywhere. God, she was beautiful. He felt a desire rising in him.

Quickly he closed the gap between his fingers and pushed his feelings back into submission. Maybe this was a trick of some sort to seduce him. Or maybe it wasn't. Maybe she simply trusted him and believed his promise not to peek. He kept his fingers pressed together tight and his eyes shut even tighter. He was embarrassed he had looked in the first place.

"You can open your eyes now," she said when she was fully dressed. "How do I look?"

"Khun suay dee mak, khun suay khun. You look absolutely terrific," he answered, moving his hand from his eyes. He knew she was asking about her new clothes, but his answer was for what he had seen just minutes before. He blushed at his thoughts.

Math's face beamed at the compliment. "Khun phut bpak wahn, you talk with a sweet mouth," she said.

"No, really," Mike said, his face still blushing. "You really do look beautiful."

Her beaming face softened to a demure smile. "Thank you, Mike. You don't know how much it means to me for someone to say I am beautiful."

He said nothing. It seemed there was nothing more to say. He just smiled at her. He wondered if his lust and desire was showing. He hoped not. How would he react if he made an advance toward her and she rejected him? He hated rejection of any sort and went out of his way to avoid situations where he may be rejected.

That reminded him of what Math had said earlier. She said he had asked Lek to go home with him last night. He had never done that before. When Lek went with him in the past, it had always happened as a mutual decision which needed no asking or answering. Considering his intense dislike of rejection, it was out of character for him to set himself up like that, whether drunk or not. "Did I really ask Lek to go home with me last night?" He regretted speaking the words even as they left his mouth.

Her smile faded into nothing. She looked up and nodded.

"I guess that wasn't very nice, was it?"

"No, it wasn't polite." A short silence grew long. Then she asked, "Do you love that lady?"

Mike paused before answering. "Not so long ago, I loved Lek as my girlfriend. But that has all changed. Now, I love Lek as my very best friend in Pattaya. Well, until last night anyway. Maybe now she is my worst enemy."

"Have you ever gone for a short-time with her?" Math used the new word she had learned.

"That's none of your business. Even if I had, I wouldn't tell you. Where did you learn that word anyway? Are you sure you're not a bar-girl?"

"I learned it from my friend Som Jai, and I already told you I'm not a bar-girl. Or did you forget."

Sharp quiet echoed through the room. Mike wished he could take back his words. "I'm sorry."

Math fidgeted with the remote control, but didn't answer. In a moment she perked up, "Can I change the TV to another program?"

"Good idea," he said, glad the silence had ended. "I think I'll read for a while. You can watch anything you want."

Mike tried to concentrate on his reading while Math found a program she liked. The show must have been funny because she laughed a lot. His book on the other hand was nothing more than pages with words. His eyes went through the motion of reading, but his mind saw only images of Math getting dressed after her shower. He closed his eyes for a moment and fell asleep in his chair.

Chapter 11

Math watched TV all afternoon while Mike slept. She wondered how anyone could sleep sitting like that. More than once she had wanted to move him to the bed, but didn't. He might become angry if she woke him. It was best to leave him alone.

By seven o'clock, the sun had set and Math had called Mon at the restaurant. Her brother hadn't come home yet and Ziriwat had been gone all day. She decided it would be smart to retrieve her clothes while Ziriwat was away.

Working as quietly as possible, Math peeled and cut the pineapple into bite sized chunks and then put them on a plate and into the icebox. She ate her share in the process. By the time she had finished Mike still hadn't stirred. Before she left the condo she wrote him a note. As she pulled the door shut, she wedged the note in its closing.

Outside, she flagged down a motorcycle-taxi and gave directions to her brother's house. The Sunday evening traffic was calm and the ride was uneventful. She arrived at the restaurant at eight-fifteen. It was more crowded than it had been the day before. She sat at a table and waited. In a minute Mon saw her and walked over.

"Sawasdee ka. Good evening," Math said. "Pehn yung ngai ka? How are you?"

"Sabai dee, khop khun ka. I am fine, thank you," Mon answered. "I'm surprised to see you. Have you heard from Anan?"

"No, I haven't. After I talked to you, I decided to get my

clothes while Ziriwat is gone. I hope the door isn't locked, or there's an open window so I can get inside."

"Getting your clothes while he is gone is a good idea, and getting in won't be a problem. I have a key to your brother's house."

"You have a key?" Math said, excited. "I don't believe it."

"I think you should take your brother's motorcycle, too," Mon continued. "That Ziriwat drives like a madman. Someday he'll wreck and your brother won't have a motorcycle. I have a key for it if you want to take it."

Math was jubilant. "Yes, I will take it. Thank you, thank you, thank you."

Mon smiled. "Are you hungry? I can cook some food while you get your clothes."

"Yes, I am hungry. Give me the keys, I think I should hurry."

Inside her brother's house, Math exchanged her new shorts and tee shirt for a pair of jeans and a long sleeved pullover. She found a couple of plastic shopping bags and filled them with as many clothes and personal toiletries as they would hold. She didn't want to try riding the motorcycle while holding a suitcase. Finished, she locked the door and strapped the bags to the motorcycle seat. She drove to the restaurant to eat the food Mon had prepared.

Her meal was papaya salad and it was delicious. After she finished eating, she told Mon she should leave before Ziriwat returned. She said her goodbyes and promised to call every day. Then she sped down the highway toward Pattaya.

It felt good to be riding the motorcycle, to be in control of her fate and destination. Cruising down the road with the wind blowing in her face, she felt free.

At a traffic light on Sukhumvit Road, she glanced at her watch. It was nine-fifteen. She decided to go to Soi 2 before returning to the condo. She wanted to ask Som Jai a few questions about Mike. She seemed to know him very well. Surely, Som Jai would be at work by the time she arrived.

When Math parked in front of Toy's, she saw Som Jai sitting

at the far end of the bar and deep in conversation with Mike. They looked serious. Neither smiled. She wasn't sure what to do. Mike looked in her direction, but didn't recognize her through the helmet. After a second she decided to leave. She couldn't imagine what Mike and Som Jai were talking about, but she was sure it had something to do with her.

Math drove aimlessly down Beach Road, turned left on South Pattaya, then north on Second. Ten minutes later she was in front of Mike's condo. After a moment of debate she decided she would stay there for the night. She wanted to hear what Mike and Som Jai found so interesting to talk about.

~~

Earlier that same day, Mike was awakened by a click-thud sound. At the time he didn't realize the noise was the door pulling shut. It was almost eight o'clock and it was dark outside. The girl was gone and the TV was silent. He did a quick search of the room. Everything seemed in place.

In the crack between the door and jamb he found a note. It read, "I went to my brother's house to get clothes. He hasn't come home, so I will need a place to sleep. If I can't stay here, I will stay with Som Jai. I'll be gone for a while because I think you want to spend time with your friends. I cut the pineapple for you and put it in the icebox. If you don't leave the key for me with the lady in the lobby, I will understand and wait until you come home. If my brother comes home while I'm there, I'll stay at his house. I borrowed 100 baht from your wallet for taxi money. I will pay you when my brother comes home. Thank you for your kindness. Math."

He reread the note. The words 'I borrowed 100 baht' jumped out at him. He checked his wallet. If anything was missing, he couldn't tell. At least it wasn't all gone.

He ate a few pieces of the pineapple, and then took a shower. Yes, he would go out to see some friends, but not the ones Math had in mind when she wrote the note. He wanted ask Som Jai who Math really was. He decided he would leave his key with the lady in the lobby, in case she returned before he got home.

He took a quick shower and put on fresh clothes for the second time that day. By nine o'clock he was at Toy's Bar sipping on a Carlsberg beer and waiting for Som Jai to arrive. She strolled in a few minutes later. He gave her time to stow her purse behind the bar and then motioned for her to join him.

Som Jai smiled as she reached his seat. "Sawasdee ka, Mike."

"Som Jai," he smiled in return, "How are you? You look very beautiful today. May I buy you a drink?"

She eyed him suspiciously. "Yes, you can buy me a drink. And what do you want? I know you want something to be so flattering and to buy a drink for me already." She paused for effect. In her near perfect English she continued, "Do you want to know what you did last night when you were drunk, or do you want to know about the girl you took home?"

Mike stammered for a moment before saying, "Nothing gets past you, does it Som Jai? I guess I want to know about both."

Som Jai smiled smugly. "Last night you were very drunk. You asked Lek to go home with you, and you were very noisy about it."

He cringed. Everyone in the bar must have heard him. "Did I ask her to have sex with me?"

"Not in those words, but your meaning was clear."

Everyone must have seen Lek's blatant rejection, too. He changed the subject. "Okay, let's forget about that. Tell me about that girl, Math. How well do you know her? Is she a bar-girl or what? Can I trust her?"

A motorcycle roared to a stop on the street just outside of the bar. The noise caught Mike's attention and he looked up. The driver, obviously female, didn't remove her helmet and didn't get off the motorcycle. He couldn't see the rider's face through the opening in the helmet. After a second, the motorcycle continued down the street. He turned his attention back to Som Jai. "So, tell me about the girl."

J. F. Gump

"She said she's the sister of an old friend and that we met seven years ago. I don't remember her, but there are a lot of things I don't remember after seven years. Actually, she looks like a girl who used to work at the Mercedes Bar on Soi 8. How can I tell you to trust her when I don't even know her? Maybe she really is the sister of my friend, but maybe she is just another lady who knows her. I don't know. You must find out for yourself. But I think it would be best if you were careful, at least until you get to know her. I guess I'm not helping much, am I?"

"No," he answered, "I guess not. I thought you knew her better."

"Sorry, I don't," Som Jai responded.

Mike ordered another beer. He sipped it slowly as he listened to the music and tried to recall everything that had been said and everything that had happened since he met the girl. He looked for something to make him feel more at ease, but found nothing. Then he looked for anything that should make him be concerned, but found nothing there, either. Som Jai was right, he would just have to wait and find out for himself. It was possible that she wouldn't come back. That thought repeated itself over and again.

He finished his beer and paid his tab. As he stood to leave, he saw Lek coming toward the bar. He turned and walked in the opposite direction. He didn't want to see her today. He wasn't in the mood to face what he'd done last night. Maybe tomorrow he would apologize.

Once away from Lek and the bar, Mike took his time walking back to his condo. It was more like an apartment, but condo sounded classier. He stopped at the service station as usual and went through his routine of buying water, beer, and cigarettes. He also stopped at the Music Lover Bar which sat along Second Road just outside of his condo. The girls asked him so many questions about the 'lady' he had taken with him last night that he hurried through his drink, left a small tip, and went home.

His key was at the front desk. Maybe she had already been here and taken everything he had. Or maybe she had come to get her things and left. Or maybe she hadn't come back at all. Each thought shot a different emotion through his body. He took the elevator to the third floor.

Inside his condo the air conditioner hummed and spit out coolness. The stove light lit the kitchen. He didn't remember turning it on, but he didn't remember turning it off either. On the desk was a note. He picked it up and read, "I left the key at the front desk so you could get in. Thank you very much for your kindness".

He wasn't sure what to make of the message. He turned on the overhead light and looked around. His laptop computer was still beside the desk and everything else looked normal. He went to the closet and checked for his passport and return plane ticket. Both were still there.

As he turned away, he did a double take back to the closet. Hanging beside his clothes were dresses, blouses, and ladies slacks. He slid open one of the drawers. Inside he found ladies panties and bras. "Oh man," groaned. "She has moved herself in."

There was a knock at the door. Mike walked to the entryway and pulled it open. There stood Math, a wide smile on her face. She held a newspaper wrapped package in each hand. He stepped aside and she strutted in, looking happy and confident.

"I bought you barbecue chicken for supper," she announced. "After you eat, I have a surprise to show you."

She put plates and silverware on the table then unwrapped the chicken and divided it between them. She wasn't hungry and gave him the biggest portions. Neither spoke much as they ate, but the smile never left her face.

Mike noticed she had changed clothes again and was no longer wearing the shorts and tee shirt he had bought her. The chicken was delicious, but it worried him. If anyone ever saw how some street vendors handled their food, they would never eat from the sidewalk food stands in Thailand. He would know in a couple of hours if the chicken was safe to eat or not. In the meantime, he would enjoy his supper.

After they finished eating, Math took him by the hand. "Come with me. I want to show you my surprise." She led him out of the condo, down the elevator, and into the parking lot. "There," she said pointing proudly at a crotch-rocket style motorcycle, "Very nice, don't you think? It belongs to my brother."

"Yes, it's very nice. Does your brother know you have his motorcycle? It looks a little big for you. Did you ride it here?"

She couldn't contain her excitement over having her own transportation. "My brother won't care. I have my own motorcycle at home and I'm a very good driver. Want to go for a ride?"

Mike was sure he didn't want to go for a ride with her tonight, maybe never. He glanced at his watch without noticing the time. "It's getting late. Maybe you can give me a ride tomorrow."

"Okay," she said, "Tomorrow." She headed back toward the elevator.

Inside the condo, Mike really did look at his watch. It was ten-thirty. He had to get up for work at the crack of dawn. He turned on the TV, opened a beer, and sat down at his desk. He would be asleep by eleven. Math commandeered the remote control and found a station she liked. He would make her turn it off when he was ready to sleep.

From inside the top desk drawer, Mike pulled out a half-smoked marijuana cigarette. He had picked up the habit a long time ago when he was in Vietnam. He didn't smoke a lot and abuse it. He would smoke about three small tokes from a joint every night to relax him. He lit the J and took a short drag.

"What are you doing?" Math asked when she smelled the smoke.

"Smoking ganja. Want some?"

"I don't smoke ganja," she said. "I've never even seen anyone smoke ganja. Can I watch you smoke?"

Mike shrugged as he exhaled. "Up to you."

She watched as he smoked his usual three hits, anticipation clear in her expression. She wasn't just watching him, she was studying him.

"Waiting for me to go crazy, or turn into some kind of freak?" he finally asked.

"You don't look any different." A hint of disappointment tinted her words. She continued her expectant staring.

Mike sighed. "I do this to relax. I'm not going to turn into some kind of strange UFO alien or anything. I think you should go to sleep now because I want to read for a few minutes before I crash. You can use the bed since you get cold so easy. I'll sleep on the sofa."

Math turned off the TV, returned to the bed, and slid under the blanket. Once covered, she removed her jeans and shirt and laid them on the floor beside the bed. She then pulled the covers over her head and stopped moving.

Mike watched the bed for a few minutes, hoping maybe her bra and panties would follow the jeans and shirt, but they didn't. He picked up his book, found where he could last remember stopping, and resumed his reading. Again, he couldn't concentrate on the story.

After a few minutes he set the alarm clock, turned out the lights, and lay down on the sofa. He had his clothes on and figured that was enough to keep warm. The air conditioner blew directly on his feet. He covered them with a towel but it didn't help. He was freezing, but he refused to turn off the air conditioner. He didn't want a repeat of last night's sweat bath. Finally, after ten frigid minutes, he relented. "It's my fucking bed," he mumbled to himself.

He got up from the sofa and walked to the side of the bed away from Math. He stood there thinking for a minute. At last he decided he wasn't going to sleep with his clothes on. He pulled off his shirt and then let his jeans slide to the floor. He sat quietly on the edge of the bed and gently eased his body into a lying position. He shifted a little to make himself more comfortable. Suddenly he was falling. There was a loud thud as the bed slats hit the floor and he bounced against the wooden side rails. Math was rolled from the other side of the bed and came to rest against his naked body.

"What happened?" she asked in the darkness.

"I think I broke the bed," Mike said laughing.

"Poom poi, fat man," she said, laughing with him.

When he turned to look at her, her face was only inches from his. Without thinking, he kissed her. Without thinking, she kissed him back. Their kiss was brief, but it was enough.

"I think I should fix the bed," he said, feeling embarrassed. He started to get up.

On impulse Math took him by the arm. "I think you should stay here." She hadn't been with a man for a long time and she had never made love with a farang. She wondered what it would be like.

When she pulled him back into the bed, he resisted, but only a little. They eased over to her side where the mattress still looked and felt like a bed. After a moment of embarrassed hesitation, Mike unsnapped her bra and slipped it from her arms. Tenderly, he touched her breasts. Math felt a flame course its way from her chest to her thighs.

Slowly, patiently, he explored her body, touching everywhere, lingering nowhere. He put his lips to her cheek. Inch by inch, he kissed his way across her face, down her neck, and into her cleavage. He felt the scar on her chest but said nothing. His tongue darted quick laps around her nipples. He gave her right breast a soft but firm bite, then continued down her stomach, kissing at every stop. He paused briefly at her womanhood and inhaled loud enough for her to hear. He left her panties untouched. His lips and tongue paid special attention to her inner thighs and the inside bend of her knees while his hands kneaded and massaged the nipples of her breasts into tight, hard knots. Suddenly, he stopped and rose to his knees. He reached out and took her by the hand. "I need you," he whispered.

"I need you too," she whispered back, breathless.

He eased her panties down over her hips and she didn't protest. In a moment, the panties joined the rest of their clothes on the floor. Mike stretched out on the bed next to her. His hand slid toward her womanhood for the first time.

Math tensed but didn't push him away. She was not on birth control pills. What if he used no protection and she got pregnant? She felt his hardness throbbing against her side. She parted her legs for his hand to touch. She knew she should stop but she couldn't. She was a kaleidoscope of emotions.

Math had only been with two men in her life and she had never been with a farang. One part of her was terrified while another was excited beyond anything she had ever felt before. This farang, this man named Mike, kissed her and held her and stroked her with such confidence and desire. He knew what he was doing and he did it well. Each touch, each caress, each kiss pulled her deeper into the throes of irrepressible lust. Within minutes she was responding with a passion she had never felt before. However much he thought he wanted her, at this moment she wanted him twice as much.

Mike hadn't been with a woman for months. Math felt so good beside him. Tonight he had had just the right combination of alcohol and marijuana, and his need was overpowering. He let go of his inhibitions and lost his soul to the heat pulsing through him. At that instant he wanted her more than anything in the world. Just when he thought he would burst from the passion, he rose up and positioned himself to take her. Then he eased himself into her, slowly, gently, eagerly.

Math's desire was an inferno by the time he took her. She climaxed even before he had completely entered her.

He felt Math tense and heard her moan softly as he joined with her body. It was all he could do to keep from ending this perfect moment before it had even started. He stopped briefly to hold her tight and whisper 'you are so good' into her ear. In a moment the urge to climax passed and they made love. Soft and easy one minute, hard, thrusting passion the next. To never end would have been too soon. Finally he gave in to the ecstasy of their union. He couldn't remember the last time he had had such a strong orgasm. Every cell in his body sang with the joy of Math. He wished the waves of release would never end.

Math climaxed for the second time as she shared Mike's powerful orgasm. She climaxed one last time as he slowly, reluctantly, withdrew from her. For some reason, she wanted to cry.

"Thank you," Mike whispered. "You were wonderful." He paused, realizing how easily he had made love to her. No half-assed erection or mid-stream shutdown. It was the best he had felt about his lovemaking and himself in a very long time. "No, you were more than wonderful, you were absolutely perfect."

Math smiled to herself and tried to respond but couldn't. Her tears kept her voice silent.

Mike reached over and touched her face. He felt the dampness. "Are you crying? Did I hurt you? I'm so sorry if I hurt you." The tone of his voice rang true.

"No," she said. "I'm crying because I am so happy. I've never had a man be so good to me. I felt very good, Mike. You will never know how good." For no apparent reason, she giggled through her tears. "Please hold me, Mike. Please, just hold me for a little while."

He pulled her close to him and held her tight. They fell asleep holding onto each other. Mike's sleep was deep and peaceful. Math dreamed of a baby with white hair and blue eyes.

Chapter 12

The next morning, Mike complained silently to himself when the alarm went off. As he dragged himself to the bathroom, he noticed that Math hadn't stirred at the sound of the alarm or of him getting out of bed. He brushed his teeth, scanned the newspaper, and took a quick shower. He left a note and 200 baht on the kitchen table. 'For Food' was all he wrote.

He took one last look at Math still asleep on the bed, then left to catch his ride. He wondered if she and his clothes would still be there when he came home. In the elevator he glanced at his watch. Damn, he was late, really late. Between being late and what had happened Saturday night, he dreaded what was to come on the van.

Being late wouldn't be a big dea except he shared the ride with four other people. He was the next to last pickup and everyone gave him shit when he was late. He wasn't a morning person and was late on a regular basis. Everyone thought it was because he went out to party every night. The truth was that no matter what time he went to bed, getting up and moving was pure hell.

As expected, the van was waiting. He slid the door open and snaked his way to his seat at the back of the van. He had been in Thailand longer than the other riders and everyone knew which seat was his. Newcomers were promptly, and sometimes rudely, informed of his seating preferences. He didn't mean to hurt anyone's feelings with his bluntness, but he felt his seniority deserved a little respect. *His seat* was where the powers of his seniority ended. Outside of that he was open to shit like anyone else. Sometimes he dished it out; sometimes he took it. Usually, he just shrugged it off. After Saturday night, he wasn't sure what today would bring.

As the van pulled away from the curb, Randy, his friend and co-worker, started. "Hey, Mike. The girls at Toy's told me you had quite an exciting weekend. You and Lek having problems?"

Mike didn't respond to Randy's question. He shut his eyes, slumped down into his seat, and laid his head back against the headrest.

Randy was the second longest term ex-pat from his company to Thailand. Mike had him out-timed, but only by a month or so. Too little to make any difference. Randy knew everyone Mike knew and then some. Randy, along with a few of his other co-workers, were known as "butterfly boys" by the bar girls. They changed girlfriends more often than some tourist changed underwear. Every night they would party until very late, but they always managed to go to work the next day. Mike could keep up with them about once a week then had to stop for rest. Randy and the other *butterfly boys* were a few years younger than Mike, which he figured explained how they could keep up that pace while he couldn't. Mike knew for sure that the hangovers hurt a lot more than they used to.

When Mike didn't answer, Randy said, "So, tell me about your new woman."

Probably stealing me blind about right now, Mike thought. Aloud he said, "Catch me at lunch. I'll tell you about it then." Mike crossed his arms to signal the end of the conversation.

Randy took the hint. He would wait until lunch to satisfy his curiosity about Mike's new affair.

The rest of the day went like that. Sly winks and innuendoes from Randy and his other co-workers. Mike told Randy everything during lunch. Randy was uncharacteristically understanding about Mike's concern over the things the girl might steal. He said a girl had once stolen a shirt from him and then actually had the nerve to wear it to work the next day. Randy was sure these Thai girls were capable of anything, from screwing your brains out to stealing you blind. His attitude did nothing to improve Mike's mood.

Mike spent most of the day fantasizing. Sometimes he thought about last night's ecstasy, and at other times about what he would find missing when he got home. He had vivid mental images of his condo being completely empty. No clothes, no suitcases, no CD player, no nothing. Everything he had wasn't much, only a few hundred dollars worth of replaceable items. Still, it was all he had in Thailand and the potential loss toyed with his mind.

By the time Mike got home it was almost dark and his nerves were frazzled, more from worrying about his condo than from his day at work. The door key had been left at the front desk. The boy on duty spoke no English and Mike's questions about who might or might not be in his condo were answered with non-comprehending smiles. He rode the elevator to his floor. The door was unlocked. He entered the condo expecting the worst. Instead, there stood Math. She was dressed in a short-cut nightgown. Her long, silky-black hair fell seductively across her shoulders. She had put on just enough make-up to be noticed. A candle burning in a glass jar on the table cast an eerie, provocative glow about the room.

"Sawasdee ka, Khun Mike," she said in a low voice. "Welcome home. I'm happy to see you." She pulled him inside the room, pushed the door shut and locked it behind him. She reached up with her face and kissed him quickly, tenderly, passionately on his lips. "I have been waiting for you," she whispered as she edged him to the bed. "Tonight, right now, I want to make you feel as good as you made me feel last night."

Without hesitation or embarrassment, she undressed him. When he was completely naked, she held him in her arms and eased him back onto the bed. Using only her hands and her mouth, she brought Mike to the verge of ecstasy within a matter of minutes. She stopped just before he climaxed. After a long pause, she slipped off her nightgown and mounted him, slowly yet firmly. This time she was in control. Over and over again she teased him to the point of eruption before stopping her self-absorbent undulations. Just as she felt his climax begin, she withdrew herself from him. Without hesitation she took his manhood into her mouth. She didn't flinch or pull away. Neither his wife nor any other woman had ever done that before.

"Thank you," he said when he could speak.

She smiled and kissed him. She was satisfied knowing she had made him happy. "I'll shower now."

Mike could taste the saltiness of himself from where Math had kissed his lips. He used the back of his hand to wipe across his mouth. His lips still tasted salty, but this time it was more like sweat. He lay there basking in a contented glow. A few minutes later Math emerged from the bathroom fully dressed and looking as if nothing had happened only minutes before.

"I'll cook dinner," she announced and proceeded to make kitchen noises with pots and pans and knives and water.

Mike slipped into the bathroom while she was busy in the kitchen. He stood under the shower for a long time. As the water washed away every last trace of their lovemaking, he tried to decide what he thought about her.

She was half his age and actually more beautiful than he had first thought. She seemed to like him or at least she seemed to like having sex with him. Maybe she was a nymphomaniac or something. She had come home with him so easily on Saturday that he thought she might be a bar-girl. On the other hand she had never asked him for money, and now she had moved in with him, clothes and all. How could a regular Thai girl go with a stranger so easily? And an old farang at that! Maybe she had a thing for older men. How could she be so trusting or so stupid to think nothing would happen to her? He mused over the situation while the water poured down on his body. He couldn't figure it out. He decided he would just enjoy the moment until he found a good reason not to.

Mike was surprised at the food Math cooked for him that evening. He had never liked Thai food much, but what she cooked was delicious. It was much better anything than he had ever eaten in a Thai restaurant.

After dinner Math asked if he would go out with his friends from work. She explained she didn't want him to stop seeing his friends because she was there.

He thought a long time before he answered. "No, not tonight," he said. "I would rather stay home and learn about you. I want to know who you are. I want you to tell me about you. Where you are from, what your childhood was like, and all about your family. I want to know your hopes, your dreams, and your fears. I want to know the girl who is sleeping in my bed and making love with me. I want to know you."

"I want to know who you are, too," she said back. "I saw your photo album today. Tell me about yourself first."

"Okay." He retrieved a cold beer from the refrigerator, smoked what was left of the joint, and then proceeded to talk. He told her about his childhood and his family. He talked about his mother and his sister. When he spoke of his father's death, he didn't tell the whole truth. When he recounted his time in Vietnam, he didn't tell her everything about that either. When he talked about his life today, he didn't mention his wife or his son. Finally, he stopped talking.

They sat in silence for a long, uncomfortable minute. Mike knew they were both thinking the same thing. Math broke the quiet. "I saw a farang lady's picture in your album. Is she your wife?"

"Yes," he blushed, but offered no further explanation.

She knew he didn't want to talk about it, so she changed the subject. "When you were in Vietnam, did you kill anyone?"

"I hope not," he answered. "If I did, it wasn't on purpose."

"Did you ever make love to a Vietnamese lady?"

"What kind of a question is that?"

"I just wondered if making love to a Vietnamese lady is the same as making love to a Thai lady."

He laughed. "Oh no, Thai ladies are much better, and you are

J. F. Gump

the best of all."

Math flushed with pride. "Khop khun ka, thank you," she said, smiling.

"Now it's your turn," he said. "Tell me about your life."

Math told him her life story. She told him about her brothers and sisters and growing up. She described the river behind her house in Phitsanulok where she and Anan would swim. She told him about her heart operations and her schooling. She talked about her career which had started and ended within six short months. She spoke of her dogs as if they were her babies. But she didn't mention her mother's failed abortion, or her father's brutal beatings. She didn't tell him about running away to Pattaya when she was sixteen and she didn't tell bout her secret lesbian desires. Nor did she mention her affair with the married policeman. Especially she didn't tell him about shooting her ex-fiancé. Finally, Math stopped talking.

"Your life hasn't been easy, has it?" Mike said when she finished.

"It could be worse," she replied.

"Or better," he added.

"Yes."

They sat there for a long time, not talking. Finally, Math reached across the table and took him by the hand. "Would you make love with me again tonight?" she asked.

He stood and pulled her gently from her chair. He led her to the bed. "I would like that more than anything in the world," he answered.

Their union was long and slow. Full of closeness without thought for physical release. Sweet, human desire without the animal lust. He would have melted and fused his very soul into hers if he could. Just when he thought the bliss would never end, it did. Together they reached the height of their passion in toe-curling ecstasy. They held onto each other for a long time.

As his hormone levels waned, Mike began to have other thoughts. What about her brother? What would he think of his

88

sister sleeping with a farang? Especially a married farang. And when was he coming back? Math would probably leave when her brother came back. For some reason he the thought disturbed him. He pulled her tighter against his body, "I don't know how, but you are doing something to my mind. I haven't wanted to be so close to anyone for a very long time. If I didn't know myself so well, I would think I am falling in love with you."

"Mike, you can't fall in love with someone so quickly. I think you are just lonely."

He thought about that for a while. She was right; you can't fall in love with someone in just two days. He was confusing physical pleasure with love. He changed the subject. "Did you call your brother today?"

"Yes," she answered. "He didn't come home again."

Math's brother didn't come home for another five days. For Mike, it was five days of happiness. They went out to a different place for a couple of hours every night, except Saturday. On Saturday night, they were out until very late doing everything Math wanted to do.

During that week all of his friends and co-workers met Math. No one made jokes or rude comments, meaning they liked her and accepted her as a friend. One night they went to Toy's bar, but the stares Math got from Lek made her uncomfortable and they never went back.

As often as not, they would go to the Music Lover Bar just outside of his condo. Math had befriended a couple of the girls there and she enjoyed talking to them. Mike was happy when she was happy so they spent a lot of time at the Music Lover Bar.

On Sunday, as they were getting dressed for dinner, Math's cell phone, her handy, rang. From her smile and the tone of her voice she was obviously happy. Mike didn't have to understand Thai to know it was her brother. Anxiety filled the pit of his stomach.

After talking for a couple of minutes, Math turned the phone off and looked over at Mike. Her smile faded as she watched his face. "Are you okay?" she asked. "I think maybe you are sick or something."

He tried to laugh but couldn't. "I'm not sick. Not yet anyway. Was that your brother?"

She nodded.

"So, you will be moving to his house now?"

She stared at him, unsure how to answer. "Not unless you want me to go."

A heady rush filled him. "I would like it very much if you stayed with me."

"I would like that very much too." Math could tell by the look in his eyes that he was indeed falling in love with her and she didn't know why. She knew he didn't know why, either.

That night Mike took to her to an expensive restaurant and they both ate until they were stuffed. They talked about everything and nothing. They laughed like teenagers on their first date. When they got home, they didn't make love. Instead they held onto each other and enjoyed warm feelings of togetherness without the need for more.

When Mike came home from work the next Tuesday evening, he knew immediately that something was wrong. The lights were off and Math didn't greet him at the door. He flicked on the kitchen light and looked around the condo. In the dim light he saw a familiar lump under the blanket. He went the edge of the bed and touched her lightly. "Math? Are you awake?" he asked in a soft whisper.

A small sob came from beneath the blanket.

"Hey, are you okay?" his voice was higher, more urgent. He pulled the blanket away from her face. Tears had caused her mascara to run. "What's going on? You act like you just lost the love of your life, and I know that's not true because I'm still here."

She didn't laugh at his weak joke. In a moment she sat up in bed and held onto him. "There is something I didn't tell you," she managed between sobs. "I'm a very bad person. I think I will go to jail soon, and no one will ever see me again."

Her words assaulted his senses. He had the sensation of falling. "What you are talking about? What could someone like you have done that is so bad that they would go to jail?"

He listened as she told him about her ex-fiancé, the lady-man, the gun, and the shots. She left nothing out. When she finished her story, she added, "I'm supposed to check with the police in Phitsanulok every two weeks until everything is settled one way or another. Today I called the police and asked if I could miss this time. They told me no. I must be there Friday. I don't know what will happen. It's very close to the time that Sawat must make up his mind. I'm afraid he will decide I should go to jail. I can't live caged like an animal. I will die in a Thai jail."

"Just how bad was Sawat hurt?" Mike asked. "How long was he in the hospital?"

"He wasn't hurt much. He was out of the hospital and back to work in three days."

"Are you sure you shot him?"

"Yes, I saw the blood on his shirt. The police said I hit his stomach – two times."

"It couldn't have been too bad if he was back to work in three days. You probably just nicked him."

"Maybe, I don't know what *nicked* means."

"Never mind. Have you talked to Sawat since then?"

"Only once," she answered. "I asked him to tell the police to never mind about everything."

"What did he say to that?"

"Sawat just laughed and said that if he couldn't have me, then he would make sure no other man had me either. His words were not polite."

Mike thought for a long time. "I don't know what to say. Unless Sawat changes his mind, this could be very bad. Do you think he still has feelings for you? Does he still love you?"

"I don't know," Math said. "I only know what he said."

J. F. Gump

"The only thing I can think is to call him and beg for mercy. Tell him if he ever loved you, he wouldn't make you go to jail. Tell him anything he wants to hear to make him change his mind. Tell him you will come back to him if you think that would help."

"But I don't want to be back with him. I don't love him. I love..." her words trailed away.

He looked at her expectantly, but she didn't finish her sentence. "I don't know what else to suggest," he said.

They sat on the bed in silence. It was nearly dark outside. After a long while Mike spoke, "I'm glad I don't have a gun in the house." His tone carried a large hint of humor.

"Ah, but you have knives." Math responded, laughing for the first time that evening.

Later, after Math had fallen asleep, Mike hid the knives. Later still, he put them back where they belonged. He felt guilty for hiding them in the first place. He lay back down next to her and slept.

On Wednesday evening, Mike bought Math a new suitcase. On Thursday morning, he gave her money for her trip then kissed her goodbye. He left for work, knowing he might never see her again. That evening when he got home, she was gone.

Chapter 13

Math caught the nine o'clock bus north toward Bangkok and her hometown. Dark thoughts haunted her every kilometer of the ride. She didn't know what would happen but she was certain it would be nothing good. She spent most of the trip wondering how she would survive in prison.

The traffic was unusually light and they made good time. She changed buses in Bangkok, and continued onward to Phitsanulok. Ten hours after leaving Pattaya, she was at her house. Her younger brother was there.

"Hello, Yai," she shouted.

Yai spun around at the sound of her voice. "Math! You're home. I'm happy to see you." He threw his arms around her. "I missed you, sister."

"I missed you too," she hugged him back. Her dogs sprinted around, yapping and jumping in excitement. "I see you've been taking good care of my babies. Thank you very much."

"Mai pen rai, never mind," he said. "I like to play with your dogs. Tell me about Anan. Is he okay? Tell me about Pattaya, too."

Math laughed. "Anan is fine and his business is very good. I think he will be a very rich man some day. You wouldn't believe Pattaya. It's right on the ocean and is very beautiful. Millions of farangs go there on holiday. There are many restaurants and discos and things to do. I think you would like Pattaya. Someday when you're older, I'll take you there.

"Would you, Math?" Yai asked, almost pleading. "I would like that very much. I have never seen the ocean. Did you help Anan with his business?"

"I helped him a little," Math answered. "Anan was away for the first week I was in Pattaya. When he came back, I went with him on sales calls so I could learn his business."

"Anan wasn't there for a whole week?" Yai asked. "Where did you stay? Weren't you afraid to be in a strange city by yourself?"

She hesitated, wondering what she should say. Finally, she answered, "I stayed with a friend." Yai accepted her answer without question.

"Did you meet any farangs? What are they like?"

Farangs, foreigners, were an uncommon sight in Phitsanulok. Their sister, Itta, was married to a farang, but Yai had never met him. Itta had married the man from Scotland and moved away without ever bringing him home to meet her family. Math always figured it was because Itta was embarrassed by her family's poorness. "I met a couple of farangs," she chose her words carefully. "The ones I met were very nice and didn't smell bad at all."

Yai laughed in disbelief. All of his life he had heard that farangs smelled bad. "But they were fat and ugly, weren't they?" he asked, still laughing.

"Oh, yes," she said, laughing with him. "Very fat and very ugly." She waited until Yai stopped laughing and then changed the subject. "How is school? You're studying hard, I hope."

"School is okay," he answered. "I don't like to study, but my grades are good anyway."

"You need to study hard so you will grow up you can be an important businessman like your brother. I would be proud to have two brothers who can help take care of our family."

"Watch this," Yai said pointing at the dogs. "Lay down," he ordered. The dogs obeyed and Yai gave each a piece of dried fish from his pocket. Math laughed and clapped her hands.

They chatted idly while they played with the dogs. Later, Math told Yai he should go home before it got too dark.

After her brother had gone, Math sat alone inside her corrugated tin house. It was little more than one room with a bed, a dresser, and a chair. It wasn't much but it was her home. She sat on the bed and stared at her cell phone, her handy. In a while she built the nerve to call Sawat. She dialed his number but hoped he wouldn't answer. She almost hung up when she heard his voice.

"Hello, Sawat. I am Math," she said, as nice as possible. "How have you been?"

"I'm fine, thank you," he replied, hesitant. "I'm surprised to hear from you. Are you okay, too?"

"Yes, I'm fine," she said and then fell silent, not sure what to say next.

After a long pause, Sawat said, "You're very quiet. That's most unusual of you."

"I'm nervous, and very sad. I'm sad because I might go to jail soon. I'm nervous because I need you to do something for me."

"What do you want me to do, Math?" Sawat asked. "Do you want me to call the police and tell them to never mind?"

"Yes," she said, barely above a whisper, "That is what I want. Please say you will. If you have ever loved me and if you have any caring for me now, please ask the police to stop investigating me. My life is turned upside down. I can't get a job and I have no money for rent or food or anything. Please, Sawat, please ask them to stop. All you have to do is tell them and they will stop."

It was Sawat's turn for silence. Finally he spoke, "Math, really, I don't want you to go to jail, but I want you to be punished for what you did to me, for my pain and embarrassment. I think you have learned your lesson, but I'm not sure what I will tell the police. Maybe I'll tell them to stop or maybe I won't. The decision is up to you."

"What do you mean, the decision is up to me?" Uneasiness crept through her.

His laugh was cold, almost cruel. "It's simple. I want to get back together with you. Maybe I'm stupid but I still love you. If you promise to come back to me, I will tell the police to stop."

J. F. Gump

Math thought furiously for an answer which would be neither committal nor offensive. After a moment she answered, "I think it's too early to tell you if that would be possible or not. I think I need a little time to get my life back together. Right now I'm not sure I can love anyone. My life feels numb. I'm sure you can understand that."

"No, I don't. I don't understand how you cannot love me or how you could have shot me, no matter what I've done." He paused, waiting for a response. When none came, he continued, "Since you're too stupid to understand anything, I'm going to make this very clear. You are going to come back to me and you will do everything for me, no matter what. Do you understand me Math?"

His words rasped against her ears. The last thing she wanted was to be back with him. Images of Sawat with the boy caused her stomach to spasm. She fought the urge to vomit. "Yes, I understand," she forced humbleness into her voice. She hated the words, even as they left her mouth. "But you must please give me time."

Sawat sighed into the phone. "Okay, I will give you time. I will tell the police to stop, but first you must do something for me."

"What?" she dreaded his response.

"Anything I ask. Now that we are getting together again, tonight I will come to your house and you will make love with me. In the morning we will go to the police and I will sign papers telling them I don't want to press charges against you. Then, tomorrow night and any night after that, you will make love to me whenever I ask. I'll give you six months to get your life back together and then you will marry me. That's what I want from you, Math. Do you understand me? That is what I want."

Every cell in her body screamed no, but she managed to keep her voice calm. "Okay, Sawat, if that is what you want, then that is what I will do for you."

"I'll be there in fifteen minutes. Make sure you are clean, naked, and in bed. It's been a long time." He hung up his phone.

Math's stomach rolled from the tension. Her nausea came to fruition and she rushed outside to vomit. After a few minutes, the nausea passed and she went to the communal bath to wash herself and brush her teeth. She didn't put on make-up. Sawat hadn't asked for that and she didn't want to give him the pleasure of thinking she was making herself beautiful for him. But she would make love to him if her body let her. She hoped that after he was finished he would leave her for the night. She dried the water from her body and slipped under the covers to wait for Sawat. She waited a long while.

After an hour had passed, she decided he wasn't coming. That pleasant thought was shattered by a knock at the door. She didn't get out of bed to answer it. She didn't want him to see her naked. "Come in," she shouted at the door. "It's not locked."

The door opened and Sawat entered, a bottle of Mekong Whiskey in his hand. "Looks like you're ready for me," he smiled. "I knew you would be waiting."

Without further words he stood the whiskey bottle on her small dresser and then walked over and sat beside her on the bed. He stared at her for a long minute before leaning over to kiss her neck. He slipped his hand under the cover and pawed at her breasts.

Math could smell the odor of sour whiskey on his breath. His groping hand was hard and chafed. She resisted the urge to shove him away.

Sawat sat up straight. "Guess you need a little warming up. It's been a while since you had me. Maybe you have forgotten how good I am." He gave her breast one last squeeze and stood. Slowly he removed his clothes as if putting on a strip show for her.

His body was as lean and hard as she remembered. She looked for a scar from his gunshot wound but saw none. When he removed his jeans, she saw he was already aroused. Against her will, she felt her own body responding to the sight of his excitement. When he finally lay down beside her, she was ready to accept him. His hand slid between her legs and he felt her wetness.

J. F. Gump

"I knew you wanted me again," Sawat said.

"You must use a condom; I don't want to get pregnant." Her fertile cycle had passed over a week ago, so she knew there was little danger of pregnancy. But she was keenly aware of Sawat's sexual adventures with the lady-man and Buddha only knew who else. She was terrified of catching some disease, especially AIDS.

"I don't want to use a condom and I will not," he snapped. Without foreplay, he positioned himself on top of her and pushed her legs apart. In one quick lunge, he forced himself into her body.

Math made a small moaning sound. It wasn't from pleasure but from the pain of such quick penetration.

"I'm glad you still like it," Sawat said, misinterpreting her moan. "The best is yet to come." He continued his rough assault.

At first she just lay there thinking he would finish quickly as he always had. After three minutes she decided the Mekong had desensitized him and he might go on for a long time. Worse, her initial arousal had waned and she could feel herself going dry. She didn't want to see what his reaction might be if he realized she wasn't excited for him. She began moving in rhythm with Sawat and faking low moans of sexual pleasure, hoping it would hurry him along. Within a minute she felt his member increase in rigidity and begin pulsing in the early stages of orgasm. In one swift motion she rolled him onto his back. Now she was in control. She tightened every muscle in her womanhood, working to bring Sawat to a climax. Within a moment he was on the verge of release. At the last moment she pulled herself from him and twisted around and took his straining member in her mouth. She didn't want him to climax inside of her.

As if understanding what she was doing, he grabbed her hair and pulled her away. "I don't think so bitch," he said. "It's been a long time and I'm going to fill you with my seed." He pushed her back onto the bed and forced her legs apart. For the second time he made a quick penetration.

Within seconds Sawat was in the throes of orgasm. Math moaned softly and said she was climaxing too. She was afraid not

98

to put on one final display of pleasure. She didn't want to risk the repercussions if he thought she hadn't enjoyed his lovemaking.

In a minute his manhood turned flaccid and slipped from her. She was happy it was over. "Sawat, darling," she purred falsely in his ear. "I must go to the toilet."

She got up from the bed, put on a robe, and hurried to the communal bath. She was thankful no one else there. She washed Sawat out of her body as best as she could. Over and over again she washed herself out. Even after she had finished washing, she still felt dirty. She put her robe back on and returned to her room.

Sawat was asleep. The bottle of Mekong lay empty next to the bed. She was tired, but she didn't lie down. Instead she sat in her only chair and waited for the night to pass.

By seven o'clock in the morning Sawat still hadn't stirred. Math put on fresh clothes and make-up. At seven-thirty she sat on the bed and shook him gently.

"Darling," she said, when he opened his eyes. "Thank you for last night. I forgot how good you can make me feel. You were wonderful both times." It was a lie of convenience.

"Both times?" he asked. "I can only remember one."

"Oh, Sawat," she said coyly. "How could you forget the second time? You were even better than the first."

He sat up and puffed out his chest. "I knew you would like it."

"Teeluk," she said, "I promised to do many things for my mother and my brother today, and you must go to work before ten o'clock. We must hurry to the police station before it gets too late. When you finish work tonight, you must come back to me. I can't wait to have you make love to me again."

She smiled and pulled him into a standing position. She could see he was becoming aroused. She wished she hadn't laid it on so thick with the 'how wonderful you were' line. She changed the subject. "I must go to my mother's house before she leaves for work. I'll be back by the time you've cleaned up and dressed."

She left Sawat and his growing arousal behind, but she didn't go to her mother's. Instead she drove her motorcycle aimlessly through the streets of Phitsanulok. When she arrived back at her house, Sawat was dressed and waiting. He was neither smiling nor frowning. She wondered what thoughts were going through his head. "We can ride on my motorcycle," she said. "After the police station, I'll drive you to your house."

Sawat nodded, climbed aboard the motorcycle, and wrapped his arms around her body. She ignored his hands fondling her breasts and consoled herself with the thought that in an hour or so it would be finished. She was relieved when she finally parked the motorcycle at the police station and extracted herself from Sawat's groping. As she started toward the door, he grabbed her by the arm and pulled her around.

"Remember Math, after I do this you and I will be a couple again, and you'll keep your promise. Don't make a fool of me, because I'll hurt you if you do. I swear to Buddha, I will hurt you bad." His glare was unmistakable proof that he meant what he said.

"I would never do that, Sawat," she replied, keeping her feelings in check.

Together they entered the police station. Everyone was expecting Math's arrival but they hadn't been expecting Sawat. They stared in wonder at Math and Sawat arriving together. After a moment one young officer broke the silence. "May I help you?" he asked, looking first at Math, then at Sawat, and then at Math again.

"I've decided not to press charges," Sawat said, his tone flat and monotone. "What papers do I need to sign to give Math her freedom?"

"Are you sure...?" the young officer started, but then stopped just as quickly. "Never mind. Please have a seat. We'll finish this as fast as we can."

Math had always been a favorite of the police at the station. Always open and very polite. They had decided a long time ago that if she had shot Sawat, it was for a good reason. The officer was glad that this was ending in Math's favor.

With record-breaking speed for the Thai police, the officer soon had everything ready for Sawat's signature. He signed everywhere the policeman pointed while Math stood by in muted excitement.

"That's it," the officer announced, face beaming. "Good luck to both of you and especially to you, Math. I'm happy we don't have to lock you up like a common criminal."

Math pressed her hands together in prayer-like fashion, placed her fingers high on her face and presented the officer with a wai of deep respect. The officer smiled but didn't return her wai.

Outside, Sawat grabbed her by the arm again. "Don't forget what I've done for you, and don't forget what I told you. I'll hurt you if you ever make me lose face again. I'll hurt you real bad. Now take me home."

She didn't react to his threats. She started her motorcycle, waited for Sawat to board, and then drove toward his apartment. This time he didn't fondle her breasts or anything else. When they arrived at the shabby complex, Sawat dismounted the motorcycle.

"I'll see you at ten o'clock tonight," he said. "You had better be there or you're in big trouble. Do you understand me?"

She nodded. "Of course I will be there. I'll be waiting for you clean, naked, and in bed."

Sawat smiled and slid his hand across her thigh to her crotch. It wasn't polite to do that in public, but he didn't care. He had little respect for old Thai customs and taboos. He would do what he wanted when he wanted. He didn't care what anyone else might think. He turned and walked toward his apartment.

Math watched until Sawat was out of sight, and then sped toward home. Relief and happiness swept through her. Free, she thought, I'm free. Without warning, tears formed and flooded down her face. She laughed aloud from sheer joy. Unable to control herself, Math shouted at the top of her lungs, "I'm free. Thank Buddha, I am free."

Chapter 14

By the Friday after Math had left for her appointment with the police, Mike's waking thoughts were flooded by the cold reality that she might never return. If the situation with her ex-fiancé and the police was as bad as she'd said, she could be sitting in jail by now. Images of Math in a filthy Thai jail haunted him all day.

By the time he arrived home, his mood had turned from gloom to depression. He puzzled over his feelings. Math really didn't mean anything to him. He had known her for less than two weeks, and at times he wished he had never met her at all.

He drank a couple of beers and smoked a joint, hoping to lighten his frame of mind. It didn't work. He tried watching TV but couldn't concentrate on it. At nine-thirty he walked to Soi 2 hoping his old routine would ease his mind. When he arrived at Toy's, Lek didn't even acknowledge his presence. The other girls at the bar smiled cordially, but none came over to talk. Lek's doings, he was sure.

He drank one beer at Toy's and left. He walked across the street to the Classroom. He didn't really like the Classroom because the prices were high and the owner was an asshole. But his *friends* at the Toy Bar were being assholes too, so it didn't matter. He had several beers in the Classroom while he watched the unenthusiastic dancers gyrating out of beat with the thumping re-mix dance music. He'd had about all of the place he could take when Randy, his friend and co-worker, walked in.

"Lek told me you were here." Randy sat down and ordered beers for both of them. "Thought you didn't like this place."

"I don't like it," Mike answered. "But tonight it seems a hell of a lot better than Toy's. I must have really pissed-off everyone there. No one will even talk to me."

Randy laughed. "Ah, the life of a butterfly. I wouldn't worry too much. After all, Lek is the one who asked me come and make sure you're okay."

"Yeah, right. She's probably worried about all of the money she'll lose if I happen to croak or find another bar to hang out at."

"Well, probably that, too," Randy agreed. "But I think she is really worried about you. She said you looked very sad. I have to agree. Are you okay?"

"I'm fine," he answered. "I've had one beer to many, but other than that I'm just fucking fine. I'm going home after this one."

Together they watched the dancers and talked about work. Randy tried to buy Mike another beer, but he declined. Finally they paid their tabs and left the bar.

Outside, Randy said, "Sure I can't buy you a beer at Toy's? Lek really is your friend. I'd like to see you two kiss and make up as they say."

"Bad idea. I think I'll just go home."

"Mike," Randy stopped him, "it's none of my business, but where is that girl you've been hanging around with? What was her name again? Math or something like that?"

"Yeah, Math. She went home."

"When's she coming back?" Randy pursued the subject.

"I think maybe never," he answered.

"Why not?"

"It's a long story." Mike knew he could never explain Math's predicament with the police and her ex-fiancé. "I don't want to talk about it right now."

The two men stared at each other. After a moment Mike walked away.

"Take care of yourself," Randy said.

"Thanks for the beer," Mike answered over his shoulder.

"Mai pen rai, never mind," Randy replied too low for Mike to hear. "Mai pen rai."

Chapter 15

Math was still excited when she arrived at her house from the police station. She went inside, turned on the fan, and sat down in her only chair. She took a few deep breaths trying to compose herself. Sometimes when she was very excited or under a lot of stress, her heart didn't work right. She could feel it happening now. The palpitations, the weakness, the nausea.

She wanted to lay down and sleep but she couldn't, not on the bed where Sawat had violated her just hours ago. The thought made her nausea worse. Besides, she had too much to do to even think about taking a nap. She had to get away from Phitsanulok. Everything she had promised Sawat was a lie. She had no intentions of being there when he came for her tonight.

"Calm down," she said aloud, forcing herself to relax. "Just breathe deep and be calm." The palpitations, the weakness, and the overwhelming exhaustion persisted. Without even knowing it was happening, Math fell asleep in her chair.

The room was a bake-oven when she awoke. The fan blew only hot air and she was drenched with sweat. She looked at her watch: it was two forty-five in the afternoon. Her little brother would be home from school within the hour. As much as she wanted to see him before she left, she couldn't wait. She had to be long gone by the time Sawat finished work.

Math pushed herself from the chair and went outside. The mid-afternoon heat was cool compared to her room. In a minute, she felt better. She went back inside long enough to get her robe and a towel, and then went to the bath. She made plans while she ladled herself clean.

She knew the smartest thing for her to do would be go to Chiang Mai and stay with her sister for a while. She was sure Nuang could help her find work there. On the other hand, there was still the possibility of working for her brother in Pattaya. As of yet, he hadn't said either yes or no about her working for him full time. She had made a few sales calls for him and she had signed up two new customers. Anan hadn't paid her for the new customers or any of her time, but she was sure he would.

Also, there was that new attraction in Pattaya that entered her mind more often than it should. Mike was never far from the center of her thoughts. She wasn't sure why. True, she'd had a really good time while she was with him, but that was all. She had known him less than two weeks and it couldn't be anything more than that. Love was not even part of the equation. Never again would she let a man be a deciding factor in her life. To prove the point to herself, she decided to go to Chiang Mai and forget about her brother, Pattaya, and the farang.

Math repacked her suitcase, turned everything off, and locked the house on her way out. She put a note under the seat of the motorcycle for her little brother to find. The note didn't say much, only that she was going to Chiang Mai and that she would call later. She walked to the main road and hailed a taxi to the bus station.

As she rode, she noticed how different Phitsanulok was from Pattaya. No beer bars, fancy hotels, or expensive condos. Also, there was almost a total absence of foreigners. That was good because most of the people in Phitsanulok were anti-farang.

The bus terminal was crowded with passengers and Math had to stand in line to buy her ticket. While she waited, she watched the people milling about the terminal. She tried to guess where they were going, even though she would never know if she was right or wrong.

After fifteen minutes of waiting, it was her turn at the ticket window. "A one way ticket to Chiang Mai, please," she told the lady.

"All of the buses leaving for Chiang Mai today are full," the ticket agent said. "We have seats available for tomorrow."

So that is where everyone is going, she thought glumly, her shoulders slumping. "What about Pattaya?" she asked on impulse.

The ticket agent paused, "Pattaya, you say?" It was more of a statement than a question.

Math said nothing. Her mind and her heart raced with unexpected anticipation.

"There's a seat on the bus to Bangkok in 30 minutes," the agent replied. "You can connect to Pattaya from there."

"I'll take it," she said without hesitation, surprised at how quickly she had changed her mind.

The agent gave her a strange look but said nothing.

Suddenly it dawned on Math how stupid her request must have sounded. Chiang Mai and Pattaya were far apart and in opposite directions. Certainly she must seem like someone with no place to go; or someone running away to anywhere as long as it wasn't near Phitsanulok. Or, perhaps, the agent thought she was a bar-girl. Math blushed at her realization. No one spoke in the brief silence.

"My daughter, Tana, works in Pattaya," the agent started then stopped in mid sentence.

Math saw that the agent, too, was blushing.

Without further comment the agent prepared the ticket and told Math the bus would be boarding in twenty minutes.

Math paid and hurried from the ticket window. She found a seat near her boarding gate. She hoped this trip would be better than the last. At least this time she would be traveling at night, and if the bus did break down it wouldn't be so hot. She'd be arriving in the daylight, too, which made her felt even better about the trip.

When her bus was announced, Math checked her luggage, climbed on board, and sank into her seat. The events of the last couple of days caught up with her. She leaned the seat back and got comfortable. Within a few minutes she was asleep.

SIAM NIGHTS

Her first dream was a short and fleeting one about Mike and herself. They weren't in Pattaya – they weren't even in Thailand. In her dream she knew she was in another country and that Mike was her husband. They were walking down a sidewalk; it was clean and unbroken. Big, non-Thai houses lined the street. It was cold. "Are you happy?" Mike asked her in the dream. She woke up before she could answer, but in the brief time she was awake there was a smile on her face.

Her second dream was even shorter than the first. It was one she had dreamt before. She dreamed of a baby with white hair and blue eyes. It was a very beautiful baby. She couldn't see its face clearly, yet the baby looked familiar. Again, she awoke with a smile on her face.

The next dream started very nice. She was at her mother's house and her father was there. If Math had been awake, this would have seemed strange. Her mother and father had been separated for several years and were together only for weddings and funerals. But in her dream, it all seemed normal. Her younger brother and her sister from Phitsanulok were there, too. It was Sunday and her mother was cooking.

Suddenly the door of the house burst open and a monkey-man straight from Thai legends bolted in. He was dressed in bright yellows, reds, and greens. His gruesome, half-human / half-monkey face stared out from the elaborate gold helmet on his head. He walked bent-kneed and slightly stooped over. A tail snaked out from the back of his warrior attire. He slashed the air wildly with his razor sharp sword. Whistling sounds echoed through the room. Suddenly he stopped and looked directly at Math. A torrent of words sprang from his monkey-human mouth. She didn't understand anything he said and it terrified her. The monkey-man repeated himself. This time she recognized one word, and the word was "Dead". Panic and dread clutched her entire body. "Who is dead?" she screamed.

The monkey-man pushed his ugly face within inches of her own; his sour breath assaulted her nose. "You know already," he spat out the words as if they were poison. Then he laughed.

"Who is dead?" she screamed again, louder than before.

Her scream woke her. She glanced around the bus, but no one was looking at her. Her heart pounded like a jackhammer. Pounding and fluttering like the heart of the little chick she had tried to save when she was ten years old. Math slid back into a restless sleep.

It was such a tiny chick. Its mother had been run over by a truck and Math decided it needed help. Even though it was hot outside, she was sure the chick must be cold without its mother to huddle under. She had felt its little heart quivering as she grabbed it up. She wrapped the chick in a towel and sat beside it in the sun.

Presently, her brother came by and asked her to play badminton. Math was very tired but wanted to play, so she went with him. She left the chick wrapped in the towel and sitting in the broiling Thailand heat. When she came back, the chick wasn't moving. It was dead. She knew it was her own selfishness and not the sun that had killed the chick. She cried over the dead chick for a long time.

Her memories of the chick faded, and the monkey-man with his warning of death returned. As the bus traveled through the dark night, the dream of the monkey-man came back over and over. Finally, she couldn't face the dream again and forced herself to stay awake.

She wondered what the dream meant. The monkey-man seemed so real. Was it an omen of some sort? Was someone really going die or was there some other hidden meaning? Why did the monkey-man say she already knew who was going to die? How could she possibly know? Maybe it was herself. Maybe her bus was going to crash or something. She shuddered at the thought.

She was glad when the bus entered the outskirts of Bangkok. Here, the streetlights and nighttime activity distracted her thoughts away from the bizarre dream. By the time they reached the bus station, her nightmares had faded into vague memories.

It was a long wait for an empty seat to Pattaya. She tried to sleep in the terminal but couldn't. After what seemed like an eternity, her bus was announced. As the bus moved south out of Bangkok, Math drifted off to sleep. This time she didn't dream.

She was still asleep when the bus arrived at the station on North Pattaya Road. The man sitting beside her shook her awake. Math was groggy but managed a polite thank you. She sat on the bus for a minute to let her head clear. Shortly she left the bus and collected her suitcase. She glanced at her watch. It was six-fifty in the morning.

The city of Pattaya was already alive with people going about their morning routines. Motorcycles, cars, and taxis moved up and down the streets toward scattered destinations. She hadn't taken the time to consider where she would go after she arrived in Pattaya. She had only been concerned about getting away from Phitsanulok and Sawat. She knew it would be best if she went to her brother's house, but the thought of going to Mike's condo held a stronger appeal. It was Saturday and Mike would have to work, but if she hurried she could get to his condo before he left. Maybe he wouldn't go to work if she was there. And maybe he would be happy to hear her good news about the police.

Math flagged down a baht-bus going in the direction of Mike's condo. In less than two blocks the traffic stopped. She leaned her head out the side of the baht-bus and looked down the street. She couldn't see anything but assumed there must be an accident. She looked at her watch. Mike would be leaving for work soon, but if the traffic started moving, she could still make it.

Her patience ebbed as the seconds ticked past. She was about to forget the baht-bus and walk when the traffic inched forward. At the next intersection the baht-bus turned right. It was the wrong direction. "You're going the wrong way," she shouted at the driver.

The driver pointed toward the middle of the intersection. There stood a policeman directing traffic to turn right, detouring them around a closed stretch of road. As the baht-bus completed its turn, she saw what had caused the traffic to jam. It was an accident. From what she could see, it involved a truck and two motorcycles. The scene was gruesome. Bloody bodies and twisted motorcycles lay bent and broken on the blacktop. She looked away. After the dreams she'd had the night before, she didn't want to see more. It might be someone she knew.

The detour took longer than she hoped. By the time the baht bus reached Mike's condo it was seven-fifteen. She paid the driver, grabbed her suitcase, and ran inside the lobby. "Is Khun Mike here?" she asked the boy at the front desk.

"He left already," the boy answered.

Bad luck lady, Math thought. The boy had seen her with Mike a couple of times when she came down to see him off to work. She hoped he remembered her. "You already know I'm Mike's girlfriend and that we live together," she stretched the truth confidently. "Give me the key so I can leave my suitcase. I will only be a minute and then I'm going to my brother's house."

After a barely noticeable pause, the boy handed her the key.

Math went to the room and unpacked her clothes. She put the clean ones onto hangers and into drawers, while the dirty ones went into the laundry basket for the maids to collect and wash. She pushed her suitcase atop the closet, out of sight and out of the way. She took a quick shower, dressed, and shoved a change of clothes into her oversized handbag. She started to write Mike a note, but changed her mind. She would be back before he came home.

Downstairs, she handed the key to the boy. "If Khun Mike comes back before I do, please don't tell him I was here," she said. "I want to surprise him."

"Okay," the boy smiled.

She left the condo and caught a motorcycle-taxi to her brother's house. She felt a shiver of anxiety, as they drove past the place where she had seen the accident. There was still blood on the pavement, but the truck, motorcycles, and bodies were gone. She wondered how many people had died.

Chapter 16

As they often did on Saturdays, Mike, Randy, and the rest of their crew decided to leave work early and go to the Tahitian Queen for afternoon happy hour. Randy made arrangements with the driver to be there at two o'clock.

Everyone had cleared their desks and was waiting when the van picked them up. There wasn't much traffic and their ride home was faster than usual. Mike was anxious to go with his co-workers to the bar. He had finally admitted to himself that he was depressed because he missed Math. He hoped that a few beers with friends would help him forget about her for a while. He arrived at his condo at two thirty-five.

The boy at the front desk smiled when Mike asked for his key. Mike smiled back but said nothing. Neither did the boy.

Mike was in his room just long enough to drop off his computer, wash his face, and put on fresh deodorant. He didn't shower or change clothes; he would do that later. He hurried downstairs, left his key with the smiling boy, and then caught a baht-bus to the Tahitian Queen. He was the last one to arrive.

The TQ was Mike's favorite go-go bar in Pattaya. They didn't play that thumping, re-mix dance music so loved by the other go-go bars. Here they played good old rock and roll classics. The music was good, the beer was cold, and the dancers were hot.

The afternoon slid past filled with jokes and laughter and half-naked ladies. Their refrain of "just one more beer" lasted until the evening happy hour started. By then everyone was in the middle stages of drunkenness, so their decision to drink through the second happy hour was an easy one. At eight o'clock the dancer's changed shifts and everyone stayed for that. At eight thirty Mike announced that he was going home while he could still find it.

J. F. Gump

Randy decided to leave with him. They shared a baht-bus home.

Randy thought Mike seemed more relaxed and happier than he had been for the last couple of days. It had probably helped just getting him out of his condo. The six or more beers that Mike had consumed probably didn't hurt too much either. Why stop now? Randy felt obligated to keep his friend occupied for the evening so he wouldn't have time to think about that girl. "Got any plans for the night?" he asked.

"I don't know what I'm gonna do. Maybe I'll just go somewhere and get drunk."

"I've got news for you Mike, you're drunk already."

Mike laughed. "No, I mean seriously drunk. Falling down, shit-faced, puking drunk. Want to come along?"

"Actually, I was going to ask you the same thing," Randy said. "I have a new girlfriend on Soi 8. Her name is Tana."

"Another girlfriend?" Mike asked without expecting an answer. "No wonder the girls call you a butterfly. What is that, the third one this month?"

Randy ignored Mike's comments. "I'm going to see her later. You're welcome to come along if you want. I'd like you to meet her. She's really hot. I think she might be a keeper."

"Bet that will go over real big with your wife," Mike needled.

"Fuck you," Randy retorted. "You're not exactly a saint, either."

"What time are you supposed to meet her?"

"About ten o'clock or so."

"Okay, I'll go. Guess I should meet this hot little home-wrecker. I just need enough time to shower and change clothes. Where do you want to meet?"

"Soi 2?" Randy suggested. Over the months, Toy's bar had become the regular meeting place for most of the guys from work.

Mike sighed. "I don't think that's such a good idea. My welcome there seems to have worn a little thin. Why don't you meet me at the Music Lover Bar? You know, the bar in front of my condo." He pulled a ten baht coin from his pocket and handed it to

Randy. "For the baht-bus to the Music Lover," he said.
"You got it," Randy agreed.

Mike buzzed the driver as they neared his condo. He looked at his watch; it was nine o'clock. "See you in forty-five minutes or so. He stepped from the baht-bus, paid his fare, and headed home.

Chapter 17

Math had spent that same Saturday morning telling her brother Anan about her trip to Phitsanulok, and Sawat's decision not to press charges. She spent the afternoon watching TV and thinking how surprised and happy Mike would be when she told him everything that had happened. At four thirty she showered, changed clothes, and put on new make-up. She wanted to smell clean and look beautiful when he saw her. By five o'clock, she was on her way to Pattaya.

At her request, Anan had left his motorcycle for her to use. She would never admit it, but his motorcycle was a little big for her. It was too heavy and her feet barely reached the ground. But it was better than catching taxis everywhere, and it gave her a feeling of freedom and independence.

Sukhumvit Road was busy with afternoon traffic. Math took no chances and yielded the right-of-way to everything larger than her motorcycle. She arrived at the condo at five thirty-five.

The boy who had been working at the desk in the morning was gone and had been replaced by the girl who worked evenings. Her name was Jahl. Jahl had seen her with Mike many times. She had always gone out of her way to be polite and friendly with Jahl.

"Sawasdee ka, good evening," Math said, in her most polite tone. "Is Khun Mike in his room?"

The girl checked for Mike's key. It was there. "He must not be home from work yet," Jahl said, holding up the key.

"Oh, good," Math said. "I just returned from Phitsanulok and want to surprise him. I'll take the key just long enough to unlock the door, and then I'll bring it right back. When Mike comes home, he won't know I'm here. When he walks in, I'll be waiting for him. He'll be surprised."

The girl handed over the key without question. Math went upstairs, unlocked the room, and then returned the key to the front desk.

Back in the condo, she slipped into a short sexy nightgown. She combed her hair and double-checked her make-up. Mike would be home at any minute. Her excitement rose at the thought. She noticed his computer beside the desk. She hadn't noticed it earlier, but thought nothing of it. He didn't always take it to work with him anyway.

By six thirty her initial excitement had worn off and she had turned on the TV. She flipped through the channels but couldn't get interested in any of the shows. Finally, she left it on MTV. She sat on the edge of the bed, staring stupidly at the music videos without really seeing or hearing them. Mike must have had to work late, she thought.

By seven thirty she began to feel stupid sitting around it the short nightgown. She dressed in her street clothes and put her nightgown back into the drawer. Maybe Mike had stopped for a beer with his friends.

By eight thirty she was hungry and irritated. She had wanted to surprise Mike, but she was the one being surprised.

At eight forty-five she turned off the air, the TV, and the lights. She left the condo. Jahl smiled as she walked past the front desk. She didn't return the receptionist's smile.

Math knew Mike used to like hanging around with that witch Lek at Toy's bar. Maybe he had started going there again after she had gone home to Phitsanulok. The thought made her blood boil. There was only one way to know for sure. She would go and look.

Outside, she couldn't get the motorcycle started. After five minutes of trying, her leg hurt and she was sweating.

The security guard, who had been watching her efforts, finally came over and offered his help. As if to add insult to injury, he had the motorcycle running on his second kick. She blushed with embarrassment and thanked the man for his help. He only nodded and smiled. Math put on her helmet and drove toward Soi 2. It was eight fifty-five.

Mike walked into the condo parking area at nine o'clock. The guard, who didn't speak any English, waved for Mike to stop. The man pointed at the parked motorcycles and made riding motions and girlie shapes with his hands.

What in the hell was he trying to say? Mike wondered. He decided the guy was wondering if he was going to ride a motorcycle and pick up women tonight. Mike laughed and shook his head. "Mai, pom maow mak mak. No, I'm drunk," he said to the guard.

They looked at each other for a long moment. Mike in bewilderment, and the guard in frustration. Finally Mike shrugged his shoulders and walked into the lobby. The night girl wasn't there, but the manager was. "Jahl bai nai, krup, where is Jahl?" he asked politely.

The manager smiled at Mike's heavily accented, badly spoken Thai. "I have relieved her so she can eat dinner," she answered in near perfect English and handed Mike his key.

"Okay, see you later," he said and went to his room.

He didn't have much time. Randy would be at the Music Lover's Bar before long. He rushed through his shower and put on fresh clothes. He left the room without noticing the female clothes in the closet or Math's suitcase resting on top.

In the parking lot, the guard again went through his hand motions. Mike smiled and made walking motions with his fingers. The guard shook his head and smiled back. At the Music Lover Bar he was given his usual warm welcome. He was a good customer, one who never caused problems and always paid his bill. Wan, the bar's mama-san, sat across from him and asked him many questions about his new girl.

He answered most of them before telling Wan that Math had gone back to Phitsanulok and probably wouldn't return. On hearing that, Wan introduced him to a new girl at the bar and suggested he take her home. He only smiled and shook his head. Wan knew he never took girls from the bar.

Ten o'clock came but Randy hadn't arrived. Mike ordered another beer. At ten fifteen Randy was still absent, so he ordered one more. *Where in bloody hell is Randy?* he grumbled to himself. Maybe Randy had received a call from his home or from the office. Not likely on a Saturday night but certainly possible.

By ten thirty Mike had finished his third beer and had ordered the fourth. His soberness from the shower had faded and the numbing cloud of alcohol had returned. At ten forty-five Randy arrived and he didn't look happy.

"Who pissed you off?" Mike asked as Randy took a seat.

Randy didn't answer. Instead he ordered a beer for both of them. After the beers arrived and Randy had had a healthy swallow, he turned to Mike, "When did your friend Math go to Phitsanulok?"

In spite of the hot night, Mike felt a cold chill start at the base of his neck and work its way down both arms and up across the top of his head. "Two or three days ago. Why do you ask?"

"No reason, really," Randy answered, nonchalant. "Just curious."

"Bullshit," Mike blurted. "First you show up forty-five minutes late, second you start your conversation with a question on something you don't even care about, and then you act like it means nothing. God damn you, Randy. What the fuck is going on? What in the hell are you getting at?"

Randy didn't reply. He sipped on his beer and looked like he was in deep thought. Finally he turned to Mike and sighed. "It didn't take me long to shower and change clothes. I had some time to kill so I decided to walk here and save the baht-bus fare. By the time I reached Soi 2, the beers drank at the TQ had kicked in and I had to piss like a racehorse. I went to the two-baht john on the south side of the bars on Soi 2. You know the one I mean?"

Mike nodded.

"Well," Randy continued, "After I finished in the john, I had to walk through the bars to get back to Second Road. That's where I saw her." Randy hesitated.

"Saw who?" he asked.

"Well, you know," Randy stammered.

"You mean you saw Math?"

"I'm not sure, but I think it was her. If it wasn't, it was her twin sister."

"What did you say to her? What did she say?"

Randy paused before answering, "I didn't say anything. I didn't stop. She was with another man, a farang."

Mike felt as if his heart had been ripped from his chest and thrown on the bar in front of him. "Are you sure it was her? I know you have met her, but maybe it wasn't her. You know how many of these people look alike to us."

Randy sighed and slumped in his seat. "I don't know 100% for sure, but it really looked like her. I might be wrong, and god knows I hope I am. I can tell by the way you have been acting lately that you like her very much. If you weren't my friend, I would just laugh and forget the whole thing, but I can't. I wouldn't want you to hide anything like this from me. I don't want you to believe something that isn't true. We've both seen these girls set guys up just to get money from them. I'm not saying that's what's going on or anything. I don't know what to think. Maybe I'm wrong. Maybe it wasn't her." For a moment Randy was silent, then he muttered, "I almost didn't come to meet you. I wasn't sure what to do. Now I wish I'd never said anything."

Mike picked up his beer, finished it in one long swallow and then ordered another. He sat there drinking, thinking, and moping. He had fleeting images of Math sitting with another man and it made his scrotum tighten in reflex. His anger built each time the thought entered his head. He chugged the beer. "Thanks for telling me what you saw," he said, setting the empty bottle on the bar. "Don't worry about telling me because it's not important. She doesn't mean anything to me. She can do whatever she wants. I'm not her father or her husband or her boyfriend."

Randy knew Mike was lying. His voice and his face betrayed his words.

Mike asked for his bill to be totaled and stood up from the barstool. He wobbled slightly.

"Where are you heading?" Randy asked. "You're still going to Soi 8 with me, aren't you?"

"Maybe, maybe not," he answered. "Right now I'm going to Soi 2." Without waiting for his bill, he threw 500 baht on the bar and walked away.

Randy reached for his wallet, threw another 500 baht on the bar, and hurried to catch up. "Hey Mike. I still have that ten baht piece. What say we take a baht-bus to Soi 2?"

Soi 2 was only three blocks away, but tonight it seemed like a very long three blocks. Mike agreed and they flagged down the next baht-bus that passed by.

When they arrived, Mike asked, "Which bar? I want to see her, but I don't want her to see me. Know what I mean?"

Randy nodded. "It's down here." He led the way.

On Randy's cue they stopped. Randy pointed and Mike looked. The girl's back was toward them and he couldn't get a good view, but from this angle it surely looked like Math.

"I can't see her face," Mike whispered, his words slurred.

"Just wait a minute," Randy said. "Maybe she'll turn around."

The girl was sitting beside a foreigner, a farang - a very big farang. She appeared to be talking to the man and a girl behind the bar. Sometimes Mike could hear them laugh, but he couldn't hear their conversation. Three times the farang put his arm around the girl and she didn't pull away. After what seemed like an eternity, she turned and looked in the direction of the Toy Bar. Mike got a perfect look. It was Math. For a moment he thought he was going to either hyperventilate or burst into rage. "I've seen enough. I'm leaving now."

"Where are you going?" Randy asked. "Let's go to Soi 8 and forget about that whore-bitch."

Mike gave Randy a look that could kill. "She's not a whore and she's not a bitch. She is a cunt. I don't know where I'm going, but right now it's anywhere but here."

Randy's face flushed. "Do you want me to say anything to her? I will, if you want."

"Tell her to go fuck herself," Mike said, then turned and walked away.

Randy watched his friend leave and debated what to do next. He was already in trouble with his new girlfriend because he was late. On the other hand, another couple of minutes wouldn't make much difference. He walked toward the bar where Math sat with the big farang.

Chapter 18

When Math left the condo earlier that evening, she went directly to Soi 2. By the time she'd parked her motorcycle, it was nine o'clock. Lek cast an evil glare but said nothing. Som Jai was there and Math motioned her over to the side of the road. "Have you seen Mike?"

"I haven't seen him tonight," Som Jai answered, glancing at Lek. "And I shouldn't be talking to you. Lek has threatened to fire anyone who talks to you or Mike. I don't know what her problem is. She acts like she owns him. I think she is crazy. There's a girl working here on Soi 2 who knows your sister. Her name is Yui. She works at Peter's Bar. It's near the toilets. I told her I've seen you and she wants to meet you. She has a letter from your sister. Something about her falling and breaking her foot. Maybe she cannot walk right again. Why don't you go talk to her?"

"Someone has a letter from my sister?"

"Her name is Yui," Som Jai said. "I have to stop talking to you now. I can't afford to lose my job." She pointed towards the toilets and Peter's Place, and then she turned and walked away.

Math walked in the direction that Som Jai had pointed. She knew nothing about her sister being hurt. But she had been away from home for two weeks and hadn't spoken with her mother while she was in Phitsanulok. Anything can happen in two weeks.

Peter's Place was easy to find. Math took a seat at the bar and ordered a coke. When she asked if anyone knew Yui, one girl responded immediately. Math explained that she was Itta's sister. After they talked for a few minutes, Yui showed Itta's letter to

Math.

Math knew it was from her sister, because she recognized the handwriting. For some reason Itta was telling this girl things she had never told her own family. She knew her sister was unhappy, but she never knew how cruel her husband was. Itta had never told her family of the beatings Ian gave her. Nor had she ever mentioned him making her have sex with his friends for money. She wanted to cry for her sister but couldn't in such a public place. She was relieved when a customer, a farang, came to the bar and sat down. He was a distraction from her thoughts.

At first the farang sat a few bar stools away, but he moved closer when he discovered she spoke English. His closeness made her uncomfortable, but she said nothing. She was waiting for Mike to show up at the Toy Bar, and she couldn't wait for him there because of Lek.

From her seat she had a good view of Toy's. Every few minutes she would look to see if Mike had arrived. The farang put his arm around her from time to time, but he was being very nice and didn't ask her to go with him, so she ignored his actions. Yui was fun to talk to and Peter's Place seemed like as good a place as any to wait for Mike. She had already decided that if Mike didn't show up by eleven thirty, she would go back to his condo and wait.

When eleven thirty came with no sign of Mike, she asked Yui for her check. She was getting money from her purse when someone behind her said her name. She turned and came face-to-face with one of Mike's friends. "Oh," she said surprised. She recognized his face but couldn't remember his name. "How are you? Have you seen Mike?"

Randy only stared, a look of disgust on his face.

"Are you okay?" Math asked. "You look ill."

"Mike said you went to your home. Now all of a sudden you are here, and with a farang." He nodded in the direction of the foreigner.

"What do you mean?" she asked. Panic nipped. "I'm not with anyone. I waited for Mike at his condo for a long time but he didn't come home. I came to find him. Lek at the Toy Bar doesn't like me so I'm waiting here. This lady knows my sister. She had a letter for me to read." She waved the letter in front of Randy as evidence. "Where is Mike?" she demanded.

"You Thai women must think all farangs are stupid. With as many people as Mike knows in this town, didn't you think he'd find that you are out whoring around?"

The farang sitting next to Math stood up. He wasn't just big, he was huge. "Is this man bothering you, sweetheart?" the big farang asked.

Math turned to the man. "You shut up," she ordered sharply then turned back to Randy. "I'm not with him. Just ask him."

Randy looked at the man. "Well?" Randy asked. The man said nothing.

Math looked at the big man. "Why don't you answer him?" she demanded.

"You told me to shut up," the farang said.

"I was only joking," she shouted shrilly. "Just tell him the truth."

"Okay," the big man said, stepping back from her outburst. "The young lady is right, I don't know her. She was sitting here talking to Yui when I came in. I noticed she spoke good English and I wanted to talk to her. In case you haven't noticed, good English is somewhat of a rarity around here. She told me she had just come back from Phitsanulok and was waiting for her boyfriend to get home from work. This girl isn't with me. I have a Thai wife who wouldn't be very happy if I was with another lady. My wife isn't very big, but she is meaner than hell when she's jealous."

"Well, now what do you think?" Math asked contemptuously.

Randy sputtered, "I think maybe I made a mistake." He hesitated for a minute before adding, "Mike saw you with this man."

"Mike saw me?" she asked wide-eyed. Panic bit hard. "How could he see me? He hasn't been here. I've been watching for him all night."

Randy's faced flushed. "Actually, I saw you first, earlier, and then Mike and I sort of sneaked up on you."

"What do you mean, *you sort of sneaked up on me*?" she shrieked. "I can't believe you men. I never thought farangs were stupid before, but I'm sure thinking it now. Do you know where Mike went?"

"I don't know," Randy answered. "Maybe he went to Soi 8 or maybe he went home. I don't know."

"Well, let's find him," she said, calming herself down as much as she could. "Let's start at his condo. I have my brother's motorcycle. I'll take us there."

Randy agreed. He paid for Math's tab and they left.

~~~

Mike was angry when he left Randy at the bars on Soi 2. He couldn't clear his mind of the image of Math sitting next to that man, laughing and having fun. It was even worse than he had imagined while sitting at the Music Lover Bar. The scene he had just witnessed repeated itself over and over in his head. The farang putting his arm around Math, and Math smiling at the attention. He tried to shut the image off but he couldn't. Instead his throat cramped tight and his eyes filled with tears.

Mike didn't understand his feelings, they didn't make sense. He hardly knew the girl. She shouldn't be affecting him like this. He was a married man. This was crazy.

After a few moments, and as hard as it was for him to admit it, he realized he had fallen in love with that girl. How could he have let himself be fooled into loving a common bar-girl? He had a sudden urge to hurt her, but it faded quickly. He took a deep breath. The cramp in his throat eased and his eyes stopped tearing. As he continued his way home, he decided that tonight he would drink until he had erased her from his head. Tomorrow he would get an AIDS test.

He stopped at the gas station and bought a liter bottle of beer. It was gone before he reached the condo. He threw the empty bottle on the sidewalk but felt no satisfaction at its shattering.

Inside the condo, the afternoon guard was gone but Jem, the manager, was still on duty. "Is Jahl still eating dinner?" Mike asked, trying to smile.

"Not really," Jem answered. "Right now I think she is getting rid of her dinner. Seems she ate something not so good for her. I'm stuck here until my night boy comes to work. I called him to come early, but he isn't here yet."

"That's too bad," he said. "I feel sorry all three of you."

"Never mind," the manager responded. "I guess you want your key?"

He nodded and Jem handed it to him. He removed the key from its oversized ring and dropped it into his pocket. He handed back the empty ring. She raised her eyebrows in question.

"I'm taking it with me. I want to be sure my ex-friend, that girl named Math, doesn't get the key to my room. I don't want anyone letting her in with a master key, either. Make sure you tell your night boy that. I don't want her here. Do you understand me?"

Jem blinked at the force of his words.

"I'm sorry for how that sounded," he said, trying to soften the impact. "I'm a little upset. I just don't want that girl to have access to my room. That's all."

"Okay," the manager said. "I'll make sure she doesn't get into your room. And I'll make sure the night boy understands too."

"Thank you," Mike said. "One more thing. If I happen to show up with a girl tonight, keep an eye on me. Okay? Seems like I'm not very good at picking trustworthy friends." Without waiting for a reply, he turned and left the lobby.

℘

Math steered her motorcycle into the condo parking area less than ten minutes after Mike left. The guard stared suspiciously.

She ignored him and pulled into a parking spot. The night boy was on duty. "Have you seen Khun Mike?" Math asked politely in Thai.

"No," the boy shook his head.

"Is his key here?" she asked.

The boy reached up and pulled down the ring, minus the key, and held it out for her to see. "He isn't here and you're not allowed here either."

"What do you mean, I'm not allowed here?" she demanded, surprised at his words.

"I don't know what I mean. All I know is that Ms. Jem said you weren't allowed here. She didn't say why. She just said it. Maybe you should go now."

"What's going on?" Randy asked, seeing the expression on Math's face.

She explained, her voice filled with questions and confusion.

"Mike must have been here already," Randy said. "Ask him how he knows Mike isn't here, if he hasn't seen him."

Math asked and the boy gave her an extended answer. She interpreted for Randy. "When he came on duty, the condo manager told him that Mike had taken his key and gone outside. She said he looked very drunk and not happy. She told the boy that he should alert the security guard if Mike came home with a girl. The manager also said that I am not allowed in his room and that I should be asked to leave if I come here."

"That's Mike," Randy said. "100% pure Mike. Come on, let's go. Maybe he went to Soi 8 like we planned. I was taking him there to meet my new girlfriend. I don't know where else to look. First, let's ask the girls at the bar out front if they have seen him or know where he went. If they don't know, then we'll go to Soi 8."

They left the condo and walked to the Music Lover Bar. The girls had seen Mike go into the condo, but they hadn't seen him leave. As far as they knew, he was already in bed. Randy and Math caught a baht-bus to Soi 8.

SIAM NIGHTS

~~~

Mike had left the condo lobby just seconds before the night boy came on duty and only minutes before Math and Randy had arrived. When he left, he took the side road that bypassed the bars out front. He didn't want to see anyone he knew and he especially didn't want to see Randy. When he thought about their earlier conversation, he realized that Randy had somehow known his feelings for Math, even before he knew them himself. Were his feelings always so clear to everyone except himself? He was embarrassed at the way Math had fooled him. Randy and the others were probably having a field day laughing at him. He didn't want to see any of them tonight. He had lost face. He walked to Soi 6. No one he knew ever went to Soi 6.

Mike had walked down the street often enough, but he had never stopped at any of the bars. These weren't your normal go-go's or have-a-good-time beer bars. These were short-time bars where you could get cold beer at reasonable prices and a hot piece of ass for just a little more. He stopped at the third bar on the left.

Inside was much better than he expected. He had only seen these bars from the outside and he'd never been impressed. This one was air-conditioned and it was clean. There was only one other customer in the bar. Mike found a stool facing the TV and ordered a beer. An attractive young lady came to sit on the stool beside him. She looked at him expectantly. He took the hint and offered to buy her a drink. As soon as he had ordered for them both, the girl stood up and proceeded to give him a very nice neck and shoulder massage. He wondered why he had never stopped here before. The massage ended when the barmaid delivered their drinks.

"Choke dee ka. Cheers," the girl said.

"Choke dee krup," he answered automatically. They both drank; Mike his beer and the girl whatever her nasty looking green stuff was.

The girl leaned against him and touched his crotch. "I want to make love with you," she said, getting to the point and wasting no time about it.

He took another drink of his beer but said nothing.

The girl continued to rub and stroke his crotch, but he didn't respond.

Finally she said, "Are you okay? I think maybe he is asleep"

Mike finished his beer and ordered another before answering, "I hope he's dead." He wasn't into the Pattaya sex thing and certainly not into the short-time scene, so he added, "He doesn't like girls anyway. He likes boys." He thought that would end this whole weird affair.

Instead, a second girl appeared on Mike's other side. "I'm a boy," she said.

Mike turned and looked at the second girl. She was sexier looking than the first. "No fucking way," he said. "I don't believe you."

She took his hand and pulled it to his/her crotch. Mike touched briefly then snatched his hand away. "No shit!" was all he could think of saying. In one quick chug, he finished his second beer. "I have to go now." He stood and walked toward the door.

The girl/guy grabbed his arm. "You didn't pay," he/she said, now sounding like a man.

Mike pulled out his wallet and threw money on the bar. He wasn't even sure how much it was. "If that's not enough, it's too damned bad. I'm outta here." He staggered from the bar.

Outside he took a deep breath hoping to clear his mind. It didn't work. If anything, it only intensified his drunkenness. He toe-heeled his way forward, his gait off balance. He teetered his way toward Second Road and his condo.

Before he was halfway home, images of Math and the big farang returned. The thoughts pushed him over the edge. He began talking to himself. "Stupid whore, cunt, bitch, Thai slut, mother-fucker."

He stopped and was silent for a moment, pissed that he couldn't think of more cuss words. He stumbled forward, repeating the same words over and over. His depression and his anger built with every replay of the scene at Soi 2. By the time he reached the Music Lover's Bar, he had reached the threshold of unbridled loathing. He was shit drunk.

When he staggered into the Music Lover Bar, he almost knocked over a stool just trying to sit on it. Wan, the bar manager, watched his weaving arrival. "Sawasdee ka," she said politely. "I'm glad you came back. Your friends came here looking for you."

"I don't want to talk about it," he cut her short. "Bring me a beer."

"But...," Wan started.

"I said I don't want to talk about it," he repeated louder, nastier. "Now bring me a beer, or you and your bar can get fucked."

Wan opened her mouth to say something else then clamped it shut. She didn't need any trouble and she didn't want to lose a customer. He was obviously very drunk and in a very bad mood. Wan brought him a beer. He downed it in seconds and ordered another.

As he waited for his next beer, he felt himself swaying on the barstool. The faces of the girls behind the bar were little more than a blur. The whole bar seemed to be tipping sideways. His mouth watered. His unbridled loathing gave way to unbridled nausea.

"I'll be back in a minute," he muttered and stumbled at a fast pace toward the toilet.

~~~

As Randy and Math rode the baht-bus toward Soi 8, Randy said, "I guess you know that Mike really likes you."

"I never thought about it," Math lied.

"Well, I've known Mike for a long time and he likes you a lot." Randy paused for a moment. "How do you feel about him?"

"I guess I like him a little. It's too soon for anything more than that. He's been very nice to me and I think someday I could like him very much."

Randy watched her face as she talked. When she finished, he said, "I think you love him already."

Math neither confirmed nor denied. Instead she blushed and changed the subject. "What's your girlfriend's name?" The baht-bus turned right on Pattaya Klang.

"Her name is Tana," he answered. "She works at the Wunder Bar. Have you ever been there?"

"I've only been to the places in Pattaya where Mike has taken me," she replied. "If I've been there, I don't remember." The baht-bus turned left on Beach Road.

"Well, you've been there now," he said, buzzing the driver. "This is where we get off." He paid the driver and they walked to the Wunder Bar.

Randy roamed around the bar looking for his girlfriend and Math followed. Finally he stopped and pointed. "There she is, with that farang over there." He waved at Tana, but she didn't wave back and she wasn't smiling. Math felt uncomfortable.

"Let's sit here," Randy said. "She'll come over in a minute."

They sat down and ordered drinks. Randy glanced toward Tana. "She looks like she doesn't feel well," he observed. "Either that or she's in a really bad mood. She's probably pissed at me for being late. When she comes over, you be quiet and I'll explain what's going on. Okay?"

Math nodded.

By the time their drinks had arrived, so had Tana. "Where have you been?" she demanded of Randy. She glared at Math.

"My friend Mike..." he started.

"Bullshit," Tana cut him short. "Why are you with that woman?" She pointed at Math.

"What do you mean, why am I with this woman? I am not with this woman. I..."

"Bullshit," she cut him off again. "You think I'm blind? What do you call that?" She pointed at Math, again.

"Math," he pleaded, "Please tell her in Thai what's going on."

Math said nothing. There was a long pause.

"Why don't you tell her what is going on?"

"You told me to be quiet while you explained," Math said, a smug look on her face. "Maybe now you understand how I felt at Peter's Bar."

"Okay," Randy said, remembering Math and the farang at Peter's. "I understand. Now, please tell her what is going on."

Math turned to Tana. "He is telling..." she started and then stopped, staring. "I just realized I know you from somewhere," she said in Thai.

"Me too," Tana said back. "Ever work at the Classroom?"

"I'm not a bar-girl," she answered. "Have you ever been to Phitsanulok?"

"Now I remember," Tana said. "I met you at the bus station in Bangkok."

The two women talked with each other in Thai for several minutes, and Math explained everything. Tana looked over at Randy every once in a while and gave him ugly looks just to keep him wondering what they were talking about. Eventually, they ran out of things to say.

"Everything okay now?" Randy said hopefully, laughing nervously.

Both women looked at him and smiled. Tana threw her arms around Randy. "I love you," she said.

Math looked at her watch. It was after one o'clock in the morning.

"Tana," Math said, "Mike must not be here or we would have seen him by now. I'm going back to his condo and wait. I have to explain everything to him."

Tana nodded, "I understand."

"Randy," Math said, "Thank you for your help. I must leave now. Maybe Mike is at home already."

"I hope so," he said. He pulled a ten baht piece from his pocket. "Here, for taxi fare. When I see Mike, I'll talk to him."

"Thank you," Math said and left.

She arrived at the Music Lover's Bar just as Mike was returning from the toilet.

Mike felt better now that he had vomited his last several beers. His mouth tasted like shit, but he felt a lot better. He reeled his way back to the bar and reclaimed his seat. He washed the nasty taste from his mouth with a swallow of beer. He looked around the bar and then toward the street. That's when he saw her. She was at the curb, staring at him. He turned away quickly and tried to clear his head. If there was going to be some sort of confrontation, he needed to be ready.

He tried to think what he would say if she came over to him, but his mind wouldn't work. His brain felt numb. Maybe he was still drunk. No, maybe he was just on edge. Maybe he just needed something to calm him down. He wished he had a joint – that would do the trick. But he didn't, so he downed his beer in one quick chug instead. When the earth didn't start weaving and rolling, he ordered another.

Math watched him from the street. She shook her head when she saw him chug his beer and order another. The girls had noticed Math and were waving her over to the bar. She ignored them and walked straight to where Mike sat. "We have to talk," she said, very calm, very polite.

For a long moment he didn't say anything or even acknowledge her presence. His mind was replaying the scene from Soi 2. But now, his alcohol-pickled brain was adding its own little twists to the story. What did the farang do while Mike wasn't watching? Probably grabbing her tits or more. His mind showed a picture of the farang squeezing Math's breasts. And what was she grabbing? His mind dutifully played a scene of Math's hand at the man's crotch. "I've got nothing to say to a stupid little whore, cunt, bitch..." Mike rattled out all of the names he had thought of earlier and then some.

Math had heard some of the words before, and knew the rest weren't polite either. From the corner of her eye, she could see the bar girls looking at her and then at Mike and then at each other. As his verbal assault pounded her ears, her mind turned white hot with anger and embarrassment.

"Why are you doing this?" she asked, when he ran out of new things to call her. It was all she could do to keep from screaming the words.

"I just told you why," he said, his words slurred. "Or weren't you listening?"

"I just want to get my clothes and I will leave you alone."

"What clothes?" he sneered.

"The ones I left in your room."

He knew she was lying. She had taken all of her clothes when she left a few days earlier. "Then get them," he shouted.

"They won't let me. You took the room key. Or are you too drunk to remember?"

"I'm not too drunk for anything," he shot back. "It's none of your fucking business anyway. Yeah, I have the key. I would be more than happy to help you get rid of anything you left in my room. The sooner the better. You didn't leave any clothes behind when you went to see that farang... oh, excuse me... I mean when you went to Phitsanulok. Khun kow jai mai? Do you understand?"

"Mai kow jai, I don't understand," Math answered, then added the polite "ka", but her tone was sarcastic.

"I don't care anyway," he said. "Come on, you can have anything you want except my clothes and my computer." He stood up from the bar. "I'll pay you later, okay?"

Wan nodded yes, afraid to say no.

It was a short walk from the bar to the lobby of the condo. Mike led weaving a path only a snake could follow. Math walked behind him, praying to Buddha he would fall and hurt himself. She fought back a strong urge to push him. As they entered the lobby, the night boy stood and stared at them, confused panic etched his face. He called to the guard in the parking lot.

"You can not go up there," the boy said in carefully spoken English.

"Bullshit," Mike said shouted. "It's my room and I'll go up there when I want."

The boy didn't understand any of what Mike said except *bullshit* – an angry farang *bullshit*. The guard arrived and positioned himself between Mike and Math and the elevator. The boy picked up the phone and called his boss.

The manager must have been awake because she was there faster than Mike could think of anything else to say to either the boy or the guard. "What's going on?" she demanded.

"I'm going to my room," Mike grumbled.

"Good boy," the manager responded to Mike, as if a mother to her son. "You go to bed now because that's exactly what I'm going to do." She spoke to the guard and the boy in Thai, then turned and walked away. Mike and Math rode the elevator to his floor.

Inside the room, Mike said, "Okay, get your stuff and get out."

"Why are you being like this?" I've done nothing wrong except want to see you."

Again the mental images of Math and the farang flared through his head. "Because..." Mike tore off into the same verbal assault as he had at the bar.

Math's practiced calm disintegrated. The white-hot anger she had felt earlier exploded. Mike looked away for just a second. When he looked back, it was at Math's fist coming at his face. He didn't have time to duck, think, or react. Her fist caught him square in the mouth.

The blow knocked him backwards against the wall and he almost fell. He felt no pain, but his thoughts scattered as if his drunkenness had suddenly intensified. He pushed himself back upright. His eyes blinked rapidly, trying to refocus. Then he walked toward Math, his face red with anger, blood trailed from the corner of his mouth.

Math was surprised at how she had almost knocked him down. He was coming at her now, but she held her ground. If he got one step closer, she would have to hit him again – harder this time – and then she would run. She balled her hands into tight fists and held them at her sides. He took another step forward.

Just as she started her swing, Mike reached out and grabbed her by both arms. He picked her off the floor, shook her roughly, and threw her on the bed. "You don't ever hit me, you little bitch," he yelled.

He jumped on the bed beside her and pulled his fist back as if to strike her. At the last moment, he checked his swing. Instead, he ripped her clothes away.

Math could feel her heart going into spasms. "Mike, don't," she pleaded. "I'm not feeling well. Please stop this."

"Fuck you," he spat out, "I don't believe anything you say." Without love, passion, or consent, he raped her.

Math didn't respond to his assault. She just lay there, not moving. She was having one of her "heart attacks". There was no pain, only overwhelming tiredness. Her anger was replaced by efforts to catch her breath. Her heart palpitated in asynchronous rhythm. She barely noticed Mike's hips thrusting between her legs. Please, dear Buddha, don't let me die like this, she thought as she slipped into a surrealistic world of semi-consciousness.

Math first became aware that he had finished when she heard water running in the bathroom. Her heartbeat was more regular now and she was breathing easier. She could feel Mike's seed seeping from her body and oozing down the crack of her buttocks. She tried to sit up but couldn't; she was too weak. She lay there embarrassed that she couldn't clean herself. After a minute, she managed to roll to her side and dropped her legs over the edge of the bed. It took all her strength to push herself into a sitting position. She tried to stand but couldn't.

Mike came out of the bathroom. His head had cleared a little from the sex and from the water he had splashed on his face. He had put his clothes back on. Math was sitting on the edge of the bed. "Get dressed and get out," he ordered, his voice cold.

"Why did you do that to me?" she asked, shaken and scared. She folded her arms across her small breasts.

He glared at her. "It's all you deserve after what you did with that... that... that farang!"

"I didn't do anything."

"You're a liar. All Thais are liars."

"Ask your friend Randy," she said, fighting back tears. "He knows everything. He knows the truth."

"Fuck Randy, too," he sneered. "Now get dressed and get out."

"I'm too weak. I..." Math started, but didn't finish her sentence. Instead, she leaned forward and forced herself into a standing position. Immediately her legs buckled and she fell. The marble floor was a bone chilling cold against her bare flesh. Her heart palpitations started again. In a moment, she began to cry.

"If you think that little act of yours will get any sympathy from me, you're wrong. Now get up and get out of here."

Math didn't respond. She sobbed weakly for a minute and then stopped moving.

Mike nudged her thigh with the toe of his shoe, the ultimate insult for a Thai. Math didn't stir. He stood by the bed and watched her, wondered how long she would play sick. After a few minutes, he began to have other thoughts. What if he was wrong? What if she was really sick? What if she hadn't actually gone with that farang? What did Randy know that he didn't know? He was sobering fast. What if she was dying and needed help? Now he was thinking all of the things he hadn't thought of before. What if he had been wrong about everything?

She hadn't moved for minutes. Worry and panic overtook his anger. He knelt on the floor beside her, put his hand on her shoulder and shook gently. "Math?" he said, very soft. "Are you okay?"

She didn't respond. For the briefest moment Mike thought she was still faking. That thought was quickly replaced by another which insisted something was terribly wrong. Carefully, tenderly, he gathered her in his arms and lifted her to the bed. Her body was limp and cold. He put his ear to her chest. He could hear her heart beating, but in an irregular fashion. Her breaths came short and shallow. He folded the blanket double and covered her. Then he lay down beside her, wrapped his arms around her, and held her tight, kept her warm.

"I am so sorry, Math," he whispered. "Please be okay. I really do love you."

When Math awoke, it took her a moment to realize where she was. She was in Mike's room. Everything was gray with the first hint of daylight. Mike was asleep beside her. Her memories of last night were jumbled and fuzzy. She wracked her brain to put all of the pieces together. One by one she remembered all of the names he called her. Quietly, she repeated them to herself. She remembered hitting Mike to shut him up. Only vaguely did she remember him having sex with her, but she didn't remember him finishing. The rest was such a blur that she couldn't tell what was a dream and what was reality. Whatever had happened, she knew it wasn't pleasant. She wanted to leave now.

She slid from under Mike's arm, grabbed her clothes from the floor, and went to the toilet. She made sure the door was shut and locked before she turned on the light and sat down to relieve her over-stretched bladder. When she wiped herself, there was a trace of blood on the tissue. Her period. Thank Buddha she wasn't pregnant.

She caught a glimpse of her left arm as she reached for her blouse. Blue-purple bruises in the shape of fingers wrapped around the upper part of her arm. She looked at her right arm. It was the same. She checked the rest of her body but those seemed to be her only bruises.

She had slipped into her blouse before noticing there were no buttons down the front. Another of her questionable dreams landed on the side of reality. He really had ripped her clothes off. She continued to get dressed, missing buttons and all.

She made plans as she put on her clothes. She would be very

quiet, then she would get her suitcase and her clothes and leave without waking Mike. As drunk as he had been last night, he would probably sleep for a long time. She would put on decent clothes someplace outside.

She was careful to make no sound as she took her clothes from the closet and put them on the floor in the hallway outside. She did it in two trips. She made one last trip for her suitcase. It was on top of the closet. She had been barely tall enough to push it up there and getting it down wouldn't be easy. She stood tiptoe as her fingertips inched the suitcase from the top of the closet. It teetered and fell, eluded her grasp and landed on the floor with a loud thud.

Mike jerked and sat upright in bed. "What's that?" he asked, his voice thick with sleep.

"Never mind," Math whispered, lifting the suitcase from the floor. "Go back to sleep."

"What are you doing?" In the dim light he saw the suitcase in her hand. "Where are you going?"

"I'm leaving, like you want."

"I don't want you to leave. We need to talk."

Mike took the suitcase from her hand and put it back on top of the closet. "Math, I had a dream I did terrible things last night."

"It wasn't a dream."

His face twisted to a look of anguish. "Dear God, I was afraid you would say that. I don't know what I might have done to you, but I'm very sorry if I did anything to hurt you. I was drunk. That's no excuse, but it's the only one I have. When I saw you with that man last night, it killed me. I went crazy with jealousy. I wanted to hurt you as much as I was hurting. I guess that sounds childish, doesn't it?"

She nodded but didn't say anything. Sawat had said almost those same words.

"I know you won't believe this," he continued, after a short silence, "but last night I realized something – I realized I have fallen in love with you. I don't even know why. I think that is why I was so angry. I don't want you to leave, Math. I want you to stay.

Please, can you forgive me?"

She didn't reply. She couldn't. She turned and walked toward the door.

"Please don't leave."

"I'm getting my clothes from the hallway," she said. "You're right. We need to talk."

They sat on the bed and talked until well past dawn. She told her story and Mike listened without interruption. When she was finished, Mike told his story. When Mike quit talking, Math laughed.

"What's so funny?" he asked.

"Your lip is very big."

His lip was puffed out and his constant probing with his tongue made it more noticeable. He could feel impressions of his teeth along the inside edge of his lower lip. "Oh, you think that is funny, huh?" he said. "I'll have you know it hurts very much."

Math laughed harder, feeling better now. She didn't hate Mike. He had said he was sorry and that he loved her. Her anger and bitterness faded and she realized that she loved him too. Somehow, she knew she would love him until the day she died. "Let me kiss it and make it better." She kissed his lips softly. "Is that better?"

"Much." He kissed her just as tenderly in return. "I love you, Math."

"Chan lak khun. Chan lak khun mak. I love you very much, too," she said back.

~~~

The next day at work Randy confirmed everything that Math had said. That evening Mike and Math talked for hours. She told Mike about Sawat agreeing to drop the charges against her, but she did not tell him quite everything. Some things were better left unspoken.

She also told Mike more about her heart problems. Using hand-drawn pictures, she showed him where a blood vessel had grown from the vein entering her heart to an exiting artery. It was maturing and getting bigger every day. It was starving her heart for blood and she already had damage. It was much the same problem she had been operated on for twice before. Without another operation to repair it, the doctors were saying she could expect to live maybe five more years or so. She had insurance but it was only for emergencies and, like before, it wouldn't pay for her surgery. She prayed that someday soon she would win the lottery.

That evening Mike talked about his family in America. He had always had a hard time telling anyone the whole truth about his family and his feelings, but Math was patient and encouraged him at just the right times. When he finally opened up, he told her everything. He talked about his wife and how she had changed after they got married. Also, he talked about how he would divorce her one day. Later he talked about his son's never ending flirtations with drugs and regular brushes with the law. Mike said he loved and hated his family at the same time, but he didn't miss them.

Math hadn't been able to understand Mike's feelings entirely. She knew from her own life that families were not always happy, but she had a hard time accepting the idea that American families could be unhappy, too. Finally she said she understood, even though she didn't. Later, they held each other close and fell asleep without making love.

The days turned into weeks and their life together was good. Mike gave Math the home she had always wanted and she gave him a renewed understanding of togetherness. He went to work every day and could hardly wait until it was time to come home to Math.

During the day Math worked with her brother. He never paid her, but he did let her use his motorcycle. She was always home before Mike. She made sure of that. Some nights they went to a movie or a restaurant. Most nights they stayed at home and talked. Sometimes they made love.

Mike still drank beer, but only in moderation and never got drunk. On the nights he did drink, they didn't go to Toy's Bar or Peter's Place. Instead, they went to the Music Lover Bar just outside the condo. Not once did they argue.

Christmas came and went, but Mike didn't go home to America. He didn't want to. Susan had begged and cried, but Mike was unmoved. He sent cards and presents, but that was all.

Math was thrilled with the gold necklace he bought for her as a Christmas gift. It was New Year's Eve when he first introduced Math to people as his wife. He could tell by the way her eyes lit up that it made her happy. Someday, he promised, he would buy her a ring.

As much as Math tried to tell herself it couldn't be true, she knew she had fallen in love with a farang. She dreamed of the day when she and Mike would be married and have their own family. More than anything else in the world she wanted a happy family and home. Until they could be married, she would be satisfied being his mia noy, his minor wife, his mistress. But in her heart, she was already his true and legal wife.

Chapter 19

It was eight o'clock on a Sunday evening when their lives were turned upside-down. Mike was working on his computer and Math was watching a Thai comedy show on TV. Her cell phone rang and she answered, still laughing from the jokes. In an instant her laughter ended.

Mike watched as Math paced the room. Her voice became weaker with each passing exchange of conversation. Within seconds, she burst into tears and dropped the phone to the floor. He hurried to her side. "What's wrong?" he asked. "What's going on?"

Between sobs she babbled in Thai. It was as if she had forgotten every English word she knew. He couldn't follow what she was saying. Finally, he understood enough words to know that someone in her family had died, but he couldn't understand who. She was inconsolable. After a minute, she pushed him away and ran to the bed. She curled into a tight ball and refused to talk.

Mike sat next to her on the edge of the bed and tried to calm her. He suspected she was in shock, but he wasn't sure what to do. He thought of her brother. Yes, maybe he could help with whatever was happening.

He pulled her into a sitting position and handed her the phone. "Call your brother."

She gazed stupidly at her handy.

"Do it now," he ordered. "Call your brother."

Numbly she took the phone and dialed. When she began talking, she broke into sobs again. Mike wondered how her brother could understand anything she said. In a while she turned off the phone and stared at nothing. A steady stream of tears cascaded down her face.

For the next half hour Mike fidgeted about the condo. He brought her water and tissues. He tried holding her hand and comforting her, but she was non-responsive. She just sat and stared. He was relieved when there was a knock at the door. It was Math's brother Anan, and another man Mike had never seen before. He invited them in.

Math and Anan and the other man talked so fast in Thai that Mike didn't understand anything they said. Every once in a while Anan would look at Mike, but he never once smiled. Mike felt uneasy. He wished his understanding of Thai was better. At least Math had calmed and seemed to be talking coherently.

Finally, Anan turned to Mike and said in English, "My sister's husband and her son have died in a drowning accident. Tomorrow we must go to Phitsanulok. We will take a bus in the morning. It's a very long ride to Phitsanulok, maybe ten hours or more. I will come for Math by seven o'clock. Math wants to stay here for tonight because she feels it is her home. I don't want her to stay with a farang at a time like this, but I can't change her mind."

"And I don't want Math to have to ride on some stupid bus for ten hours *at a time like this*," Mike said curtly at Anan's snide comment about Math staying with a farang. "I will pay for a taxi to Bangkok and airfare to Phitsanulok."

Math looked up in surprise. "Oh Mike, you don't have to do that. It's very expensive." It was the first complete English sentences she had spoken since the phone call.

"I've made up my mind." He turned to Anan. "When you come in the morning, Math will have enough money for both of you to fly to Phitsanulok." He looked at Math, "How much do you think?"

"About 5,000 baht," she answered.

"Nit noy money," he said pointedly. "I'll take care of it. Thank you for coming, Anan. I'm truly sorry about the death in your family. I'm even sorrier your sister is spending the night with a farang." He didn't like the sound of his own words, but he couldn't stop them from coming out. He hoped Math didn't hear his sarcasm. Mike showed Anan and his friend to the door. He was as happy to see them leave as he had been to see them arrive.

Mike helped Math pack her suitcase and then ordered her to bed. He held her close all night. Her sleep was fitful. Every time she awoke, Mike was staring at her. He was still awake and watching when the alarm sounded at five o'clock.

Math spent a very long time in the bathroom that morning. When she finally came out, she told Mike her stomach was upset and she had been vomiting, but she felt better now. Probably nerves, she suggested, and he agreed.

Anan called from the lobby at seven o'clock. He didn't say anything except that it was time to go. Mike escorted Math downstairs. He made sure Anan saw him give Math the 5,000 baht.

Just before they left, Mike slipped another 10,000 baht into Math's hand. "For an emergency or in case you need extra money for anything," he said.

When no one was looking, she kissed him on his lips. "Thank you, teeluk, sweetheart," she whispered. "I promise, I will return to you in quickly time."

Mike wasn't to hear from Math for eight days.

~~~

Math and Anan took a taxi to Bangkok and bought airline tickets from there. They could never have afforded to fly home without Mike's help and they both knew it. Math asked for, and was given, a window seat. She felt guilty for satisfying her own wants at a time like this, but it was her first flight and she was excited. The flight was perfect, the sky cloudless, and the view spectacular.

Math and Anan arrived in Phitsanulok at one o'clock in the afternoon. By one thirty they were at their mother's house. Already, it was full of mourning friends and relatives.

Immediately Math looked for her sister Neet. It was Neet's husband and son who had died. She found Neet and her two-month-old baby in their mother's bedroom. She was crying.

"Oh Neet," Math held her sister close, "I am so sorry. Jabal was a good husband and Sadayu was a beautiful son. It isn't fair that this happened, but you will be okay; I promise I'll take care of you no matter what."

"You have your own life," Neet replied. "You must take care of yourself."

"Never mind," Math said. "When I help you, I will be taking care of myself." She truly felt sorry for her sister. Neet was the only one in the family who hadn't finished school. When Neet had been old enough for high school, there hadn't been enough money to pay her tuition. Instead of school, Neet had gone to work as a common construction laborer. That turned out good, because it was at work where she met Jabal.

Jabal, too, was uneducated, but he was very clever and a hard worker. He had become a supervisor by the age of twenty-two and earned more money than most laborers ever dreamed about. He wasn't rich, but he was able to take care of his new bride. Now that he was gone, Neet wouldn't be able to take care of herself and her new baby unless someone helped.

"Tell me what happened. I know Jabal and Sadayu are good swimmers. I don't understand how this could have happened."

Neet composed herself as best as she could and repeated the story for Math. Two days ago, on Saturday evening, Neet and her family had visited their mother Nui. Little Sadayu had made a comment about how much he liked one of his grandmother's special fish dishes. Nui promised to cook it for dinner, if Sadayu would catch the fish. Yesterday, Sunday morning, Jabal and Sadayu had gone fishing. They didn't go to the river as they usually did. Instead, they went to a pond owned by one of Jabal's bosses. His boss kept the pond stocked with fish and had invited Jabal to fish there whenever he wanted. Jabal figured they would have better luck there than the river, and that the fish would probably taste better too.

But according to a young girl who lived near the pond, the fish weren't biting as good as usual that day. From a distance, she had watched Jabal and Sadayu as they fished. Sadayu had soon bored with holding the pole and catching nothing. Before long he'd stopped fishing and started exploring the banks of the pond. Sadayu was on the other side of the pond from his father when he saw a large fish in the water.

The girl had seen the fish too. It had been swimming near the surface, acting as if it was dying. Sadayu hadn't been able to resist the temptation and jumped into the water determined to catch the fish with his bare hands. The fish moved away just as Sadayu made his grab. He swam after it. He hadn't gone far when it happened. He seemed to be cramping or something. Sadayu screamed to his father for help. Without even thinking, Jabal jumped into the water after his son. Immediately, his muscles spasmed and he was unable to swim. Sadayu saw his father sink into the water and swam toward him to help. But the closer Sadayu came, the more his muscles tightened. Suddenly Sadayu turned and started back toward the shore. He didn't get far before he lost his struggle with the water and drowned. The girl had gone for help, but it was too late.

"There was a power line down in the pond, Math. Jabal's boss had already informed the electric company, but it hadn't been repaired. Jabal didn't know, his boss had never told him."

"Oh Neet," Math said. "What a tragedy. The electric company should be made to pay. It's their fault. They killed your husband and your son. I will make them pay."

Neet laughed grimly and shook her head, "Papa called them this morning. They said it wasn't their fault. They said they were sorry, but they will do nothing."

"The dirty bastards," Math said, using one of Mike's English phrases. "I will make then pay. You just watch me."

Math and Neet walked together into the living room. Her mother and father were standing beside each other talking.

SIAM NIGHTS

Suddenly Math remembered her monkey-man dream. Dear Buddha, so this was who the monster meant. She should have told everyone about her dream. If she had, maybe none of this would have happened. But how was she to know the dream meant anything? There was nothing to do about it now. It was too late to do anything except feel guilty. If she ever had a dream like that again, she would tell everyone she knew.

Later that day, Math and her family went to the temple to begin their mourning. Jabal and Sadayu were in their decorated caskets. Someone had placed the teddy bear Math had bought for Sadayu's last birthday into the casket. Little Sadayu looked like he was asleep holding onto the bear. He can't be dead, she thought.

There was a flash. Someone was taking pictures. Math turned to see who it was but saw no one. Whoever it was had already put the camera out of sight.

She looked back at the caskets. She felt dizzy, light-headed, like she was floating on air. She could hear people talking but couldn't make out their words. She turned to look. Everyone stared, their faces blurred and distorted. She turned back toward the caskets and lost her balance in the motion. She took a staggering step forward to keep herself from falling. The last thing she remembered was blackness closing in and the sense that she was flying. She landed hard on the marble floor of the temple.

Math awoke to a damp cloth wiping her face. She was nauseated, and exhausted. She opened her eyes and saw a monk sitting beside her. It was her old friend Jum, the monk who seemed to always be there whenever she needed someone.

She reached up to take Jum by the hand, then stopped herself. It was not polite to touch a monk, and she never had even though he sometimes touched her. Also, it wasn't polite to talk to a monk, unless they spoke first. She had broken that rule of etiquette many times, but Jum had never seemed to mind. She hadn't seen him for a long time, so today she waited for him to speak.

Jum continued wiping Math's face with the cloth for several

minutes after she had awakened. "Are you feeling better?" he finally asked.

"I'm not sure," she answered. "I feel a little sick and very tired. I guess I'll be okay."

"I saw you fall, Math," he said. "You fell very hard. You should be more careful with yourself. You are a very special person right now, and I don't want you to get hurt."

"I don't feel very special," she said. "I only feel sick and my arm hurts."

Jum didn't respond. Their silence went on for a long while. Finally, Math whispered, "Why did God allow this to happen to my nephew and my brother-in-law? They were too good to die so young."

"Everything happens for a reason," he whispered back. "Their bodies are dead but their spirits live on. I can feel them around us now. Pray for them but do not mourn for them. Someday they will return, and they will have a better life to replace this one that ended so soon. This you must believe, Math."

"I do believe," she said. "I should be with my family now. They must be wondering if I'm okay. They have enough to worry about without having to worry about me."

Jum nodded but said nothing.

Math stood to leave. She felt sick and dizzy but much better than she had earlier. "Thank you for you kindness," she said and presented Jum her most respectful of wai's. As expected, Jum nodded but didn't return her wai. She smiled then turned and walked away.

Jum's voice stopped her as she reached the doorway. "Someday, I have something I must... uh... I mean, if you ever need to talk, you know how to find me. Please take care of yourself." This time Jum presented Math with a wai.

Math was shocked at his gesture. Monks never wai'ed anyone, not even the king. Though she couldn't understand why he had done such a thing, it made her feel good. Indeed it made her feel special. Not knowing what to do, she smiled and wai'ed in return.

The sympathy ceremony was nearly finished by the time Math rejoined her family. She removed her shoes and sat on the floor next to her sisters and her brother. She was careful to not show the bottom of her feet to the nine monks performing the ceremony.

Her gaze wandered around the temple as she listened to the chanting. The flowers, the flickering candles, smoking incense, and the caskets that held the dead bodies of Jabal and little Sadayu, it was all very emotional. She held back a strong urge to cry. It was bad luck to cry at the ceremony. The spirits wouldn't move on as long as loved ones were grieving for them; they cannot swim against a river of tears. It was best to cry later, alone in the privacy of her home.

Math saw Sawat standing to one side as she and her family left the temple for the night. He didn't say anything, but his glare was frightening. She took Anan by the arm and walked close beside him. She didn't look back at Sawat.

Her mother's house was crowded with relatives who had come for the funeral. There weren't enough places for everyone to sleep. Math knew she would have to stay at her own house for the night and the thought made her uneasy. Sawat and his threatening stares lay heavy on her mind.

After the commotion had calmed, Math asked her oldest sister Nuang and her husband to sleep at her house. She was relieved when they agreed. It was after eight o'clock before she, Nuang, and Surat went to her home. Surat fell asleep soon after they arrived.

Math tried to call Mike but her cell phone battery was dead. She opened her suitcase for the charger but it wasn't there. "Damn it," she said, using words she had heard Mike say when he was irritated.

"What's wrong?" Nuang asked.

"My phone battery is dead and I left the charger in Pattaya," she answered.

"Who would you be calling this time of the night anyway?"

"It's a long story. You probably wouldn't believe me, even if I told you."

"Maybe or maybe not," Nuang said softly. "Tell me, and then I'll tell you if I believe you."

They talked late into the night. Math told her older sister everything about Mike. How they met, how they fought, and how they loved. Nuang was totally engrossed.

As Nuang listened to Math talk, she felt a deep sense of envy. She had always been attracted to farang men. She had often wished she had waited to meet one instead of marrying Surat. He was a nice man, but he didn't care much about Nuang's family. Over the years, Nuang and Surat had stopped being husband and wife. They had never had children. They stayed together out of financial need rather than love. In a while, Math stopped talking.

"Sister," Nuang said honestly, "I think you're a very lucky lady."

Math laughed. "If I'm lucky now, it's the first time in my life."

"I want to meet this Mike person someday. If he is to be my brother-in-law, I should meet him."

"Brother-in-law?" Math asked. "Who said I would marry him?"

"Do I look stupid?" Nuang asked, then added, "Never mind, don't answer that." She stared at Math for a moment. "I can tell you're in love with that man by the way your eyes shine when you talk. I think you'll marry him someday. By the way, does he have any brothers or cousins or friends who would like a nice Thai wife?"

Math and Nuang laughed together at her question. Their laughter was interrupted by a knock at the door. Nuang glanced at the door and then at her husband. He didn't move. When she looked back at Math, she saw terror on her face. "What's wrong?" Nuang whispered urgently. "Who is that?"

"It must be Sawat. Please answer the door and tell him to go away. I don't want to see him."

"I thought you and Sawat were finished. Why would he be

here?"

Another knock came - louder this time.

"Please Nuang," Math pleaded softly, "Just answer the door and tell him to go away."

Nuang walked to the door and opened it a crack. It *was* Sawat. He leaned against the door jamb, his face inches from Nuang.

"Who are you?" Sawat asked, surprised it wasn't Math.

Nuang could smell Mekong on his breath. "I am Nuang and I have seen you before," she said. "It's late. What do you want?"

"I want to see Math," Sawat answered. "Tell her to come now or there will be a big problem."

"Math is asleep," Nuang said. "This isn't a good time. There's been a death in our family. You must leave and let us mourn in peace." She started to push the door shut.

Sawat pushed back with the heel of his hand. "You don't seem to understand. Math owes me something and I've come to collect. I want to see her now."

"You're the one who doesn't seem to understand," Nuang hissed back. "There's been a death in our family and you are being rude. My husband is here and he is asleep. If you wake him, then you're correct, there will be a big problem, but it will be your problem, not Math's. Do you understand me?"

Sawat moved his hand away from the door. "Tell Math this isn't finished. Tell her I will be back to collect what belongs to me." He turned and walked away.

Nuang shut and bolted the door. "Would you mind telling me what that was all about?" she demanded of Math.

Math told her everything, leaving nothing to the imagination.

"You're not safe here," Nuang said. "Sawat has been drinking tonight and you know how Thai men can be when they're drunk. He might hurt you. You must get out of Phitsanulok."

"I can't leave until the funeral is over, and I can't leave until I know our sister is okay. I don't think Sawat would hurt me, but he does scare me."

"He scares me too, and I think he would hurt you," Nuang

J. F. Gump

said. "I don't trust him. I'll stay until you leave Phitsanulok."

"No, you can't stay here." Math said. "A wife belongs with her husband. When the funeral is over, you must go home and take care of Surat."

"Surat is no longer my husband. He is just the man I live with. Our love died a long time ago. I'll stay here until everything is settled and you leave Phitsanulok. There'll be no more discussion. Am I clear?"

Math nodded. She felt lucky to have a sister like Nuang.

That night they all slept in the same bed. Surat on one side, Nuang in the middle and Math on the other side. Math didn't like to sleep alone and knowing her sister was beside her made her feel good. She fell asleep quickly.

In the early morning hours, she dreamed of the monkey-man again. "They're not the ones," he laughed. "You are so stupid," he mocked her. "You are so stupid." He danced around her, his sword sliced the air. "It's someone much more important." He laughed again and swung his sword straight at her.

Math jerked awake. She was sweating. Outside, a rooster crowed. The early light of dawn seeped through the window. She shook Nuang lightly.

"What?" Nuang mumbled, still mostly asleep.

She told Nuang about her dream. It was almost the same dream she had dreamt on the bus weeks earlier. She was sure it meant something. Didn't recurring dreams mean they would come true?

"It doesn't mean anything," Nuang said, "except you probably ate too much spicy food. Now go back to sleep. We have a busy day coming."

Math couldn't sleep. She got out of bed and wrote down everything she remembered about her dreams of the monkey-man. She would show it to Mike when she saw him again. He was very smart and maybe he would know what it meant. As she made her notes, she had an eerie feeling that it was Mike who the monkey-man was talking about. The thought sowed seeds of terror in her chest. Before she had time to think about what might happen to

Mike, she was sick. She rushed outside and vomited. She thought she saw blood.

The next few days passed like a blur. The ceremonies, the relatives, the food, the coffins, and everything filled each day from morning to night. Every day, Math tried to call Mike from a pay phone but either he wasn't home or the phone lines to anywhere from Phitsanulok were out of order.

Sawat showed up at the temple every day, but didn't say anything to anyone or make any more threats. He never came back to her house.

Jum, the monk, seemed to be everywhere Math went, but he didn't talk to her. Always, he just stood and stared.

Every morning Math was sick and threw up. She decided she had grown an ulcer from the stress. Nuang insisted Math see a doctor as soon as the funeral was over, and Math promised she would.

Each evening before they went to sleep, Math and Nuang would talk. Nuang talked about her dreams that had never arrived, while Math talked about her future and the dreams she hoped would come true. During those few days, Math and Nuang built a sister-to-sister relationship stronger than they'd ever had before.

Late at night, after the lights were off, Math would think of Mike. She hoped he was safe. Also, she hoped he was alone. She knew he must be wondering what was happening in Phitsanulok. She prayed he wasn't too lonely. She knew he had become accustomed to having female companionship during the time she had lived with him. She also knew that men sometimes decided they needed a woman every night, even if it wasn't someone they loved. He isn't like that, she would think to herself, he doesn't go with bar girls. Those thoughts helped some, except the times when she thought about Lek. She knew Mike had once liked Lek very much. In fact, she often felt like she had stolen him away from Lek. He had always denied it, but she thought it was true. As long as he didn't go near Lek, he would be okay.

Chapter 20

On Saturday, the seventh day after their deaths, Jabal and little Sadayu were cremated. Exhausted, everyone went home and cried.

When Nuang told Surat she was staying with Math for a few days and wouldn't be going back to Chiang Mai with him, a heated argument ensued. Surat shouted and made threats. Nuang screamed back louder. In the end, Surat got into his car and drove home to Chiang Mai alone. Nuang cried, but only a little. She wasn't sure if her tears were from sadness or relief.

Math was happy that Nuang had decided to stay, even though she was sad about the argument.

Together, Math and Nuang took care of Neet's young baby so Neet could get some much needed rest. Math was like an old mother hen. If the baby whimpered, even a little, Math would swoop it up and make cooing noises or feed it until the baby was quiet. Nuang chided Math gently for spoiling the baby, but she didn't interfere.

The next morning, after her daily sickness, Math went to the temple. The monk, Jum, was participating in a ceremony and she had to wait to see him. She passed the time strolling the temple grounds. No one said anything or tried to stop her. The temple was quiet except for faint chanting. For the first time in a week, she felt at peace. She didn't hear Jum when he approached.

"How are you, my daughter?" he said, surprising her.

Math turned and wai'ed respectfully. "I am fine," she answered, then added with an impish grin, "And how is my father?"

The monk allowed himself a small smile. "Your father is fine, too. You wanted to see me?"

"Yes," she said. "I need advice and I don't know who to ask. You have always been very kind to me and I think you're very wise. I hope you can help me know what I must do."

Math explained how Jabal and Sadayu had died. Then she told Jum how the electric company had denied all responsibility for their deaths. She told him about Neet's lack of education and about her two-month-old baby, who now had no father or brother. How could Neet and her baby survive without Jabal? Shouldn't the electric company be forced to help?

Jum listened until she had finished. When he spoke, his words were slow and deliberate. "I have known your family for a very long time, even before you were born. I know your sisters and your brothers. I know your father and your mother. Everything they have done was not always good, but they are not bad people. Of all the children, you are my favorite. We have always been close to each other. I will help you however I can. I already know what happened to your brother-in-law and your nephew. Truly, it is a tragedy. I have given it much thought."

Jum paused for a moment, choosing his words carefully. "My brother is a lawyer and knows many people in the government. I've talked with him about the deaths, and I think he can help. Here is his number." He handed Math a piece of paper. "Call him in the morning. He'll be waiting. There will be no cost for his help."

Math hadn't expected what he was offering. Tears filled her eyes. "Thank you for doing this. How can I ever repay you? I came for advice, but you have given me hope. I am no one, yet you help me like I am somebody. I don't understand why you are doing this."

A sadness pulled at the monk's face. "Because you are special, Math. More special than you know." His voice choked and he stopped speaking for a moment. He took a deep breath and then stood. "I have things I must do for the temple today. You must leave now." He turned and walked away. When he reached the doorway, he stopped and turned back to Math. "I will be leaving this temple soon. I wanted you to know that."

"Why would you leave here?" she asked, wiping at her eyes. "This is your home. You have lived here as long as I can remember."

Jum sighed. "There are many reasons, but mostly because I haven't been a very good monk. I've let personal wants and desires enter my mind."

"What do you mean? You're the kindest person I know. How can you say you're not a good monk?"

"I've allowed myself to love you as my daughter," he said, barely above a whisper. "I swore to Buddha I would never do that. I've asked to be transferred to another temple. Someday you will understand." He motioned as if he had something more to say, but no words came. Abruptly, he turned and hurried away.

Math stared as he disappeared into the temple. She tried to make sense of what had just happened. Why should his feelings for her make him want to leave his home? Suddenly she felt very sad. Maybe it was from being in the temple again so soon after the funeral, or maybe it was because Jum had seemed so sad. She wasn't sure which it was, if either. Maybe it was neither. Maybe it was because she would miss her friend. She sat in the temple for a while, saying prayers and giving thanks to God and Buddha. Later she shoved Jum's note into her purse and went home.

Math spent the rest of the day wondering at what Jum had said. None of it made any sense. Still, she had the piece of paper with the phone number. She would call in the morning.

That evening, Math and Nuang had dinner with their mother. When Math mentioned the monk and what he had said, her mother excused herself and left the room.

"What's that all about?" Math asked, looking at Nuang.

"I'm not sure," Nuang shrugged. "Maybe she doesn't like your monk friend. She seemed to be fine until you mentioned him."

"Maybe," Math replied, "But I can't imagine anyone not liking Jum."

Again, Nuang shrugged.

Early on Monday morning Math called the number Jum had given her and asked for Isara, the name on the paper. A man came on the phone.

"Sawasdee ka," she said very politely. "I am Tippawan Bongkot, Math. My friend Jum said I should call you. He said maybe you can help me."

"I am Isara," the man responded. "I've been expecting your call. Can you be at my office by nine o'clock?"

"I think so," she answered.

"Good. I have some calls to make before you arrive." He hung up the phone without saying goodbye.

Math dressed as quickly as she could and was at the lawyer's office by nine o'clock. Suddenly everything was happening with lightning speed. By nine thirty they were in Isara's personal car driving across town. By ten o'clock Math was in a meeting with top executives and lawyers from the electric company. By noon, the electric company agreed they were marginally culpable for what had happened to Jabal and Sadayu. By one o'clock they had agreed to compensate Neet and her new son 500,000 baht for the deaths of Jabal and Sadayu. Math told Isara it was too little, but he suggested it was the best they could hope for without risking everything. By three o'clock she was home and had told Neet and Nuang what had happened. Neet was very thankful. She hadn't expected anything from the electric company. For her it was like a gift from God.

That night Math and Nuang talked about what they would do now. Neet could take care of herself with the money from the electric company, and there wasn't much more either of them could do. Nuang said she would go back to Surat in Chiang Mai. Math said she would return to Pattaya and live with Mike. Nuang agreed that was a good idea.

"When was the last time you talked to Mike?" Nuang asked. She knew of Math's failed attempts to contact him.

"The day I left Pattaya," she replied.

J. F. Gump

"That's been over a week ago," Nuang said. "He must be very worried about you. Or maybe he thinks you're never coming back."

"I told him I would be back," she retorted, but Nuang's words made her uneasy.

"Without calling?" Nuang questioned, high pitched. She shook her head. "You have so much to learn about men."

"Like you're an expert," Math shot back, harsher than she intended.

Nuang ignored her barb. "If you want to keep that man, you should go back to Pattaya tomorrow. I suggest you find the nearest pay phone and keep calling until you reach him, even if it takes you all night." She pulled a handful of change from her purse and threw it on the bed. "Just in case you don't have enough money."

Math looked at the money disdainfully. "I have enough of my own, thank you."

"Then what are you waiting on?" Nuang raised her voice, "Some other lady to steal him away? Now get out of here before you make me really angry with your stupidity."

Math grabbed her purse and stomped out of the house. Nuang was right and Math knew it, but she didn't like anyone pointing out her mistakes.

Her motorcycle was at her mother's house, so she had to walk. Except for an occasional street light, it was dark on the streets of Phitsanulok. Math paused beneath a street light to check the time. It was nine-thirty. She felt unsafe, but no one bothered her as she walked to the nearest pay phone.

The light in the phone booth was broken, but the dim street lamp gave enough light for her to dial the number. Over and over, for the next hour, she got a busy circuit signal. Between attempts at calling, she watched the traffic moving along the street. She was about to give up when Mike's phone rang.

"Hello," he said.

"I am Math," she said into the phone.

"My god, Math. Where in the hell have you been?" Mike sounded half asleep. "I've been worried sick about you. Are you

158

okay?"

"I'm okay," she whispered, breathless from hearing Mike's voice. "The funeral is over. I'm coming home to you in quickly time."

"Math, listen" Mike said. "There's something I must tell you. I have bad news. We must talk when you come home. I tried to call but your phone didn't work. Can you be here tomorrow?"

"What's wrong?" Her voice raised several octaves.

"Tomorrow, Math," was his response. "Promise me you'll be here tomorrow."

"I will be there tomorrow, teeluk," she fought growing panic.

"I'll be waiting. Call me when you arrive at the bus station."

"Call you at work?" she asked.

"No," Mike said. "Call me at my condo. I'm not working tomorrow. I'll explain later."

"Okay," was all she could think to say.

"Thank you, Math. I love you." He hung up the phone without waiting for a reply.

"I love you too, Mike," she whispered into the dead phone.

Her mind whirled as she hurried back toward her house. What was Mike talking about? Something was wrong and it was driving her crazy that he didn't tell her what it was. Her heart started doing its palpitations. Please not now, she thought. Suddenly, she was sick again. She stopped long enough to vomit at the edge of the sidewalk, and then she hurried on.

She passed a drug store that was still open. She had promised her sister she would ask about her sickness. A druggist was not the same as a doctor but it was as close as she would find at this time of night. She explained her symptoms to the man on duty. She told him about the death in her family and the stress she had been under. She suggested she needed something for an ulcer.

"Are you pregnant?" he asked.

Math was flustered. "I don't think so," she said. "Why would you ask that? I had my last menses on time." She didn't mention that during her last period she did little more than spot.

"Well, it happens sometimes," the druggist said. "I'm going to give you two things. One is a medicine for your stomach and the other is a self pregnancy test."

"I'm not pregnant," she retorted, offended.

"Try it anyway," the druggist said firmly. "It will give you one less thing to worry about."

"Okay," she conceded. She paid for the medicines and left. "Asshole." she said under her breath, using another of Mike's favorite words. "What does he know?"

Five minutes later Math was at her house. As she approached, she could see that something wasn't right. The door wasn't completely shut. Dread clutched at her chest. Nuang wouldn't leave the door open like that. A sour rush of adrenaline exploded Math's dread into cold panic. She ran to her house and flung open the door. Nuang was lying on the bed. Her blouse was ripped open. She made no sound.

"Oh my God," Math whimpered as she moved closer to Nuang. "Oh my God. What happened? Are you okay?" She pulled the hair away from Nuang's face – it was a bloody mess. Math looked around wild-eyed, looking for an attacker, but no one was there. She grabbed a towel and ran to the public toilet. She soaked it with water and ran back to her house. Gently she wiped Nuang's face. She cried as the blood came away and the true horror of Nuang's cuts and bruises appeared. Swelling had already begun. By tomorrow, Nuang wouldn't be recognizable. "I'm calling an ambulance," Math said. "And I'm calling the police too."

"No, please don't," Nuang cried. "If I look like I feel, I don't want anyone to see me. I will be okay."

"Oh, Nuang," Math said. "This is terrible. Please tell me what happened. Who did this to you?" Math was sure she knew already, but she wanted confirmation.

"It was Sawat," Nuang answered. "When he knocked at the door, I thought it was you coming back. I opened the door without thinking. He shoved his way inside. He was drunk. He started calling you names and saying bad things about you. I got very angry and hit him. He hit me back harder. He hit me many times, Math. I don't remember how many times. I must have passed out because I don't remember anything else." Nuang ran her tongue across her swollen lips and touched her face with her hands. "How bad do I look, Math?"

"Not too bad, sister," she lied. "You look as beautiful as ever."

"I don't believe you," Nuang said.

"Did he rape you?"

"No, I don't think so," Nuang whispered. "I don't know." Her tears started again. "I don't remember."

"I will kill that son-of-a-bitch for hurting you," she said matter-of-factly.

"Math, he'll be coming back for you. You must get away from here. Promise me you will go away now, tonight."

"Not without you," she said. "We will both go away. I know a place where we'll be safe. Come, let's pack our clothes." She took another look at Nuang. "Never mind. I'll pack for both of us."

Within five minutes Math had everything ready. Nuang had put on clean clothes and dabbed a heavy coat of make-up on her face.

"I'm ready," Nuang said.

"The next time I shoot Sawat, I will kill him." Math promised.

Together, they left the house. They walked to the main road and caught a taxi. Math directed the driver to the temple.

"Why are we going to the temple?" Nuang asked.

"I lied to you before," she answered. "Your face looks very bad. I hope nothing is broken. I'm taking you to my friend Jum at the temple. They have a safe house there for women. You'll have your own room and everything. They will take care of you until you're better. I don't think your husband should see you like this. In a couple of days you can go home."

"This doesn't seem right," Nuang protested, touching her face tenderly.

"It is best, Nuang. Please trust me." Math opened her purse,

"Mike gave me some extra money in case of an emergency. I think this is an emergency." She counted out 3,000 baht. "Here's enough to buy you a plane ticket to Chiang Mai."

"What about you?" Nuang asked.

"Don't worry about me. I have enough for myself."

Everyone at the temple was asleep except for one lone monk. After some coaxing, Math convinced him to get Jum. When Jum arrived, he didn't look well. He agreed that Nuang should stay at the temple, just to be safe. Math gave Nuang a hug and left.

The taxi dropped Math off at the airport. She bought a ticket for the next flight to Bangkok. Then she sat and waited.

Chapter 21

Mike's mood had been crap since the day Math went to Phitsanulok for the funeral. He had become accustomed to Math meeting him at the door when he came home. He missed her smiling face and their conversations, as broken as they sometimes were. He missed having someone he could love. Mostly, he missed having someone who loved him.

Mike wasn't worried when Math didn't call to let him know she'd arrived. After two days without a call, he started to worry, but only a little. After all, there had been deaths in her family, and he wasn't important compared to that. By the time four days had come and gone he was worried shitless and totally depressed. He stayed home every night waiting for the phone to ring.

When Randy had found out that Math had gone home for the funeral, he had started pestering Mike to go have a beer with him and his new girlfriend from Soi 2. Not the same girlfriend he had a few weeks earlier but a new lady, the third one since the girl at Soi 8. Mike was having trouble keeping up with Randy's love life. He had been declining Randy's offers to go out, but he knew he had to get out of the condo and stop thinking about Math or he would go crazy. He finally decided he'd go the next time Randy asked.

Mike was getting dressed for dinner when the phone rang. It was the first time his phone had rang since Math had left. His heart skipped a beat. Maybe it was her. He nearly fell in his hurry to answer the phone. "Hello, Math?" he said excitedly.

"Hey, Mike. It's me." It was Randy.

His excitement fell flat. "What's up, Randy?"

"I forgot to tell you. One of the girls at Toy's Bar is having a birthday party. A bunch of us kicked in a few baht to help her out. There's gonna be lots of free food. You should come down. It'll be a good chance to meet my new girlfriend."

Mike sighed. "The Toy Bar, huh? I'm not sure I want to go to Toy's bar. I'm about as popular there as airborne AIDS."

"Oh, come on," Randy persisted. "Get your head out of your ass. It stinks there and it's so dark you can't see anything very well. You need to get out and quit your brooding. If you're worried about Lek, you can forget that. She's been asking about you every night. She said she feels bad about everything that's happened. She told me she'd buy you a couple of beers next time you come in. I'll even buy you a couple myself. What do you say?"

"Typical Lek," Mike answered. "She thinks the way to a man's heart is through a beer bottle."

"You mean it's not?" Randy asked, sounding surprised. "Damn, I always thought it was. So, are you coming or not?"

"Oh, what the hell," Mike answered. "Yeah, I'll be there."

Mike left the condo but didn't go directly to Soi 2. Instead he stopped at the Music Lover Bar. It was the first time he'd been there since Math had left. The girls asked him a million questions about Math. They had all gotten to know her and wondered where she had gone and when she would return, or if she was coming back at all. Had she called? Had she taken all of her clothes and things? He suffered their prying through two beers and then left for Soi 2.

Most of the night was great. Randy and the others were there, the food was good, and Mike got more than a few free beers. Lek spent a most of the evening smiling at Mike but she never came close.

He was pretty well buzzed by the time Lek finally came and sat beside him. She was very nice, very polite as they went through the 'How have you been?', 'You look well', 'I missed seeing you', and the other polite things people say when there's nothing else to say. In a while they ran out of idle things to talk about.

After a short silence, Lek said, "Where is your new girlfriend?

She's a very beautiful lady. I forget her name."

"Math," he answered. "Her name is Math. She had to go home for a family funeral."

"I'm sorry to hear there was a death in her family. Is she coming back soon?"

"I think so, but I don't know for sure. I don't know how long these things go on in Thailand. In America I would expect her to be gone for four or five days. But here I don't know."

"It's never the same," Lek said. "Sometimes in one or two days the body is burned. Sometimes it's ten days or a month. It depends on the family. The King's mother wasn't burned for a year after she died. Next time your girlfriend calls, ask how long she'll be gone."

"She hasn't called yet," he mumbled, barely audible over the music.

"Oh," Lek paused, letting his words register. "Well, I'm sure you'll hear from her soon. Or maybe she will just come back and not call. Sometimes Thai people do things different from farangs."

"I'm starting to feel not so sure about everything."

"You never know what Thai people are thinking. I am a Thai and I don't know what I think myself most of the time." Lek laughed at her own humor then continued. "She might decide she must stay to help the family. Family is very important to Thai ladies. If it comes to a choice between love and family, the family will come first."

"Do you think that's what's happening?" Mike asked.

"I don't know," she said sympathetically. Then she leaned over and whispered erotically in his ear, "Don't worry, darling, if she doesn't come back, you still have me." With that she stood and added, "I must go say hello to my customers. I'll be right back." She ordered him another beer and left.

Mike went to the toilet. By the time he returned, Lek was already in the seat next to his. "That was fast."

"I told you I'd be right back," she smiled. "By the way, let me know when you're ready to go home and I'll give you a ride."

"You don't have to do that, but it's nice of you to offer."

"Never mind. I have to go buy some things for the bar anyway."

"Well, okay," he said. "I guess I'm ready to go now."

Randy gave Mike a thumbs-up sign as he and Lek left the bar together. Mike frowned and shook his head in response.

As they neared the condo, Lek said, "Mike, I'm embarrassed to ask you this, but could I use your toilet?"

He didn't know what he could say without seeming impolite, so he told her it was okay.

The guard and Jahl gave Mike a questioning stare when they saw him with Lek. They had never seen Mike with anyone but Math. In the past, Lek had been to the condo on a few occasions, but it was always on a Saturday night and it was always very late. By that hour Jahl and the guard were off-duty. Mike felt a need to explain, but didn't.

Once in his room, Lek excused herself and went into the bathroom. Mike turned on the TV and flipped through the channels deciding which bad station to watch. He finally settled for MTV. Lek was in the bathroom for a long time. "Are you okay?" he finally shouted toward door.

"Yes, darling," came her answer.

A couple of minutes later the bathroom door opened and Lek stepped out. Her work clothes had been replaced by a very revealing nightgown.

"What are you doing?"

She didn't answer. Instead she sauntered over to Mike and kissed him on the mouth. "I miss being with you," she said. "Truly I do." She kissed him again and let her hand slide down his stomach and beyond.

He felt himself reacting to her touch. He could literally feel the hormones racing through his body. If she didn't stop soon, he wouldn't be able to stop himself. He wasn't sure he wanted her to stop. Of all the times Lek had gone home with him, they had never had sex. He had wanted her very badly before, but his body had never cooperated. "We shouldn't be doing this," he said huskily. His heart pounded.

"I think we should," she whispered urgently, "I have wanted to make love with you for so long." She touched him lightly through his jeans. "I think you want to make love too. We shouldn't waste this chance."

He let her seduce him. For the first time ever, Mike and Lek made love.

Later, after Lek had returned to work, Mike sat at his desk thinking. He held a picture of Math in his hand. Why hadn't she called? If she had been calling every day, he wouldn't have gone to Soi 2 tonight and none of this would have happened. Lek wouldn't have come here, they wouldn't have had sex, and he wouldn't be sitting here feeling pissed at everyone. It was all her fault. He fell asleep in the chair staring at the picture and waiting for the phone to ring. It never did.

At work on Monday morning, Mike and the others from his company received a fax from their home office. It was short and blunt. "Come back as soon as possible. Take what time you need to pack and ship your personal belongings, but get it done in the next few days. Don't bother going to work tomorrow and don't plan on going back to Thailand."

Everyone was in shock. They had no idea what was going on? Mike called their boss at home in America. The problem turned out to be a matter of pure business. The Thai company they were working for was very overdue on payments and Mike's company was cutting its losses. They would leave Thailand for now and come back only if the payments were caught up.

Without informing the Thai company's management, Mike and the others stopped everything they were working on and packed their personal belongings and the company-sensitive files. At noon they told their driver they were taking off early for the day. They loaded everything into the van and left work with no intentions of going back.

On the way to Pattaya they agreed to meet later at the Tahitian Queen to discuss their plans. By two o'clock they had all arrived, and they were a solemn bunch. The beers slid down easier and faster than usual. Their conversations were as sullen as their tones were depressing.

"I'm not ready to go home," Randy announced after his fifth beer. "I just found a new girlfriend and I'm really in love with this one."

A chorus of *me too's* echoed above the music.

Mike felt obligated to respond because of his tenure and his position. "It's fucked up, that's for sure. But what are any of you going to do? If the company decides to send us home, then we go home. It's that simple. I don't think any of us have the money to stay in Thailand forever, no matter how much we like it. Our jobs may not be finished here, but I think we are. As for me, I'm going to have one more beer and then go back to my condo. I'm really tired."

The others looked at Mike and then at the girls on stage. At last they all nodded their heads in agreement. Mike was right. None of them could survive here without a job. If they didn't go home as they were told, their paychecks would eventually stop. They had no choice.

"On a brighter note," Mike added, "I think it will probably take us at least two weeks to pack our things and get out of Thailand. I'll call our boss and tell him that. I'll tell him it's my decision. If they want to give anyone shit, they can give it to me. I know two weeks isn't very long, but it's enough time to say goodbye to your friends." Mike thought for the briefest of moments about the absence of calls from Math, and then continued. "I really don't have that much stuff to pack or any real reason to stay here. I'll leave this weekend. When I get home, I'll make sure our boss understands you guys are right behind me. No more than two weeks. Is that okay with everyone?"

They all nodded.

"Thank you," he said. "I really am not feeling well. I think I'll just go home, pack my things, and go to bed." He turned to Randy and added, "I assume you will be going to Soi 2 later. Tell Lek I won't be coming by tonight, and that she shouldn't come to my condo either. I have a lot of thinking to do."

Randy nodded his understanding.

Mike paid for everyone's drinks and left the bar.

He went straight back to the condo but he didn't go directly to his room. The sun had slipped over the horizon but it wasn't yet dark. The Music Lover Bar in front of his condo was open but there were no customers. The two girls tending bar were absorbed in a Thai soap opera on the TV. He walked past them and went to the bar in the lobby. He ordered a beer and then glanced at his watch. It was almost seven o'clock. That meant it was seven in the morning in Pennsylvania. The office wouldn't open for another hour.

He passed the time sipping his beer and rehearsing what he would tell his boss. It would be the truth mixed with a dose of exaggeration about how long it would take for everyone to pack and leave. Two beers and an hour later, Mike went to his room and called his boss in Pittsburgh. He was surprised that he received no flak about anything.

With that out of the way, he called a local travel agency. By nine o'clock he had airline reservations for Saturday morning, just four days away. By nine-thirty he had packed everything except what he would need until his flight. With nothing left to do, he sat at his desk and read. By ten o'clock he was asleep.

A ringing woke Mike at ten thirty. It took a moment for him to realize it was the phone. He picked up the receiver on the fourth ring. "Hello," he said.

"I am Math."

"Math," he said struggling to come awake, "Where in the hell have you been? I've been worried sick about you. Are you okay?"

"I am okay," he heard her whisper. "The funeral is over. I'm coming home to you in quickly time." Even in his sleepiness, he almost laughed at her English.

"Math, listen." he said, still groggy. "There's something I must tell you. I have some bad news. We must talk when you come home. I wanted to call you, but your phone didn't work. Can you be here tomorrow?"

"What's wrong?" her voice raised several octaves.

"Tomorrow, Math," he responded. "Promise me you'll be here tomorrow."

"I'll be there tomorrow, teeluk," she said.

"I'll be waiting for you. I'll explain everything then. Call me when you arrive at the bus station."

"Call you at work?" she asked.

"No. Call me at my condo. I'm not working tomorrow."

"Okay," she said.

"Thank you, Math. I love you." There was a soft knock at his door. He hung up the phone without waiting for Math to reply.

He started toward the door and then stopped. He knew it was Lek and he wasn't in the mood to deal with her. She continued to knock for another few minutes before slipping a note under the door. When was sure she was gone, he picked up the note and read, "Please come see me at my bar before you leave. I want to tell you goodbye."

He lay in bed thinking of everything that had happened since he arrived in Thailand, and what was happening now. He fell asleep wondering what tomorrow would bring.

Mike awoke at his regular time for a work day. He had read the paper and was halfway through the puzzles before he remembered he didn't have to go to work. By the time he finished his shower, a small bud of uneasiness had blossomed into full pitch alarm. He had ignored Lek last night, but he wasn't convinced she wouldn't just show up again tonight or even this afternoon. Math had said she would be here today but didn't mention a time. Probably, she didn't know herself. He was leaving Thailand in less than three days. His mind raced.

By eight o'clock, he had made up his mind – he would leave Pattaya today, as soon as Math arrived. He would take her with him and go to Bangkok.

Mike found an ad in the Pattaya Mail newspaper and called Min Travel. He made reservations at the Novotel Lotus for two nights and for one night at the Amari Airport Hotel. He packed the rest of his things and talked to Jem, the condo manager. She would hold his room for two or three weeks. If he didn't come back by then, she could make no promises.

At ten o'clock, Mike went to the bank and got a lot of extra money on his Visa card. He paid his condo bills, then he sat in his room and waited for Math.

~~~

Math's flight left Phitsanulok that same morning at eight forty-five. She hadn't slept all night. She was worried about her sister's health and she was consumed with Mike's words, "I have some bad news." It was driving her crazy. What could he be talking about? Maybe he was going to tell her he didn't love her and that she would have to go away.

She tried to sleep on the plane, but the monkey-man dreams kept entering her thoughts. Maybe Mike was sick and dying or something. The idea terrified her. She was exhausted, but thoughts of the monkey-man kept her awake.

She collected her suitcase from baggage claim at ten thirty. She had enough money left so she hired a taxi to drive her straight to Pattaya instead of taking the bus. She didn't want to waste a single minute. As she rode, she prayed everything was okay with Mike.

She arrived in Pattaya at two o'clock in the afternoon. Mike had asked her to call when she arrived, but she didn't. Instead, she had the taxi take her directly to his condo. No one was at the front desk when she arrived. The manager was in her office and didn't notice Math as she walked to the elevator.

She rode to Mike's floor and knocked on his door. When he opened it, she rushed inside and pulled him close to her. "I missed you so much. Please, just hold me for a minute." And he did.

After a moment, she loosened her hug, stepped away, and stared at him, hands on hips. "So, what's this terrible problem you told me about?"

"I'm so happy you're here," Mike smiled. "I missed you very much, too."

"You didn't answer my question," she said. Seconds passed.

His smile faded. "I'm going home in three days."

Math felt like she had been hit with a sledgehammer. Her knees weakened, and she sank to a kneeling position and cried. Mike sat on the floor beside her and they cried together.

When no more tears would come, they lay on the bed and talked. Math told Mike all about how Jabal and Sadayu had died. She told him about the funeral and the monk. Finally, she told him about Sawat, and what had happened to Nuang. Then she didn't talk for a long time, but she wouldn't let Mike talk either. Every time he started to speak, she would press her fingers to his lips. At last, after many minutes of silence had passed, she told Mike about her agreement with Sawat and why he had decided not to press charges against her. Then she told what Sawat had done to her. Lastly, she explained why Sawat had beat Nuang. When she finished talking, she asked, "Do you hate me?"

"No, I could never hate you, Math."

"Can you forgive me?"

Mike thought of what he had done with Lek while Math was at the funeral. "There's nothing to forgive," he said. His eyes avoided hers. "You've done nothing wrong compared to what I have done."

"I don't understand what you mean," she said. "Can you say it again?"

"I have betrayed you," he answered. "I made love with another woman while you were gone."

He waited for her response, but she said nothing. After a

moment he told her about Lek. He told her everything down to the smallest detail. When he finished speaking, he looked at her and asked, "Can you forgive me?"

She answered very slowly, as if reciting something she had read or heard before. "There can be no love without forgiveness. For if there is love without forgiveness, then it is not a true love." She turned and kissed him ever so gently on the lips. "Yes, I can forgive you, because I love you truly."

Mike thought he had no more tears left in him, but he was wrong. He held onto Math and cried at her forgiveness. Later, he called for a taxi.

The ride to Bangkok and the two days that followed were quietly somber. They talked a lot but said very little. They didn't speak of his leaving, or if he would ever return. Math told him about her monkey-man dreams and he laughed at her. The dreams, he said, meant nothing.

Math tried the home pregnancy test and the results were positive. But the directions said there could be false indications and that two positive tests were required to be 100% sure. She wasn't worried. She would try again in a couple of days. They made love only twice, but it was enough. Saturday morning came with surprising swiftness.

At the airport Mike promised to call her when he got home. He made her promise she wouldn't go to Phitsanulok. Math agreed and said she would go to her sister's house in Chiang Mai. Also, she promised she wouldn't cry when he left. Mike waited until the last possible moment before stepping through the doorway into Immigration Control.

Once he was out of sight, Math was overcome by a feeling of complete emptiness. She sat on a bench in the airport and cried until she was physically sick. When she stopped vomiting, she went to the domestic terminal and bought a ticket to Chiang Mai.

Thirty minutes after exiting Immigration Control, Mike was

airborne and headed east across Cambodia and Vietnam. The plane was packed and the cabin air was bone-dry. Mike supposed it was the airlines way of keeping body odors to a minimum

Flying coach was not his first choice but all of the business class seats were already booked. Luckily, he managed to get an aisle seat. He passed the time thinking about his life.

He had been working in Thailand for nearly three years. His company had been contracted to expand an oil refinery. It was a cake job and everything had been going as planned. Now, it was all falling apart. The Thai company had over-extended itself and ready cash had become a problem. It would probably work out, but only after the banks and investors had extracted their pound of flesh from the developers.

His thoughts drifted to Math. How long had he known her? Five months? Six? He counted forward from the day he'd. It had been grand opening day for a new restaurant in Pattaya. Mike had treated Lek, Toy, and Toy's boyfriend, Eduardo, to dinner that night. He had still been vying for Lek's attention then. He had met Math that night by accident. He could hardly believe it was less than four months. He felt like he had known her all his life. It all seemed like a dream. The most improbable thing was that he had fallen in love with her. On the other hand, maybe he hadn't. Maybe he was just lonely as she had once said. Or maybe he was only caught up in a fragile time of his life. Then again, maybe he really did love her. He couldn't decide. Math and his feelings were enigmas he couldn't explain. He fell asleep and dreamed of Math.

Chapter 22

While waiting for her own flight, Math watched the outgoing planes wondering which one was Mike's. She watched and wondered until it was time for her to board.

Her flight to Chiang Mai was only the third airplane ride of her life and it wasn't a good one. They flew through a violent storm. As big as the plane was, it still jumped and bucked like a wild water buffalo. She was grateful the airlines had been thoughtful enough to put air sickness bags in the seat pouch with the magazines.

She was still queasy when she stepped off the plane in Chiang Mai. Instead of collecting her suitcase at the baggage pickup, she went directly to the women's toilet, washed her face with cold water, and then sat in a stall until she felt better. When she went to the baggage carousel, her suitcase was nowhere to be found. Probably an employee had picked it up, thinking it wasn't going to be claimed. Or maybe it had been stolen. She tried to push that thought aside but couldn't. She went to the airline counter.

"Kaw thort ka, excuse me." Math said calmly, not wanting the lady behind the counter to know how worried she was.

"Sawasdee ka, good morning," the woman replied, just as polite. "May I help you?"

"I've lost my luggage," Math replied. "I was late getting to the baggage claim. When I arrived, my suitcase wasn't there. I'm afraid it's been lost."

The lady smiled comfortingly. "I'm sure it was picked up by one of the attendants as forgotten baggage, or it was put on the wrong flight by mistake. We can check in the separated baggage area. If it's not there, it will probably show up later today or tomorrow."

The lady led the way and Math followed. The lost baggage room was filled with an incredible mixture of boxes, bags, and suitcases. Math searched through them all. Her suitcase wasn't there.

Now she panicked. Almost everything she owned was in that suitcase. Her clothes, her shoes, her make-up, her stomach medication, and the charger for her handy. More than just the things she needed for Chiang Mai; it was everything she needed for anywhere. On the verge of tears she explained how badly she needed her bag.

The woman was sympathetic and promised she would do everything possible. She asked Math for a number where she could be reached when they located her suitcase. Math started to give the lady the number for her handy then realized that without the charger, the cell phone could be dead by tomorrow. She said she had no phone number and asked if she could call the airlines instead. The woman gave her a business card and said to call later. Outside the terminal she took a taxi to her sister's house.

No one was home when Math arrived. She asked some of the neighbors if they had seen Nuang. One woman had seen Surat as recent as yesterday, but no one had seen her sister for several days. Math was worried. Nuang might be in the hospital for all she knew. But there was no way for her to know for sure. The monkey-man dream entered her mind. She pushed it away and prayed her sister was okay.

Math stood in front of Nuang's house, fretting over what to do next. She could wait for Surat to come home, but she didn't feel comfortable staying at his house with him if Nuang wasn't there. She trusted Surat and wasn't afraid anything would happen, but she was sure the neighbors would talk. Gossiping was the one thing Thai people liked to do more than eat. Nuang would be embarrassed if Math stayed in their house alone with her husband.

She decided to get a hotel room for the night and worry about what to do later. Maybe Nuang would be home tomorrow, and maybe her suitcase would show up and she'd have clean clothes to wear. She flagged down a motorcycle-taxi and asked the driver to take her to the nearest and cheapest hotel. Mike had given her money before leaving, so paying for the hotel wouldn't be a problem. Still, she didn't want to waste it. If Mike never came back to Thailand, the money would have to last her until she found a job. Mike had given her as much as she could make in two months, but it would disappear quickly if she wasn't careful.

The hotel turned out to be a dump, but it was cheap and within walking distance of Nuang's house. The hotel clerk made her pay in advance for the night. The room was hot and it had no air conditioning. There was a TV but it only had sound and no picture. There was no telephone. She supposed it was better than sleeping in an airport or a bus terminal, but not by much. She took a quick shower and then put the same clothes back on. She hadn't eaten since early in the morning and she was hungry. She decided to go out for dinner. Maybe the room would be cooler by the time she returned. She checked her cell phone, the battery was still charged. She clipped it back onto her waistband and left the hotel.

Math found a street-side restaurant and ordered a Thai noodle soup with chicken. She spiced it up with sugar, mild fish sauce, and a generous helping of ground, red-hot peppers. When Mike had heard about her ulcers, he had made her stop eating spicy foods. She knew the hot peppers wouldn't be good for her ulcers, but Mike wasn't here to make her feel guilty. After she had finished eating, she waited for the meal to do something nasty to her stomach but nothing happened. Maybe Mike was wrong about the hot peppers.

Math called the airlines from her handy, but her suitcase hadn't been found. The man who answered the phone said it was early and that she should try again later.

It was still daylight and Math knew the room couldn't have cooled down much. She decided to walk to the shopping center located not far away. That would help pass the time and it would be cooler there than on the street or in the hotel. She browsed through the store but didn't buy anything. By the time she looked at her watch again, two hours had passed.

Outside, darkness had fallen. Math started back toward the hotel. The street was mostly deserted, and she didn't feel safe. A Thai lady walking alone at night wasn't a good idea, especially in a strange city. As much as she hated to spend the money, she flagged down a regular taxi to take her back to the hotel.

She called the airlines again. This time she was informed that the lost baggage department had closed for the day and that she should call back in the morning. "Damn it," she said to herself in the same tone that Mike used.

The room was cooler than before, but not much. She removed her blouse and inspected the armpits with her nose. They smelled awful. If she had to wear the clothes another day, she knew she would truly smell like a farang, especially without her deodorant to help hide the odor. She washed the armpits of her blouse as best as she could in the bathroom sink. It helped, but she could still smell the sour stench.

Later, she took a long shower. At least she would smell clean for the night. She tuned the TV to a station playing music and then lay down on the bed with the overhead fan blowing down. In ten minutes she was asleep.

Chapter 23

Mike awoke as his flight was preparing to land in Tokyo. It dawned on him that he hadn't called to tell Susan he was coming home. He wasn't sure if was forgetfulness or if he had subconsciously forgotten on purpose. Whichever it was, he didn't care.

Many of the men who worked in Thailand became excited at the thought of going home. Mike couldn't understand why. He only got depressed whenever he thought about going home. He hadn't even gone home this past Christmas. He had called and sent presents, but he hadn't gone home. He used the excuse that it would screw up his tax break. It wasn't true but he didn't care. Math had been living with him then and he hadn't wanted to leave her. He felt only mildly guilty at his decision.

On his flight from Tokyo to the U.S. he toyed with the idea of getting a motel room and not going home at all. By the time he reached Detroit, he had decided the motel idea was pretty stupid. He considered calling Susan during his layover, but he never did.

At the Pittsburgh airport he rented a car and drove to his house. It was snowing but the streets were mostly clear. He hadn't driven a car in several months and now he was driving in the snow on the hilly streets of Pittsburgh. He hit a few slick spots but arrived without incident.

It was Mike's Saturday night, but twelve hours away in Thailand it was already Sunday morning. His body couldn't decide what time it was. Traveling west to east always played hell with his internal clock.

He rang the doorbell for several minutes but no one answered.

J. F. Gump

It was mid February, the snow was blowing, and he didn't have a coat. He was freezing. He unzipped his suitcase in the trunk of the car and rooted around until he found his home-side key ring. Shivering, he tried the keys one by one. He had almost decided that Susan had changed the lock when the last key opened the door.

After warming up for a few minutes, he retrieved his suitcase from the car. Next he explored the house. They had moved in only a few days before he had left for Thailand the last time. He had been gone before they had finished unpacking. It was a nice house, but it didn't feel like home.

He found a note laying on the kitchen table. It was addressed to their son. 'Josh - I went out with my friends from work. If the streets are bad later, I'll probably stay at Marsha's house. If I don't come home tonight, I'll be there in the morning. I'm leaving this note in case you decide to come home tonight and wonder where I am. Love, Mom.'

He read the note twice. Who was Marsha and what did she mean *in case Josh decided to come home*? It sounded like maybe neither of them would be coming home. Oddly, he felt relieved he wouldn't see either Susan or Josh tonight. He checked the fridge. No beer! Susan was a wino, so he wasn't surprised. He would buy some later.

He went to the bedroom, stripped off his traveling clothes, and took a long shower to wash off the smells of the last 26 hours he had spent in busy airports and overcrowded 747's. Even after showering, shaving, and brushing his teeth, he could still smell and taste the trip. And he was cold. He pulled on a warm sweater and turned the thermostat up a few degrees. He looked outside, it was still snowing. He dumped his dirty clothes in the washer, put on his coat, and then went out for beer and cigarettes.

Pennsylvania isn't a very progressive state when it comes to alcohol. While most states sell beer in every store and gas station imaginable, Pennsylvania restricts their beer sales to distributors and bars. The distributors were closed this time of the night, so

SIAM NIGHTS

Mike was stuck going to a bar.

There were several neighborhood bars near the house, but since no one was home he decided to make the best of his last night of freedom. He went to a bar he remembered having a decent crowd and its fair share of good looking girls. More importantly, it was the only place where he knew the bartenders well and they would charge his credit card fifty bucks for a ten dollar tab and give him the rest in cash.

The crowd seemed smaller than he remembered for O'Shanes on a Saturday night. Probably the snow, he thought. He didn't recognize the bartender either. She wasn't the same night-time bartender who had been here the last time he was in town. If she was the same one, she had certainly gained a lot of weight. He took a seat at the bar and ordered an American beer. It didn't taste nearly as good as he remembered, but he ordered another anyway.

Mike looked around the immediate bar area. A lot of yuppie types filled the seats. None of the women looked as good as he thought they should. Their faces were all wrong. They were pale and hard, quite unlike the tanned, fine features of the women he had just left. He'd first noticed this phenomenon when he arrived in Detroit, and then again when he had landed in Pittsburgh. At the time, he figured he was still half asleep and no woman would look good. Now he was wide awake and they still didn't look too hot. He quit looking.

Mike motioned for the bartender to come over but she either didn't see him or was ignoring him. After a few hard taps of his empty bottle on the counter, she finally noticed.

"Need another beer?" she asked blandly.

"Maybe," he answered. "I was wondering where Teresa was."

"Who is Teresa?"

"She used to work here in the evenings."

"Then she must have quit a long time ago because I don't know any Teresa and I've been here for over six months. Nice tan you got. You been to Florida or California or something?"

"Yeah, or something," he answered. "Teresa used to let me

overpay my tab with my charge card and then give me change. I always left her a nice tip. Can you do the same?"

The bartender looked Mike over carefully. "Where're you from?"

"Just down the road, the River Bend subdivision."

"Oooh, nice area. If you have an ID, I guess it would be okay."

"Thanks," he said, "you're a sweetheart."

"Where did you say you got that tan?"

"I didn't," he responded. The bartender stared at him for a moment, then walked away.

Mike wondered how he could have ever thought this was a neat place to go. It was clean and well decorated but it was boring. This bar would never survive in Pattaya, he decided. He looked around the room. The women would never survive in Pattaya either. Too much competition.

He finished his second beer and ordered six to go. He paid his tab, received his change, left a nice tip, and went home. After just one beer, Mike fell asleep on the sofa.

Chapter 24

When Nuang awoke in the temple on the morning after Sawat had beaten her, the first thing she did was look at her face in the mirror. She couldn't believe how bad she looked. She found the toilet, washed herself, and then went directly back to her room. She didn't come out the rest of the day, not even to eat.

She lay on her bed, listening to the sounds of people shuffling past her door and the occasional faint sound of the monks chanting their daily prayers. From time to time she would touch her face ever so lightly and feel the swollen soreness.

By nine o'clock that evening, the old monk Jum had become concerned about Nuang. He went to her room and knocked softly.

"Who's there?" Nuang asked without opening the door.

"I am Jum," the monk answered. "I saw you last night when Math brought you here. I wanted to make sure you were okay."

"I'm very ugly right now," she said through the door, "but I'm okay."

"You didn't eat today," the monk persisted. "I'll bring you some food if you'll eat."

She was taken aback. She knew that monks didn't bring food to people; people brought food to the monks. She wondered at his offer but said nothing. "I will eat tomorrow," she replied.

"Okay," Jum said, "in the morning, then." There was an urgency in his voice as if he had more to say.

She listened for the monk to continue but heard only his footsteps as he walked away. When she knew he was gone, she went to the bath area to relieve herself and wash up. Afterwards, she lay in bed and thought for a long time about the old monk's offer to bring her food. She didn't understand. In a while she fell asleep.

Nuang awoke as dim shades of red edged the early morning sky. She pushed herself from the bed and went to the toilet. She was the only one there, so she took time to wash herself thoroughly. Back in her room she looked at herself in the mirror again. The swelling had gone down some, but the bruises hadn't disappeared. She applied more make-up than usual to cover them. In the dim light of the room, she thought she looked almost normal.

Nuang was hungry but didn't know where everyone ate or what the routine was. She opened her door so she could see out. She decided she would ask the next person she saw. Her wait was short. The old monk came by less than a minute later.

"Sawasdee dee krup, good morning," the monk spoke first.

"Sawasdee dee ka." She presented him a wai of respect.

Jum smiled. "You promised you would eat today. But before you can eat, you must help with the cooking. Come with me."

She followed the monk to the temple kitchen area. Three other women were already there, busily preparing food.

"These nice women will show you what you must do," he said and then left.

Nuang felt awkward but the women were very nice. Soon everyone was talking as if they were old friends. No one asked why she was at the temple and no one mentioned the bruises on her face. She was grateful for their silence.

By the time the sun broke over the horizon, Nuang and the three women had finished cooking. The monks served themselves from the bowls the women had set on a table. They didn't speak to the women, not even to say thank you. Only after the monks had finished their meal did the women eat.

Nuang was famished. She thought she must look like a pig, the way she gobbled her food. She cared but didn't care at the same time. The other women watched and smiled as she devoured her breakfast, but no one said anything.

By nine o'clock the kitchen utensils had been washed and put back into their proper place. Nuang was informed there would be no lunch, but that she was expected back in the kitchen later to help with the afternoon meal. The rest of the day she could do whatever she wanted. One woman suggested that Nuang say a few prayers or attend one of the daily ceremonies. Nuang smiled and thanked them for everything and then went back to her room.

She had been there for a just few minutes when there was a soft knock at the door. This time she opened the door, instead of talking through it like the night before. It was the old monk. She waited for him to speak.

"I've asked for a free day and it has been granted," Jum said. "I would like very much for you to spend some time talking with me."

She didn't understand why the monk would want to talk with her, but she couldn't refuse. "Thank you," she wai'ed politely. "It would be my honor."

"Please come," he said and walked away.

Nuang followed as he led her to a garden area just outside of the temple. The garden was small but exquisite. Brightly colored flowers, laid out in intricate patterns, were in bloom everywhere. Someone had taken a great deal of time nurturing the garden to near perfection.

"It's beautiful," she said, honestly impressed.

"It's something the temple has allowed me to do. I'm not allowed to be proud of it, but I am anyway. I think Buddha will forgive me for this one self-indulgence. After all, every rock, flower, and blade of grass in this garden belongs to God. I'm only helping to make them as beautiful as he intended."

Nuang walked slowly, stopping here to touch a leaf and there to smell a flower. "I think God and Buddha are both proud of what you've done. Otherwise, they wouldn't allow it to be so beautiful." After a minute she went back to the monk. "What did you want to talk about?" She was sure she had done something wrong at breakfast, and that the old monk had been sent to reprimand her.

Jum sat cross-legged in the shade on a small area of grass. "Please, sit here," he said, motioning at a spot in front of himself.

Nuang sat cross-legged like the monk.

"I have many things I want to tell to you. I'm not sure I can even say them all, but I feel I must try." Jum fidgeted nervously with the edge of his robe. "My soul is being eaten by secrets, and I think Buddha is pushing me to cleanse myself before I die." He paused and sighed.

Nuang waited expectantly, wondering what secrets he was about to tell her.

After what seemed like an eternity he continued, "I have known your family for a long time. I've known your mother since I was a boy. We used to play together when we were children. When we became teenagers, I decided I was in love with your mother and I wanted her to be my wife. But my family had money and your mother's family was very poor. My father was furious that I would even think about having a wife from a family of peasants. My love for your mother caused many problems in our house."

Nuang was surprised at what she was hearing. Her mother had never mentioned loving any man except her father. She didn't know what to say, so she said nothing. She studied his face as he talked.

"When I was seventeen, my father sent me to school in Bangkok. It was my punishment for loving your mother. I didn't stay long, but it was long enough. By the time I decided my father was wrong and I came back for your mother, she had married your father and she was pregnant with you. I was devastated. I had spent most of my time in Bangkok dreaming of the day Nui and I would be together, and now it would never happen." The monk fell silent. He closed his eyes and bowed his head.

Nuang wondered if he was saying a prayer. In a moment he lifted his face toward her.

"Please don't hate me for what I'm about to tell you," his eyes pleaded. "There was a time when I hated you for being Nui's first baby. You were supposed to have been mine. My hate didn't last long, only a month or so. Still, even today, it bothers me that I had those thoughts. Do you hate me for my feelings?"

"No," she answered honestly, "That was a long time ago and for only a moment. I could never hate anyone for that."

"Thank you," Jum said, breathing a sigh of relief. "I think I was actually angry with your father for getting your mother pregnant. I hope you understand when I say I never liked your father much. It was partly my jealously, but mostly it was because I considered your father a brute and a drunk, and I believed he would never make a proper husband.

"I watched your family through the years and your father proved me right. What little money he earned he spent on drinking and gambling. He used to beat your mother and sometimes he would even beat you and your brothers and sisters. I truly hate your father. Once I even thought about killing him for what he was and what he was doing. Of course I never did, but I thought about it. I have never understood why Nui stayed with him as long as she did. As much as I loved your mother, sometimes I think she was a fool."

"You don't understand," Nuang snapped at the monk who wasn't talking so much like a monk. She felt compelled to defend her family. Even if the monk was right, he had no right to call her mother a fool and her father a drunk. "My mother's family arranged her marriage to my father. She had no choice. And you don't know what you are talking about, my father is not a drunk and he never beat any of us." It was a lie and she knew it was a lie, but she said it anyway.

"Nuang," the monk continued patiently, "your mother used to tell me everything; I know what happened in your house. Your father was a bully, and everyone paid the price when he drank. And your mother did have a choice about who she married. She could have just said no. I know that's not easy for a traditional Thai lady like Nui, but sometimes traditions aren't worth much.

"When my father arranged a marriage for me, I refused. He

disowned me for my refusal but I didn't care. I am Thai and I respect tradition, but I knew I didn't want to live with someone I didn't love. In the end I never married anyone because I loved only your mother. Even when she was married to your father, I loved her. I never interfered with your family but there were many times when I wanted to. Instead, I kept my silence and went about my life and my work.

"When the Americans came to our country during the war in Vietnam and Kampuchea, I made a lot of money supplying them with things they needed. Also, I made a lot of money from the soldiers at the bars I owned in Bangkok. I'm not proud of the bars, but at the time I wanted only to make money. I wanted to prove to my father that I didn't need his help to be a success. He had disinherited me and I had something to prove to him, and to myself."

Nuang listened wide-eyed. She could hardly believe this old monk had once owned bars in Bangkok. For some reason she found the thought funny, but she didn't laugh. Nor did she interrupt.

"When the Vietnam War ended and the Americans went home, my business died. I didn't care. I had saved a lot of money and had more than enough to live. I opened a small store not far from your house and was satisfied with what I had. Your mother often came to my store to shop. When she had no money, I sold her things on credit and never expected to be repaid. Sometimes she would come to my store just to talk. I know almost everything about you and your brothers and sisters."

Jum paused. He spent a moment trying to read Nuang's face. He saw only confusion. He sighed deeply and continued, "By the time I decided to become a monk, my brother was a successful lawyer. I took all of the money I had saved and gave it to him to take care of things. It wasn't for him to spend on himself and he knew that. It was for other things. Like when your sister had her first heart operation when she was twelve, and the second when she was nineteen. Do you think your father and his insurance paid for those operations? My brother made it look like that is what happened, but it was a lie. And when your sister went to college, do you believe the little money she made selling perfume, clothes, and jewelry to her friends covered all of her costs? The school took what she had and my brother paid the rest. Do you think the job she got in Bangkok was by luck or by accident? My brother arranged that too. I helped your sister every way I could."

The old monk paused again. This time there were tears in his eyes. "I helped Math until the day all of the money was gone." He stopped talking. A small shudder shook his body.

Nuang looked at the old monk, trying to understand everything he was telling her. She couldn't. Something was wrong. Something was missing. "Jum," she said, using his name, "There is more, isn't there?"

The old monk nodded. His body shuddered again. A small, unmanly sob escaped his throat.

"Please tell me everything, Jum," she urged gently.

After a moment, he recovered his composure and continued, "One night your mother came to my shop. Your father had come home very drunk. He had been hitting you and your mother and she had run away. That night, your mother was afraid Supit would kill her. She wanted to be someplace safe and she needed someone to talk to. I held her and comforted her for a very long time. I don't remember why it happened, but before that night was over we made love. Please understand me Nuang, we didn't just have sex, we made love. During all of the years I'd loved your mother we had never done that. Somehow that night it felt so right, so that is what we did.

"I didn't see your mother again for nearly eight months. The next time she came to my shop she was very pregnant and she was crying. She told me the baby could only be mine from the night we made love. She said she had tried to abort the baby at four months but it hadn't worked. She was scared; terrified the baby would be some sort of monster because of what she had done."

His words came faster now. "I didn't know what to do. I made

J. F. Gump

her an appointment with the best doctor in town. He pronounced
the baby in fine health. A month later your sister, Math, was born.

"As soon as I knew your mother and your sister were safe and
well, I sold my shop and became a monk. I could no longer live as
a person, knowing the shame I had caused your mother. I isolated
myself here at the temple. I had my friends and my brother watch
your family and let me know when Math needed anything. When
she finally had the job in Bangkok, I thought everything would be
okay. How was I to know what would happen to the Thai
economy? There is no more money and I cannot help her anymore.
Your sister is cursed because she's a bastard child. She's double
cursed because she is my bastard child."

Jum broke down and cried openly.

Nuang's heart ached at the old monk's pain. She discarded all
rules of politeness and took him in her arms. She held him tight
and cried along with him.

After a long while his tears stopped. He raised his head and
said, "I'm very ill. I need someone in your family to forgive me
before I die. Can you forgive me?"

"You're a good man, Jum," she whispered. "But you know it's
not my forgiveness you need. You need your daughter's
forgiveness. I will find Math and bring her to you." She hesitated
then asked very softly, "How long will you live?"

"The doctors always say something different. Sometimes they
say six months and sometimes they say a year or longer. Only God
and Buddha know for sure."

"I promise that before you die, I will bring your daughter to
you. I'll leave tomorrow to find her."

"Please," he begged, "When you bring Math to me, don't tell
her what I've told you. I should be the one to explain everything."

"Why didn't you tell her before? I know you have talked with
her many times."

"I don't know. I wanted to, but I was afraid. I was afraid she
might hate me."

"Then you don't know your daughter as well as you should.

Math could never hate you. I'll respect your wish, though. When I find Math, I'll bring her here."

"You can't bring her here. I'm leaving tomorrow. I have asked to be moved to another temple. I'll visit with my brother for a few days and then I'm going to the temple on the mountain above Chiang Mai."

"Then Math and I will find you there," she promised.

"Thank you. I must go now. I have many things to do before I leave."

"I must go, too," she said. "I've decided to find Math starting today."

She knew her face still looked bad and she wasn't quite ready to go home, but she didn't want to stay in the temple any longer, either. Finding Math gave her a good excuse to leave without seeming impolite.

Nuang went back to her room and recounted the money Math had given her. More than enough for the bus fare to Pattaya and back to Chiang Mai. She repacked her suitcase, said quick prayers for safety, and then left the temple.

She knew Math had gone to Pattaya to be with Mike. She went directly to the bus station and bought a ticket to Bangkok. It was Thursday afternoon. She would be in Pattaya by Friday morning.

Nuang fretted as she rode the bus. She had never been to Pattaya and she didn't know where her brother lived. She had his address but it didn't say Pattaya; it said Banglamung. She knew it had to be near Pattaya but she didn't know in which direction. She fell asleep praying for Buddha to guide her safely to her brother's house.

At four o'clock in the morning Nuang changed buses in Bangkok for the final leg of her journey. She arrived in Pattaya at six forty-five. She called Anan but there was no answer. Probably still asleep, she thought.

She flagged down a motorcycle-taxi and showed him the address. The driver read the address several times, then told her he knew where it was. He had taken another lady to that address before. At seven she was knocking on Anan's door. When he answered, it was obvious she had awakened him.

"Nuang," he said, staring at her in sleepy-eyed surprise. "Is that you? What are you doing in Pattaya?"

"I'm sorry to wake you, but I need your help."

"Come inside," he said. "Are you hungry? Would you like something to eat?"

She shook her head no. "I've come to find Math. Is she here?"

"Why would Math be here? The last time I saw her was at the funeral. What's going on?"

"I'm sorry, but I can't tell you right now. I think Math came to Pattaya to stay with a farang. His name is Mike. Math said you know him."

"I know him," Anan said curtly. "I don't like my sister sleeping with a farang. It's not polite."

"Shame on you, Anan," Nuang said sharply. "Your sister loves that man. He's very good to her. How dare you say something like that? You should be glad your sister has found someone who makes her happy."

"I know," Anan responded. "It's just that I see so many farangs with Thai ladies that I'm sick of it. Most of them are no good. All they want is to have sex with a Thai woman."

"Well," she said, a little softer, "This is different. Math is in love with this farang and from what she told me, I think he loves her too. I may be wrong, but I think I'm correct. Do you know where this Mike person lives?"

"Yes, I can take you there."

"Thank you. Can we leave soon?"

"What happened to your face?" Anan asked, not moving.

"I had an accident," she lied. "It's not important. I'm okay. Now, please get dressed so we can go."

Anan and Nuang arrived at the condo at nine o'clock. The manager informed them that Mike had checked out of his room three days earlier. He was going back to America. No one had seen Math since she had gone to Phitsanulok for the funeral.

"What can we do?" Nuang asked as they left the condo.

"I don't know," Anan answered. "I think there's nothing we can do. Do you think the farang took Math to America with him?"

"I wish it were true," she replied, "but Math doesn't have a passport or a visa. It would be impossible for her to go to America."

"Maybe she went back to Phitsanulok," he suggested.

"I don't think so, not now. Math is too smart for that."

"What do you mean?" he asked. "It's her home. Why wouldn't she go there?"

"Never mind," she answered. "It's a thing between us women. I just don't think Math would go to Phitsanulok right now."

"Maybe she went to visit you in Chiang Mai?"

She looked at him like a light had just clicked on. "Yes, that has to be it. Math must have gone to my home. Let's go back to your house and call my husband. Even if Math isn't in Chiang Mai, Surat must be wondering where I am. We argued before he went home from the funeral. I haven't talked to him since he left. He must be wondering what's happened. I'm not a good wife."

Using Anan's phone Nuang called again and again for nearly four hours before Surat finally answered. "I am Nuang," she said when she heard his voice. "I'm sorry I haven't called you. Many things have happened and I'm in Pattaya looking for Math. Please don't be angry."

"I'm not angry," Surat said, relief in his voice. "I was only worried that you would never come home. I called to your mother's house, but no one has seen you or Math. Are you okay? Are you coming home soon?"

"I'm okay," she answered, thinking of the bruises that still showed on her face. "I'll be home on Sunday. If you see Math, please call Anan right away. It's very important."

"I'm working for the next few days," Surat replied. "But if I see her, I'll make her stay here. What time will you be home?"

"I don't know. I don't know anything about the buses from Pattaya to Chiang Mai. I don't know what time, but it may be very late. Thank you for not being angry teeluk." She hung up the phone and looked at Anan. "Please take me to buy a bus ticket home."

She spent the rest of Friday and most of Saturday sleeping. When she was awake, she spent most of the time praying her bruises would be gone by Sunday. She spent the rest of her time thinking about Surat. She was surprised by how much she missed her husband. Maybe she loved him more than she thought.

At six o'clock on Sunday morning, Nuang's bus left the Pattaya terminal on its fourteen hour trip north to Bangkok and onward to Chiang Mai.

Chapter 25

On the same Sunday morning that Nuang was leaving Pattaya, Math awoke early in her hotel room in Chiang Mai. She showered and went out for breakfast. After eating she waited for the usual morning vomiting but it didn't come. She felt slightly nauseated, but she didn't vomit. Maybe Mike was wrong and the hot peppers she had eaten with her supper had cured her ulcers. She found a pay phone and called the airlines. Her suitcase was still missing.

She went back to her room and contemplated what do next. Without even sniffing she could smell odors coming from the armpits of her blouse. She was glad no one was there to share her embarrassment. She decided to buy some clean clothes. At least a blouse and underwear.

Math took her money from her purse and counted it. Seventy-three hundred baht and some small change was all that was left. She would have to be very careful about the money. It was going too fast. Now she regretted her decision to fly to Chiang Mai. If she had taken the bus, she wouldn't have spent so much and she would still have her suitcase. "Not bad luck lady", she thought, "but stupid lady".

She slipped 1,300 baht and the change into her pants pocket. The rest she rolled into a tight wad and hid it in her purse. She didn't want to be flashing her wad of bills for everyone to see. It wasn't safe. She checked out of her room.

Not far from the hotel, Math stopped at a small shop and bought a shirt, bra, and panties. She paid for the clothes with the money from her pants pocket. She asked the sales lady if it would be okay to put on the new clothes and wear them from the store.

J. F. Gump

The lady agreed. Math changed her clothes in the dressing room and put her smelly clothes in the plastic bag. She felt better just knowing she didn't stink anymore.

She called the airlines again. Her suitcase had arrived. Instantly she was angry with herself for buying the clothes. She was even angrier that she had worn them from the store. Now she couldn't take them back for a refund.

"Damn it," she said, disgusted with herself. She took a motorcycle-taxi to the airport.

The airline lady in missing baggage was very apologetic. Mai pen rai, never mind, Math told her. She went through the suitcase and everything was there. She put on deodorant before zipping the suitcase shut.

Outside the terminal she there were no motorcycle-taxis, only regular taxis and a couple of tuk-tuks. She decided on the tuk-tuk because it was cheaper than the regular taxi. She gave the driver directions to her sister's house. In fifteen minutes she had arrived. The door was still locked and there was no sign that anyone had been there during the night.

She wondered and worried why Nuang wasn't home. She could think of no reason why her sister would still be at the temple in Phitsanulok unless something really bad had happened. Maybe Sawat's beating had hurt Nuang worse than she thought. Maybe that was where Surat had gone, too. Maybe someone had called him with an emergency about Nuang. A wave of uneasiness swept over her. At that moment she decided to return to Phitsanulok to find her sister. She had no other choice. She had to make sure Nuang was okay.

Math counted the money in her pocket. There was still 600 baht. Math thought it would be enough for the bus fare and a meal or two, but decided to put another 1,000 in her pocket just in case. She probed her fingers into the secret hiding place in her purse. She didn't feel the money. She probed harder and deeper. Still nothing. Her breath came in short gasps. She groped frantically through her purse. Finally, she dumped everything onto the ground and sifted through the things laying on the sidewalk. The money was gone. Slowly, she pushed everything back into her purse. Tears welled in her eyes. How could she live on just 600 baht?

As she sat crying, she retraced her every movement since she'd checked out of the hotel. After a few minutes she knew it had to be the lady at the clothes shop. She remembered she had already paid the lady and had left her purse on the counter for just a minute while she put on her new clothes. That had to be it. The sales lady had stolen her money while she changed clothes.

She grabbed her suitcase and ran awkwardly down the street to the clothes shop. When she arrived, the store was closed and the door was locked. She exploded into a rage. She kicked repeatedly at the shop door. "Whore, cunt, bitch, Thai slut, mother-fucker," she shouted every nasty Thai word she knew and every evil English word she had learned from Mike.

A policeman saw her kicking and screaming at the door. He ran over and grabbed her by the arm. "What are you doing?" he shouted. "You do that one more time and I'll arrest you."

Math's knees buckled and she dropped to the sidewalk. Her curses gave way to sobbing. "She stole my money. The lady in that store stole my money. You must do something."

The policeman looked at the shop. "It's closed," he said. "You must be mistaken. Are you drunk or on drugs?"

"No," she protested, "I'm not on anything. I'm telling you the lady stole my money and then she closed her shop."

The policeman noticed the suitcase. "Where's your home in Chiang Mai?"

"I don't live in Chiang Mai. I live in Phitsanulok."

The policeman regarded her coldly. "Then I can't help you. If I see you kick that door one more time, I'll arrest you." He walked away, looking back at Math every few steps.

She stood and glared at the door. As the policeman turned the corner, she kicked it one last time. "Fucker," she shouted, picked up her suitcase, and headed back toward the hotel.

As she walked, she decided she had to contact Mike. He would know what to do. He would help her. Ten minutes later she arrived at the hotel hot, tired, and sweating.

Math told the man at the hotel desk what had happened. In her most pitiful tone she begged him to send a fax for her to America. At first he refused, but after listening to her pleading for a while he relented and said he would do it. But she would have to pay 50 baht for the phone cost. She agreed and promised to make it a very short fax.

"Call me on my handy," she wrote. "I have something important to tell you. Love, Math."

The man tried to send the fax while Math waited. In a moment he came back shaking his head, "I can't get through to America. I'm getting busy international circuits."

"I can't wait; I must go to Phitsanulok today. If I give you an extra fifty baht, will you keep trying until it goes through?"

"Yes, of course," the man agreed. "I promise I'll try until the fax has been sent."

"Thank you." She counted out the money carefully and left the hotel lobby.

Outside the hotel Math repeated her story to a motorcycle-taxi driver until he finally agreed to take her to the bus station for just five baht.

She bought a ticket on the eight o'clock bus to Phitsanulok. She spent the next few hours counting her remaining money over and over. She could hardly believe it. Just yesterday morning, when Mike left Thailand, she had ten thousand baht and now she was almost broke. "Stupid lady," she mumbled to herself.

As her bus left the Chiang Mai terminal, it passed another bus just arriving. She didn't know it, but that bus carried a special passenger. It carried her sister, just arriving from Pattaya.

An hour later she passed another bus moving north toward Chiang Mai. That bus, too, carried a very special passenger who wore saffron robes and was headed to the temple on the mountain above Chiang Mai.

Chapter 26

Mike awoke in America at four o'clock on Sunday morning. His first thoughts were of Math. He wondered if she was okay. With the kind of luck she had, anything was possible. She believed she was cursed woman, a bad luck lady. He had always pooh-poohed the idea and made fun of her about it, but he had to admit things weren't exactly going her way. He had no way of knowing that at that very moment Math was busy kicking down a dress-shop door in Chiang Mai. Even if he did know, he wouldn't have been surprised.

Unable to sleep, he got up and looked through the window. The streets were covered with snow and it was coming down hard. A quick tour of the house proved that no one had come home during the night. With the snow outside, he figured they probably wouldn't be home any time soon.

He made himself a cup of instant coffee, which he hated almost as much as Thai coffee. It tasted like shit, but it had caffeine and he needed a healthy dose of that. He puttered around the house for a while, and then read some recent newspapers left laying here and there. At ten thirty he took a nap.

At noon, he woke up and drank a beer. He was glad he hadn't drank them all the night before. He turned on the TV. It had more channels than his TV in Pattaya, but the shows seemed just as bad or worse. He flipped idly through the stations but never found anything that held his attention for more than a few minutes.

As the afternoon wore on, he slowly but surely finished his small supply of beer and cigarettes. He searched the house upside and down but found neither; he wanted both. He looked outside again for the hundredth time that day. The snow had let up some, he tried to convince himself. Besides, it would only get worse if he waited. Fuck it, he mumbled to himself, as he put on his coat and walked to the snow-covered car.

The trip to the nearest bar wasn't far, but the streets were a disaster. Mike's rental car slipped and skidded over the road but he made the trip without accident. At the bar he bought a twelve pack of beer. Pennsylvania's antiquated liquor laws wouldn't allow him to buy more than that at one time from a bar. After putting it in the car, he went back inside and bought another twelve pack. It was his way of thumbing his nose at stupid laws. Next he stopped at a gas station and bought a carton of cigarettes. He wouldn't run out of anything tonight.

When he got home from his beer run, there were three messages on the answering machine. One was from Susan telling Josh she was still at Marsha's. The second was from Josh saying he was still at Nick's. Neither wanted to drive in the snow. The last message was from his boss. It was addressed to either Mike or Susan. He wanted Mike to call him as soon as possible.

Mike sighed and shook his head. He drank a couple of beers and smoked several cigarettes. Finally he dialed his boss's number.

"Hello," Jess Ankrom answered his phone.

"Hi, Jess. It's me, Mike."

"Thank god. We didn't know what happened to you. Thought maybe you had gone native on us or something. Where are you?"

"I'm at home," Mike answered, confused. "Where did you think I would be?"

Jess sighed aloud. "I was hoping you were still in Thailand."

"Well," Mike said defensively, "You're the one who said for us to come home right away."

"Forget about that. What's important is that you get back to Thailand by Wednesday morning. Not our Wednesday morning, but their Wednesday morning. Can you do that? It's important."

"You're kidding, aren't you?" Mike asked. "First you tell me to come home as soon as possible, and then you tell me to go back as soon as possible. Christ, to get there by Thailand's Wednesday morning, I would have to leave tonight or tomorrow morning at the latest. I haven't even seen my family yet."

"Maybe that's better," Jess said. "I called your house Friday evening. Susan had no idea you were coming home and I didn't tell her. I got the impression you didn't tell her either. Did you?"

"Well, no," he answered, embarrassed.

"Then she'll never know you were home. You can call her when you get back to Thailand. If she's tried to call you, tell her that you and some of the guys went touring for a few days. She would believe that."

He thought of Math. He could be back with her in 24 hours. Jess's idea was sounding better by the minute. "I'm willing to leave on the next available flight, but I'm totally exhausted from my last trip. I need some rest and I don't sleep very well in those business-class seats. First class seats are much better for sleeping plane."

"Okay," Jess sighed, understanding exactly what Mike was doing. "Just get there by Wednesday morning and I don't care how you do it. Oh, by the way, there is one more thing."

"What's that?"

"You're to finish what you're working on now and then get home. How long do you think?"

"You're a prick," Mike sighed. "Maybe six weeks give or take another six. I'll get it done as soon as I can, but I'm not going to kill myself to do it." He hung up the phone without waiting for a response. He had never talked to his boss like that before, but the whole situation sucked and Jess Ankrom knew it.

He called the airlines until he found one with an open first-class seat leaving at eight thirty that evening. He looked at his watch. It was Sunday, five-fifteen. He would have to hurry because of the snow but he could make it. He hoped the airport didn't shut down because of the weather.

He erased his boss's message on the answering machine and undid everything he had done to the house. He put his new carton of cigarettes in his computer bag and the twelve-packs of beer in the rental car. He worried for a moment about his charges at O'Shane's and for the rental car, but with as much as Susan charged on the credit cards, he figured she would never notice. He pulled his still-dirty clothes from the washer and packed them back into his suitcase. Last, he hung his coat back in the closet then left the house as if he had never been there. The blowing snow would cover his foot tracks soon enough.

The ride to the airport was winter hell. Once he did a complete doughnut with the car, but ended up going in the right direction. It was then that he decided he would never again complain about Thailand's hot weather. He arrived at his gate at eight o'clock. He boarded the plane twenty-five minutes later. It felt good to be going home.

Mike arrived in Bangkok at eleven thirty on Tuesday morning. The trip had taken over twenty-four hours. He hired a taxi and was in Pattaya by two o'clock in the afternoon.

After checking back into his condo, the first thing he did was call Math. He had no problem making a telephone connection, but he kept getting the Thai version of, "The phone you are dialing is out of the area or out of service". After the fifth try he gave up.

Math had said she would go to her sister's in Chiang Mai, but he didn't have that phone number. Maybe her mother could help if he could find her number. He rummaged through his old receipts and finally found a telephone bill from the condo. He knew Math had used his phone to call her mother's house among other places. After a brief process of elimination, Mike had the phone numbers narrowed down to two.

At both numbers, the person on the other end couldn't speak or understand English. Also, they couldn't understand his brand of Thai no matter how slowly or how clearly he spoke. He wasn't sure anyone ever understood anything he said, but he kept trying.

Every night he would call the numbers. Then he would sit by the phone waiting for it to ring. After three agonizing days the phone did ring and it was Math.

Chapter 27

Math arrived in Phitsanulok at five thirty on her Monday morning. She had no way of knowing that Mike was just now leaving his house in America and was on his way back to Thailand. It was too early to be calling her mother or anyone else, so she spent half of her remaining money for a taxi to her house.

Nothing had changed since she and Nuang had left a week earlier. Her first priority was her cell phone. The battery had died sometime during night. She put it in the charger. Next, she went to the public toilets to bathe. The water was cold but it felt good to be clean. After she dressed, she walked to her mother's house. The sky was growing pale with the first hint of daylight.

Thank Buddha, she said to herself, when she saw the motorcycle on her mother's porch. And thank God, too, she said when she checked the gas tank and found it almost full. She wrote a short note telling her mother and her brother that she was taking the motorcycle. She slipped the note under the door. She coasted her motorcycle from the porch to the street where she kick-started it to life. In less than two minutes she was back at her house.

Her handy wasn't yet charged, but she clipped it to the waistband anyway. It made her feel whole again. Math knew she couldn't stay here because of Sawat, but she hadn't considered what she would do beyond going to the temple to look for her sister. For a moment she considered tying her suitcase to the seat on the motorcycle, then changed her mind. She didn't want to be riding around Phitsanulok with a suitcase in tow. She grabbed her purse, locked her house, and drove to the temple.

The monks were already busy with their morning routines.

J. F. Gump

Against all politeness, Math approached one of the monks and spoke first. "I need to talk to the monk named Jum or my sister, her name is Nuang."

The monk looked at her with mild disdain.

"I'm sorry for my boldness," she apologized, "but this is very important. I must make sure my sister is okay."

The monk's stare softened. "Jum left here three or four days ago. I'm forbidden to say where he went. I don't know about your sister. If she's the woman with braided hair, she left the day before the monk. I'm sorry I can't tell you more."

"Thank you. Please forgive me for interrupting you," she said, wai'ing respectfully as she backed away from the monk.

Math pondered what to do next. If Nuang had left here three or four days ago, where could she have gone? For that matter, she didn't even know where she would go. With only seventy-five baht left in her pocket, she knew it wouldn't be far.

She wondered if Mike had received her fax. The man at the hotel said he would keep trying until it was sent. Surely Mike would have called by now. She had told him it was very important. She knew if Mike would only call, he would take care of everything.

For a moment she worried if the man at the hotel had just pocketed her money and thrown the fax away. That thought faded as she realized the battery in her handy had been dead for hours. How could Mike call her if her phone was dead? She pulled the cell phone from her belt and turned it on. The low-battery light glowed an irritating yellow. "Toh woi, damn it," Math muttered.

She sat on her motorcycle for a few minutes deciding what to do and where to go. Because of Sawat she didn't feel safe staying at her house or her mother's house. She considered her father's house, but discarded that idea also. On impulse she drove to the nearest pay phone and called an old friend from school, her ex-roommate. As the phone rang, she practiced what she would say when Kallaya answered.

"Hello," a female voice answered the phone.

She recognized the voice immediately. A rush of forgotten excitement coursed through her body. Math pushed her feelings aside. "Hello, Kallaya," she said, almost whispering. "I am Math. Do you remember me?"

"Math," the voice on the phone shouted excitedly, "Of course I remember you. How could I ever forget you? Where are you? How have you been? I haven't heard from you for so long. I've missed your company."

"And I've missed you too," Math said. "I'm in Phitsanulok. I was thinking I would like to come and visit with you for a while. Would that be possible?"

"Of course," Kallaya said. "I would love to see you and talk about old times. Do you know where I live? Can you come today? Today would be perfect. My husband had to go to Bangkok on business and I have no one to talk to. Please say you can come today and keep me company."

Math cringed when Kallaya mentioned her husband but she kept her voice steady. "I can be there in twenty minutes. Would that be okay?"

"Yes, please. I'll be very happy to see you again," Kallaya answered.

"I'll be there soon," Math said and disconnected the call.

After Kallaya had married, Math had always kept track of where she was. Math knew it was because of the feelings she had for Kallaya. As hard as she had tried to kill the feelings, they had never quite gone away. Kallaya was an emotionally strong woman and Math admired her greatly. As she drove toward Kallaya's house, she could almost feel the woman taking her in her arms and telling her everything would be okay. In her mind she could feel Kallaya holding her and stroking her hair and her body, keeping everything evil away.

She skidded the motorcycle to a halt. She had to stop the thoughts and the feelings coursing through her. Kallaya is married and has a baby, she told herself. Kallaya was only her friend and not her lover. After a few minutes, she had her emotions under control and she continued on her way.

Kallaya and Math had a joyous but tearful reunion on Kallaya's front porch. They spent the rest of the morning and most of the afternoon talking about old times, taking care of Kallaya's baby, and bringing each other up to date on their lives.

Math didn't tell Kallaya about the things she might not understand. She was sure Kallaya didn't tell her everything about her life either. When they finally ran out of things to say, she decided it was time to ask Kallaya for a big favor.

"Kallaya," she began, "Is it possible I could spend a few nights at your house."

Kallaya cocked her head and looked at Math curiously. "Well, of course you can, but I thought you and your family lived here in Phitsanulok. Wouldn't you rather stay at your own home or at your mother's house?"

She told Kallaya just enough about Sawat and his recent violence that Kallaya would understand her reasoning. "I think he might hurt me or my family. It would be best if I stayed away from my house and my mother's house for a while. Really I want to go to Chiang Mai and live with my sister, but she's away right now. I think she'll be home in a few days."

"Then you can stay here until my husband comes home this weekend. Do you have clothes and everything?"

"Yes, but they're at my house," Math answered. "I can go and get them now."

"Never mind," Kallaya responded. "You can wear some of mine. Tomorrow or the next day, I will leave the baby with my mother, and I'll go with you to your house. If Sawat is as crazy as you say, I think it would be safer if we went together."

The next afternoon they did go and get Math's suitcase. The trip was uneventful. Back at Kallaya's house, Math tried to charge her cell phone, but something was wrong. No matter how long she left it plugged in, the battery would only last for a few minutes. She wished she had money to buy a new battery.

Using Kallaya's phone, Math contacted Nuang in Chiang Mai. Her sister was evasive about where she had been, but assured Math she was well. Math told Nuang about her adventures since she had left the temple. Nuang insisted that Math come to see her as soon as possible but she didn't say why, other than her worries about Sawat. Math promised she would come to Chiang Mai as soon as she could, probably this very weekend.

Math spent the next three days helping Kallaya cook and clean and tend the baby. Kallaya was thankful for the company and the relief from constant babysitting. She and Kallaya renewed the bond they had formed when they were in school.

Math had stopped vomiting every morning, even though she didn't take her ulcer pills. In fact she felt really good. She decided her problems had been caused by stress and not from an ulcer after all. Except for missing Mike, it was a very pleasant three days.

On Friday afternoon, Kallaya suggested they go to a movie. Her mother could take care of the baby and they would be back long before Kallaya's husband returned from Bangkok. Math agreed and they went to the movies.

Math drove them to the theater on her motorcycle and Kallaya paid their admission to the movie. They watched a tragic Thai love story that made them both cry. While exiting through the theater lobby, Math slipped on a wet spot and fell hard on her buttocks. She laughed, even though the pain brought tears to her eyes. As they left the building, she felt a dampness at her crotch. For a moment she thought she had lost bladder control when she fell. She reached down to feel her pants hoping she wasn't so wet that everyone would see. When she pulled her hand away, her fingers were covered with blood.

"Oh my God, Kallaya," she swooned, faint from the sight of her own blood, "I think I have hurt myself." She held her hand out for Kallaya to see.

"Dear Buddha," Kallaya said when she saw the blood. "You have to go to the hospital. Stay here while I get a taxi."

"What about my motorcycle?" Math shouted as Kallaya ran

toward the street.

"Forget the motorcycle," Kallaya yelled back. "I'll get it later."

In less than a minute Kallaya returned with the taxi. The driver seemed irritated that a bleeding lady would be sitting on his seat, but after one look at Kallaya's face he said nothing. Within ten minutes they were at the hospital. Kallaya guaranteed payment for everything.

Presently the nurses on duty told Kallaya that Math would be okay, but she would stay overnight for tests and observation. They let her see Math for just a few minutes.

Math gave Kallaya her purse and handy to take back to her house and then told her she should go home to be with her baby and her husband. Kallaya agreed and promised to check on Math in the morning.

On Saturday morning Kallaya phoned the hospital several times, but Math refused to take her calls. Saturday afternoon she went to the hospital but Math had left instructions that she didn't want any visitors. Kallaya was bewildered, insulted, and angry.

On Sunday morning Math called Kallaya and asked if she would come to the hospital. They were letting her leave. Kallaya agreed without hesitation.

"What did the doctors say was wrong?" Kallaya asked, as they rode from the hospital toward her house.

"I don't feel like talking about it right now," Math answered.

Kallaya was surprised at Math's response. Her first thought was that Math must have cancer or something equally dreadful. "Are you going to be okay?" she probed gently.

"I don't know," Math said. "I'm a bad luck lady. How can I ever know?"

After a short silence Kallaya asked, "You're not going to die or something, are you?"

"If I die," Math answered, "it will be from a broken heart. I wish you would stop asking me stupid questions."

Kallaya was irritated at Math's response. "Listen to me," she raised her voice. "You and I have been friends for a long time.

We've been through a lot together. Now stop playing little children games and tell me what's going on."

Math looked at Kallaya. She tried to answer but the knot in her throat wouldn't let her words come. She threw her arms around Kallaya and buried her face against her shoulder. "I'm pregnant," she said through heavy sobs. "I should be happy but I'm not."

"Math," Kallaya said softly, stroking her hair, "I think it's wonderful. Certainly nothing to cry about."

"You don't understand," she moaned, "When I fell, I hurt myself very much. The doctors said there is a 50-50 chance I will miscarry the baby. They said if I don't miscarry, there's a 50-50 chance the baby will not be healthy when it is born. The doctors said I should let them abort the baby for my safety."

"Oh Math, you poor thing," Kallaya said. "I am so sorry. Have you told the father?"

"No, I cannot."

"It's only right that you tell him," Kallaya urged. "You know who the father is, don't you?"

"I know," Math answered, miffed at Kallaya's insinuation. "His name is Mike. He's a farang. He's at home in America and I don't know how to connect with him."

"Oh," Kallaya said pausing, allowing Math's words take full effect. "What will you do?"

"I think I would like get my clothes and go to my mother's house," she replied, withdrawing into herself.

"What about Sawat?"

"If he comes close to me, I will kill him."

Her words were so final that Kallaya knew they were true. She held Math tight. "Everything will work out for the best, Math. I'll take you to my house to collect your things, and then I'll have the taxi take you to your mother's home. Your brother can come back with the taxi to get your motorcycle. I will pray for you and your husband."

"Thank you for being my friend," Math said. "I want to go home now."

Chapter 28

When Math arrived at her mother's house, her mother Nui was all excited. Some farang had been calling but she couldn't understand what he said. Nui didn't speak English or German or whatever language the man had been speaking. Math knew at once that it had to be Mike.

"Mama, listen," she said anxiously. "Did you understand any words? Did you hear the man say America or Thailand or Pattaya or anything? Think very hard mama."

"Oh Math," answered Nui. "I'm not sure. I think I heard him say Pattaya."

Hoping beyond hope, she used her mother's phone to call Mike's condo in Pattaya. She nearly fainted when he answered.

"Teeluk, sweetheart," Math shouted into the phone, "I'm so happy to hear your voice. When did you get back from America? I thought maybe you would never come back."

"I'm happy to hear your voice, too," Mike responded. "I miss you very much." He explained everything about his company sending him back to Pattaya. He was happy to be back, but sad that it wouldn't be for long. "When can you come to Pattaya, Math? I want to be with you every minute."

Math's excitement faded. "I have many things to tell you." She told him about her trip to Chiang Mai and about losing all the money he gave her. Then she told him about seeing her old friend from school. At last she said, "There's one more thing I must tell you." She paused and took a deep breath. "I 'm pregnant with your baby."

There was a short silence before Mike said, "Math, that is

wonderful. I'm honored for you to be the mother of my child."

She almost cried knowing that Mike was pleased. She took another deep breath and continued, "I wish it was all wonderful, teeluk." She repeated what the doctors had told her. When she finished, Mike said nothing. Math thought she heard him crying. "Teeluk," her words barely a whisper, "Are you okay? I'm very sorry if I make you sad."

"I'm okay," he answered. "This is very hard, Math, and I know someday I will hate myself for saying this, but I think we should do what the doctors say is best and safest for you. Someday we can have another baby. Promise you will have another baby for me someday. I would like that more than anything."

It was her turn to cry. "I promise I will teeluk. All you have to do is tell me when you are ready and I'll give you as many babies as you want."

"Thank you, Math. You are the sweetest, most wonderful woman in the world. I love you."

"I love you too, Mike. Tomorrow, I will go to the hospital and see the doctor and..." She hesitated, unable to say *abort your baby*. "... and I will come to you as soon as the doctors say it's safe for me to travel."

"Just take care of yourself. You're the most important person in the world to me. Don't travel until you're sure it's safe. Tomorrow I'll deposit enough money into your account for everything."

"Thank you, teeluk. I'll come home to you in quickly time. I must say bye for now. I love you. Please dream of me when you can." She hung up the phone sobbing.

"I will, Math," Mike said into the dead receiver. "I will dream of you."

That evening Math called her sister, Nuang, in Chiang Mai to tell her she wouldn't be coming to visit this weekend as planned. She would be going to see Mike in Pattaya instead.

Nuang pressed Math to come to Chiang Mai first, but her mind was made up. Nuang dropped the subject.

A few days later, when Mike came home from work, Jahl, the receptionist, and Jem, the manager, gave him a warmer than usual greeting. He shook his head in bewilderment as he stepped into the elevator. Women, he thought, are so weird than no one can figure them out. He went to his room.

When he opened the door, there stood Math, looking more beautiful than he remembered. He dropped his briefcase and computer bag and hurried to her. "Oh God, Math," he said taking her in his arms, "I'm so happy you're here. Are you okay?"

"Yes, teeluk," she answered smiling broadly, "I'm okay. I wanted to surprise you."

"Well, you certainly did," he laughed. "Now shut up and kiss me."

She did just that. They stood there for many long minutes holding and kissing and touching each other.

"Jesus, Math, you feel so good," he whispered between kisses. "You will never know how much I love holding you."

When the excitement of their reunion had calmed, he said, "Come and lie down and hold me so we can talk."

Math stiffened noticeably.

"What's wrong, sweetheart?" his voice was filled with worry.

"Nothing really," she said hesitantly. "It's just that the doctor said I shouldn't make love for a few more days."

He laughed but wanted to cry. "My dear sweet Math, don't you know by now that you don't have to have sex with me to make love to me. Just having you hold me and talk to me is often the best lovemaking you could ever give. For now, just having you with me is more than enough."

"Thank you, teeluk," she said very quietly. "I'm very lucky to have a man like you. You are the best man in the whole world."

He could feel himself blushing. "That may be pushing things a little. I can think of several people who would disagree with you."

"Then they are stupid people," she responded. "Now you shut

up, so we can lie down and hold each other."

They lay in bed and paid intense attention to one another. Their hunger for each other was apparent, but physical sex was neither a motive nor a goal. It was a very satisfying evening of lovemaking.

The following weeks passed quickly. Mike refused to work late or on weekends. He even left work early a number times. What was his boss going to do? Make him come home? That would happen soon enough anyway. He wasn't sure what would happen once he left Thailand. He wasn't even sure if he would ever return. He wanted to be close to Math every minute. He took her to dinner, he took her shopping, he took her to movies, and he took her dancing. He was very careful to not make her jealous and he was especially careful to not let anything she did upset him. Any casual observer would have said he was a doting lover.

The only evening he left her alone was the night Randy and the others had a farewell party for themselves. They didn't have it at Soi 2, so Mike agreed to go. Even then he stayed for only hour or two before going straight home to Math.

The weekend Randy and the others left Thailand was the beginning of Mike's depression. Their leaving was his personal omen of what was to come. His depression had nothing to do with Math. It had only to do with the knowledge that he, too, would be leaving soon. He became edgy and irritable. He even allowed himself to argue with Math once or twice, and those moments intensified his depression.

"Mike, are you tired of being with me?" Math asked one evening after a small spat.

"No," he answered truthfully. "Why would you ask something like that?"

"I don't know," she replied. "Sometimes you don't seem happy with me anymore. Have I done something to displease you?"

"No Math," he said. "You have been perfect. I'm just upset and depressed. I know I'll be leaving soon and it's killing me. You have no idea how it makes me feel. I've finally found someone I love with all my heart and I'm so very afraid I'll never see you again. I'm sorry if I haven't been as loving as I should have been."

She bowed her head and was silent for a moment. "Never mind, teeluk. I understand. I'm feeling the same. I love you, too, and I never want to lose you either. But you shouldn't worry. I will wait for you to come back to me. I'll wait until the day I die." She paused for a brief second. "Teeluk, can we make love right now? Suddenly I want you very, very much."

Mike didn't answer. Instead, he picked her up in his arms and carried her to the bed. Then, with complete and total abandon, they joined with each other in heart, body, and spirit. A fiery passion seldom felt by two people burned in their souls. They succumbed to each others needs and desires with unbridled rapture and nurturing compassion. They made pure, selfless love as only God could have intended between a man and a woman. The sweet satisfaction of their union left them exhausted and fulfilled.

For the next few days they went through life knowing they had experienced a togetherness unmatched by anything they had ever felt before. Math had blushed and smiled when Mike called it a religious experience and suggested they put a shrine in the room as a memorial.

It was three days before they made love again. They both were worried that anything less than that night might seem like failure. They were wrong. They never again matched the magic of that one night, but it was never a disappointment either. Their lovemaking varied only by degrees of ecstasy.

Mike stretched his six-week stay into three months by wasting as much time as possible. Eventually, the job he was there to wrap up was finished. Reluctantly he submitted his final report. Along with the report, he sent a note saying he would not be back for a week or two. He wanted to visit other parts of Thailand while he was there and had the chance.

That night he told Math his plans and she realized just how little time they had left together. "Teeluk," she said, "Now I know 100% when you will be leaving me, and I'm very sad and very afraid. Sometimes, I feel I will never see you again."

"Not that monkey-man dream again, is it?" Mike tried to sound light-hearted but failed.

"That might be part of it," she said. "I wish you would stay with me and never go home."

"Math," he spoke softly, "If I could stay here with you, I would do it in a heartbeat. If only I had a job and could take care of you, I would never leave. But don't worry, someday I'll come back for you. That's my promise to you. If you wait for me, one day I'll marry you and take you back to America. That is, if you will go with me."

"Mike, I'd go with you anywhere. All you have to do is ask."

"Let's not talk about my leaving anymore," he said. "I think it might make me cry."

"Me too," she whispered. Then she perked up. "Let's talk about where we can visit in Thailand. I have a good idea. We can go to Chiang Mai and visit North Thailand. You'll like it there. It's beautiful this time of the year, and it's not so hot. They have beautiful mountains, long neck people, hill tribes and everything."

"Do they have Carlsberg beer there?" he interrupted.

She hit him playfully on the arm. "Yes, they have Carlsberg beer. Now shut up and let me talk. My sister, Nuang, and her husband live in Chiang Mai; they can show us around. Nuang's husband, Surat, drives a car for tourists and farang businessmen. If he isn't busy, he can drive us himself. If he is busy, we can get a discount from his company. What do you think teeluk?"

"It sounds great," he answered. "I'd like to meet your sister. If she's half as beautiful as you, I might fall in love with her, too."

This time Math hit him harder. "Bad idea," she said and pretended to pout.

Mike laughed. "I only meant fall in love with her as my future sister-in-law. Now, let's make plans for our trip."

Together they made a list of things they wanted to do and see while in North Thailand.

That night Mike made plane reservations for their trip to Chiang Mai. Later he boxed the documents from work for shipment to America while Math called her sister to make arrangements for a hotel and car with a driver.

"Sawasdee ka," Math said politely when Surat answered the phone. "I am Math. Is my sister there?" There was a pause and she heard talking in the background.

"Hello, Math?" Nuang came on the line.

"Hello, Nuang," she answered back. "I'm coming to visit you in Chiang Mai in two days, and I'm bringing a surprise."

"Oh, Math," Nuang was excited, "I have a surprise for you too. What's your surprise?"

"I'm bringing my future husband to meet you."

"You mean the farang?"

"Yes," Math answered, "and you're going to love him. He's very anxious to meet you. What is your surprise?"

"I think it's not as important as your surprise right now." Some of the excitement disappeared from Nuang's voice. "I'll tell you later, after you get here."

"Nuang, you know how much I hate secrets," Math said, "but I guess I'll wait. Mike and I want to visit many places while we are in Chiang Mai. Do you think you can get us a hotel room near the night bazaar, and can Surat drive for us?"

"Yes, I can find you a good hotel at a discount," Nuang answered. "And Surat is not busy now, so he can drive you around. If it would be okay, may I travel with you and your friend?"

"Mike and I would like that very much," Math said. "I want him to know you. If you're going to have a brother-in-law, you should get to know him too. Then, when you come to visit me in America, you will feel more comfortable."

They both laughed at the thought of Nuang visiting Math in America. The idea excited them. Nuang promised to take care of everything. Surat would meet them at the airport.

Chapter 29

The next day, Mike shipped his boxes to his office in America. The day after that, they left for Chiang Mai and Northern Thailand. Mike wanted to go in style so they rented a Mercedes limo to the Bangkok airport. Math had never been in a limo before and she was thrilled. Mike had never ridden in a Mercedes before, either, but he didn't admit it. He just enjoyed watching Math act like a rich lady.

At the airport they checked their bags and had lunch from the KFC counter. Not much later they boarded their plane. The flight went smoothly until the moment they were landing. Then they hit turbulence and the plane started bouncing dangerously. Math told Mike she was afraid the plane was going to crash. The plane didn't crash, but Math did. In her fear and panic, her heart went spastic. By the time they landed she was nearly comatose in her seat.

Mike had seen her reaction before. He tried to tell the stewardesses to give her a little time and she would be okay, but they didn't speak English and they couldn't understand his Thai. They called an ambulance. Within minutes Math was being exited through the service entrance.

Mike stood inside the plane wondering what to do. He was being separated from Math and he couldn't explain that she was with him. He didn't know what Math's sister or her husband looked like. He was going to be stranded at the Chiang Mai airport without Math.

He elbowed his way through the knot of stewardesses, determined to go wherever Math went. The airline employees pushed him back just as hard as he pushed them. Desperate he

J. F. Gump

shouted, "Teeluk, pom lak khun mak. Sweetheart, I love you very much."

One of the stewardesses looked at him and said something in Thai that he didn't understand. He nodded anyway. They let him go with Math to the ambulance. He tried to explain to the ambulance crew about Math's heart condition but it was useless. They only smiled, nodded, and ignored him. Ten minutes later, sirens blaring, they arrived at the hospital. Math was wheeled into the emergency room.

Much to hospital staff's dismay, Mike refused to let go of the gurney. Everyone eyed him suspiciously but he stood his ground. He followed Math into the examining room and stood watching while the doctors and nurses went through their routines.

After a few minutes a lanky Thai man, obviously not a doctor, rushed into the examining room. He looked at Mike and then at the doctor before hurrying to Math's side. The man said something to her but Mike didn't understand his words. Math mumbled something back but her voice was so low that Mike couldn't hear. The Thai man turned and said something unintelligible to Mike. Mike stared stupidly while he tried to remember the Thai words for "who are you". The words wouldn't come. In a moment the man exited the room. Math seemed to be semi-lucid so Mike went to her and kissed her softly on her cheek.

"Are you okay, sweetheart?" he asked.

"I'm not sure. I hurt and I can't breathe well. I'm very tired, teeluk. Can you hold my hand?"

Gently, he took her hand in his. "Is this the same thing that has happened to you before?"

"I think so," she answered, "but I'm not sure."

"What did the doctor say?"

"I don't know the English word. Maybe you should ask him."

Like he can speak better English than you, Mike thought. He turned to the doctor and said, "Alai, nah? What?" while pointing at Math.

The doctor spoke rapidly in Thai.

"Mai kow jai, I don't understand," Mike answered.

The doctor picked up a book and leafed through it. In a moment he said in English, "Panic attack".

Mike laughed as tears of relief filled his eyes. He pointed at Math. "Math bai, chai mai? Math can go?"

The doctor smiled and nodded his head.

"I will pay for everything," Mike said, but the doctor just stared. "Tao lai? How much?"

The doctor thought for a moment then said, "Five hundred baht." His English was perfect.

Mike tried to pay the doctor but was directed to a cashier's window. He paid the fee and hurried back to the emergency ward. He arrived just as Math was exiting the examination room. The lanky Thai man he had seen earlier was helping her walk.

"This is my brother-in-law," Math said weakly. "His name is Surat."

"I'm pleased to meet you," Mike said in English.

"He doesn't understand English," Math answered for him. She spoke to Surat in Thai. Surat nodded politely and then motioned that they should leave. Mike tried to take Math in his arms, but Surat didn't release his hold. Mike didn't persist. Instead he followed behind. Math was part of his family and Mike respected that.

In the car Surat and Math had a brief conversation. Then Math told Mike they would go to the airport to collect their suitcases and then go to the hotel. Ten minutes later they were at the airport and fifteen minutes after that they were at the hotel. Surat said goodnight, and Math and Mike went to their room.

Math was exhausted and wanted to lie down. After making sure she was comfortable, Mike took a beer from the room's mini-bar and went out onto the balcony. The view of Chiang Mai at night was terrific. He sipped at the beer as his eyes soaked in the sight.

Later, after his beer was finished, he went inside. Math was asleep. He sat on the edge of the bed and watched her for a long time. She was very beautiful. He wondered what she saw in him. Whatever it was, he was glad. He lay down beside her and slept.

The next morning Math was up early. She showered, dressed, and put on her make-up while Mike slept. He was awakened by the sound of the hotel room door opening and closing.

"What time is it?" he asked, struggling to wake up.

"Time for lazy farangs to get out of bed." Math said, walking into the room with her hands full. "I bought you a newspaper and American coffee already. I'm going to the balcony to drink my tea and enjoy the morning while you wake up."

She knew his morning moods and had learned that it was best to leave him alone until he had finished his shower. "My sister and brother-in-law will be here in an hour," she added as she stepped out onto the balcony.

Math had a terrible fear of heights, but the view from the balcony was too hard to resist. She stood by the railing and looked at the morning city for several minutes before she backed away. By the time she finished her tea, Mike was in the shower. Ten minutes later they went downstairs to the lobby restaurant to wait for Nuang and Surat.

Mike was nervous. He had met Surat at the hospital the night before but he had never met Math's sister. "I hope your sister likes me," he said, fidgeting in his seat.

"Of course she'll like you. Why would she not like you?"

"Because you're her sister and I'm a farang. A farang old enough to be your father. Maybe old enough to be her father, too, for that matter."

Math laughed. "Yes, you are a very old man," she teased. "For our first anniversary I will buy a walking cane."

"Very funny," he said. "Okay, maybe I'm not that old, but I'm a lot older than you." He raised his eyebrows in mock question, "You were only joking about the cane, weren't you?"

"Oh, no. I'm serious about the cane, but it's not for you. It's for me to beat you with if I ever find you with another lady."

He smiled and kissed her on her neck. "You can buy the cane but you'll never have to use it. You're the only woman I want."

Math smiled and kissed Mike on his lips. Their kiss was interrupted by polite cough. They both looked up to see Surat and a lady standing by their table.

"Sawasdee ka," said the lady softly, distinctly. "Chan cheur Nuang. My name is Nuang."

Math got up and hugged her sister. "Nuang, this is my friend Mike."

Mike stood clumsily, almost knocking his chair over backwards. He could feel himself blushing. "Sawasdee krup," he muttered in his worst Thai. He wanted to say it again, clearer, but figured that would only make him look stupid. Nuang giggled and his blush increased to the point that small beads of sweat popped out onto his face.

"Pom cheur Mike. My name is Mike" He held his hand out for Nuang to shake. It was an automatic action. He knew Thais didn't shake hands as a custom. He wanted to run away and hide from his bumbling.

Nuang wai'ed to Mike then politely shook his hand. "Are you okay, Khun Mike?" she asked in broken English. "Your face is very red and you seem nervous and upset." Then she smiled.

"Just making an idiot of myself," he replied hoping Nuang didn't understand.

Nuang looked questioningly at Mike, then at Math. Math translated, and Surat and the two girls laughed. Not knowing what else to do, Mike laughed with them.

"Please sit down and join us for breakfast," Mike invited, still laughing. Again Math interpreted and everyone sat. They ordered their food and passed the time getting to know each other. Math interpreted from English to Thai and Thai to English as was necessary for everyone to understand. It was awkward but effective.

"I'm studying English," Nuang volunteered. "By the time you and Math get married, and I come to visit you in America, my

English will be almost perfect."

Mike eyed Math curiously.

"I told Nuang that you are the man who will be my husband," she said shyly. "I told her she should come to visit us when we move to America. I hope you don't mind, teeluk."

Mike smiled, then leaned over and whispered into Math's ear, "I don't mind, sweetheart, but only as long as you never change your mind about marrying me." He kissed her softly on the cheek. When he looked up, he saw Nuang observing intently.

"Pom farang ngoh ngoh. I'm just a stupid foreigner," he said to Nuang, laughing.

Nuang nodded her head in agreement and laughed with him.

Thus started their adventure in Northern Thailand. It turned out to be seven days Mike hoped would never end, seven days he would remember for the rest of his life. Together they went elephant trekking through the mountains, watched men defy death in pits of cobras, visited exquisite floral gardens and orchid farms, toured ancient Buddhist temples, traveled to Myanmar (Burma), traveled through Southeast Asia's infamous Golden Triangle, saw Hill Tribe villages and Long Neck people and more. At the end of every day Mike and Math were exhausted but still found the energy to love each other.

Nuang had many opportunities to tell Math her secret about Jum, but remembering her promise to the old monk she held her tongue. Math looked so happy to be with Mike, yet so sad knowing he would be gone in a few short days. She wouldn't ruin the time Math had left with Mike by telling what she knew. She had been to visit Jum at the temple and for now his health was okay. There would be time enough later for Math to learn about her true father. Nuang decided it could wait until Mike had gone home before she said anything to Math. For now she would keep her secret.

On their seventh day in Chiang Mai, Mike announced that he wanted to see Phuket Island in South Thailand, and that he and Math would leave the next day.

Everyone, including Math, was surprised. Mike had never mentioned going to Phuket, but Math didn't mind. She had never been there and was excited at the thought. She would have been excited and happy to go anywhere as long as it was with Mike.

That evening Mike and Math took Surat and Nuang to a very expensive restaurant for dinner. Nuang dressed in her finest traditional Thai clothing and she looked absolutely ravishing. Surat's ego practically burst at the seams when Mike told him he was married to the second most beautiful lady in Thailand. Second only to Math, of course. Both Math and Nuang smiled bashfully at his words. At that moment Mike knew he had made up for that awkward and embarrassing first day in Chiang Mai. Math capped off the evening by making slow love to him.

The next morning Mike made flight and hotel reservations for Phuket. Later, Nuang and Surat drove them to the airport. Nuang cried and hugged Mike and Math goodbye. "I will come to visit you and Math in America," she said to Mike. "I promise."

"You'll always be welcome in my house, Nuang," he replied, meaning it.

They arrived at their hotel in Phuket just as the sun was setting. They walked the beach until dark, holding hands and saying nothing. It was quiet except for the sound of the waves rolling across the sand.

In a while Mike stopped and took Math in his arms. He held her close and said, "I don't want to go home, Math."

"I know. I don't want you to go either. Please say you can stay here with me, teeluk."

"We should get something to eat and go to bed," he changed the subject. "I feel very tired. I think I could fall asleep just standing here."

She knew he wasn't tired. She had seen him in these moods before. She knew he was depressed. She hoped it was only for tonight. Please dear Buddha, she said silently, let Mike feel happier tomorrow. "I'm tired too," she lied. "Maybe we can order our dinner from room service. Then we can be alone with each other. I don't feel like seeing a lot of people right now."

"Me too," he responded.

She knew she had said the right thing.

Altogether they stayed six days in Phuket. Mike's depression faded but never disappeared. They spent most of their time walking the beaches, shopping, eating, and lazing around the room. They made love whenever the mood struck, and as the remaining days grew fewer the mood struck more often and with increasing passion. Sometimes they talked, but less often than one might have expected. When they did talk, it was never about Mike's leaving. It was always about anything but that.

At the end of the sixth day, Mike told Math he was making reservations for his flight to America. He couldn't put it off any longer. She responded by locking herself in the bathroom while he called the airlines. She didn't want to listen to him talking about leaving. After he had finished with the airlines, he knocked on the door and she came out. She had been crying.

"We'll go to Bangkok tomorrow," he said. "I leave for America the day after that."

She said nothing. She could not. Instead, she pulled Mike down onto the bed with her and held him tightly for a very long time. She did not talk, she did not cry, and she did not make love to him. She just held him and touched his face and his hair and his arms and everywhere. When she finished, she said, "I never want to forget what you feel like, teeluk. I hope you don't mind."

"I don't mind," he replied. Then he did the same to Math.

Later that evening, they made love. They didn't know it then, but it was to be the last time they would make love with each other before he went home.

By five o'clock the next day, they were at the Amari Airport Hotel in Bangkok. They both knew they had less than twelve hours left to be together. Mike took Math shopping for some new clothes, hoping it would brighten her mood. It seemed to help, but only a little.

Later they had a pleasant dinner at the hotel and tried to pretend that nothing was happening. They tried to ignore how quickly their last hours together were passing. Mike had already decided he wouldn't sleep that night. He could do that on the flight. He wanted to spend every last minute awake and with Math.

By ten o'clock they were back in their room. Math needed no words to tell Mike she wanted to make love. Within minutes they were in bed kissing, touching, and caressing.

"Please take me now," she whispered urgently.

He needed no further encouragement. He positioned himself between her legs then paused for the briefest of moments to kiss her neck and tease her breasts. Suddenly, and without any forewarning, he felt his manhood softening, going limp. He had had this problem before, but never with Math. He went into a panic which only hastened his flaccidity.

Math waited patiently for Mike to take her. She didn't know what was happening to him at that moment.

Mike, realizing it was hopeless, stopped everything. He moved from Math and sat on the edge of the bed. He faced away from her to hide his embarrassment.

"What's wrong, teeluk? Don't you want me?"

"I don't know what's wrong," he said, tense.

"Are you angry with me? Did I do something wrong? I only want to love you one more time before you go to America. Don't you want me anymore?"

"Damn it, Math," he snapped. He forced his voice lower. "Yes, I want you. I want to make love to you more than anything in the world but I can't. I don't know what's wrong with me, but I can't make love now. See?" He pointed at his flaccid manhood.

"Just lay down, teeluk," she said, reassuring him. "Maybe I can make it better."

Mike lay down on the bed and Math used every trick she knew

to make him erect. Three times he almost made penetration and three times he failed.

After the third attempt she said, "Never mind about me, teeluk. I only want to make you happy." Using only her mouth, she skillfully brought Mike to a climax. Afterwards, he did the same for her. They spent the rest of the night lying in bed, holding each other, and talking about the future.

"I will come back to you, Math. I don't know how long it will take, but I promise you I'll come back. As sure as I'm leaving in the morning, I will be back."

"And I will wait for you. As long as there is a breath in my body, I will wait for you."

At three o'clock in the morning, Mike showered and repacked his suitcase. At four, they checked out of the hotel and walked across the freeway overpass to the Bangkok International Airport.

Math watched as Mike went through security and checked in with the airlines. She met him by the entrance to Immigration Control. There they held each other until Mike said, "Math, leaving you today is the hardest thing I have ever done in my life. I don't want to stop holding you but my plane is leaving very soon. I'm sorry, sweetheart. I must say goodbye."

"No, please, teeluk. We will not say goodbye. We will only say bye for now, until we can be together again."

He kissed her long and hard. "Yes, teeluk, only bye until we are together again." He kissed her one last time, and then walked toward Immigration Control. He didn't look back.

"I will wait for you, teeluk," she whispered to herself as she watched Mike disappear through the doorway. Then she sat down on her suitcase and cried. "Please God," she prayed silently, "keep my love safe and send him back to me in quickly time."

In a while she took the shuttle to the domestic terminal and bought a ticket to Phitsanulok. Really, she didn't want to go there because of Sawat. But Mike had been adamant that he didn't want her living in Pattaya. He wanted her to go to her sister's house in

Chiang Mai and she had said she would. But except for Nuang, there was nothing for her in Chiang Mai. At least in Phitsanulok she had her own house and her mother, father and little brother. By now a long time had passed and maybe Sawat had forgotten his anger. If he bothered her, she could always leave again. At that moment, Phitsanulok seemed her best choice.

On the plane, she wrote a letter to Mike telling him about her decision to go back to her own house. She begged for his understanding. She told him she missed him very much already and prayed he would return soon. She reaffirmed her love and her promise to wait for him. At the end she signed it, "I Love You, Teeluk. Your Future Wife, Math."

In Phitsanulok her first stop was Phitsanulok Communications. There she faxed her letter to the number Mike had given her. As she continued her way home, Math wondered where Mike's fax machine was and who else might read her letter before he arrived in America. She hoped her fax wouldn't cause any problems for him.

Chapter 30

Even though Math hadn't been to her house for a long time, nothing had changed. Well, almost nothing. Her two dogs were now living at her mother's house but everything else was the same. Mike had been paying her rent so no one had removed her meager furniture or padlocked the door. The room was small compared to Mike's condo, but it was her home and she was comfortable.

Before Mike left, he had given her as much money as she could earn in three months, but she knew how fast money could disappear. She had to find work to make the money last until Mike returned. She didn't know how long that would be, but she knew it might be forever.

That evening she visited her mother, brother, and sister to make sure they were well. She told them about her adventures in Pattaya, Chiang Mai, and Phuket. She also told them about Mike and their plans to be married. Her mother wasn't pleased but said nothing. As far as Nui was concerned, all farangs were bad people. Nui never stopped to remember the beatings she had suffered at the hands of her own Thai husband.

Math stayed at her mother's house watching TV until very late. She was happy when her mother suggested she stay for the night. Math didn't want to be alone, especially tonight. She slept with her little brother. It gave her comfort having someone near, even if it wasn't Mike.

The next day she went job hunting. It was a totally dejecting experience. The collapse of the Thai economy had left thousands—if not millions—of Thais out of work. Competition for the good jobs was fierce with most of them going to relatives or friends of the employer. The only employment she found was menial labor that demanded long hours and paid less than 100 baht per day. After paying her rent and her insurance, there would be little money left for food and clothes.

Math took one of those jobs only because she had no choice. That first week she worked three days on a construction site clean-up crew. It was the hardest work she had ever done. It left her body exhausted and her hands bleeding. After the third day, she decided she would rather work as a bar-girl in Pattaya than to go through that every day.

She wrote a fax to Mike telling him about the job and that she was going to quit and find something easier. She looked but found only a few hours of work at a laundry. It paid less than construction, but it at least it didn't make her hands bleed.

Two days later she received a fax from Mike. He was back in America and had received both of her letters. He agreed that she shouldn't work as a laborer again. He would deposit money into her bank account so she could live. She was relieved to read his words. His company was sending him to another job away from home but still in America. He said he would write as often as he could. He still loved her, the fax read. He missed her very much and prayed every day he could come back for her soon. She read his letter over and over until she had memorized every word. That night she dreamed Mike was with her again.

In the morning she put on her best business clothes and resumed her search for a decent job. She hoped desperately to find a full time position with a good company. She would still consider part time and temporary jobs, but only the ones that wouldn't make an old woman out of her.

By mid afternoon she had filled out six applications. She was near the movie theater and decided to apply there. A wave of sadness swept over her as she entered the theater lobby. It was where she had fallen and killed Mike's baby. Instantly, she decided she could never work there and turned to leave. As she reached the door, she heard someone calling her name. She turned to look. It was Sawat.

"Math, please wait," he shouted. "I have something important to tell you."

She wanted to run but knew he would easily catch up with her if she did. She stepped back inside the lobby where there were more people. She watched Sawat cautiously as he approached. He was smiling.

"I don't think I want to talk with you," she said, her voice tight. "What do you want?"

"Math," he said softly, "I only want to tell you I'm sorry for the way I treated you and your sister and your family. Please understand, I was hurting very much and I wanted you to hurt the way I did. I know I was wrong. I beg for your forgiveness."

She moved a step away from him. "Maybe you should be telling that to my sister. You know what you did to her. If I could have found you that day, I would have killed you."

"I don't blame you. I would have deserved it too. If your sister were here, I would beg her forgiveness, too. I've had a lot of time to think and now realize what a bad person I've been. I don't know why I was acting like that. I guess I was feeling sorry for myself. I had been taking a lot of drugs and drinking. I think I was a little crazy. But I have stopped all of that now. I haven't taken drugs or had anything to drink since the night I... ah... Well, you know, what I did to your sister."

She was suspicious. She stared at him but said nothing.

"Please, Math. Please forgive me. I promise I'll never do anything like that ever again. Please, say we can be friends."

He seemed so sincere that she said, "Okay, Sawat. I know you were once a nice man and I loved you. I can never love you that way again, but I can forgive you." She paused. "And I guess we can be friends, but only friends. I have someone else I love now. I want you to know that."

His face beamed. "Thank you, Math. I understand. I have someone else I love too. I have a new girlfriend. I would like for you to meet her someday. She is really nice. By the way, where are you working now?"

"I don't have a job. I'm looking for work but I'm not having much luck. Seems all of the good jobs are taken."

"Maybe I can help if you'll let me," he offered. "A woman at Big C is pregnant and will be quitting her job in a couple of days. The manager is a friend of mine. If you want, I can ask him to hire you. The pay isn't much but the work is very easy. What do you say?"

She wanted to say no but she needed a job. "Okay. What do I have to do?"

"Come to the Big C tomorrow morning at nine o'clock. I'll introduce you to my friend. I can't promise anything, but I think there won't be a problem."

"Thank you, Sawat," she said. "This is very kind of you."

"Mai pen rai, krup, never mind. It's the least I can do to make up for the hurt I caused. I must go now, but I'll see you tomorrow at nine." He smiled and left the theater.

Math spent the rest of the afternoon wondering at the change in Sawat. He had never been so nice to her. Maybe he was finally becoming a man, she thought, or maybe he wanted something. She wasn't sure which. She would have to wait and see what happened. That evening she wrote another fax to Mike saying she thought she had found a good job. She didn't mention Sawat.

Early the next morning, she went to Phitsanulok Communications and sent her fax. At nine o'clock she met Sawat in front of Big C. As promised, he introduced her to the manager and gave her a very good recommendation. Twenty minutes later she was offered a job starting the next Monday, and at three times the salary she had made as a laborer.

When she left the interview, she tried to find Sawat to tell him the good news and to thank him. He was nowhere to be found. On impulse she decided to go to the temple and say prayers. On the way she bought food and gifts for the monks, and offerings for Buddha.

After saying her prayers she started to look for Jum, but then remembered he had gone to another temple. She would miss her conversations with the old monk. She roamed the grounds of the temple in no hurry to go home. She felt content now that she had a decent job lined up.

On one side of the temple Math found a garden which probably had been very beautiful at one time. Now it had fallen victim to a lack of care. She spent the rest of the morning and most of the afternoon in the garden pulling weeds and picking up the leaves that had fallen onto the stone pathway. When she finished with the garden, she headed home feeling she had done her part to help keep the temple beautiful.

On the way she stopped at Phitsanulok Communications. There was a fax from Mike. He told her he was now at his new work assignment and gave her a fax number where he could be contacted. If he had received her last fax, he didn't mention it. Math paid to have her earlier fax sent to the new number.

That evening, as she sat watching TV with her younger brother, her cell phone rang. It scared her because it was the first time it had rang in weeks. It was Mike. "Teeluk," she screamed, "I'm so happy you called. I have much to tell you."

"I love you, Math," he said, laughing at her excitement. "Sweetheart, I can't talk long because it's very expensive from America. I just wanted to tell you how much I love you and miss you. Also, I want you to know that I have deposited some money into your bank account."

"Thank you, teeluk. You're too kind to me. I love you, too. I want to tell you that today I have found a job and it pays enough for me to live. You must save your money and take care of yourself and your family. If you want to send money once in a while to buy me new clothes or something, you can, but I can't ask you for money while I'm working."

"Never mind. I will send you money as often as I can because I love you. I don't want you to go without anything. I'll be at this work assignment for a while, but then I don't know where I'll be."

"Teeluk, do you have a phone number where I can call you?"

"It's very expensive to call, Math. You need to save your money, too."

"Okay, teeluk. I think you know what's best. I'll send you a fax every day anyway."

Mike laughed. "That would make me happy. I must say bye for now. I'll call you again as soon as I can. I love you, Math."

"I love you too, Mike. Bye-bye teeluk, please take care of yourself."

As much as she hated the sound of the phone clicking disconnect, she was on cloud nine. It was the first time she had ever received a call from America. She was beside herself with excitement. She told her mother and her brother about their short conversation until her mother finally told her to stop. Then she told them one more time.

Later she lay in her brother's bed but couldn't sleep. She spent most of the night thinking about Mike. She missed him terribly. In the morning, after her mother had gone to work and her brother had left for school, she lay in bed touching and rubbing herself pretending it was Mike. Her climax left her feeling ashamed.

For the next few weeks everything was as good as Math could have hoped for. Her work, as Sawat had said, was very easy and the pay was lot more than what she had made at construction and laundry. Sawat worked at Big C too, and she saw him nearly every day. He was always a perfect gentleman.

Mike sent faxes almost every day and deposited money into her bank account every week or so. Not a lot of money, but enough to make a difference between existing and living. She was able to live.

Math began spending more time at her own home. Her dogs had come home from her mother's house, so she had company even when she was alone. Sawat stopped by from time to time just to say hello and to play with her dogs. He never threatened anything and she was comfortable with his visits. Once he brought his new girlfriend with him. She was indeed a very nice girl.

233

J. F. Gump

Math's life settled into a normal routine and she was happy.

Then, in a single day, her world was turned upside down. It began when she received a very long fax from Mike telling her that his company was 100% finished working in Thailand and he wouldn't be returning. The only way he would come back was if he could save enough money to do it on his own. That wouldn't be easy because it took nearly all of his salary just to pay his regular bills. What little extra money he managed to save he had been sending to her so she could live. He had saved none for himself. The last lines of his fax were the most devastating of all.

"Sweetheart," his words read, "You are a very young and very beautiful woman. You know I love you very much. I don't want to say this because it hurts me too much, but I think you should find a nice Thai man to love. I'm afraid I may never be able to come back for you. I know this isn't what you want to hear, but I think it will be best for you. Everything at my home is very complicated right now. I don't know how to explain what I'm going through. I don't know what to do. I don't even know if I'll ever see you again. I love you but I cannot be so selfish as to make you wait for me until I have fixed my own life. Please don't hate me. I'm doing what I think is best for your life. I will always love you and I will never forget you. Mike."

She read the fax several times to make sure she understood. Her emotions ran rampant from anger to sadness to self-pity. She was so confused she wasn't sure what she felt. She wondered what was happening in Mike's life. He had not explained anything. She forced herself to sit down and write a reply.

"Teeluk," she wrote, "I know from your fax that you are going through a very difficult time in your life. You're a good man and I know you will do what is correct for everyone. Please believe me when I say that I love only you, and if I cannot have you I don't want another man. I understand your life is very confused right now, but one day soon things will be better. In my heart I know you'll come back to me. I will wait for you, teeluk. I will wait for you forever. Please forgive me, but I will continue to send you faxes, even if you do not send any to me. I believe in you and I believe in our love. In my heart I am your loving and devoted wife. Math."

With tears streaming, she drove to Phitsanulok Communications and sent the fax. Then she went home.

At nine o'clock that same night, her handy rang. She just knew it was Mike. "Hello, teeluk," she answered.

"It's me, Nuang," she heard her sister say.

"I'm sorry, Nuang. I was hoping Mike would call me today. How are you?"

"You must come to Chiang Mai," Nuang said, bypassing customary Thai pleasantries. "It's very important."

Math heard the urgency in her voice. "What is it, Nuang?"

"I can't tell you over the phone. Just trust me when I say it's important. When can you come? Can you be here tomorrow?"

Math's mind whirled with questions. "How can I? I have a job. If I don't go to work, I might be fired. Maybe I can come this weekend. What's so urgent anyway?"

"Please, Math," Nuang pleaded. "Ask your boss if you can have a few days off."

"Are you well, Nuang? Is your health okay?"

"It's not me, but it's very important. You must come to Chiang Mai. Please don't ask more questions. Just ask your boss if you can have a few days off."

"Okay. Tomorrow, I will ask."

"Thank you," Nuang said and hung up the phone.

Almost immediately, Math heard her dogs fighting outside. They did this about once a week, but she had never figured out why. "Damn it," she shouted. "Why do you stupid dogs have to fight tonight?" She ran outside to pull them apart.

As she reached her door, she heard a man's voice and the fighting stopped. It was Sawat. She saw him pick up the smaller of the two dogs and look at its right front leg.

"He's bleeding pretty heavy," Sawat said.

"Let's take him inside," she said, worried about her dog. The small one was her favorite.

Sawat had visited her house several times recently, but this was the first time he had been inside since the night he had assaulted Nuang. Together, they doctored the dog's injured leg. In a while the bleeding stopped and the dog wanted down. Reluctantly, she let it go. A few minutes later, the injured dog and the larger dog were lying together as if nothing had happened.

"Stupid dogs," she said, disgusted.

They sat in silence for a few minutes, waiting to see if the dogs would behave themselves. There was no further commotion.

"Math, I still love you," Sawat said, abruptly.

Math was caught off guard. "We're just friends, Sawat," she said trying to laugh off his comment. She didn't need any more complications in her life. "Your girlfriend wouldn't be happy if she heard you saying that."

"I finished with her tonight, Math."

"I'm sorry, but we're still only friends."

"Yes, I know." Sawat paused a long moment then asked, "Who is the farang?" He pointed at the picture sitting on the nightstand.

She tensed. The way he said *farang* made her teeth itch. She bit back her immediate response and kept her tone nonchalant. "Oh, him? Just someone I met in Pattaya."

Sawat picked up the picture and stared at it for a long time. Finally he gripped an edge with the thumb and forefinger of both hands, as if to rip it in half. "Just someone you met in Pattaya?" He tore the picture just a little.

Her heart leapt to her throat. "Give me that." She reached for the picture.

Sawat pulled away from her. He tore the picture a little more. "Just someone you met in Pattaya?"

"He's the man I love. Now give me the picture."

Sawat shook his head. "I can't believe you dumped me for this farang. He is ugly and he is old. Where is he now, Math?"

"He's in America but he'll be back soon," she answered.

"You know he's never coming back, don't you? I think it's time you forget about him."

"Sawat, please, give me the picture." She reached again.

Sawat held one hand in place and allowed the other to be pulled away by Math. He held tight with both hands and the picture ripped in half.

Math went into a rage. "Ee hia. You lizard," she spat, "I will kill you." Her fist hit him hard, high on his cheekbone. Her blow knocked him to the floor.

Immediately he was up, his fists pelting wildly at her. His assault forced her backwards. She covered her face with her arms, but his blows knocked them aside. She let her knees buckle to fall away from his onslaught. As she fell, she swung her fist upward into his crotch. That quick, it was over. Sawat fell gagging to the floor.

Math scrambled to her feet. Already, dark bruises were forming on her arms. She could only imagine what her face looked like. There was a taste of blood in her mouth. She grabbed Sawat by the hair of his head and dragged him out of her house. She knew she had to get away before he stopped hurting.

She hurried back inside the house and threw a change of clothes and a few essentials in her oversized purse. Then she locked her door and ran toward her motorcycle. As she passed Sawat, she kicked him savagely in the groin to make sure he didn't get up any time soon. She drove to the bus station leaving Sawat moaning in the dirt.

Math washed the blood from her face in the ladies room at the bus station. She had cuts and bruises on both cheeks. An ugly knot protruded from her forehead. She covered everything as best as she could with make-up, and styled her hair so it hid the worst spots. Then she left the restroom and bought a one-way ticket to Chiang Mai. She stood near a security guard while she waited for her bus to leave. She was worried Sawat might show up, but he never did.

Chapter 31

When Math arrived in Chiang Mai the following morning, she called home and told her little brother where to find her motorcycle. Next she hired a taxi to her sister's house. Fifteen minutes later she knocked on the door.

"Oh," Nuang said, surprised at Math's unexpected arrival. "I didn't expect you so quickly." She stared at Math for a moment before asking, "What happened to your face and your arms?"

"I think you know already," she answered. "It was Sawat. I'll be okay."

Nuang nodded her understanding.

"Last night, when you called me, what was so important?" Math asked.

Yesterday, before calling with her urgent message, Nuang had been to visit with the old monk Jum as she did every two or three weeks. She was shocked to see how his health had deteriorated since her last visit. She thought he might not live until her next. She had known immediately that she had to bring Math to him as soon as possible. What had been only important before was critical now. "There's someone you must see before it's too late."

"I don't understand, Nuang." Who is so important?"

"Please, it's not easy to explain. Just come with me now. I want you to see an old friend." She took Math by the hand and led her from the house.

They took a taxi to the temple on top of the mountain. As they rode, Math caught an occasional glimpse of Chiang Mai in the valley below. It was a spectacular sight.

The taxi waited while Nuang led Math toward the temple.

"Why are we here?" Math asked. "Why have you brought me to this temple?"

"Gniap. Be quiet," Nuang said sharply. "You're in a very sacred place. For once in your life, just be quiet."

Nuang's tone irritated her, but she held her silence and followed her sister. They stopped at a door.

"This is it," Nuang announced.

"This is what?" Math asked.

"Go inside. A friend is waiting to see you."

Math pushed the door open. On the bed lay an old man, a monk. From the doorway and in the dim light she couldn't see who it was. She took a few steps closer. Suddenly she recognized her friend from Phitsanulok. "Jum?" she said without waiting to be spoken to. "Is that you?"

The old monk slowly turned his head to look at her. "My daughter," his words were barely a whisper. "I'm happy to see you. I knew you would come before I died."

"You're not going to die, you foolish old monk," she said softly.

Jum reached out and took Math by the hand. "Please sit down here beside of me," he said. "I have many things to tell you."

She sat carefully on the edge of the bed. She was surprised at the firmness of his grip. He didn't let go of her hand, even after she sat.

After a long silence Jum said, "Do you remember the first time I called you my daughter?"

She thought for a long moment. "I'm not sure. I think I remember you calling me daughter at the funeral for my brother-in-law and my nephew, but I'm not sure."

"You're right, Math," Jum said, "that was the first time. Do you remember what you said?"

"Honestly Jum, I do not," she replied shaking her head. "I'm sorry I don't remember. Why do you ask?"

"You said, 'I am fine today, and how is my father?' Do you know how that made me feel?"

J. F. Gump

"Jum, I apologize if I said the wrong thing," she replied, remembering what she had said. A feeling of guilt washed through her. "I didn't mean to insult you or anything. I would never do that to a monk. Please forgive me."

"Math, there is nothing for you to forgive." The old monk paused, his eyes squeezed shut and his lips pursed.

For moment she thought he was going to cry. She wondered if he was in pain.

After a short minute he took a deep breath and continued, "When you called me father, it made me the happiest man alive. I knew you were only joking when you said it, but your words filled me with a joy I've never known. For that, I thank you."

She stared at the old monk. Her mind whirled. "I'm sorry. I don't understand any of this."

"Look at my face, Math," he ordered in a quiet but demanding tone. "Have you ever seen this face before?"

She looked at him, more confused than ever. "Jum, I have seen you many times. Since I was a little girl. You know that already. You remember all the times we talked at the temple."

"No, Math, look very close. Ignore the old man wrinkles and the sagging skin. Look at the shape of my face. Look at my nose and my eyes and my ears. Have you ever seen those before, besides on my own head?"

Then, as she looked at Jum, she knew she had seen them before. A cold chill shot down her back as the shock of her own realization assaulted her mind. "I have seen them in my own mirror," she said in whisper so low it was almost inaudible. "What's going on? What does this mean?"

"I am your father, Math," Jum said, almost as quiet, "and you are my daughter."

"Why are you lying to me?" she denied what she was hearing and seeing. "Why are you saying these things?" She tried to pull her hand away, but Jum held fast.

"It's not a lie, Math. Sometimes I wish it was just an old man's fantasy, but it's not. Maybe I should keep my silence but I cannot. I have my own selfish reasons for confessing to you. Please, just stay here with me for a while and let me tell you everything. Consider it a wish from a dying man. Then, when I'm finished, you can believe what you want, and you can do whatever you think is best. Will you please do that for me?"

She let her hand relax in his. "Yes, I will listen."

Jum repeated the story he had told to Nuang just a few months before. He told Math about his love for her mother Nui, and the night she was conceived. He told her about his secret attempts to help her through her life. He told her everything.

Math listened without interruption. As his words spilled out, she knew they were true. As she heard each new revelation, her emotions ran the gamut from anger to love for the old monk, and from self-pity to a newfound understanding of herself. By the time Jum finished his story there were tears in his eyes. Long before he stopped talking, she was crying openly.

Finally the old monk ran out of words and sighed. "Daughter, I had to tell you this for two reasons. The first, but not the most important, is that I wanted you to know who had caused the curse on your tender life. I wanted you to understand what a horrible creature I am. As hard as I tried to fix everything I had caused, I could not. My feeble efforts only made me more vile and despicable. The second reason is that I need to know you can forgive me before I die. Buddha knows I don't deserve forgiveness. I deserve only to be spit upon and made to live with snakes and lizards. Still I'm asking you to forgive me. No, Math, I'm not asking your forgiveness, I am begging you for it." He fell silent.

She leaned over and hugged the old man hard. Through heavy sobs, she said, "Jum, I once told you that you are the kindest person I know. Since I was a little girl, I have loved and respected you as my friend. Today, all of that has changed. Now I love and respect you as my father. Yes, father, I can forgive you for anything and everything. And now that I have found you, I cannot let you die. I will stay and take care of you. I will not let you die."

Jum hugged her in return, "Thank you, Math. Thank you for

your forgiveness. I feel like the sins of the world have been lifted from my heart. But you can't stop me from dying. Only God can do that and I think he's made up his mind already. I would like it very much if you would come to see me once in a while."

"Yes, father," she savored the taste of the word on her tongue, "I will come to see you every day, even if it's forever."

He smiled. "Daughter, you have better things to do with the rest of your life than to worry about an old monk, even if he is your father. Like that man you're in love with."

She looked at him in surprise.

"Yes, I already know," Jum continued, "Your sister told me everything. He will come back for you, Math. I can feel it in my heart. Take care of him and he'll take care of you. He will make you happy. But there is another thing I would like you to do for me. It will take some of your time, maybe more time than I have left, but it's something that's important to me. It will make me happy."

"I will," she said earnestly, "Tell me what it is I can do that will make you happy."

"It's something you must see to understand," he said. "Right now I'm too tired to take you, but your sister knows. Have Nuang show you what I want you to do." He squeezed her hand tight. "Math, you should go now and let an old monk get his rest."

"Okay, father, but I'll come back to see you again tomorrow, and the day after that and the day after that, too." She hugged him one more time. "I love you, father," she said.

"I love you too, Math. Today you have made your father very happy. Thank you."

"Mai pen rai, ka," she said, standing.

Jum allowed Math's hand to slip from his grasp.

"Until tomorrow, father." She wai'ed to Jum in a manner reserved only for those she loved and respected most. Then she turned and left the old monk's room. Outside, she cried on her sister's shoulder for many long minutes. Nuang held her but said nothing.

After Math had calmed, she said, "Nuang, my father said there was something he wanted me to do for him. He didn't say what, but he said you know. Please tell me."

"Come with me," Nuang said and led the way. They had walked just a short distance from the temple when Nuang stopped. She waved her hand in a sweeping motion. "This is it, Math," she said. "This is what your father wants you to do."

She looked at Nuang's face, wondering if she was playing some sort of joke on her. "This is what, Nuang? Except for a few flowers someone has planted, there is nothing here."

"But someday there will be," Nuang stated, confident in her words. "When Jum was in Phitsanulok, he showed me a very beautiful garden about this size. It was filled with flowers and shrubs and rocks and neatly cut grass. He had done it himself. He said God and Buddha allowed him that one indulgence because he was helping to make the world more beautiful. He wanted to do the same thing here in Chiang Mai. He started his work on the garden but became very sick before it could be finished. He wants you to finish the garden for him, Math. That is what he wants."

"I know the garden at the temple in Phitsanulok," Math said. "I saw it the same day I got my new job. You're right, it's very beautiful. I'm not sure if I can make anything like it. I've never done such a thing. I have no flowers or anything. How can I make a garden without flowers? I want to do it for my father, but I want it to be perfect. What if I do it wrong?"

"You will do it perfect, Math," Nuang said. "And I'll help you. I don't know where we'll get the flowers but we will, even if I have to steal them. Together we will finish this garden for your father."

After Jum was sure Math and Nuang had left, he got up from his bed and wrote a short note to his brother. "Isara. Today is the happiest day of my life. I have confessed everything to my daughter and she has forgiven me. Now I can die in peace. I have two favors to ask of you." Jum wrote down his requests then called to a fellow monk.

J. F. Gump

"Friend, I need to get this message to my brother in Phitsanulok but I'm too weak to go to a phone. Could you please call my brother and give him my message? It's very important and I would be most thankful."

The other monk agreed. He took Jum's note and left.

That afternoon, Math and Nuang went to a few greenhouses begging for flowers and shrubs. The responses they got were dismal. Depressed, they went back to Nuang's house to decide what they would do. On the way, Nuang began plotting where she would steal flowers. A man was waiting for them when they arrived.

Nuang had never seen the man before. She wondered if there was some sort of trouble. Maybe someone, somehow, knew about her plans to steal flowers. "Who are you?" she asked.

"My boss told me to come here. You are to make a list of what you need, and then I'm to return to him."

"What are you talking about? You must have the wrong house."

"I don't know. My boss only gave me this address and told me that you need flowers and things for a garden. Anything you need will be provided. I assumed you knew already."

"We do need things for a garden, but I don't understand how your boss would know. Who is he anyway?"

The man named his boss and the nursery that he owned. Nuang knew the nursery; it was the largest in Chiang Mai. It was also the most expensive. Neither Nuang nor Math recognized the name of the owner.

"How much?" Nuang asked. This was too good to be true. She knew there had to be a catch.

"I don't know," the man answered. "My boss didn't mention money. He only said for me to get your list and return it to him."

"I still don't understand," Nuang said. "But we'll take everything your boss will give."

Math and Nuang looked at each other and giggled in their

excitement. God and Buddha work in mysterious ways. They went inside Nuang's house and made their list and a sketch of what they hoped the garden would look like. The man thanked them for their time and took their needs to his boss.

The next morning when Math and Nuang arrived at the temple, the man was there with a truckload of flowers and shrubs. He also had a note from his boss offering suggestions on building the garden. Math and Nuang began their work in earnest.

Each morning, more flowers and more suggestions awaited them. Every day they worked from sunrise to sunset. In the evening before they went home, Math would visit with Jum, no matter how tired or dirty from her labors.

Each time she saw him, he seemed a little weaker, and she would redouble her efforts in the garden, racing against a clock she could not stop. Finally, after two weeks, they planted the last flower and positioned the last rock in place. They were finished.

"We must show my father, now, today," Math said.

Nuang nodded her agreement, and they went to Jum's room. He was asleep.

Math hesitated for a moment, then shook him gently awake. "Father," she said, "The garden is finished. I know you want to sleep, but I want you to see what I've done for you."

"Soon, I will have more than enough time for sleep," Jum said. "Today I want to see your garden." He tried to get out of the bed but couldn't. "I think this old monk is too tired to walk by himself. Please help me, my two daughters. Please help me to walk to our garden."

Together, with one on each side, Math and Nuang helped Jum out of his room and down the short path to the garden they had made. When they arrived, Jum stared at everything for a very long time.

"It is perfect," he announced, smiling in satisfaction. "It's the most beautiful garden I have ever seen. I'm very proud of you, Math, and of you too, Nuang. I would like to sit here for a while and admire what you have built for me. Help me over there, where I can sit. Then you two should go and wash the dirt from your hands. When you've finished, I would like you to come back and pray with me for a while before I sleep."

They helped Jum to a cool place in the shade on a small area of grass. He sat with his back resting against a smooth rock. Once they were sure he was comfortable, they went to wash themselves.

When they returned, Jum was still sitting in the same position as they had left him. Math and Nuang sat on the grass just in front of Jum. His eyes were closed and he didn't seem to notice their arrival.

After a few minutes, Math said, "Father, are you sleeping?"

Jum didn't move or answer. An uneasy feeling clutched at her. "Father, are you okay?" she asked, reaching out to touch his hand. It was cool and unresponsive. She knew immediately her father was dead.

She moved close to Jum and pulled him against her chest. She held him like that for a long time, rocking back and forth, crying. Finally Nuang pulled Math and her father apart.

"Let him sleep now, Math," Nuang said gently through her own tears. "Your father would not want you to mourn his death. His spirit cannot swim against the river of your tears. He would want you to remember the happiness you gave to him before he died. Come with me, we must tell the other monks what has happened. Then we must get some rest for ourselves. Tomorrow will be a very busy day."

Nuang lead Math away from her father's garden.

Surat came home that evening but he was tired and went to bed early. As he slept, Nuang and Math sat awake and talked about Jum and everything he had told them. Math was still coming to grips with all of the implications. As they talked, she realized for the first time that she now had another family by blood. She had already met Jum's brother, the attorney, her uncle.

How strange, she thought, to have relatives you never knew

existed. She knew she could never tell anyone because some people might not understand, and look down on Jum and her mother with shame and disgrace. She couldn't do that to the memory of her father, and she could not allow the public humiliation that might fall upon her mother.

Math and Nuang agreed it was best to say nothing. She would tell Mike but no one else. He would understand and, like Nuang, he would keep her secret.

That night Math dreamed of the monkey-man again. This time the monkey-man said nothing. He appeared in her dream from out of nowhere, swinging his sword at her. Over and over the tip of his blade swished toward her, missing only by a hair's breadth. She backed away until she bumped into a wall. There was no place to run. The blade touched on her chest just below her right breast. Math clutched at the wound with her left hand. She could feel the blood pouring through her fingers. Then his blade cut across her forehead just above her left eye. She put her other hand to her head but felt no blood. She knew her head was bleeding, but she couldn't feel it.

Abruptly the monkey-man stopped his attack. He stood back, laughed at her, and then disappeared. She woke up breathless. She sat up and grabbed at her chest, expecting to find a bloody gash. There was nothing. It had been a dream.

"Are you okay?" Nuang had awakened at Math's stirring.

"I dreamed about the monkey-man again. I'm scared, Nuang. Every time I dream about the monkey-man, someone dies or something bad happens."

"You're wrong," said Nuang. "You only dream about the monkey-man after someone has already died."

"Why did he cut me, Nuang?"

"It doesn't mean anything," Nuang reassured. "It's only a bad dream. Nothing is going to happen."

She nodded but she wasn't convinced. She would tell Mike about the dream. He had only laughed at her before, but maybe this time he wouldn't.

In the morning Math and Nuang went to the temple to see what the funeral arrangements would be. Jum's body, they were informed, had been sent to Phitsanulok at the request of his brother. Jum's family was taking care of the funeral. The monks at the Chiang Mai temple were having a simple Buddhist ceremony for Jum tomorrow, and Math and Nuang were welcome to attend if they wanted.

"What will you do, Math?" Nuang asked, as they left the temple.

"I will go to Phitsanulok and say my last goodbye to my father," she said without hesitation.

"What about Sawat?"

"What about him? I'm not afraid of him."

"I know you're not afraid Math, but Sawat is a dangerous man to you. He can't be trusted and you can't believe anything he says. I'm afraid he might hurt you really bad the next time."

"I've decided I'll stay at my other father's house. Sawat won't bother me as long as my father is around. I will leave Phitsanulok as soon as the funeral is over."

"You know, Math, you're a lucky girl."

"What do you mean? You call this lucky?"

"You're lucky to have another father to protect you after the first one has died. Where will you go when you leave Phitsanulok? Will you come back here? You know you're welcome."

"I don't know what I'll do. When I get to Phitsanulok, I will pack my clothes and things, and then I'll decide where I'll go."

"What about Mike?"

She hesitated remembering Mike's last fax and her answer to him. "I don't know about that either. Right now I'm very mixed up and I don't know what to do. Sometimes it seems like there is so much on me that I can no longer bear it. I cannot stay in Phitsanulok. It's my home but I can't stay there. The father who loved me and was so kind to me is dead. I know I have another father, but he's the same one who used to beat our mother and all of us, his own children. The man I love is on the other side of the world and may never come back to me. I have no job and just a little money. Sometimes everything is too much. I feel so tired. Sometimes I wish the monkey-man would take my life so I could rest."

"That's crazy talk," Nuang said pointedly. "You've lived through worse things and you will live through this. There's a man who would be crushed if you were to die. He's coming back for you, and you have much to live for. I don't know when Mike will be back, but I can feel in my heart that it will be soon."

"I hope you're right, Nuang. I pray to Buddha that you are right. But I'm so afraid something terrible will happen and I'll never see Mike again."

"Nothing terrible is going to happen," Nuang said, comforting. "Everything will be okay." She put her arms around Math and held her tight.

Math was silent. Memories of her last night with Mike in Bangkok flashed through her head. She would do anything to have that night back. To do it over and do it right. She would do anything to have Mike in her arms again. She would never let him go until he had made love to her one last time. She shook off the thought. "Sister, if it turns out that you are wrong and the monkey-man dreams are real, could you do something for me?"

"I'm tired of you worrying about that stupid dream," Nuang said, irritated. "I told you it means nothing."

"I know you're right," Math responded. "But just in case you're wrong, will you do something for me?"

Nuang gave in and promised that if anything bad happened, she would do whatever Math asked.

Math told Nuang what she wanted her to do, and Nuang nodded her agreement.

Chapter 32

Math arrived in Phitsanulok at seven o'clock the next morning and went directly to the temple where Jum had once lived. The monks there would know about the family's plans for her father's funeral. She dispensed with customs and asked the first monk she met. He didn't seem insulted at her brashness. Instead, he motioned for her to follow him.

He led her to the garden where she had spent an afternoon cleaning. Her father's garden. A small tent had been erected in the center of the grassy area. Under the tent, an ornate wooden casket held Jum's body. Just outside of the garden was a much larger tent with rows of folding chairs and stacks of flowers on a long table. The family had spared no expense. It will be a fitting farewell for my father, Math thought.

"May I walk down and look?" she asked. The monk nodded.

She walked to the casket, glad she had come early. She was the only one there. She stood beside Jum, saying silent prayers and crying for her loss. She would miss the old monk, her friend, her father. In a while she returned to where the monk waited. "When is the funeral?"

"Tomorrow morning at ten," he replied.

"Thank you for everything." She wai'ed to the monk and left.

From the temple she went to her house and packed her suitcase with everything she thought she might need. Then she went to her father's barbershop. He had turned to barbering three years ago when he'd hurt his back and could no longer work as a laborer. His shop was little more than a hole in the wall, but the business made enough money for him to live.

"Sawasdee ka father," she wai'ed as she entered his shop.

"Math? What are you doing here?" he looked up, surprised.

"I was wondering if I could stay at your house for a while."

"Of course," he looked at her curiously. "May I ask why you don't stay at your own house, or at your mother's house like you do sometimes? Is everything okay?"

"I think someone has been inside my house," she lied. "I'm afraid to stay there in case they come back. I only need to stay with you for a day or two."

He fished his house key from his pocket and handed it to her. "Stay as long as you wish."

That night Math and her father talked, but not much. They never did. She mentioned Mike just to see her father's reaction. As expected, he was negative. Her father, like many people in Phitsanulok, was anti-farang. Rather than argue, she agreed with her father that the best thing would be for her to forget Mike and find a nice Thai man to marry. It was a lie, but she wasn't in the mood for confrontation.

The next morning she went to the temple at nine. The garden was filled with monks and Jum's family and friends. She knew she had every right to be there, and that no one would think anything other than that she was just a friend coming to pay her respects, yet she held back. She couldn't bring herself to walk to the casket or mingle with the other mourners. These people had money and she was intimidated. She stayed at the edge of the crowd and paid her respects from a distance.

At ten o'clock the monks began their services. By eleven it was over. A member of the family announced that Jum's body would be cremated at noon and told them where the burning would take place. Math wanted desperately to attend the burning of the body, but she knew it was only for family and very close friends. She would never be allowed to attend. With head hung low and tears in her eyes she said one final prayer for her father.

As she turned to leave, a strong hand gripped her arm. She turned around expecting to see Sawat, but it was Jum's brother, the attorney. The same man who had helped her with the electric company when Jabal and little Sadayu had been killed.

"I am Isara," he said, "in case you don't remember my name. Please, I would like for you to come with me."

"I do remember you. Where do you want to take me?"

"I'll explain later," he spoke softly. "You'll be safe."

He led her to a car. Everyone stared as they passed among the mourners, but no one said anything. Isara opened the door and motioned her inside. She looked up at her uncle then climbed into the back seat. He slid in beside her. He gestured to his driver and they drove away from the temple.

It was a fancy car, a Mercedes, much like the one Mike had rented to Bangkok. Leather seats, a small bar, and a compact TV. A sliding glass window separated the front seat from the back. She had no doubt this car cost more than she would make in a lifetime. Isara pushed the window shut for privacy.

"I know everything, Math," he began. "I have known for a long time. Jum was my older brother. He was my hero while I was growing up. Even when our father disowned and disinherited Jum, I kept in contact with him. He told me about you when you were less than a year old. You probably don't know it, but I've had people keeping track of you most of your life. I lost you for a while when you moved away from Phitsanulok, but I know some about that because Jum told me.

"A couple of weeks ago I received a short message from Jum. Then, just a few days ago, I received a long letter from him. He told me about many things, including your American friend. Jum said he had confessed to you and that you had forgiven him. Because of you, Math, he died a happy man. Thank you for making my brother happy and giving him peace. Did you finish the garden before he died?"

She looked at Isara questioningly. "Yes, I think my father willed himself to live until it was finished. He said it was very beautiful. He died sitting in the garden on the day we planted the last flower. How do you know about the garden?"

Isara blushed then stammered, "He mentioned it in his letter. He said you and your sister were working very hard. I'm happy he got to see it before he died."

Math accepted Isara's answer, even though his face said it wasn't completely true. "Where are you taking me?" she asked.

"I want you to be with me today because you are my brother's daughter, my niece. Most of the relatives at the funeral today are hypocrites. They are the same ones who disowned Jum when my father did. They're here out of politeness but not respect. I knew you had returned to Phitsanulok and I knew you were staying at your father's house. I was sure you would be here today, but if you hadn't come this morning I had someone ready to bring you. I arranged everything for the funeral and I have reserved a seat for you next to me. As Jum's daughter, you should be allowed to take your rightful place among the relatives at the burning of the body. I would be proud if you join with me to honor and say goodbye to someone who was special to both of us."

"Thank you for your kindness, Isara, uncle," she said, "but aren't you worried what the rest of your family might think."

He snorted and said, "I don't care what they think."

"Then I would be proud to sit next to you at the final ceremony for my father."

Math sat tall next to Isara through the ceremony at the crematorium. Everyone stared at them and whispered amongst themselves. After the ceremony ended, members of the family filed past Jum and dropped flowers into his wooden casket.

Isara held Math back until they were the only ones who hadn't passed the body. Then he handed her a large bouquet of roses and orchids, and walked toward Jum, motioning for her to follow. Isara dropped his single rose into the casket. He turned and waited for Math.

She laid her bouquet on Jum's resting body. His blank face stared up at her. Even in death she looked like him. She glanced up at Isara. Tears streamed from her eyes. Her knees weakened. Isara took her by the arm and escorted her away from the casket.

J. F. Gump

Moments later, Jum was pushed into the pyre. Everyone stood respectfully for a while then started milling away from the crematorium. It was time to go home.

"Thank you uncle," Math said. "How can I ever repay you for what you did today?"

"You can come with me again tomorrow morning at nine," he answered. "There's one more thing you and I must do."

"What is that?"

"I'll tell you tomorrow," he answered. "I'll have my driver take you home now. He will pick you up there again in the morning."

"No," she said. She was embarrassed by her father's house. It was shabbier than her own. "Not home. I'll show him where to drop me. He can pick me up at the same place tomorrow."

Isara nodded and spoke to his driver.

Math had the driver stop by Phitsanulok Communications and asked him to wait while she went inside. She had several faxes from Mike. She paid for them and shoved them in her purse. Next she had the driver take her to the place where she would meet him in the morning. At her father's house, she sorted the faxes into chronological order and read them in turn.

In his first fax, Mike said he had received her last fax. He still loved her but didn't want her to become an old maid waiting for him. He promised to come for her as soon as he could, but he didn't know when that would be. He asked her to fax him and reaffirm she would wait for him.

The next fax was dated two days after the first. He hadn't heard from her and asked if her health was okay. He was worried. Again, he asked her to fax him as soon as possible.

The third fax had come about a week after the second. Mike asked if she still remembered him. Since she hadn't replied, he wanted to make sure she still knew who he was. His fax begged her to let him know something, even if it was bad news.

His last fax was just two days old. In that fax Mike said he wouldn't be sending more faxes. Since she hadn't confirmed she would wait for him, he believed she had decided to move on with her life and to forget about their future plans. He said he was sad, but he understood her decision. He said he still loved her and would never forget her, but he wouldn't stand in the way of her happiness with someone else.

Math cried as she read his words. She cussed herself for not sending him a fax before now. She found a piece of paper and sat down to write. Halfway through the first sentence her pen ran out of ink. She searched desperately through her father's house but didn't find another. Finally, she gave up the search. She was physically and mentally exhausted by everything that had happened during the last two weeks. She lay down and fell asleep.

The next morning, Isara's car was waiting as promised. Isara was inside. "Thank you for coming. We're going back to the temple. After today, Jum will be at rest."

At the temple Isara took an urn from the trunk of the car. Math followed as he walked to Jum's garden. "In this urn are the remains of your father, my brother. Jum never asked me to do this, but I know he would want to become one with this, his special garden. I want you to help me spread Jum's ashes among his flowers."

She nodded but said nothing. Together, they carefully placed a piece of Jum next to every flower. When they were finished, they said a short prayer and left the temple grounds.

"Math," Isara said as they rode toward her meeting place, "If there's anything you need, now or ever, all you have to do is ask. Do you need money or anything?"

She needed money but her pride wouldn't allow her to say that. Instead she asked. "Can you help me get a passport and a visa to America?"

Isara chuckled. "I think that can be arranged. It might take me a while, but I know the right people to make it happen. Here's my business card. Call me in three or four months." He noticed the frown on her face. "I hope that isn't too long."

"It's okay," she replied. "I've waited this long; another few months will make no difference. Do you need papers or anything from me for the passport?"

"Don't worry. I have ways to get whatever I need."

The car pulled to the curb. "Don't forget Math, if there's anything you need, you call me at the number on my business card. I will always be there to help you."

"There is one more thing, uncle. Do you have a pen I can borrow? Mine ran out of ink and there is a letter I must write."

Isara laughed softly and handed her a very fine pen from his suit pocket.

She got out of the car and wai'ed to Isara. "Thank you for everything. I will never forget you." The Mercedes pulled away and disappeared down the street.

That evening she called a friend, a girl she had worked with at the finance company. She asked if she could come to visit with her in Bangkok for a few days. The girl agreed without questions. Next she called Mike's office in America. He wasn't there and the lady who answered refused to give a number where he could be reached. She didn't leave a message. Later, she finished the fax she had started the night before.

"Teeluk," she wrote, "I'm sorry you haven't heard from me for so long. You must think I've forgotten about you. My life has been very mixed up lately and I haven't been able to write. I still love you and I'm still waiting for you. I will explain everything later.

"You will not be able to connect with me for a while because I can't live in Phitsanulok any longer. I'm going to Bangkok in the morning to visit with a friend. I don't know where I will go after that, but I will write to you every chance I get. If you send faxes to Phitsanulok Communications, I will get them when I can. Please teeluk, trust me and what I do. I am not with another man. I love only you. I wait for you as your devoted and faithful wife. Math."

Chapter 33

During the following weeks, Math became a gypsy, living for a few days with a friend here and a relative there. Whenever she had money, she sent Mike faxes telling him where she was and what she was doing. It was nearly two months before she returned to Phitsanulok. When she finally came home, she went to her mother's house.

Her mother had an oversized envelope addressed to her from Isara. Inside was a passport, an official looking form, and a letter. Math was so excited about the passport that she forgot about the letter until her mother asked what it said. Math read it aloud.

"Here is the passport I promised. You will sign the attached form and return it to me to make it official. I'm still working on the visa. Maybe two more months. There was a person in Phitsanulok who hurt you in the past; he won't bother you again. With my help, he is now in the army near Kampuchea. I think he'll be there for a long time. Call if you need anything. Isara."

She was ecstatic. She danced around laughing excitedly and babbling to her mother and brother about her passport and Sawat's new career. It was the first good thing that had happened to her for months. Maybe her life was finally changing for the better.

After she finally calmed down, she called Phitsanulok Communications and asked about her faxes. She had had quite a few, but since she didn't come to pick them up for such a long time, they had started throwing them away. She was irritated but too excited to be angry. She sat down and wrote a fax to Mike.

"Teeluk," she wrote, "I have just come back to Phitsanulok. I know you have sent me faxes but the communications company has thrown them away. I don't know what you've said to me. I need to tell you that today I received my passport. If you still want me, I'll be ready to go whenever you ask. I have no job and no money, but I still have my dreams. Please answer me soon. Let me know if you still want me after all of this time. I love you with all of my heart, Math."

She borrowed money from her mother and then drove to Phitsanulok Communications. She asked if she could wait for the reply and they agreed. By closing time there had been no reply. The next morning, Math was there when they opened. She waited all day for Mike's fax. She knew it was nighttime in America, but she waited anyway. At eight o'clock that evening, his fax came.

"Sweetheart," it read. "I was out of the office yesterday and just now got your fax. I'm excited about your passport. I think we can make use of it very soon. My own life here in America is turning upside down. So many things are happening I don't where to begin. If all goes as planned, I'm coming back to Thailand and I think I have a good job for you. I thought I would never say this, but I want you to go to Pattaya as soon as possible. When you get there, let me know where I can contact you. I'll explain everything then. Try to set up an email account if you can. I love you, Mike."

"Quick, give me piece of paper," She demanded. She scribbled her reply, "I will wait for you in Pattaya, teeluk. I love you, too. Math." She handed the attendant her fax, threw a hundred baht bill on the counter, and left without waiting for her change.

She felt better than she had in a long time. Everything was going to be okay. Mike was coming back to her, she had a passport, and soon she would have a visa. She stopped at the bus station on her way home and bought a ticket to Pattaya. It cost every last baht her mother had loaned her. That night she told her mother and brother she was going to visit with Anan and work at his company. In the morning she left for Pattaya.

Anan still owned her and he knew it. She convinced him to let her work for him in exchange for food, a place to sleep, and the use of his bigger motorcycle. She even got him to throw in a little spending money.

Pattaya was full of places to send and receive faxes. Math picked one at random and sent a fax to Mike saying she had arrived and was waiting for him. The shop owner helped her set up an email account but she didn't understand how to use it. Faxes were much easier.

Every day she would check to see if she had faxes. Sometimes she did and sometimes she didn't, but she checked every day just in case.

Mike had explained about a friend who was starting a tourist business and needed an assistant in Pattaya. He had suggested Math, and his friend had agreed. The man had also agreed to pay Mike's airfare to Thailand if he would help set up their office in Pattaya. Mike asked her to find prices on office space and on condos similar to where he had lived.

Math was happy to do whatever Mike asked. If it meant him coming back to her, she would do anything.

As the days passed and his faxes continued to be more positive, she knew Nuang had been right. Mike was coming back for her.

At long last, the day she had been praying for arrived. It started just like any other day. She had two sales calls lined up for that morning. They were both in Jomtien Beach. She would stop for her faxes after she finished with business. At eleven o'clock she arrived at Kafe Net and she had a fax.

"My darling Math," Mike had written, "Everything is set. My airline tickets are confirmed. I will be with you again in six weeks. I must go to a meeting now and have no time to explain. I'll send another fax later today or tomorrow. I'm excited about seeing you again. I have much to tell you about my life. I love you. Mike."

She squealed out loud and reread the fax. Then she read it one more time. "Six weeks,' she told the girl behind the counter. "He'll be here in just six weeks." She squealed again and ran from the office without paying her bill.

She was beside herself with excitement and happiness. She was floating on air as she rode to her brother's house. She couldn't wait to get there and tell Anan and everyone that Mike was coming back to her. She would call Nuang first thing. Nuang would want to know.

Traffic was light, so she pushed the accelerator hard. She was going make it to her brother's house in record time.

In her hurry, Math almost missed her turn-off from Sukhumvit Road. She braked abruptly to make the turn. The driver behind her couldn't slow as quickly and his car hit her motorcycle hard in the rear.

Math pitched backwards from her motorcycle, bounced off the windshield on her right side, and then flew over the top of the still moving car. Her head hit the chrome plated bumper just before her body landed on the pavement. She was still conscious. In a panic reaction she stood. She was surprised she was alive. There was a piercing pain in her right side when she tried to breath. She put her hand over the pain and could feel a sticky wetness. Her head hurt terribly, throbbing above her left eyebrow. She reached up but there was no blood. Suddenly, she felt herself reeling. She stumbled and fell. Everything was going blurry and dim. The sun was fading. She heard someone shout something about an ambulance. She struggled desperately to stand again, but couldn't. She lay there giving in to the darkness that was engulfing her. Just before everything faded away, her last thoughts were of Mike and a baby with white hair.

Chapter 34

Mike arrived at his office on Wednesday at 8:15 a.m.. Fifteen minutes late again. He was famous for never being at work on time. He waited for someone to make their usual snide remarks but no one did. Instead, everyone just stared at him – no smiles, no good mornings, nothing. He went into his office wondering what was up with them. The receptionist was directly behind him.

"What is it, Laura?" he asked.

"You've had three phone calls and one fax from Thailand today already." she said, her voice cracked slightly. "I thought you would want to know. Here is the fax."

"Thanks, Laura," he said. "Was the caller a man, woman or child?" He smiled at his question. He was sure it was Math with some crazy thing to tell him.

"It was a man," Laura said and dropped her eyes away from him. "I'm sorry, but I read your fax. I think you should read it right away. I'll hold your calls." She turned and walked away.

An unwanted terror gripped his chest. Adrenaline pumped into his bloodstream by the gallon. He sat down and read the fax. He read it over and over hoping the meaning of the words would change.

"Dear Sir," the fax read, "Math has had an accident and it is very serious. She is in intensive care at the Bangkok-Pattaya Hospital. The doctors want 90,000 baht to operate and I have only 20,000 baht. Without the operation, she will die. Please help me. I am the brother of Math. Anan." The phone numbers for the hospital and Anan were included.

Mike stared at the fax. This couldn't be happening. Someone

had made a mistake or was playing a nightmarish trick on him. A thousand thoughts raced through his head but he couldn't focus on any of them. He tried desperately to think but couldn't. A dense fog of numbness invaded his head. Everything within his scope of awareness became surrealistic, dreamlike. He entered a state of acute mental shock. He didn't move, he didn't think, and he didn't react.

"Mike," Laura said.

Mike gave no indication that he heard her.

"Mike," Laura said louder, almost shouting.

He lifted his head. "What?" His voice was monotone.

"That Thai man is on the phone again. Do you want to talk to him?"

He nodded lifelessly. "Please shut the door on your way out."

He didn't pick up the phone right away. Instead he stood and started talking to himself. "Come on, you stupid son-of-a-bitch. Snap out of it. You've got to think. Math may be dying and you're acting like a stupid asshole."

He paced back and forth across his small office, slapping himself hard on the face. The pain cleared his head a little. He hit himself again and again until a wedge of anger and awareness pried loose the grip of emotional shock. He picked up the phone. "Hello, this is Mike."

"Hello, sir. I am Anan. I am Math's brother. Do you remember me? Did you receive my fax?" The man was obviously Thai, and more obviously he was crying.

"Yes, I remember you, and I have your fax," Mike said trying to remain calm. "Anan, please tell me what has happened."

"Sir, Math, she have accident. She hurt head very bad. If doctor no operate, maybe she die. I have not money. Please sir, can you help?" His words were a repeat of the fax.

"How much money do you need?" Mike asked.

"Seventy thousand baht, sir," Anan answered. "Please help me, sir. I want my sister's life back." Anan broke down in unintelligible sobbing.

Mike could feel his own eyes watering. He took a deep breath. "That's a lot of money, Anan, but I'll get it. I just don't know how I can get it to you by tomorrow. With banks and foreign countries it's not easy. What about her insurance? I know Math has insurance because I paid it every month."

"The insurance company no pay," Anan answered. "I not understand, sir."

Mike could barely hear his words because of his crying. "I don't understand either. Anan, please listen carefully. I'll do everything I can. You must fax me your bank account number and your bank's international routing number." He knew he was talking more complicated English than most Thais would understand, but he couldn't think of the Thai words. "Do you understand what I said, Anan?"

"Yes, sir," Anan replied, "Tomorrow I fax my bank account number."

"And the international routing number," Mike repeated, almost shouting. "I need the routing number or I cannot send you money. Tell the bank you are getting money from America. They will understand and give you everything I need. Remember, Anan, account number and international routing number. Okay?"

"Okay, sir," Anan answered, "Thank you, sir. Goodbye now, sir." The phone clicked dead in his ear.

His mind was working again. He called the number of the hospital from the fax. The lady who answered didn't speak English and after a minute of non-communications she hung up. He called back. This time he was connected to ICU but ran into the same language problem. He called again. Again, he was connected to ICU. This time the lady said, "One moment, please."

He waited on the phone for nearly ten minutes. He was about to hang up when another lady came on the line. Her English wasn't good, but it was better than anyone else he had talked to. Very slowly and very distinctly he asked his question, "Khun Tippawan Bongkot sabai mai? Is she okay? Tippawan Bongkot."

"One moment please," the new lady said. After a short wait,

the nurse continued, "Miss Tippawan have very much head injury. Prognosis not good. Will die in one or two days."

The woman's words ripped at him. Shock crept back with a vengeance. "Are you sure? Are you sure 100%?"

"Yes, sure, 100%," the lady responded. "Maybe die already, but have machine to help breathe. Prognosis not good," the lady repeated. "Will die in one or two days."

"Thank you," he said and hung up the phone. His mind turned into a mass of confusion. What if the lady in ICU was wrong? What if Anan was right, and all Math needed was an operation? What if there was still time?

He had an overpowering urge to catch the next flight to Thailand. He fought the impulse down. Flying in a plane for the next twenty-four hours wouldn't help anyone. He had to get the money. Whether it was for an operation or to help the family pay for Math's funeral, he had to get the money.

He also needed someone in Thailand to help him find out exactly what the facts were. But who? Everyone he knew and trusted had been gone from Pattaya for a long time. Who, damn it, he forced his mind to think, who could he call? Montharee. The name popped into his head. His friend Montharee from the Thai company. She had given him her home phone number once. Surely he had it somewhere. He was a packrat and never threw anything away. Systematically he went through every scrap of paper in his wallet, his laptop computer case, and his desk. After a thirty-minute search he found it. He looked at his watch. It was ten o'clock. That meant it was ten at night in Thailand. Not too late. He dialed Montharee's number hoping beyond hope it hadn't changed. She answered on the fourth ring.

"Hello, Montharee," he said, "This is Mike. Do you remember me?"

"Khun Mike?" she asked, surprise filled her voice. "Yes, I remember you. I'm very happy to hear from you. Are you okay? How have you been?"

"Actually, I'm not well. I need your help. Can you do

something for me?"

"I'll help you if I can. What do you need?"

He explained everything. He told her about Math, he told her about Anan, and he told her about the lady at the hospital. He told her over and over until he was sure she understood.

"Tomorrow," she promised, "I'll go to the hospital and see for myself. Khun Mike, I'm very much worried because some Thai people are not honest. I want to be sure 100% about your friend Math, before you send money to Anan. Maybe he's not honest man. Please don't be angry for me to say that, but I know how some Thai people are."

"I understand, Montharee," he said, "and I'm not angry. I understand. Thank you for your help. I'll call you tomorrow. Okay?"

"Is okay, Mike," she answered. "I will take care everything. Goodbye for now, Mike."

"Goodbye," he said and hung up the phone.

The money, he thought franticly, where do I get the fucking money? With Susan's spending and his regular bills and the retainer he had paid the lawyer, he barely had two quarters to rub together. How could he come up with that much money on a minute's notice? He pulled out his wallet and eyed the credit cards. Dear God, he prayed, please let one of these be worth something. On his way out he told Laura he didn't feel well and was going home.

It took three of his four credit cards to get all of the cash, but by one o'clock it was done. If Susan said anything about him taking loans on the credit cards, he would tell her to go fuck herself. He figured he would be inheriting her debt soon enough anyway.

Mike started to go home then changed his mind. He was too emotionally stressed deal with Susan and Josh and all of the bullshit that went on around his house. Today he needed solitude and something to calm his nerves.

He stopped at a redneck joint not far from his home. The place was seedy but the beer was cheap. He sat by himself drinking beer and thinking about Math. Images of her lying in a hospital bed kept parading through his head. The sad country music on the jukebox matched his mood. After his fourth beer he broke down and cried for the first time since he had received the fax.

"Are you okay?" the barmaid asked.

"Bring me another beer," was his reply.

He stayed there drinking and thinking and crying until the barmaid finally refused to serve him. He stumbled out of the bar so drunk he could hardly walk. So drunk that nothing mattered to him. Not even his own life.

He drove with one eye closed because when he opened them both he saw two of everything. Two roads, two street signs, and two sets of headlights coming toward him. He knew he shouldn't be driving but he didn't care. He drove off the edge of the pavement and nearly hit another car head-on when he pulled back onto the road. He found the whole thing hilarious and laughed until he cried. In a while, only his laughter had stopped.

It was eight thirty when he arrived at his house. He vomited heavily in his driveway and then went inside and up the stairs. He passed out in the guest bedroom. If anyone said anything to him, he didn't notice. He slept like the dead.

Mike woke up at five o'clock the next morning. His stomach was queasy and his head felt like it might explode at any moment. It was going to be a long day. He was showered, dressed and out of the house by six-thirty. Susan didn't get up and he didn't wake her. He stopped at a Seven-Eleven store and bought a breakfast sandwich, a carton of milk, and a bottle of aspirin. As he drove, he ate the sandwich, then chewed up five aspirins and forced them down with the milk.

He was forty-five minutes early for work and the first one to arrive. There were no messages for him on the answering machine but there was a fax from Anan. It contained his bank name and account number but no routing number.

"Damn you, Anan," he shouted out aloud. He went to his office and called Montharee.

"Hello." She answered on the first ring.

"Hello, Montharee," he said. "It's me, Mike. What did you find out?"

"It's not good news. The people at the hospital confirmed what they told you yesterday. The doctors say Math will die. It's not a problem with money. She has much bleeding inside her head and it's too late for operation already. I'm sorry about your lady, Mike."

Her words struck Mike like an emotional pile driver. "Did you see her?"

"Yes," Montharee answered, "She looked very beautiful and perfect. She looked like she was asleep except for the things in her nose and her mouth. Did you receive a fax from the hospital?"

"No," he replied numbly, his eyes filled with tears, "I received only a fax from Math's brother. What is the fax from the hospital?"

"I asked the hospital to send you a fax about your friend's condition. I'll tell them again tomorrow."

"Thank you, Montharee," he said. "Thank you for helping. I need you to do two more things. I need you to check with the hospital every day and send me a fax when Math dies. Also I want you to call Math's brother and tell him I can't send money because he didn't give me all of the information I need." He gave her Anan's number.

"I'll do that for you, Mike," she said. "Please, take care of yourself, okay?"

"I will, Montharee," he answered listlessly. "I will."

Mike struggled through the day trying to act as if nothing was wrong, as if nothing was happening inside his head. The stares he got from his co-workers told him he wasn't succeeding. Finally, at three o'clock in the afternoon, he went home.

He was relieved no one was there. He was physically and emotionally exhausted. He turned to his old friend alcohol to numb his pain. Within an hour he had drank an entire six-pack of beer.

He was grateful when his exhaustion allowed him to sleep.

On Friday, Mike was up and out of the house before anyone else was awake. He skipped breakfast and went straight to work. Laura was already there but avoided looking directly at him. She handed him two faxes. One was from the hospital and the other was from Montharee. He carried them to his desk. He read the hospital fax first.

"Tippawan Bongkot was admitted to the hospital at 12:00 noon with a history of a motorcycle accident. She had one compound fractured rib and a contusion above her left eye. She was semi-conscious. Two hours after arriving, her condition changed to complete coma. A CAT scan was performed. There has been heavy intra-cranial hemorrhaging. The patient displays dolls-eye reaction to deep pain. Diagnosis is brain death condition and the patient will likely die in one or two days."

Brain death condition, the patient will die in one or two days. Mike repeated the words over and over as images of Math dying in a hospital bed invaded his head. A small whimper escaped his mouth. He laid the fax down and picked up the one from Montharee. Instinctively, he knew he didn't want to read it. It was very short.

"Math died today at 12:00 noon, Thailand time. My sympathies are with you."

He got up and left the office just as his whimpering sobs exploded into gut wrenching wails of grief. He stopped in the toilet and threw up until nothing but dry heaves remained. He left the building, got into his car, and drove from the parking lot.

He didn't know where he was going and he didn't care. He only wanted to run away and hide from the searing pain that was wracking his soul. All of his hopes and dreams had vanished with the arrival of those two worthless pieces of paper. His life, as he'd planned it, had just ended.

As he drove, he realized he would never see Math smile again. Thoughts of her played through his mind like an endless video.

With crystal clarity he could hear her saying "Hello, teeluk, I am Math", as if he couldn't recognize her voice on the phone. Her odd way of saying "in quickly time" instead of soon. He could see the way her face lit up when she was happy or proud. The way her lips pouted when she was upset or angry. The way she cried when she was sad. He could almost feel her hand on his, soft and gentle. He could almost hear her voice saying, "I love you, Mike. Please come back to me in quickly time." Never again would he see her face or hear her voice or feel the touch of her hand. Never again would he ever love anyone the way he had loved Math.

An ugly thought entered his mind. He had killed her. He was the one who had told her to go to Pattaya. If she hadn't been there, she wouldn't have had the accident. Except for him, she would still be alive. Cold, sharp blades of guilt sliced through him. He had killed the one thing he loved more than anything in the world. Without warning, tears erupted like torrents of blinding rain. He pulled to the side of the road. As he sat there crying, dark thoughts of suicide ravaged his mind. It would be so easy and the pain would end in quickly time.

Suddenly he heard Math speaking to him. It sounded so real, as if she was in the car with him. "Please take care of yourself, Mike. Take care of yourself and your family. Chan lak khun, teeluk. I love you, sweetheart. Chan lak khun talod bai. I will love you forever." Her words eased his soul. He looked in the back seat expecting to see her, but he was alone.

At that moment he knew he had one more thing he must do, and then what happened in his life was up to fate. He had to make one more trip to Thailand to say goodbye to Math. He knew if he didn't do that, his soul would die as surely as the sun would rise tomorrow. His tears slowed and he turned back toward his office. As he drove, he made plans for his journey to say goodbye to Math. When he walked back into the office, everyone stared but no one said anything. He wrote two faxes, one to Anan and one to Montharee.

"I'm very sorry about what has happened to Math," his fax to

J. F. Gump

Anan read. "I can feel your pain. You will never understand how much I loved your sister. You will never know how much I hurt inside. Please say a prayer for Math from me at her funeral. I'm coming to Thailand as I had already planned. I would like very much to have a Buddhist sympathy ceremony for Math to pay my own last respects and to tell her goodbye. If you can help me, I would be forever grateful. I will pay for everything. If your sister Nuang can join us, I would be very pleased and happy to see her again. My thoughts and my sympathies are with you and your family. Mike."

To Montharee he wrote. "I'm coming to Thailand in less than six weeks. I've asked Math's brother to help me arrange a sympathy ceremony for Math. Please contact Anan and make sure he has received my fax, and tell me if he will do what I've asked. Thank you for your help and kindness. Your friend. Mike."

He sent the faxes, and then left the office.

Mike went home and did something he hadn't done for a long time. He rolled two marijuana cigarettes and smoked them both. It dulled his senses and took the sharp cutting edges from his pain. In a while he lay down and dreamed of Math, alive, happy, and smiling.

In the morning he again had two faxes. One was from Anan and the other was from Montharee. Everything would be arranged as he had requested. He sent a note of thanks to both, and promised to send his travel details once they were final.

The next few weeks were the weeks from hell. He struggled through each day merely going through the motions of living. After the first week he cried only once in a while. Usually it was at night when he was alone, and had too much time to think and too much beer to drink. His appetite disappeared and during those six weeks he lost nearly ten pounds. But he survived and the day for him to go back to Math finally arrived.

Chapter 35

It was the longest flight Mike had ever taken. As hard as he tried, he couldn't sleep. His thin-padded, coach-class seat felt only slightly better than a rigid, straight-backed, church pew. He had traveled coach before, but he couldn't remember the seats being this uncomfortable. Maybe they weren't any harder; maybe he was only imagining it.

He sat there in his coach-class torture chamber, staring at the back of the seat in front of him. He ignored the movies showing on the screen just a few feet from his face. Instead, his mind replayed scenes from the last year of his life. From time to time he would shake his head ever so slightly and sigh. All the stupid clichés he had ever heard entered his head at one time or another during the flight. Life is a bitch and then you die, what doesn't kill you makes you stronger, there's a silver lining behind every gray cloud, and all of the rest of the bullshit. Probably the most inane of the bunch was 'Tis better to have loved and lost than to never have loved at all'. Whoever said that was the biggest fool of all. Obviously they had never lost someone like Math.

He arrived in Bangkok at eleven thirty at night. He knew the routine with the taxis and getting transportation to Pattaya wasn't a problem. It was very late when he arrived at the condo.

Mike hadn't been there for months, yet he was treated as if it was yesterday. Even at that late hour the manager, Jem, came to greet him. Everything was ready for him even though he'd made no reservations. He was dumbfounded at the reception.

"Your friend, Montharee called and told us you would be arriving tonight," Jem said. "We have missed your company. We

J. F. Gump

couldn't save you the same room you had before, but I've given you the best room we have available." She looked around. "Where's your friend, Math? You know, the girl who lived with you before. She's a very nice young lady. She stopped by not long ago to ask about rooms."

"Math is dead," he answered, more bluntly than he intended.

"Please don't joke," Jem said. "Your joke is not fun."

"It's not a joke, Jem." he said softer. "Math was killed in a motorcycle accident just a few weeks ago."

"Oh, Mike. I'm very sorry for you. She was such a wonderful person. She told me she loved you very much and that you would be married soon."

His voice choked at her words and he couldn't answer right away. He finished filling out the reservation form. "Yes, we were to be married soon."

The boy at the desk handed Mike his room key.

"I can find the room on my own. I need a wake up call at seven. Please tell the boy what I need."

Jem nodded her agreement and spoke in Thai. The boy nodded his understanding. "Is there anything else I can do?" she asked.

"You can say a prayer for Math's soul in her new life," Mike answered. "I would like that."

"Yes," she said. "I will say a prayer for her spirit."

Mike picked up his suitcase and went to his room. He wished he had the same room as when he and Math had lived together, but he didn't. Still, the room was similar and comfortable. He lay in the bed and thought about Math. He was extremely tired and couldn't maintain his focus. In quicky time he fell asleep.

That night he dreamt he was in Pattaya and Math was with him. She felt so close. He could hear her soft breathing, he could feel her warmth, he could smell her perfume.

Mike awoke to the sun shining through the curtains. He opened his eyes expecting to find Math beside him, but there was only a pillow. He looked at his watch. It was nine-thirty. He vaguely remembered getting a seven o'clock wake up call and just as vaguely remembered falling back asleep.

He took a quick shower and called Anan. They agreed to meet in the condo lobby at eleven.

Mike went to the lobby. He knew he should eat but ordered a Carlsberg beer instead. His body was telling him it was ten-thirty at night, regardless of what his watch and the sun said. By eleven he was on his second beer. Anan arrived ten minutes late. Nuang was with him.

"Good morning, sir," Anan said politely in English.

"Sawasdee ka, Khun Mike," Nuang said wai'ing.

"Sawasdee krup," Mike answered in Thai. "I'm happy to see you again. Please sit down."

Nuang giggled as she sat.

Mike tilted his head and stared at her. He hoped he hadn't said something stupid. "Is my Thai wrong?"

"Oh no, your Thai words are very good," Nuang giggled again and pointed at the Carlsberg. "Math said you liked to drink beer too much. She never told me you had beer for breakfast."

"Oh, that. I guess it is a little early. Would you like something to drink or eat?" They declined his offer.

"I've arranged everything for the ceremony," Anan said. "It will be at my house tomorrow morning at eleven o'clock. I hope that's not too early."

"That will be fine," Mike replied. "I'm not familiar with Buddhist ceremonies and Thai customs but I want to show respect. Is there anything special I need to do? How should I dress?"

"Don't worry, sir," Anan said. "You can wear whatever clothes you want. If you have a white shirt and black slacks, that would be polite, but it's not important. There will be a man at the ceremony to tell you everything you must do. Don't worry, okay?"

"Thank you. I appreciate everything you're doing to arrange this ceremony. You're very kind. How much does all of this cost?"

Anan told Mike how much he had spent for the monks, the flowers, the food, and everything. Mike gave Anan the money. It was a small amount to pay for what he would receive in return. He would have paid ten times the cost to show his honor for Math.

"I will be very busy in the morning making sure everything is arranged," Anan said. "Nuang will come for you at ten o'clock."

"I'll be waiting for you," Mike smiled politely at Nuang.

Nuang smiled back shyly, and then lowered her eyes, blushing.

Anan glanced at his watch. "We must go now. I have many things to do today."

"I understand," Mike said. "I'll see you tomorrow."

Mike had two more Carlsbergs before returning to his room. The beer had taken its toll and he was still tired from the trip. He lay on the bed and fell asleep.

He was starving when he awoke at nine o'clock that evening. He washed, shaved, and then went out for something to eat.

He stopped at the Music Lover Bar in front of the condo for a quick beer. Most of the girls who had worked there before had moved on with their lives. Wan, the mama-san, was still there.

"How are you, Mike?" Wan smiled. "I'm very surprised and happy to see you again."

"Hello, Wan," he replied. "I'm happy to see you again, too. I've missed my friends in Thailand."

"When did you come back?" she asked. "How long will you stay?"

"I came last night. My plane leaves in ten days. Maybe I'll stay longer or maybe I'll leave sooner. Right now, I don't know."

"Where's your friend Math? When will she join you?"

"I guess you don't know," he answered. "Math is dead."

"I don't understand what you mean," she said, shock etched her face. "I saw her just a few weeks ago. She came here to tell me hello. She said you would be coming for her soon, but she wasn't sure when. Are you sure she's dead?"

"I'm sure, Wan," he answered. "I'm sure 100%."

Tears welled in her eyes. After a long moment she said, "I'm very sorry for you and for Math. She was a nice person with a good heart. I feel much pity for her. She was my friend and I'll miss her."

"Me too," he said, a hoarseness in his voice. "Tomorrow I'm having a ceremony to say goodbye to her forever."

Wan wiped at her eyes and stared at Mike as if not sure what to say. Finally she said, "Your beer is free. I want to buy it."

"You don't have to do that for me," he said back.

"I'm not doing it for you." She picked up the wooden cup that held his bill and walked away leaving him to drink his beer alone.

Wan said something in Thai to the other girls at the bar. Everyone looked at him, but no one smiled and no one came to talk. He finished his beer and left.

He bought a sandwich at the KFC by Big C Shopping Center. When he finished eating, he crossed Second Road and went to Toy's Beer Bar. A few of the girls he knew still worked there and came over to talk. He bought them drinks just like old times and they passed the time with idle conversation. He was thankful no one asked about Math. He was paying his bar bill to leave when Lek arrived.

When Lek first saw Mike, she stared at him dumbfounded, as if she couldn't believe what she was seeing. After a second she ran to where he was sitting and threw her arms around him. She was crying.

"I'm so happy to see you," she said through her tears. "I knew you would come back for me, I just knew it."

"I'm happy to see you Lek," he said, meaning it. "You look as beautiful as ever."

"Are you working in Thailand again?" she asked hopefully.

"I wish I was but I'm not."

"Then you're here on holiday. That means you won't be here long. When do you leave?"

"I'm not here on holiday, either," he answered. "I'm here to say goodbye to someone I love."

She gave him a questioning look. "I don't understand. Who are you saying goodbye to? Do you mean me?"

J. F. Gump

Mike shook his head. "Do you remember the girl who stayed with me before? The girl named Math?"

"Yes," Lek said sourly. "I don't like her."

"She died six weeks ago, killed in a motorcycle accident. I've come to tell her goodbye. Do you understand what I'm saying?"

There was a long silence before Lek answered, "I understand, and I'm sorry."

"Never mind," he said more softly. "It's not your fault."

"I know," she replied just as soft. "I'm very sorry you have lost someone you love. I really mean that, Mike. It's never easy to lose someone special."

"Thank you Lek, I didn't think you would be so kind."

"Mai pen rai ka." She kept her tone quiet and reserved. "I can feel your sorrow. I would like to buy you a beer."

"No, not now, but thank you anyway. It's getting late and tomorrow I must get up very early. I have a ceremony to tell Math goodbye."

"I understand." She toyed briefly with the hem of her skirt then said. "I know this may not be the right time, but I would like to go home with you tonight. I think you need company. You know, someone to hold onto."

Mike hesitated for a long moment. He did need someone to hold, but tonight is wasn't Lek. "I'll come for you tomorrow."

"Okay, tomorrow," she agreed. "I'll wait for you until then."

As he walked back to the condo, he realized it had been exactly one year since he had met Math. One year since she had invited herself to go with him to South Pattaya. One year since she had helped him to his condo because he was too drunk to walk, and because she had no place to stay. So much had happened in just one year that it might have been ten.

He wondered if he would have done anything differently had he known what the past year would bring. It was a question he couldn't answer. That night he lay in bed alone and cried himself to sleep. That night he didn't dream.

Chapter 36

When Mike awoke, it was barely dawn. He showered, dressed, and went out for breakfast. He went to the same restaurant where he had taken Math on that first morning after they met. He ordered an American-style breakfast. Then, on impulse, he also ordered Thai rice soup with pork. It was what Math had ordered that day. The waiter gave him a strange look but said nothing. He felt a little foolish but didn't change his mind.

As he sat there, he had the overwhelming sensation that Math was very close, as if she was sitting at the table. He shut his eyes and let the warmth of her presence surround him. In his mind he heard her say, "I have never been to a restaurant with a farang before. I think everyone is looking at me like I'm a bar-girl."

"Screw them, if that is what they think," he said aloud, surprising himself. He opened his eyes and looked around to see if anyone was staring at him. No one was.

In a moment his food arrived, but he had lost his appetite. He ate the rice soup but left the American breakfast untouched. He paid his bill and left.

Nuang arrived promptly at ten o'clock. She was riding a motorcycle much like the one Math had borrowed from her brother so long ago. For a moment Mike thought it was the same one, but as he walked nearer he knew it wasn't. He straddled the seat behind Nuang and patted her on the shoulder indicating he was ready to go. She reached back pulled Mike's arms around her waist. "For safety," she said.

About halfway to Anan's house Nuang coasted the motorcycle

to the side of the road.

"Is something wrong?" he asked.

Nuang took off her helmet and shook her head. "No, nothing is wrong. This is where Math died. This is where the car killed her. I thought you would want to know." She put her helmet back on and drove away.

Anan's house was small, the fourth unit in a long row of one-story, townhouse-type buildings. There was no air conditioning and it was hot. Two oscillating fans in the living room offered only minor relief from the heat. Mike wished they had held the ceremony earlier, before the sun had time to turn the house into an oven.

There was no furniture in the living room except chairs with backs and seats but no legs. There were nine of these odd chairs. Mike assumed they were for the monks. In one corner, near the front door, stood a small shrine similar to the spirit houses he'd seen all over Thailand. On a small wooden table next to the spirit house sat a picture of Math dressed in a traditional Thai gown. He had never seen that picture before. She looked beautiful.

Nuang noticed Mike staring at the picture. "She had that photo and some others taken just before she died. She said they were for you. I have them now. I will give them to you before you go. She would want you to have them."

A thin Thai man wearing glasses came into the room.

"This is the man who will help you know what to do in the ceremony," Nuang said. She excused herself and left the room.

In halting but acceptable English, the thin man explained everything Mike should expect during the ceremony. It seemed more complicated than a Catholic mass. When the thin man finished, Mike said, "I'll not remember all of that."

The man smiled, "Just watch me and do what I do. God and Buddha don't care if you make little mistakes. It will be okay."

The monks arrived a few minutes later. They paraded into the room and took their seats on the legless chairs. Nuang and Anan came into the room and sat cross-legged on the floor. The thin man said something in Thai to the eldest monk, and then sat on the floor directly in front of him. Mike sat down next to the thin man.

After a moment the eldest monk said something to the thin man. The man rose but motioned for Mike to stay seated. He took a ball of white string and looped one end around the picture of Math. Then, unraveling the ball of string as he went, the he offered each of the nine monks a portion of the string to hold. Finished, he returned to his place in front of the eldest monk.

The monk chanted for a few seconds, then stopped. Again, he spoke to the thin man. The thin man took the candles and incense from the table where Math's picture sat and handed them to Mike. Mike lit them and handed them back. All but one candle and one piece of incense were placed in front of the spirit house. The final candle and last piece of incense were placed in front of Math's picture. The thin man returned to his place and the monks began chanting in earnest.

As the monks chanted, Mike remembered all of the time he had spent with Math. He remembered the good times and the bad. The happy and the sad. The pleasure and the pain. He remembered it all. Several times his eyes filled with tears, but he wouldn't allow himself to cry. Someone had said it was bad luck for the deceased if you cried at a ceremony for them. He held his composure. After about forty-five minutes the chanting stopped.

"The monks will eat now," the thin man said softly in Mike's ear. "But they won't just take the food. You and I must give it to them. When the women bring the food into the room, you will take it from them and give it to me, and then I will give it to the monks. The women aren't allowed to give food to the monks."

The women brought bowls of fish, chicken, pork, and rice and handed them to Mike one by one. In turn, Mike passed the bowls to the thin man and the monks were given food.

While the monks ate, the man explained there would be one final prayer. This prayer was to be from Mike. He would be given a small container of water and an empty bowl. He was to pour the water very slowly from the urn into the bowl while the monks sang another chant. As he poured the water, he was to say a prayer for Math and ask that she receive all of the love and everything they were giving to her. He was to wish her peace and happiness in her new life. After that, he would give the monks a "thank you" gift from him, and then the monks would go home. Mike understood.

The monks ate slowly, but within half an hour they were finished and returned to their seats. Mike, Anan, Nuang, and the thin man also returned to their places.

Mike was brought the urn of water and the empty bowl. The monks started their chant. The thin man motioned that he should start pouring.

Mike had never been a religious man, but as he poured the water into the bowl he prayed very hard for Math. He prayed with all of his heart and soul. As the last drop of water fell into the bowl, a single tear slid down his cheek. He looked up at the eldest monk. The monk smiled at him and nodded his understanding.

In a moment the chanting stopped. Anan handed Mike a large bucket filled with canned food, snacks, and candy. A paper sign on the bucket said in both Thai and English, 'Thank you for the ceremony for Math, from Mr. Mike'. He presented the bucket to the eldest monk.

As the monk received the bucket, he took Mike's hand and squeezed it gently. The ceremony was ended.

The monks rose from their seats and left the room. Mike followed them outside and watched as they disappeared up the street.

Anan came to Mike and said, "Now we will eat."

Mike and Anan and the thin man ate in the now deserted living room. Nuang ate in the kitchen area with the women. While they ate, a constant parade of neighbors passed through the living room into the kitchen and then out again, carrying plates of food. Mike figured the food he bought was feeding the whole neighborhood. He hoped it was enough.

Mike got his share of attention from the neighbors. Wide-eyed stares from the younger children, giggling glances from the older girls, and kind smiles from the adults. Anan's house was several kilometers from Pattaya and farangs were rarely seen in the neighborhood. Mike smiled and nodded to everyone.

When they finished eating, Nuang came to Mike and said, "I must help the women clean the dishes. When we're finished, I'll take you back to Pattaya."

While the women cleaned, Mike sat on Anan's front step smoking cigarettes and talking with the thin man. "Your English is very good," he said. "Where did you learn it?"

"I studied English when I was in college," the man answered. "Also when I played music in a nightclub in Bangkok. I was what you Americans call a hippie. I used to play a guitar and sing American songs. My favorites were John Denver and Bobby Goldsboro. Do you know their music?"

"Yes," Mike answered, "They were very popular many years ago. John Denver is dead now."

"I know," the man said. "It's too bad, I liked his music." He fell silent.

"You seem to know the ceremony as good as the monks," Mike said. "How do you know everything so well? Did you study the ceremonies in school?"

The thin man smiled. "After I stopped being a hippie, I joined the monastery. I shaved my head and put on the saffron robes. For five years I was a monk. I know all of the ceremonies."

"You're a most interesting man," Mike said.

Nuang came outside, interrupting their conversation. The thin man excused himself and went inside.

Nuang stood nervously beside Mike and said, "Have you ever seen these clothes before?"

He inspected Nuang briefly, "I think I've seen Math wearing them. Is that right?"

She blushed. "Yes, they are Math's clothes. I thought you would like it if I wore her clothes."

J. F. Gump

"You look nice in Math's clothes. I feel like she's with me again." The smile on her face told him he had said the right thing.

"Mike, do you know it has been exactly forty days since Math died?"

"I never thought about it. Does it mean something special?"

"Some people believe that a person's spirit is reborn forty days after they die."

"Do you believe that, Nuang?"

"I don't know; it's just what some people say. If it's true, I hope my sister is born into peace and happiness."

"I hope so too," Mike said. "After the hard life she just left, it's the least God could do."

They stood next to each other in silence, both hoping their wishes for Math would come true. Finally Nuang spoke, "Mike, I've never been to the beach before. When I take you back to Pattaya, will you take me to walk on the beach?"

"You've never been to the beach?" he asked in amazement.

Nuang shook her head.

"Then I would be happy to be the person to take you for your first walk in the sands of Pattaya Beach."

"Thank you. I'll tell Anan I will not be coming right back after I take you home. I'll tell him I'll be late returning." She darted off into the house and returned a few minutes later with Anan.

"I want to tell you," Anan began, "the ceremony today was much better than the one we had for Math at her funeral in Phitsanulok. I could feel my sister all around us. I know she received our love and our prayers. Now she is at peace. Thank you for doing this."

"No. Thank you. Without you and Nuang this would not have been possible. We must go now, I promised to take Nuang to the beach."

"I know," Anan said. "Please take care of Nuang. My sisters are very special to me now."

"I will," Mike replied. "She is very special to me too."

As they rode toward Pattaya, Nuang shouted over her shoulder, "I have the pictures of Math in my purse. I think we should take them to your condo before we go to the beach."

"Okay," he shouted back.

In his room Nuang found one excuse after another not to leave. First she wanted to show him all of Math's pictures, then she said it was too hot to go to the beach, then she had to use the toilet, and then she wanted to talk.

Finally he asked, "Are you okay, Nuang? I thought you wanted to go to the beach, but now you act like you don't care if you go or not. Is something wrong?"

"Nothing is wrong," she said. "I guess I'm a little nervous because I have something to tell you. There's something I promised my sister, but I'm afraid of what you might think."

"Unless you tell me what it is, you'll never know what I think."

She hesitated for a minute and then said, "When Math came to Chiang Mai and met her father, we talked for a very long time. Math was very afraid she would never see you again. She kept talking about dreams she was having."

"You mean the monkey-man?"

"Yes."

"I always laughed at her dreams about the monkey-man."

"Me too," Nuang said. "Maybe I should have listened. Math believed her dreams were telling her someone would die. Sometimes Math thought you would die, and sometimes she thought she would die. Math was very sure something would happen and that you and she would never be together again."

"I wish I hadn't laughed at Math's dreams," Mike said, "because now I know the monkey-man was after her."

"You shouldn't think about it. It's not good for you to think like that."

No one spoke for several minutes. Finally Nuang took a deep breath and said, "Math asked me to do one thing for her if she happened to die, and if I ever saw you again."

"What do you mean? I don't understand."

J. F. Gump

She blushed and lowered her eyes from his face.

"What?" he asked again. Gently, he put his finger under her chin and lifted her face until she was looking at him. Their eyes met. Her pupils were slightly dilated, a nervous smile played on her lips.

"I don't know the English words," she answered in a low whisper. "I will have to show you."

She took Mike by the hand and led him to the side of the bed. "Please lay with me for a while. Math wanted me to hold you like she used to do."

"Are you sure?" he asked.

"I made a promise to my sister."

He lay down on the bed with Nuang beside him. Nervously, she wrapped her arms around him and held him close. "Now you should close your eyes and think only of Math."

He lay there for a long time, shutting out everything around him. In a while only images of Math filled his thoughts. He could feel Nuang beside him. She began stroking his body sensually.

"What are you doing?" he asked. He didn't open his eyes.

"I'm doing the rest of what my sister asked," she answered softly. "Today I am Math and I love you. Today I want to hold you and kiss you and make you feel the way we used to feel. Teeluk, I want to make love with you one last time before you go home."

Her voice sounded just like Math's. It was the first time he had noticed that. He kept his eyes closed and touched her face. She even felt like Math. He kissed her soft and gentle. He caressed her body and let himself believe it was Math beside him. They made love. For a few long and precious minutes he held Math in his arms again. When he finished, he opened his eyes. Nuang was crying. He pulled her close and they cried together.

In a while he got up from the bed and went to the bath. When he returned, Nuang was gone. On the bed was a note. "My family loves you," it read. "We will never forget what you gave to Math before she died. Please never forget us. Love, Nuang."

Waves of conflicting emotions washed through him. He felt

empty yet whole, happy yet sad, lonely but loved. He wished she hadn't left without saying goodbye.

He packed his suitcase and called the airlines to change his flight. He was ready to go home. He wasn't sure what was there for him anymore, but he knew he was ready to go. Maybe someday he would return to Thailand but, then again, maybe he wouldn't. There were plenty of good memories for him here, but there were plenty of bad memories, too. He didn't know what his future might bring.

Just before the taxi arrived to take him to the airport, Mike called Anan's phone and asked for Nuang. "Thank you," he said when he heard her voice. "What you did today means more to me than anything in the world. I will never forget your thoughtfulness or your kindness."

"Mai pen rai ka, Khun Mike," Nuang said. "Mai pen rai."

After leaving the condo, Mike directed the taxi driver to the Big C Shopping Center. Inside, he bought a wedding band and a single red rose. Minutes later he asked the driver to stop again, this time on Sukhumvit Road, not far from Anan's house. It was where Math had died. Mike got out of the taxi and stood unmoving for a long time. Finally he slipped the ring over the stem of the rose then pressed them both between his hands. In Thai fashion, he wai'ed with deepest of love and respect to the last place where Math had been truly alive.

"Goodbye teeluk." Tears flowed as he laid the rose and the ring in the grass at the edge of the road. "Goodbye my wife. I will love you forever. Please wait for me. I'll come to you in quickly time."

Other Books Available
By J. F. Gump

From Bangkok Book House
www.bangkokbooks.com

Even Thai Girls Cry
ISBN: 974-93100-4-7

The Farang Affair
ISBN: 974-85123-6-3

One High Season
ISBN: 974-85129-3-2

From Sabai Books U.S.
www.JFGumpNovels.com

Thailand – Cold Rain
ISBN 10: 0971485542

Tears For The Thai Girl
ISBN 10: 0971485534

Blame It On Bangkok
ISBN 10: 1440473803

For Details Go To:

www.JFGumpNovels.com